PRAISE FOR BRANDENBURG

"Meade's second foray into international intrigue imagines that Nazis biding time in South America hatch a viable plot to take over contemporary Germany. The novel opens with a splendidly tantalizing episode of eavesdropping by a Paraguayan reporter who, before he's caught and killed, hides a tell-tale tape recording. . . . Fast, sly, and slick, this thriller delivers the goods—tension, action, plot twists—until the smoke clears on the last page."

—*Booklist*

"Sheer, nail-biting suspense . . . a rare treat."

—*Sunday Telegraph*

PRAISE FOR GLENN MEADE

"The Irish-born author teeters on the edge of genius and sacrilege with this thriller about a subject known since the time of Christ. . . . Some who have avoided Christian fiction or only dipped in will find this departure from the mold refreshing, even while some regular readers of Christian fiction may find certain passages revolting. Fans of Davis Bunn or Dan Brown won't bat an eye at Meade's unblinking look at the Vatican and the religious secrecy that fuels such novels. With a plot that screams, a controversial edge, and characters with attitude and something to prove, this has all the makings to be the next *Da Vinci Code*."

—*Publishers Weekly*, on *The Second Messiah*

"Dan Brown meets Tom Clancy—Glenn Meade sure knows how to get your pulse racing. I was gripped from page one. Whether *The Second Messiah* is fact or fiction is up for debate, but one thing's for sure—it's one heck of a thriller. You know you're in safe hands with Glenn Meade—*The Second Messiah* is a roller coaster of a thriller that lifts the lid on the inner workings of the Vatican and leaves you wondering just how much of the fiction is actually fact."

—Stephen Leather, author of *Nightfall*

"Reading similarly to both a Thoene novel and *The Da Vinci Code*, bestselling author Meade's *The Second Messiah* will keep readers on the edge of their proverbial seats. . . . *The Second Messiah* reads quickly and will hold the reader's attention with its many plot twists. In the story, Meade also addresses the problem of suffering in an insightful comment from the pope. Fans of fiction tied to news headlines will enjoy this geopolitical thriller. Recommended for readers of Joel C. Rosenberg."

—*Christian Retailing*

"This novel is a *Da Vinci Code*-type thriller, but it's far more. The secret scrolls and chases are standard thriller fare, but deftly handled. Some of the characters are particularly captivating, especially the new Pope, a true follower of God who's tormented by his past and struggling with the future of the Church. This suspenseful book is well worth reading."

—CBA Retailers + Resources, on *The Second Messiah*

"Written in the mold of *The Da Vinci Code*—sans all the erroneous claims (thankfully)—bestselling author Glenn Meade's latest geographical thriller, *The Second Messiah*, keeps readers on the edge of their proverbial seats with multiple plot twists."

—*Charisma*

"Meade knows how to entangle, and untangle, an exciting array of characters and plots guaranteed to keep the reader hooked . . . a talented storyteller, he sets the scene quickly before taking off on a rollicking ride that keeps the pages turning. It's a hard book to put down."

—Crosswalk.com, on *The Second Messiah*

"In this big-boned thriller, Meade makes his contribution to the distinguished number of first thrillers premised on the attempted assassination of a world leader (e.g., *The Day of the Jackal*; *The Eagle Has Landed*) by imagining a CIA hit man targeting Josef Stalin. . . . Meade writes with a silken pen, inking unusually sympathetic leads. Vivid cameos of historical figures, including Eisenhower, Truman, Beria and Stalin, lend credence to the story, which, according to the author, includes events of 'documented history.' The Cold War may be on ice, but through this literate, memorable story, Meade shows that it can still freeze readers' attention and chill their blood."

—*Publishers Weekly*, on *Snow Wolf*

"Meade's research is so extensive yet unobtrusive . . . that it is often easy to forget you're reading fiction and not history. This is a completely riveting thriller in the tradition of *The Day of the Jackal*. A white knuckler!"

—*The Washington Post*

"One twisting, breathless chase."

—*New York Times*

"A tremendous sense of dramatic action and page-turning excitement culminating in a riveting, thought-provoking climax."

—*The Sunday Times*, on *Snow Wolf*

BRANDENBURG

A THRILLER

GLENN MEADE

HOWARD BOOKS
A DIVISION OF SIMON & SCHUSTER, INC.

NEW YORK   NASHVILLE   LONDON   TORONTO   SYDNEY   NEW DELHI

Howard Books
A Division of Simon & Schuster, Inc.
1230 Avenue of the Americas
New York, NY 10020

First Howard Books trade paperback edition April 2013

HOWARD BOOKS and colophon are registered trademarks of Simon & Schuster, Inc.

For information about special discounts for bulk purchases, please contact Simon & Schuster Special Sales at 1-866-506-1949 or business@simonandschuster.com.

The Simon & Schuster Speakers Bureau can bring authors to your live event. For more information or to book an event, contact the Simon & Schuster Speakers Bureau at 1-866-248-3049 or visit our website at www.simonspeakers.com.

Designed by Jaime Putorti

Manufactured in the United States of America

10 9 8 7 6 5 4 3 2 1

The Library of Congress has cataloged the original edition as follows:

Meade, Glenn.
  Brandenburg / by Glenn Meade.—1st ed. p. cm.
  "A Thomas Dunne book."
  ISBN 0-312-15483-6
  I. Title
  PS3563.E16845B73 1997 96-54630
  813'54—dc21

ISBN 978-1-4516-8823-8
ISBN 978-1-4516-8824-5 (ebook)

TO MY PARENTS,
TOM AND CARMEL

So we beat on, boats against the current, borne back ceaselessly into the past.

—F. SCOTT FITZGERALD, *THE GREAT GATSBY*

FOREWORD

First books are special.

They're always a triumph of hope and hard work over despair and sloth.

They also prove something to the novice author: You've climbed Everest by writing a book—even if it felt like you were wearing carpet slippers at times. So maybe you can do it again?

Brandenburg was my first novel. It was published in Europe to far better reviews than I could ever have hoped for and translated into almost twenty languages.

Except German.

No German publisher would touch it with a barge pole because of the controversial neo-Nazi subject matter.

However, soon after the success of another novel of mine, my publisher finally decided to take the risk. *Brandenburg* became a long-running bestseller in Germany; it's a book I still get mail about from readers.

At its core is a very real and dramatic Nazi-era "secret," one that I happened upon in the small alpine town of Garmisch in the depths of a bitter winter.

In the course of writing a newspaper article, I interviewed an elderly former SS man, who, wacky as it might sound, enjoyed listening to the music of Frank Sinatra and Dean Martin as he languished near death in a local old folks' home.

He also told me a true and remarkable wartime story that provided me with the idea for *Brandenburg*.

And despite all the effort of writing it in longhand, often after already working a ten-hour shift—I remember keeping my window open most evenings to let cold air in to keep me awake—I truly enjoyed having written it.

I hope you enjoy reading it just as much.

1

When the doctors at the San Ignatio Private Hospital told Nicolas Tsarkin he was going to die, the old man nodded sullenly, waited until the men had left, then dressed without speaking another word and drove his Mercedes to the corner of the Calle Palma three blocks away.

He parked the car and walked back the last block to the small commercial bank on the corner, pushed through the revolving doors, and told the manager he wanted to see his safe-deposit box.

The manager promptly ordered a senior clerk to go down to the vault with the old man: Señor Tsarkin, after all, was a valued customer.

"Then tell him to go. I want to be left alone," Tsarkin said in his usual abrupt manner.

"Certainly, Señor Tsarkin. Thank you, Señor Tsarkin." A final, polite bow from the manager, and then, "Buenos días, Señor Tsarkin."

The blue-suited manager irritated Tsarkin, as usual, but especially so this morning, with his bowing and scraping and ingratiating, gold-toothed smile.

Buenos días. Good morning. *What was good about it?*

He had just been told he had less than forty-eight hours to live, and right now the pain in his stomach was eating into him like a fire, almost unendurable. He felt weak, terribly weak, despite the drugs to quell the pain. What had he to smile about? What was good about this morning?

The last morning of his life, because he knew now what he had to do.

And yet the truth was, Tsarkin felt a strange kind of relief: the lie would soon be over.

He caught a reflection of himself in the cold, stainless-steel walls as the clerk led him down into the cool of the vault. Tsarkin was ninety-one and, until six months ago, had looked ten years younger. He had been fit then, ate the proper foods, never smoked, and rarely drank. Everyone said he would make the century.

They were wrong.

His reflection in the stainless-steel wall showed him as he was: emaciated, looking like a corpse already, the bleeding in his stomach so bad that he could almost feel the life draining from him. But he had important things to do, no matter what the pain, no matter what the doctors had told him. And once those things were done he could sleep peacefully, forever.

Unless there really was a God and a hereafter, in which case he would pay for his sins. But Tsarkin doubted it. No just God would have let him live so long and so full and so rich a life after all he had done. No, you just died. It was that simple. The flesh became dust, and you were gone forever: no pain, no heaven, no hell. Just nothingness.

He hoped.

The clerk unlocked the metal gates and led him through into the basement chamber. It was a small room, six yards by six, silent, a cold marble floor. The clerk examined the key number he held in his hand, ran a finger along the shining steel boxes along one of the walls, found Tsarkin's deposit box, removed and unlocked the box, and placed it on the polished wooden table in the center of the room. He handed over the key, withdrew, and then Tsarkin was alone.

The vault had the coldness and the silence of a morgue and Tsarkin shivered involuntarily. *Soon I'll be there,* he told himself. *Soon there will be no pain.* As he went to sit at the table he dragged the small metal box toward him, inserted the key, and opened the lid, before removing the contents and spreading the papers out onto the polished table.

All there. The deeds to his lands, the keys to his past. He reconsidered a moment, putting off what had to be done, thought about enjoying one last orgy of indulgence, but truly there was nothing more he wanted to do. The pain made everything unbearable, and, besides, he had enjoyed everything life had to offer.

He gathered up the contents of the deposit box in his hands, sorted them neatly into an orderly pile, and placed them in one of the old, large envelopes that contained some of the papers. It made a neat, hefty bundle. Then he pressed the buzzer for the clerk to return.

The house stood on the Calle Iguazu, on the outskirts of the city. White and large and surrounded by high walls, barely visible from the road. The classiest part of Asunción, and Tsarkin had been able to afford it. He opened the wrought-iron gates with the remote control, drove up the curved sweep of the asphalt road, and parked the Mercedes on the gravel driveway in front of the house.

He grunted when the mestizo butler opened the front door to greet him. He went straight through to his wood-paneled study and locked the door. It was warm in the study. Tsarkin loosened the two top buttons of his shirt as he looked out onto the lush, manicured gardens, the pepper and palm trees beyond the window. He owned a lot of property in Asunción, and three farms in the Chaco hinterland, but this place had always been his favorite.

He sat down at the polished apple-wood desk and emptied the contents of the envelope onto the gleaming surface and began to sift through the pile.

He looked at the passport first. Nicolas Tsarkin. Fine. Except he wasn't Nicolas Tsarkin. His real name—he'd almost forgotten it—and then when it came to his lips, so unreal, he had to smile to himself, weakly. So long to live a lie. He put the passport aside.

Once he was wanted in half a dozen countries. Once he did terrible things in that old, forgotten name. Inflicted terrible deaths and terrible pain. And yet the truth was, when you boiled it down, he couldn't stand pain himself. He chided himself: it was no time for thought. *Do it.*

He sorted through the papers. Old, tired papers, tattered records of his past. He read through them once again. As in his nightmares, it all came back to him: the cold terror on the faces of his victims, the blood, the butchery. Yet he felt no remorse.

He would have done it all again. No question.

He put the papers aside, removed several blank sheets of paper and an envelope from the desk drawer, and began writing.

When he finished fifteen minutes later, he sealed the envelope and tucked it into his pocket before crossing to the fireplace, clutching the papers from the safe-deposit box in his hands, and making a neat pile of them in the grate.

He took a match from the box he kept on the mantelpiece, struck it, and set the flame to the papers. Then he crossed to the wall safe hidden behind the framed oil painting, swung back the painting on its hinges, and thumbed through the combination.

He selected the papers he wanted, making sure there was nothing left that might incriminate anyone, and crossed back to the fireplace. Watching as the flames licked the papers, he added more to the blaze, until there was nothing, only black ashes. He checked through the ashes with the poker.

The flames had done their work. Nothing remained.

When he had done all he had to do, he left the house. He drove to the post office four blocks away, bought the stamp he needed, and posted the letter, express. He drove straight back to the house, parked the car in the garage this time, and went into his study again.

Do it quickly, the voice in his head told him.

No time for thought. No time for thinking about the pain to come. From the top drawer of the polished apple-wood desk he took out the long-barreled Smith & Wesson .357 Magnum revolver, checked that the chambers were loaded, then placed the barrel of the weapon in the roof of his mouth, letting his lips form a perfect O around the cold metal.

He squeezed the trigger.

It was all over in less than a second, and Tsarkin never heard the explosion that flung him up and backward, shattering half his brain, as the bullet ripped out through the back of his skull, sending shards of bone and bloodied brain matter flying into the air behind him, spattering the white walls gray and red as the blunted lead of the bullet embedded itself in the wood below the ceiling.

Less than a second of primary pain.

All in all, Nicolas Tsarkin could not have wished for a more quick and painless death.

PART ONE

2

Sally Thornton knew she wanted to spend her last night with him.

It was raining hard as they came out of the restaurant near the opera, and when Joe Volkmann hailed a taxi to take them back to his apartment, she knew she was going to stay. Men didn't ask a girl back for a drink and then send her home in a taxi. Especially not on a rain-soaked night. At least not the men she'd known.

She wore an emerald-green blouse that hugged her slim figure and matched her eyes. Her skirt was gray and tight, and her legs were sheathed in darker gray-patterned stockings. She knew she had a shape that most women would kill for. But she wasn't quick to give her sexual favors. Though she knew little about Joe Volkmann, she liked him very much.

Sally had been in the intelligence services for five years since Oxford, and she had just finished a six-month temporary posting at DSE—Direction de Sécurité Européenne. Created eighteen months earlier by the European Union, the intent had been to form a European equivalent of the United States' FBI, with investigation and enforcement powers that crossed national frontiers. In practice, DSE didn't quite live up to that intent. Despite the European Union, nationalism had not withered away. Still, her time in Strasbourg had been fascinating. But now it was time to go home, a week's leave in London before her posting to New York.

During her time at DSE, Joe Volkmann had been her teacher and mentor. He had been friendly and warm, intense at work, but today when he offered to help her pack, she was a little surprised; still, she knew the offer was genuine and not a come-on. She got the feeling that he didn't push things, so the man was a challenge.

He'd spent the afternoon in the apartment in Petite France, help-ing her fill the wooden packing crates with her belongings and the small items of antique furniture she'd bought. When she suggested a meal to repay him, he countered with tickets to the opera and din-ner afterward.

The opera was *The Magic Flute,* music she loved. As she watched him throughout the performance, she saw that he listened to it attentively. And though he smiled at her a lot and the evening had a romantic flavor, he didn't try to make a pass. That was usually a specialty of the Italians if you ventured near their DSE offices.

His apartment on the Quai Ernest Bevin was on the first floor, and the balcony entrance overlooked a tiny, paved courtyard. It was a small, two-bedroom affair, and he kept it pretty neat for a guy. A TV in a corner, as well as a Sony sound system. Several books lay around and lots of CDs. Classical mostly, but she saw some jazz and rock. On shelves above were some photographs in frames, and more books.

Choosing a disc, he inserted it into the CD player. Edith Piaf, Sally soon noted with approval. "How about a drink, Sally?"

She went to sit on the couch and crossed her long legs. She saw him look at them briefly, and she said, "How about scotch?"

"A girl after my own heart," he said, smiling.

"With ice and a splash of water," she added, echoing his smile.

She watched him go into the kitchen. He was tall, dark-haired with a touch of gray, and well built—not handsome in a conven-tional way, but he was attractive. He looked more French than Brit-ish. And he had something, only Sally Thornton couldn't figure out what. Maybe something in his sensitive brown eyes, the same eyes she had seen in the woman in one of the photographs on the shelf.

He looked like the kind of guy who could protect a woman . . . But then, all the men she worked with looked like that—trained sol-diers and intelligence officers and hard-nosed narcotics specialists masquerading as policemen.

She figured out maybe what it was. Here was a man she could

trust. He was a hard man, but he didn't come on hard. And his smile gave him away . . . he was vulnerable, she reckoned, under the confident exterior.

He came back into the room carrying their glasses. He handed hers across and sat on the couch opposite. He loosened his tie, and as he sipped his scotch, he let his eyes fall on her, and she was conscious of his stare—and of his gentle, unthreatening smile. In the background, Edith Piaf was singing. *Je ne regrette rien.*

"You're going to miss me, Joe?"

"Sure. There's a lot to miss."

"Then why are you smiling?"

"Because they're going to love you in New York."

"Who? The people at the embassy?"

"Those, too. But I mean the Americans. The guys will be beating down your door."

She smiled, swirled her glass. "Why, thank you for the compliment. You'll come visit me sometimes?"

"If you like. But the truth is, you're better off over there, Sally. Things are turning bad in Europe, and I think they'll get a lot worse before they get better." He glanced at his watch, then the TV. "You mind if I catch the late news? It's a professional vice."

"Go ahead. I'm a news junkie, too."

He turned down the sound system and flicked on the TV. The news was pretty discouraging. The economic downturn was in its third year. Unemployment was over 20 percent. Business failures kept mounting—solid companies you'd have thought would never fail. And in Germany, where the East was never successfully integrated, the downturn was worse than in the other nations of the EU. Angry mobs rampaged through the streets. Except for the fact that the images were in color, the scenes were very like those from another age. And they both recognized that.

He flicked off the remote.

She said, "It's not starting over, is it?"

They both knew what "it" was.

"I don't think history repeats itself," Volkmann said. "At least I hope not. Especially not in Germany. But you're better off in the States, Sally," he said again.

"I'm just sorry I waited this long to get to know you," she said, smiling.

"Me, too."

She took a long sip from her glass. "Tell me about yourself, Joe. I've worked with you for months but I hardly know a thing about you. Apart from the fact you're a news junkie."

He smiled back. "What do you want to know?"

"How long have you been in DSE?"

"Eighteen months."

"You like working in Europe?"

"Sure. The problems are pretty interesting. It's the main reason I'm in the profession. I like solving problems, don't you? I'm easily bored."

She nodded assent. "And before that?"

"Intelligence—SIS."

She uncrossed her legs and stretched them. He let his eyes fall on them appreciatively. "Were you ever married, Joe?"

He sipped his scotch. "Divorced. No kids."

"And your folks?"

She glanced up at the photographs on the shelf. Two were of a couple and a young boy, one taken outside a pretty stone cottage and another on a beach. The boy was obviously Volkmann, about fourteen, and the couple was surely his parents. There was another of the boy and his father, a distinguished but sickly-looking man in a heavy overcoat. They were standing near the cottage; the beach was down a long slope below. Another photograph showed just the mother. She was sitting at a piano in some great hall, a striking-looking woman.

Then it came to her. "She's that Volkmann, isn't she? The famous pianist? Is she your mother? She hasn't played in years. Whatever happened to her?"

"Yes, she's that Volkmann. And no, she doesn't play any longer. Arthritis crippled her hands. But she still does some teaching."

"The photo was taken at Carnegie Hall, wasn't it?"

"You have a good eye."

"I remember her." Sally smiled, inclined her head toward the woman's photo. "She was up there with the best. I loved her Schubert. What about your father?"

"He died six months ago."

"I'm sorry. Were you close to him?"

"Very. He was a good man."

"I don't think you took after him," she said, staring at the other photo. "He looks a bit . . . otherworldly."

"You could say that." Joe smiled. "He was a professor."

"You never wanted to follow either of your parents' professions?"

"No talent," he sighed, and changed the subject. "I got a call from Dick Wolsey in London the other day." There was heavy concern in his voice. "He claims the Germans and the French are trying to pull out of this operation."

"You mean out of DSE?"

He nodded and took a long swallow of scotch.

Sally said, "They'd be crazy to do that. If they do, all of DSE will come tumbling down, and bang goes security cooperation in Europe."

"Did you hear any rumors?"

Sally shrugged and played with the top button of her blouse. "We've all heard the rumors, Joe. Some politicians think DSE is all a waste of taxpayers' money. Everybody's in trouble financially. You see the same news I do." She gestured toward the television set. "The Germans, the French, us. As long as the financial markets are in turmoil, they have the frights. And when nations get the frights—watch out—it's each for itself."

"Did you hear Ferguson say if he's heard any rumors?" he asked. Ferguson was head of the British section of DSE.

Sally Thornton smiled. "I hardly talk to the man. He's so darned stuffy."

He laughed. "What about Peters?" Peters was Ferguson's number two.

"All Peters tells me is that I have good legs." She paused, saw Volkmann glance at her legs again. "And that you're a terrific intelligence officer." She looked at him. "Do we have to talk about work?"

"Not at all."

She said, "Can I ask you a very personal question, Joe?"

"How personal?"

"Why didn't you ever come on to me?"

He let his eyes catch hers. "I like you, Sally. A lot. But I don't like to rush things. And I don't like to mix bed and work. Life gets messy enough."

"You're a very sensitive man, Joe Volkmann. Did you know that?"

His gaze remained on her, but he didn't say anything.

"Would you like me to stay?" Sally asked.

When he smiled, she smiled back and put down her glass. "My plane leaves at three," she said. "And yours?"

"Two-thirty, to London."

Sally was sleeping quietly beside him, nestled against him, but Volkmann was still awake, his back propped against a bunched-up pillow. The long-ago memory of his father came to him . . .

They walked along the deserted Cornish beach together. It was November; the beach grasses were yellowed and dry. Waves swept up the sand, rattling the pebbles.

He had come down from the weapons course in Scotland, soon after he joined SIS, the year before the Wall came down. The sun was shining—one of those perfect days in autumn when the air is crisp and clear and it feels good to breathe. His father looked frail as always, wrapped in the tattered tweed overcoat that looked a size too big for him. They sat on a driftwood log, and the old man regarded him with watery brown eyes.

"Mama tells me they're sending you to Berlin."

"It's a good posting, Papa. And with luck, I'll get home once a month, so it won't be so bad."

"Is it dangerous?"

He saw the dark look on his father's face. Berlin brought back bad memories. "No, Papa. Not dangerous. It's intelligence gathering mostly. Nothing for you to worry about. They're not going to send me over the Wall with a gun, I can promise you that."

"And Anna?"

"She'll join me in a couple of months."

"What's it like now?"

"Berlin? Pretty exciting. Full of energy. A little like New York, but on a smaller scale. Not like the old days . . . not like the Berlin you once knew."

He saw the old man look away toward the waves, his face drawn as if troubled by some private thought. Joseph Volkmann recognized the look, recognized the pain. The old man stood, glanced at his watch, cut off the pain before it took hold. He had had plenty of practice doing that.

"Your mama will have lunch ready. We better not keep her waiting."

"Papa."

His father looked down at him, and Joseph Volkmann was aware of the pink circle of rutted flesh on the frail man's temple, the wound indelible and permanent. The ones inside were not visible, but they were no less permanent.

He said quietly, staring at the scar, "It's all in the past, Papa. A long time ago. But sometimes I want you to talk about it. Maybe it would help."

His father shook his head. "Believe me, Joseph, talking about it does not help. I tried to talk for many years and learned that it's much better to forget." The brown eyes looked down at him. "You'll learn that as you grow older, Joseph. Bury ghosts if you can. Don't let them live. Now come, let's not keep Mama waiting."

The son watched as the old man moved away, the bony, hunched body lost in the heavy tweed overcoat.

He stood and followed his father.

* * *

The boy, Joe's father, was thirteen. The girl, his sister, was six. Drunken SS guards made them stand in front of a shallow pit, half filled with the already murdered. The girl was so frightened, she reached out her hand to her brother for comfort. The SS man told her to stay still and he jerked her hand away. When the child reached out again in fear, the SS man shot her point blank.

After that, they pushed her into the pit, then forced the distraught boy to kneel down; an SS captain shot him in the face, and then they threw him on top of his sister. The boy was horribly wounded. But the captain had been too drunk to aim properly. The boy waited, lying among the dead, more scared than he had ever been. Waited while the guards tossed dirt on top of the bodies. Waited until it was dark and at last the guards were gone, and then he began to cry out for his sister . . .

3

ASUNCIÓN, PARAGUAY. NOVEMBER 23

Rudi Hernandez waited while the woman checked in at the desk. The airport was busy, crowded with midday passengers, but his eyes were fixed firmly on the woman. Watching her figure, he wished she were not his cousin.

He told himself, *Hey, remember who she is.*

But he couldn't help it, enjoying the view of the woman's long, silky, suntanned legs and the perfectly shaped hips and thighs that filled out the creamy-white summer skirt. Her blond hair was cut short, and it complemented her pretty face, her fine cheekbones.

The view was exquisite, and he smiled to himself. It was the Latin in him. He liked women. And he especially liked Erica.

It wasn't just her looks, of course. She was smart, very smart, a good journalist for one so young—early thirties, five years younger than he was. *Maybe she's even a better journalist than I am,* he reflected. *I'm a reporter. That's it. I find stories. But she can write. She'll do books someday, just you wait,* he thought, proud of her.

But it wasn't just that she was smart. She was also a very fine person, sensible and sensitive—wise beyond her years.

Why does she have to be my cousin? He sighed inwardly. If it weren't for their blood ties, he knew he'd have rushed over to her, torn up her tickets, and taken her in his arms.

She turned and smiled at him, her business complete as she gathered up passport and tickets and picked up her carry-on luggage from the desk. She crossed to where he stood as he ground out his cigarette on the marble floor.

He smiled back. "Everything okay?"

Erica nodded. "I board in twenty-five minutes. We have time for a coffee." Her hand found his arm; her eyes were glistening. "I'll miss you, Rudi. It's a long way—and a long time—between visits."

"Hey, I know. I'll sure miss you, too, Erica."

He took her carry-on luggage and led her across the concourse to the small restaurant lounge. He found a vacant table and ordered two coffees and two brandies. As they chatted, his mind went back to the day they had spent in the mountains, up in the rain forest near the border with Brazil, the day they had taken the guided tour. Magnificent country, a splendid day. And she was so relaxed, so easy to be with. *And my cousin. Darn!*

When the waiter brought their drinks, Erica took a sip of brandy and caught his eyes.

"I'm worried about you, Rudi. I'm worried about the story."

So am I, Rudi thought. *But I can't tell you that.*

One good thing about her departure was that it took his mind—at least momentarily—off the story. It was a big one; all his reporter's instincts pointed that way. And it had many complex strands—leading only heaven knew where. Perhaps it would turn out to be the biggest story he'd worked on. And it was dangerous . . . one man was already dead, murdered. The bad thing about her departure—the other bad thing—was that he would have loved for Erica to work alongside him. Her brains would have come in handy.

"I want you to promise me you'll be careful," she went on. "Promise me that?"

He smiled easily, letting his gaze rest on hers. "I'm always careful. You know that."

"Bull." She smiled ruefully, with a shake of her head.

With her fair skin and light hair, she looked so different from the South American women, the dark-skinned women in the barrios, and the contrast had turned heads. The Indian woman selling flowers on Calle Estrella had asked to touch her blond hair. "She's beautiful," the old woman had said, smiling as she stroked Erica's hair like a talisman and looked at Rudi. "She will bring us both luck. Believe me."

And when the Latin men stared at her, he didn't blame them.

He saw her look of concern. "There's not much of a story, Erica. Not yet. Maybe it will turn into something big—"

"You know it will," she interrupted. "We both know it. My thumbs are tingling, Rudi. When my thumbs tingle"—she smiled—"well, believe them."

He grinned. "That may be, but so far, I don't have much. Really very little." He shrugged. "Only what Rodriguez has told me. And the photographs."

"But the photos connect Rodriguez with that man, Tsarkin—a very wealthy man. And my old school friend Dieter Winter." There was an ironic edge to her voice when she mentioned the last name. "And through them, the story leads to Europe. It's not local, Rudi, whatever it is. It's bigger. The lines go far." Her eyes clouded for a moment. "It's probably drugs," she said . . . which was what she had said the first time he told her about Rodriguez. "But it could be something else, too."

"We'll see," he said quietly, catching her thoughtful mood.

He remembered Rodriguez's brown body, lying on the cold metal table in the mortuary of the city hospital, the feeling of nausea when the attendant pulled back the white sheet and he had stared at the man's pulped, bloodied flesh. He suppressed the shudder of fear he felt inside and leaned closer, breathing in the sweet scent of her perfume as though it were a refuge.

"But," Rudi said, "so far, we have no idea of where the lines go. I don't have any further leads. So far, Erica, there's no story. Just suggestions. Hints."

"And a dead man."

"And a dead man," he agreed.

"So you'll be careful." She looked hard at him, her face filled with concern.

"I promise."

Erica sipped her brandy, held the glass tensely in both hands. "What about the men who killed Rodriguez?"

"What about them?"

"Won't they come looking for you? Won't they be afraid you'll tell the police?"

Hernandez smiled, seeing her fear, trying to sound unafraid, trying to reassure her. "No chance. For one thing, they don't know me; they've never seen me. They don't know I exist."

"But what happens once the story breaks?"

Rudi took a sip of coffee. "Look, I'm a reporter. We'll have to burn that bridge when we cross it . . . if there's a story," he added. "And besides, I have one or two friends—*policía*—who'll protect me if I need protection. You remember Sanchez."

She nodded. Sanchez was a detective captain in the policía. "Too bad he and I didn't meet."

"A good man," Rudi said. "Next time . . ."

Meanwhile, the woman saw him reach into his pocket and take out a bunch of keys. He played with them idly.

Rudi Hernandez was a handsome man. His brown hair, cut in

a boyish fringe, made him look younger than his years. He smiled easily, as if life were constantly fun, constantly amusing. Even the noticeable scar that ran jaggedly across his right cheek was not unbecoming. It gave him an almost dashing, swashbuckling appearance. He toyed with the keys, watching her watch them, as he slipped them between his fingers. He smiled at her. "Like I told you last night, everything solid I have on these people is in a safe place. So don't worry, Erica, I'll be okay."

She smiled back. Her hand moved to touch his, and he slipped the keys back in his pocket.

"Be sure you are. You're a good man, Rudi, and I care about you. I want you to be here the next time I come."

A loudspeaker announced her flight.

He walked with her to the departure gate, carrying her hand luggage. As they stopped at the security gate, he handed across her bag. "Give my love to everyone."

"I will."

She moved up to him to kiss his cheek. "Auf Wiedersehen, Rudi."

"Auf Wiedersehen, Erica. Have a pleasant flight."

He watched her pass the security gate. On the other side, she turned and waved. He waved back before she disappeared from view.

He heard the public-address system crackle to life again, a shrill, metallic voice filling the terminal.

"Señor Rudi Hernandez, please come to the information desk. Señor Rudi Hernandez to the information desk, please."

The girl at the desk handed him the message. A telephone number was written on the slip of paper. There was no name. He found a telephone booth and dialed the number. After four rings, there was an answer.

"Sí?" a male voice said.

"This is Rudi Hernandez. Someone at this number left me a message to call."

"Yes, Señor Hernandez, one moment please." It was more like three minutes before a second voice came on the wire. This one Rudi recognized.

"Rudi, my friend." It was Captain Vellares Sanchez. "I only have a moment."

"So what's happening?" Rudi asked quickly, not wasting time on a greeting. They were close friends; they didn't need to oil the social gears.

"This is off the record, but one good turn deserves another." There was a pause, and then Sanchez went on. "Do you remember the old man you suggested I keep my eye on?"

"Tsarkin?"

"Nicolas Tsarkin, yes, that man."

"What about him?"

"I'm up on Calle Iguazu. Number Twenty-Three." That was Tsarkin's address, in the city's wealthiest suburb. "Maybe you'd like to join me."

"Why, what's up?" Rudi asked with growing excitement. He had been there, parked across the street, watching. Watching because Rodriguez had told him to. Watching and taking photographs of the big house with the white walls where the old man Tsarkin lived, the old man Rodriguez had told him to watch.

"Tsarkin's dead," Sanchez said. "Suicide."

Rudi thought. First Rodriguez, now Tsarkin. Both dead. "I'll be right there. Give me twenty minutes."

NORTHEASTERN CHACO, PARAGUAY. NOVEMBER 23

Four hundred miles away, darkness descended as the tall, silver-haired man sat in the cane chair on the veranda. His face was wrinkled with age, his eyes deep set and intense. He wore a fresh white shirt open at the neck and his light cotton pants were crisply pressed.

Beyond the wooden veranda, the rain fell in heavy sheets. A light was on overhead, moths buzzing around the shade. The man's silver hair shone under the light, and his tanned features looked handsome.

A boy served him iced tea from a teak tray, adding two spoonfuls of sugar to the glass. Jade-green jungle lay beyond the downpour, thick with bamboo and fragrant mango trees.

As the silver-haired man stared out at the drenching rain, footsteps echoed on the veranda's floorboards.

Kruger appeared, smoking a cigarette. The security chief wore a gray sweater, the sleeves pushed up to reveal thick, muscular arms. He sat in the cane chair opposite, a paper in his hand.

The silver-haired man smiled at the servant boy. "Leave us, please, Emilio."

The nut-brown face smiled back before he left. "Sí, señor."

Kruger's stocky frame creaked the cane chair. An insect crawled across the table. Kruger flicked it away.

"A message from Meyer," he said, waving the paper, "confirming for the twenty-fifth."

"So, everything is on schedule?" The old man sipped the iced tea.

Kruger nodded. "Everything. We meet Meyer in Asunción. Tsarkin has arranged for a suite in the Excelsior. We leave here on the sixth. That's also confirmed. As is the stopover in Mexico City with Haider."

The silver-haired man spoke softly, but his voice was compelling, and Kruger listened respectfully.

"Before we leave, I want everything in this house destroyed. Everything we're not taking must be burned. Nothing must be left behind. As if we had never existed. You'll see to it, Hans?"

Kruger inflected his head in reply.

"Thank you, Hans."

The security chief moved into the house, his footsteps echoing on the floorboards.

Alone now, the silver-haired man removed his wallet from the inside pocket of his linen jacket and slipped out a photograph.

The grainy print showed a blond young woman and a dark-haired man.

He stared down at the photograph as if mesmerized.

4

ASUNCIÓN, PARAGUAY. NOVEMBER 23

A high wall surrounded the perimeter of the property, but Hernandez could see the expansive, sun-washed lawns as he drove up toward the house. *House* was not the word: the property was a large estate, barely visible beyond the pepper and palm trees that lined the long driveway. It stood on a hill overlooking the city, large, two stories high, the bland, gray-painted exterior imposing but not inviting attention.

The wrought-iron front gates were open, and Hernandez was about to drive the rusting old red Buick through when he saw the young policía step forward from behind the cover of the wall, hands dug into the leather belt that held his holstered pistol.

He raised his hand for Hernandez to stop. Hernandez hit the brakes abruptly and leaned out of the window, flashed his press identity card as he smiled, tried to look friendly.

The young policía checked the identity card, stone-faced. Hernandez said, "Nicolas Tsarkin. Old guy. Suicide. I'm here to cover the story for *La Tarde*."

The policía nodded. "Yes, Señor Hernandez. I was expecting you. Captain Sanchez left word."

Hernandez looked up at the house in the distance. "Is Vellares up there now?"

"Sí, señor, he's waiting for you." He gestured through the open gate, and Hernandez passed through.

The old guy, Tsarkin, had had money. Lots of it, for sure.

The manicured lawns stretched down from the house for more than a hundred yards. Hernandez could make out the house beneath the red, pantiled roof. He glanced to the left and right as he drove up the asphalt driveway; beyond the pepper trees, yellow and pink hibiscus were in bloom.

The gardens were something else. Mango trees, peach trees, a couple of coconut palms, their fronds heavy and limp in the breeze-less, hot afternoon air. They were the best-kept gardens he had seen in Asunción.

He kept the old Buick at a slow pace all the way up, taking in the place, remembering how he had wondered what it would look like beyond the white walls that led up from the road below, something telling him there was more to be learned here in this house than what Rodriguez had told him.

Halfway up the hill, the Buick's engine started to groan, racking the old rusted chassis.

He swore.

The big old American Buick was ready for the scrap heap. Fifteen years old, a hundred and fifty thousand miles on the reconditioned engine. It had been a trusted friend for a long time, but he badly needed a new car. He took a little pressure off the accelerator. The car stopped groaning, then started up again after another twenty yards. He was coming around the bend now, seeing the house clearly and unobstructed for the first time: big and expensive-looking.

Thirty yards from where the asphalt driveway became gravel, the Buick gave out, the engine not responding to his foot as he pumped the accelerator hard, the car coasting along now, the road still a little uphill. He swung the wheel to the left and pulled over onto the grass shoulder, slammed the steering wheel with his fist.

Hernandez swore again, switched off the ignition, and looked up at the entrance. A blue-and-white cop car was parked on the gravel driveway. The big front door of the house opened and the familiar bulk of Vellares Sanchez moved out into the sunlight, the hint of a smile on his face.

Hernandez climbed out of the car. Sanchez waved. Hernandez waved back and walked up toward the house.

Vellares Sanchez was forty, a large man with dark, hooded eyelids who always looked like he needed a good night's sleep. His thinning black hair was combed across his head in wisps. The white linen suit he wore was crumpled and ill-fitting. Everything about him looked in disarray. But Hernandez knew that was all part of the detective's act. Behind his hooded, sleepy eyes was a sharp, probing intelligence. Rudi Hernandez learned early on not to underestimate Vellares Sanchez.

He was a man of few words but of great warmth. And as Hernandez approached, he held out his hand. His grip was firm, but before he got to what was obviously on his mind, he nodded to Hernandez's car.

"What's wrong with that heap of junk?" he asked, smiling.

"The choke's been acting up. Floods the engine. It'll be okay once the sun dries it out."

Sanchez examined the young man standing before him. Hernandez was tall, brown-haired, pale-skinned, and handsome. He wore his clothes loosely, like a lecturer from the *universidad*. He could have passed for a college teacher were it not for the jagged scar that ran across his right cheek.

They had known each other for ten years. Rudi was a fine reporter. He had a dogged energy and broke more than one case before the policía did. He was also a good man, and kind. There was a girl he kept in the barrio, not for sex—she wasn't his mistress—but because she didn't have everything in the head like other people did, and because she needed help. He gave it without asking for medals.

Hernandez was looking at him now with twinkling eyes, a smile on his face, but something else, too. Excitement? Fear? Sanchez took a pack of cigarettes from his pocket and offered one to Hernandez. He lit them both and looked at the young man.

"A few days ago you told me to keep an eye on this old man, Rudi. And now he's dead. Any thoughts?"

Hernandez looked around at the lush gardens, then back at the house. The smile grew broader. "Two come to mind. You can't take it with you, and money can't buy happiness."

"It sure can't buy good health, my friend." Sanchez drew on his cigarette, coughing.

"Was that why the old guy killed himself, because he was sick?"

"He was sick for sure. But whether or not he killed himself because of that . . . well, we'll have to wait and see." He poked a thick finger in Hernandez's direction. "I'm still waiting to know what exactly made you curious about Señor Tsarkin. You said he was connected with your friend Rodriguez, the smuggler. But what's the connection? Apart from the fact that they're both now dead."

Hernandez rubbed his chin. "I don't know, Vellares. I'm still working on it. I'll need more time."

"But you'll let me know when you've got something?"

"As always," Hernandez answered.

The two men had long ago worked out a modus operandi. Some cases they worked closely together, sharing information; others they kept a professional distance. Sanchez understood that he'd be the first to know when Hernandez had found whatever it was that sent him sniffing around this very rich and now very dead old German.

Hernandez reached into the back pocket of his corduroy pants and pulled out a wire-bound notepad, searched in his pockets for something to write with. "You mind if I take some notes?"

Sanchez shook his head. "Of course not. Only, my men from the forensic department haven't finished yet."

Hernandez nodded. "How long will they be?"

"They're almost done."

"You got a pen I could borrow?"

"You still borrowing pens? Reporters are supposed to carry pens."

"I keep losing them. Holes in my pockets," said Hernandez, shrugging a smile.

Sanchez handed a pen to Hernandez. "It was the same ten years ago, in the courts. How many pens you owe me now? Holes in your head, amigo." Sanchez went to turn. "Come inside. When the men finish, you can take a look around." There was enthusiasm in his voice now as he ground out his cigarette with the heel of his shoe. "You ought to see the place. This old guy had money to burn."

"Tell me . . . ," said Hernandez, and followed Sanchez inside.

Hernandez looked around the house in amazement, but pretending more surprise than he felt, because this was how he imagined a rich man like Tsarkin might live.

The crystal chandelier in the hallway, the sweeping staircase, the dining room with the silver candlesticks and the hand-carved chairs of solid oak, the kitchen that was bigger than his whole apartment. There was a Jacuzzi with gold-plated taps, and a tennis court on the back lawn.

The servants' quarters were near the outdoor swimming pool. Four servants, Sanchez told him, and three gardeners. They had all left for the afternoon, after Sanchez's men had questioned them.

Sanchez kept the study on the ground floor until last. The forensic men were finishing as they came into the hallway from the kitchen. Sanchez caught one of the men by the arm and took him aside to talk in private. When they had finished, Sanchez crossed back to where Hernandez stood, examining an oil painting of a sleek jaguar in a jungle setting. The painting was unsigned, but not bad. *A good amateur*, Sanchez thought.

"Well?" Hernandez asked.

"Suicide," said Sanchez. "No question. One less problem for me to worry about. We have a little time before they remove the body. You want to see Tsarkin?"

Hernandez nodded, and Sanchez led the way.

The door into the study was open, the room large, like all the others. The first thing Hernandez noticed was the painting in a gilded frame swung back on hinges to reveal a safe in the wall, its gray metal door ajar. Books lined the shelves along three walls. Hernandez looked around the room but couldn't see the body. His eyes went back to the safe just as Sanchez pointed toward the window.

"He's over there, behind the desk."

Hernandez crossed to the big polished desk and looked over, saw the trousered legs of the man first, then the pools of blood on the gray carpet. The man's head was covered with a bloodied white handkerchief. Hernandez suppressed the nausea he felt in the pit of his stomach and knelt down for a closer look.

"It's not pleasant. He shot himself through the mouth," Sanchez said.

Hernandez saw that the handkerchief was soaked through in sticky blood. As he pulled back the material, he felt the congealing blood come unstuck from the dead man's face. He nearly vomited.

The face itself was almost unrecognizable above the lips, the shattered jaw set in a final, contorted grimace, as if the dead man had feared the last moment before the gun had exploded and the bullet penetrated the roof of the mouth, shattering the cranium. The old man's wrinkled claw of a hand was raised and crooked, as if he were waving a grotesque good-bye.

Hernandez let the bloodied handkerchief fall back into place and stood, seeing the gun then, big and frightening on the gray carpet a yard away.

Sanchez looked across at him. "You okay?"

Hernandez swallowed. "Sure."

"It must have been quick. No pain. Not the worst way to go, amigo."

Hernandez nodded.

"How much do you know about him?" Sanchez asked, walking over to sit in a comfortable leather chair beside the coffee table.

"Not much. No family. Retired businessman. Owned a number of businesses, import-export mainly. German, emigrated after the war.

Made very little impact in this country, despite his wealth. Except for that, you'd hardly know he was here."

"You know about as much as I do about this man, Rudi," Sanchez observed. "He was a cipher. No religion, no charities, no notable vices. He just made money. Interesting."

"Do you know how old he was?" Rudi asked, notebook open, pad ready.

"Late eighties, maybe more? I'm not sure exactly just yet." Sanchez drew on his cigarette, coughed out smoke. "He had a long life. Hope I'm as lucky."

Hernandez said, "You mentioned he might have been ill?"

Sanchez flicked ash into a crystal ashtray. "One of the servants said he was in and out of the hospital for the past six months. Also, he had an appointment at a private hospital this morning. He was pretty sick. Cancer, the servant said. He'd lost weight. He didn't look too good." Sanchez glanced over at the corpse. "He looks a lot worse now. I'm having one of my men contact the hospital he attended. The San Ignatio."

Hernandez glanced at the body again, felt the sickness return. He moved a couple of paces toward the open wall safe. "Anything in there?"

"Nothing." Sanchez gestured to the fireplace with his cigarette. "But lots of ashes in the grate. Looks like he burned a lot of papers."

Hernandez stepped toward the fireplace. It had been his one hope, finding something, anything, but the old man must have been prepared, been sure before death to burn everything.

"Not a sliver of paper left. Nothing but ashes." Sanchez stared absentmindedly at the grate. "I wonder what the old man had to hide?"

"I wonder?" echoed Hernandez.

Sanchez looked up, stared at him for a moment before looking away again. "Anyway, it's all over now. And it's a wrap." He looked away, pushed himself slowly up from the chair with effort. He took the handkerchief from his pocket and dabbed his brow. "You want a beer? The refrigerator is full. Imported beers, too. German, Dutch, you name it. The old man isn't going to drink them now. Me, I could do with one."

"A beer sounds good."

Sanchez moved away. "I'll be back in five minutes."

Hernandez nodded. The detective turned and went out the door.

Hernandez stood there in the middle of the study, trying to think. His eyes went from the bloodied body to the wall safe, then to the fire grate. Why? Why had the old man killed himself? Because of his cancer? Or because of the people Rodriguez had told him about? Or maybe they had killed the old man, too, made it look like suicide.

He crossed to the big, blackened fireplace and stood in front of it, stared down. He took a tong quietly from the stand of utensils beside the fireplace and raked the ashes. It was just as Sanchez had said. Not a sliver of paper. Only soot and ashes. What had they been, these papers?

He replaced the tong and moved toward the open safe in the wall, careful to tread softly, listening at the same time for Sanchez's return. He peered into the safe; it was empty, as Sanchez had said. He crossed quietly to behind the desk, tried not to look down at the body near his feet.

Blood covered the desk's blotting pad and polished surface. Hernandez felt queasy again. There were two drawers on the left side of the desk. He tried the top one first. It was unlocked and slid out quietly, the smell of the apple wood rising up to meet his nostrils. Inside were a pair of scissors, a letter opener, and some plain white sheets of bond paper.

He flicked through the sheets of paper. All blank. He slid the drawer shut and tried the next. More blank paper, some rubber bands, a box of staples. He closed the drawer and looked down at the drying blood that seemed to be everywhere, at the rigid corpse, at the one hand raised in the air as if waving good-bye. *So long, Señor Tsarkin.*

The old man had been careful. Very careful. Perhaps elsewhere he kept some information. Something that would point a way, open a door for Hernandez so that he might know what was happening. Gaining access to the house or study again would be difficult, perhaps impossible. This was his one opportunity. He stepped back toward the rows of shelves lining the walls.

Books on Paraguayan history, a biography of Lopez, gardening books, heavy tomes on import-export regulations. Hernandez plucked one from the shelf. It was in Spanish, its pages virgin, unread. He replaced the book and riffled through some more.

The same. No thumb marks, the smell of paper strong. The old guy hadn't been a reader.

As he replaced the last book, the telephone rang.

Hernandez froze at the shrill noise disturbing the quiet of the study. It rang a couple of times, Hernandez listening to hear if Sanchez was returning, but nothing, no sound apart from the telephone. He crossed to the desk quickly and lifted the receiver.

"Sí."

"Señor Tsarkin, please." The man's voice on the line sounded prissy. Hernandez thought he heard music playing faintly in the background, Ravel's *Bolero*. He glanced down at the body of the old man on the floor, thinking for a moment. If it was a relative, it wasn't his business to break the news.

"What is it?" Hernandez asked more loudly.

"Señor Tsarkin! I did not recognize your voice."

Hernandez was about to interrupt, but the man spoke first. "This is the reservations manager at the Excelsior Hotel. I am telephoning to confirm that everything is in order. The executive suite you requested for Friday evening is Suite 120. I am at your service and hope everything will prove satisfactory for your guests."

Hernandez said it automatically, feeling his pulse quicken: "Yes, I'm sure it will." He turned his head sharply toward the study door, thought he heard footsteps in the distance. Sanchez returning?

"There is a slight problem, however, señor," the man went on, his voice now more stilted, formal. "We have some regular guests flying into Asunción late tomorrow night. They require several suites, and we are heavily booked. You said you would require the suite only from seven until nine o'clock. If it is possible, I would like to confirm this so that our expected guests may be accommodated." There was a pause. "Could you confirm this, señor?"

"Yes. Until nine." Hernandez swallowed, hearing his heartbeat quicken, hearing the footsteps outside become louder.

"Excellent!" said the man. "Thank you, señor. Buenas tardes."

"Buenas tardes."

Hernandez replaced the receiver and looked down at the body of Nicolas Tsarkin. Maybe not so *buenas*. When he looked up again, Sanchez was standing in the doorway, two cans of beer in his hands.

"Who was that?" Sanchez asked as he came into the room.

"No one," Hernandez said with a dismissive shrug. "A wrong number."

"You're telling me the truth?"

"Sure, why wouldn't I?"

Sanchez looked at him for a moment, then offered a can of beer, watching as Hernandez cracked open the chilled can.

Hernandez took a sip of the ice-cold German beer, the brand unknown to him. He looked over at Sanchez. "Good beer."

Sanchez said with an intensely skeptical look, "You should have let me take that call."

"It's no big deal, Vellares." Hernandez smiled.

"Let me be the judge of that." The detective raised the can to his lips and swallowed. "Are you finished here?"

"I guess so."

"Drink your beer, then we'll see what we can do with that car of yours. If I were a proper cop I'd have slapped you in prison for driving a car like that."

Hernandez smiled. He finished the beer in one long swallow, then tucked his notebook into his trouser pocket and slipped the pen in after it.

Sanchez said, "The pen's mine, amigo."

Hernandez winked and handed it back. "Gracias."

Sanchez put down the empty can and nodded toward the door. "Come, let's get out of here. Dead bodies give me the creeps."

Hernandez took one last look at the old man's corpse. Then he turned and followed Sanchez outside.

Hernandez drove back to the city through the dusty, hot streets and parked his car in the office lot of *La Tarde,* the old engine running smoothly now. He promised himself he would get it fixed just as soon as he had time.

He climbed the stairs to the newsroom and greeted his colleagues before going to his desk and switching on his computer. It took him only fifteen minutes to write up a filler on the old man's suicide, the bare facts, the name, the address, and the background information, remembering it all, no need for the notebook on the desk in front of him.

It was almost four in the afternoon when he filed his copy with the news editor, time for him to finish work. He flicked open his notebook, saw again what he had written there once he had left Tsarkin's house: *Friday, 7:00 to 9:00 p.m., Suite 120. Excelsior Hotel.*

Two days away. The question was, what was happening? Why had Tsarkin booked a suite for only two hours? A meeting? It had to be a meeting.

If that was it, then what he needed was a plan, a plan to get in there, listen to what was being said. He tidied his desk, then went down to the lot and drove to the Excelsior Hotel on the Calle Chile.

The hotel lobby was busy. A plush palace of Oriental carpets and dark wood, the best hotel in the city. Hernandez took the elevator to the first floor and found the suite with no problem, noting the nearby room numbers and the layout before going back down to the lobby and out to the parking area and the old red Buick, parked twenty yards from the hotel's fire-exit doors. Hernandez took note of the doors.

The day was still hot, and he kept the windows down on the way to his apartment, smoking as he drove, trying to work something out in his head, trying to come up with a plan. The key to it all was Tsarkin. Only now Tsarkin was dead.

When he stepped into his apartment twenty minutes later, he heard the gentle whirr of the air-conditioning unit by the window. He had forgotten to turn it off that morning. The room was cool, pleasant, and his body was very hot.

The apartment overlooked the city and had a sweeping view of the river south of Asunción. Rudi loved it. A bachelor's place, compact, one bedroom, a couch in the living room, where he had slept during Erica's stay. He went into the kitchen and poured himself a large scotch, added some cracked ice, then went to sit by the window, staring absentmindedly at the riverboats plying up and down the Rio Paraguay.

He glanced up at the photograph of his mother and father on the bookshelf in the corner of the living room. Why had his mother chosen to come to such a godforsaken city as Asunción? And yet it was home for him; he fit in more easily here than he ever had in his mother's homeland. There were many things he hated about this city, many things he loved. He hated the poverty, the corruption; he loved the girls, the sun, the easygoing mestizos.

He finished his scotch quickly, placed the glass on the table. He could still smell the scent of Erica's perfume lingering in the room.

He looked at the photograph on the bookshelf again, his father dark and handsome and smiling; his mother blond, pretty, but her Nordic face set in a harsh, strained smile. She should have smiled more. But then, she had never had much to smile about. That was the one thing the mestizos had done to his blood. Made him smile more.

He smiled now, thinking of the suite in the Excelsior Hotel, the plan coming into his head with such ease, so complete, that he picked up the telephone at once and began to call the number.

Perhaps the old Indian woman on the Calle Estrella had been right. Perhaps Erica would bring him luck.

He hoped so.

Because if not, then maybe he would end up dead, too.

RICHMOND, SURREY, ENGLAND. NOVEMBER 24

There were no pedestrians in the quiet street of redbrick Victorian houses, the small park it faced empty on this winter's day.

The black taxi drew up outside Number 21, and Volkmann paid the driver and stepped out. It was cloudy and cold, the sky threatening snow as he walked up the narrow front path. The garden was overgrown, dockweed climbing between the bare winter rosebushes.

As Volkmann unlocked the door and stepped inside, he heard the faint sound of music coming from the room at the back of the house and smiled. Cole Porter's "Night and Day."

He left his overnight bag by the door and passed the small parlor, its door open to reveal the silver-framed photographs on the mantelpiece and the walnut sideboard, the bric-a-brac his mother had collected over forty years.

In the kitchen, the big Aga range was fired, its metal throwing out a blanket of heat into the small room, the door at the end open, the music louder now as he stepped toward it.

She sat by the window of the music room, her gray head bent close to the Steinway piano. The silver-topped walking cane lay on top of the black, polished wood. She looked up as he peered around the door, smiled before removing her glasses.

"You've made an old woman very happy. I was beginning to think you wouldn't come."

He smiled back warmly, crossed to where she waited, and kissed her cheek. "It's only two days, I'm afraid. I've got to be back by Saturday."

She touched his face with her palm. "No matter, it's good to see you, Joseph. How was your flight?"

"Delayed, two hours. Why don't we go into the kitchen? It's warmer there."

He handed her the silver-topped cane and helped her toward the door, holding her arm as she limped. "I managed to get some tickets for the Barbican tonight. What do you think?"

"Tonight? But that's wonderful."

"It's Per Carinni. He's doing the three Beethovens." He smiled down at the old woman. "And how's the patient?"

"Much better now that you're here. You can tell me all the gossip about Strasbourg."

It never changed, the house, remained always as he remembered it each time he returned: the same familiar smells, the same peaceful quiet that enveloped him like a warm cocoon, and always music somewhere in the background. The radio was on, Bach playing softly.

They sat in the kitchen drinking tea. She had placed a plateful of cookies beside his cup, but he left them untouched, the old guilt creeping in on him again, the thought of her alone in the big old house, shuffling around on the silver-topped cane.

Every time he returned Volkmann remembered her as younger. He glanced up at the photographs on the wall over the kitchen fireplace: his father and her, taken more than thirty years before, her dark hair falling about her face as she smiled out at the camera, himself a boy sitting on her knee outside the cottage in Cornwall.

"Tell me about Strasbourg."

Volkmann put down the china cup. "There's not much to tell. There's still a lot of work to be done, and there's a lot of distrust about. The French don't trust the English; the English don't trust the French." He smiled at her. "And the Italians, of course, don't trust anybody. So much for mutual-security cooperation."

"What about Anna? Do you hear from her?"

"She telephones now and then. She met someone. She seems happy."

He stood up and placed a hand on her shoulder, smiled down at the wrinkled face. "Come. I'd like to hear you play for me. We have some time before the concert. Then I'll call a cab and have them pick us up at seven."

It was after one o'clock when the taxi taking them home after the concert turned into the street. The snow had stopped and when they reached the park, the old woman told the driver to stop, they would walk the rest of the way; she needed the exercise. Volkmann helped her out and gripped her arm, the snow soft underfoot, his mother ignoring his protests, saying she felt better, the evening had done her good.

The trees of the park were ghostly white as they passed the entrance, snow outlining their branches, the open spaces a gray expanse in the gloaming.

She wasn't limping now as they strolled toward the house. For someone of an artistic nature who had fallen ill, his father had once remarked, the doctor ought to prescribe a round of applause, not pills. Volkmann smiled in the darkness, remembering the remark.

She looked up at him. "Wasn't Carinni divine?"

They had reached the park entrance, and Volkmann looked down at her. "I've heard you play better."

She smiled. "You're a flatterer, Joseph. But you know the way to an old woman's heart."

She stopped to regain her breath, and he watched as she looked around at the snowy park landscape, then moved toward the entrance, stepping through the open gates. He stayed close behind her.

"This reminds me . . . ," she said.

"Tell me."

"Of when I was a little girl. Of Christmas. There was always snow in winter in Budapest." She looked up at him and he could see her face dimly. "But that was all such a long time ago. Long before I met your father."

"Tell me again."

He had heard it all before, many times, her words like some comforting litany. The season of plenty in Budapest, and the anticipation of Christmas. When the blue flag was up on the frozen lake in Octagon Square, and the ice was thick enough for skaters, and the red candles flickered in the windows of warm houses, warm as an oven, the smell of burning oil lamps, great gray plumes of coal smoke rising in the cold air. Budapest long ago, the city of her childhood.

But she was silent. Volkmann looked down, saw her wipe tears from her eyes. He touched her arm gently.

"Come, you'll catch cold."

She turned her head then, looked out over the cold white park. Volkmann moved to grip her frail arm before the melancholy took hold. As he looked at her face, he remembered the young woman she had been on the beach in Cornwall all those years ago.

She looked up at him and he saw the grief in the wet brown eyes. "I miss him, Joseph. I miss him so."

Volkmann bent and took her wrinkled face fondly in both hands, kissed her forehead. "We both do."

6

The giant Iberia 747 banked onto final approach and began its descent into Campo Grande airport.

Of all the passengers on board the packed flight to Paraguay's capital that late afternoon, none was probably as tired as the middle-aged man in the dark-blue suit who sat quietly in row 23.

The flight he had endured earlier from Munich to Madrid had been tolerable, but the long haul from Madrid to Asunción had taken its toll and now his dehydrated body ached.

It was almost three months since he had last visited Paraguay. He hadn't enjoyed it then, and it was unlikely he would enjoy it now. Mosquitoes. Heat. Temperamental natives. But this time his visit would be even briefer, twenty-four hours, and for that, he was grateful.

The man in the blue suit picked up the leather briefcase from the floor in front of him and clicked it open. He flicked carefully through the documents inside, checked that everything was in order.

A pretty flight attendant moved down the aisle, a last-minute check on seat belts. The man glanced up, saw the slim hips sway rhythmically toward him. The attendant paused, said something rapidly in Spanish as she pointed to the briefcase on his lap before moving on. The man in the blue suit clicked shut the case, tucked it neatly under the seat in front, and sat back.

Beyond the port window he glimpsed the sprawling, ragged suburbs of Asunción: the flat-roofed, white- and yellow-plaster adobes and the tin-roofed shacks of the barrios. As the bowels of the big plane shuddered, he heard the whirr of the flaps extending and the dull thud of the undercarriage lowering into place.

Five minutes later, he saw the yellow lights of the runway rush up beneath him, and then came the rumble of wheels on concrete as the giant aircraft touched down.

The man—his name was Meyer—retrieved his suitcase from the carousel and passed unquestioned through customs twenty minutes later.

In the arrivals area, a tall, blond young man who stood out from the waiting crowd held a placard stiffly in front of him: Pieter De Beers. Meyer stepped forward and the young man took his suitcase and beckoned for him to follow.

A Mercedes stood parked nearby, its black bodywork muddied, and he saw the three men waiting inside. Schmidt sat impassively like a rock in front, and the two men reclined in the back.

Both wore immaculate business suits, and both smiled when they saw Meyer.

One was young, in his middle thirties, and wore a light-gray suit. He was stockily built, and his dark hair glistened. Not handsome, but ruggedly attractive, and his broad face was deeply tanned from years in the sun.

The second man was old, his wrinkled face handsome. His silver-gray hair was more silver than gray and was combed back. He was tall, and had the look of a self-assured diplomat. He wore a charcoal-gray business suit, a white shirt, and a red silk tie, and his gentle blue eyes radiated confidence and charisma. He raised a hand and smiled again as Meyer approached.

The blond young man put Meyer's suitcase in the trunk, and Schmidt got out to open the rear door for him.

When Meyer slid into the backseat, the two passengers shook his hand in turn.

"You had a good flight, Johannes?" the silver-haired man asked.

"Ja, danke." As he turned to the younger, dark-haired man, he said, "Any problems?"

Kruger glanced at him and shook his head. "No, but some bad news."

"Oh?" said Meyer, feeling uneasy now, wondering if it had anything to do with the project. *It couldn't,* he told himself. Everything was in order, he was absolutely certain.

"We'll talk about it on the way, Johannes," said Kruger as he leaned forward and tapped the driver on the shoulder.

"The hotel, Kurt."

As the car started and pulled out from the curb, Meyer sat back, dabbing his forehead and silently cursing the heat, wondering what the bad news could be.

Rudi Hernandez was tired; he had been up until two that morning. Ricardo Torres had not arrived with the equipment until twelve-thirty, and it had taken him another hour to explain how to set it up.

"It's only a loan, okay? Make sure it all comes back in one piece," Torres had said. "Otherwise, my boss kicks me out on my butt, and I'm selling nuts outside the city zoo, comprende?"

Comprende.

The equipment was expensive. Torres had gone over the operation of the components with him, asking when he had finished, as he had when Hernandez had first telephoned him, "What you going to do with all this, amigo?"

Hernandez had smiled enigmatically and said, "Undercover work."

Torres had looked at him, one eyebrow arched. "Okay. But any damage, you pay, sí? Just remember that, Rudi."

Hernandez said there was no problem. He just needed to borrow the stuff for one night. He would return it intact.

He had gone to work early at *La Tarde,* finished at three, and driven straight to the apartment. He already had everything organized but went over it one more time so there would be no mistakes, no hitches.

There was a chance that the meeting at the Excelsior was simply a business conference. In which case he was going to a lot of trouble for nothing. On the other hand, he knew he could be putting himself in serious danger. Rodriguez was dead. And before he died, he had been very worried.

So, he thought, *if it's only a business meeting, then I have nothing to worry about. If it's something more interesting, then my plan had better work.*

If it didn't, he figured he was in big trouble, unless he could get out of the hotel fast. He remembered the fire exit on the first floor that led down to the rear of the hotel. A bolt-hole. He might need it.

He stood and went into the kitchen, poured himself a tepid Coke as he sat, then lit a cigarette, thinking about the plan, trying to see flaws. No real flaws, only risks, he decided.

He stubbed out the cigarette in the ashtray and stood, aware of his restless anxiety. From the bedroom he took the suitcase, already packed with the rest of the things he needed, then came back into the living room once again.

He laid the suitcase on the couch and flicked open the catches, checked that he hadn't overlooked anything, then turned his attention to the equipment Torres had loaned him, lying on the coffee table.

He took it piece by piece and placed it carefully in the suitcase among the clothes he had already packed there, making sure the equipment didn't rattle around, remembering that Torres had said it was sensitive. When he had finished, he checked through everything again, carefully shut the suitcase, and thumbed the combination lock to another set of numbers.

He felt a shiver of fear go through him. He sucked in a deep breath, let it out slowly.

Relax, amigo. Stay calm. Otherwise you're dead even before you start.

He glanced at his watch. Five-thirty.

He just had time to change, and then it would be time to go.

The black Mercedes moved slowly through the evening traffic toward the city. The glass partition between the driver and his passengers was closed, allowing the passengers their privacy.

Meyer looked out beyond the tinted windows at the lights coming on as dusk fell, at the smaller cars moving past on either side in the three-lane traffic, drawing him closer to the city, to his final meeting in this dreadful country.

A battered yellow pickup went slowly past the window, a cowboy-hatted Indian and his fat wife sitting in front, a crying child on her lap, windows rolled down, a radio blaring out Paraguayan harp music. In the back of the pickup, half a dozen restless, brown-faced scruffy children danced about like monkeys.

Dirty, idiotic kids. Meyer turned his head away in disgust. How had his people endured it here? He glanced at Kruger.

"The news you spoke of . . . ?"

"It's Tsarkin. He shot himself two days ago."

Meyer's eyebrows rose in surprise. "He's dead?"

Kruger nodded. "It was only a question of hours, anyway. Cancer. So he decided to take the quick way. He sent a letter to Franz Lieber before he did it. Said the pain was too much to bear. He wished us well, said he was sorry he couldn't make it."

Meyer nodded, understanding, remembering Tsarkin's poor health.

"A great loss," commented Meyer. And then a thought struck him, a terrible thought. "His papers?" His face showed concern as he looked at the silver-haired man seated opposite.

The silver-haired man smiled. "There is no need for alarm, Johannes. Tsarkin burned all his papers. Everything. Nothing can lead back to us. Nothing."

"Our people checked it out?"

This time it was Kruger who spoke. "Franz called at the house after the cops left. There's absolutely nothing to worry about. He checked it out with the servants. The cops saw it as a straightforward case of suicide."

"He checked Tsarkin's study and belongings?"

"There were only some old photograph albums. He removed them."

"And Tsarkin's safe-deposit box?"

"He emptied it himself. Burned everything before he pulled the trigger." He looked across at Meyer. "I'm certain Franz has been thorough."

Meyer nodded and said, "And the arrangements for the meeting?"

"Tsarkin said the hotel was organized as usual, but Franz checked just to be certain. Everything is in order." Kruger paused. Then he smiled and said, "He was a cautious man, old Nicolas. As cautious in death as in life."

Kruger turned his face back toward the window. The silver-haired man reclined farther in his seat.

Meyer did the same, relieved.

Hernandez reached the Excelsior at five-fifty and parked the Buick twenty yards from the fire-escape doors that opened onto the parking lot.

He strolled over to the exit doors, placed his palms against the metal, and pushed. The doors were locked by sprung bars that could be opened only from the inside. He had checked already to make sure they worked. They did. He probably wouldn't have to use them, but he wasn't taking any chances. Nothing must obstruct the doors from opening onto the parking lot.

A row of metal garbage bins stood nearby, twenty yards from the kitchen's rear entrance, but did not obstruct the exit. Satisfied, he crossed back to his car, removed his overnight suitcase, and left the driver's door unlocked. He walked around to the hotel entrance. He wore tinted glasses and a gray business suit.

As he walked over to the brightly lit lobby and headed straight for the reception desk, he saw a dark-suited man standing behind the counter, busy sorting through some papers.

The man looked up as Hernandez approached. "Señor?"

"I have a reservation for tonight. My name is Ferres."

"One moment, señor." The man tapped the computer terminal

beside him. Without looking up, he said, "Señor Ferres. Room one hundred and four. The first floor." The man looked up, smiled a plastic smile. "Our last free room. You were lucky."

I hope so, Hernandez thought. He had telephoned the hotel the evening before last to make his reservation, explaining to the reservations clerk that he had stayed on the first floor before and had enjoyed the view, had a preference for it. The clerk had said yes, but only a double. Hernandez had said he would pay for the double.

"Will señor be settling his account in cash or by credit card?"

"Cash," said Hernandez. "And I would like to pay now. I intend to leave early tomorrow morning."

"Certainly."

"Also, I am having some friends come by shortly. I want a bottle of champagne and some canapés sent up to my room immediately."

"But of course, señor. At once. I will see to it."

The bellhop carrying his suitcase led him to his room at the end of the corridor, five doors from Tsarkin's suite and on the opposite side of the corridor. Having the room on the first floor was imperative. And it had been the last one free—a good omen, surely. The evening after telephoning the Excelsior, he had gone to the hotel once again to examine the corridor layout. The room he'd booked was perfect, not too close, not too far away.

As Hernandez followed the bellhop into the room, the boy switched on the lights, placed the suitcase on the rack provided, waited for his tip. Hernandez obliged; the boy smiled, bade him good evening, and withdrew.

Hernandez crossed to the window and stared out: lights coming on everywhere, darkness descending rapidly over the city. And there was real fear in him now. He checked his watch. Six o'clock. Whoever was going to use the room down the hall would be arriving soon. A sharp knock rattled the door.

He admitted the white-coated, smiling waiter, the food trolley he pushed laden with the champagne and canapés. Hernandez watched him, the way he worked, listening to the chatter. The man made a fuss of arranging the trolley in the center of the room. Hernandez requested him to leave the champagne unopened.

"Of course, señor." The waiter bowed and went to leave, but not leaving, a practiced art.

Hernandez peeled off some bills from the wad in his pocket. "That was excellent service. What is your name?"

"Mario, señor. Mario Ricardes."

"Thank you, Mario." Hernandez handed the man the money; the waiter bowed and left.

Hernandez looked at the champagne and food. The story was costing him a small fortune already. He hoped it was worth it. The champagne was French and expensive, the six sparkling glasses neatly arranged beside the bucket of crushed ice. The canapés looked exquisite: neat, crisped triangles of fresh bread with smoked salmon, anchovies, various cheeses, meat pastes, arranged splendidly on a silver tray.

He went to sit on the bed, opened the suitcase, and removed everything he needed, laid them neatly on the spread.

He went to work quickly, setting everything out in its place. When he was finished ten minutes later, he lit a cigarette, then punched in the number to call suite 120. There was no reply.

Whoever intended on using the suite had, thankfully, not arrived early. Had someone answered, he would have pretended a wrong number and put down the phone.

Hernandez checked his watch again. Six-ten. He stubbed out his cigarette in the crystal ashtray and stood up nervously.

It was time to go to the lobby.

It was a different hotel this trip, Meyer noted as the Mercedes drew up outside the Excelsior. But they had used the hotel before, many times, he and Winter. But never together. The meetings to deliver the reports had alternated between both men.

The hotels had been Tsarkin's idea; a different room each time meant there would be less chance of electronic bugging or eavesdropping. Better than using a house, where prying neighbors might pose a threat to security.

The house in the Chaco, of course, would have been ideal, but it was too remote and when the rains came, the roads were often impassable.

Schmidt and the driver stepped out of the Mercedes and opened the doors, Kruger and Schmidt leading the way into the lobby, Meyer walking beside the silver-haired man.

They waited while Kruger went to the reception desk, carrying his briefcase. Meyer glanced around at the luxurious surroundings. The lobby was quiet. A couple of nice-looking girls sat in leather easy chairs nearby. A young man wearing a gray suit sat close by, reading a newspaper.

Meyer saw Kruger return from the desk. "Which room?" Meyer asked in German.

"One-twenty," Kruger replied.

They all followed Kruger to the elevator.

Six-fifteen.

Hernandez had bought a newspaper and found a vacant chair in the lobby, facing the reception desk.

Background music played softly in the lobby, but he had a perfect vantage point and if he concentrated hard, he could understand what was being said at the desk. He opened his newspaper, pretended to read, but kept his eyes on the entrance lobby.

Ten minutes later Hernandez saw the men. His eyes flicked to the entrance instinctively as he heard them come into the lobby. Four men, all wearing business suits, all European-looking. Hernandez was suspicious immediately: the four men carried no luggage, and only two carried briefcases. They could have been simply returning from a business meeting in the city, but a gut feeling told him otherwise.

One of the men was obviously a bodyguard, a giant of a man, looking uncomfortable in his pale linen suit. He walked ahead of the group, big-chested, close-cropped blond hair. He had a swaggering, slow, awkward gait and looked as if he were made of solid granite. Not the kind of man you tackled, unless you had an army behind you.

The second man was rugged, in his mid-thirties, with dark, shining hair. He carried a briefcase and looked like a company executive. The third was middle-aged, overweight, and wore a blue crumpled business suit. He held his briefcase under his arm and he looked tired, as if he had endured a long journey.

But the fourth man was the one who stood out from the group. An old man, but tall, leanly built, his silver hair swept back off his handsome face.

One of the men approached the reception desk while the others waited nearby. Hernandez listened, trying to separate the faint, piped hotel music from the voices, but the man spoke very quietly.

"Sí, señor . . . ," came the reply from the desk clerk, and then a muttering of words in Spanish. The background music suddenly rose in pitch, almost drowning out the voices. Hernandez swore. *Speak louder, amigo. Louder.*

"All ready for you, señor . . ." More babble. *Darn!* He hadn't heard the room number.

Hernandez went to stand, to move closer, but saw one of the men, the tired-looking one in the crumpled blue suit, glance over at the girls nearby, then at Hernandez. He shifted in his seat, looked down, pretending to look at his watch. He did not want the man to get a good look at his face. He was unfolding his newspaper when he heard the voice speak faintly, in German, in his mother's tongue, the language of his childhood, the man in the steel-blue suit asking it softly of the dark-haired man, as he passed by Hernandez, moving toward the elevator.

"Welche Nummer?"

"Ein hundert zwanzig."

Which number? A hundred and twenty. Hernandez felt a shiver of excitement.

These are the men.

He watched as they crossed to the elevator. The older man, the one with the silver hair, stood in the center of the group. He made a remark and the others smiled and laughed, but Hernandez couldn't hear what was said. The men were too far away.

The door opened, and they stepped in. Hernandez stood and watched the numbers over the elevator halt at floor one.

He waited for a minute before moving toward the second elevator, reached it seconds later as the doors opened. He felt a knot of fear in his stomach as he stepped inside and punched the button for the first floor.

When they stepped out on the first floor, Schmidt led them to the suite, inserted the key card, and went in first, his big blond head touching the top of the door frame. He switched on the lights, checked the room, closed the curtains, his muscular bulk awkward but moving fast.

Kruger entered next, followed by the others. As Meyer closed the door behind him, Kruger unlocked the briefcase he carried. He took out the rectangular, handheld electronic detector, held it chest-high, turned around in a circle, watching the small red indicator light at the tip of the device. He listened for the alarm signal, but none came. None had ever come; it was only a precaution.

Kruger placed the device back in his briefcase and said, "All clear."

Schmidt took up a position in a chair by the locked door, sat down, and folded his arms, two bulges evident on either side of his broad chest, where, Meyer knew, the holstered pistol and the big, jagged-edged knife were strapped. The man was expert with either weapon and intimidating all the more because of his perpetual silence. But his presence at these meetings always made Meyer feel secure. No one would tangle with Schmidt and live.

As the three men sat around the table at the end of the room, the gentle hum of the air conditioner wafted in the air, but it was warm in the room, still humid.

Meyer dabbed his brow, flicked open his briefcase, and removed his papers.

"The report on Brandenburg first, I presume?"

The handsome, silver-haired man made a steeple of his slim, manicured fingers, and his gentle eyes sparkled.

"If you would be so kind, Johannes. I know you must be tired, so let us proceed as quickly as possible."

Meyer nodded and dabbed the sweat from his brow again. Then he looked down at his papers and began to speak.

7

ASUNCIÓN

Hernandez stood in front of the bathroom mirror. Gone was the gray business suit and the tinted glasses. The white shirt remained, but this time with a black tie. Instead of the suit, he wore a waiter's white service jacket, black trousers, and black shoes he had bought the previous day in a catering supplier on the Calle Palma. Without the glasses, his hair brushed down, he certainly looked different. He touched the scar on his right cheek. Nothing could be done about that.

If they were professionals, they would be careful to check the suite for listening devices. That was why he wanted to give them a little time. If his plan worked, he wouldn't be able to record all their conversation, but the men were going to be a while in the suite, so he should be able to hear most of it.

If the plan worked . . .

He stepped out into the bedroom and took the single sheet of hotel-monogrammed notepaper from the bedroom's desk, checking the scribbled note he had written. Champagne and canapés. Suite 120.

He knelt down and raised the white linen cloth that hung over the food trolley edge. Underneath he saw the tiny microphone he had placed there earlier with the adhesive tape, checked again that it was secure.

Satisfied, he let the tablecloth fall back into place and then turned his attention to the second part of the equipment lying on the bed. It was an old Japanese-made receiver-recorder, but no bigger than a cigarette pack. He had checked the transmitter and it worked properly, as Torres said it would.

The receiver was battery-operated, and Hernandez inserted one of the two miniature cassette tapes he had brought. Everything was ready. A spare two-hour tape lay on the bed, just in case. He stood up and checked his watch. Six-forty. The men had had fifteen minutes. Hernandez hoped it was enough time. He picked up the white waiter's towel and placed it over his left arm. He was ready.

For a couple of seconds, he hesitated, thinking of Rodriguez's hideous corpse, and a spasm of cold fear shot through him.

He forced the memory from his mind as he walked briskly to the door, opened it, and peered out into the corridor.

Empty.

He pulled the trolley out behind him, checked to see that his room key card was safely in his trousers pocket, then closed the door after him.

He listened again in the corridor for any approaching sound.

Nothing.

Hernandez drew in a deep breath and let it out quickly, then started to push the trolley toward suite 120.

It took Meyer twelve minutes to read the report. He kept to the key points, careful to highlight his hard work, the attention to detail on which he prided himself. Now would come the questions. He looked up.

The handsome, silver-haired old man seated opposite nodded his head agreeably.

They all heard the soft knock on the door, and their heads turned sharply. Meyer saw that Schmidt already had his pistol out and by his side. Another knock, louder this time, and Kruger stood up quickly and crossed to the door, Schmidt calling out in Spanish, "Who is it?"

Kruger moved the big man aside and put his ear to the door. Everyone in the room heard the voice behind it reply.

"Room service, señor."

Kruger nodded to Schmidt, and the big man stood back from the door, pistol at the ready.

Kruger opened the door a crack but kept his shoulder firmly against it. A room-service waiter stood there, a dumb smile on his face.

"We didn't order anything," Kruger said curtly. "You must have the wrong room."

"Really, señor? Oh . . . I'm sorry . . ." The waiter looked at the slip of paper in his hand, then at the room number, and said, "No, señor . . . Suite one-twenty. Champagne and appetizers. Compliments of the hotel."

Kruger opened the door. He saw the champagne wedged in a silver bucket of crushed ice, the neatly arranged appetizers. He gave the waiter a questioning stare.

The waiter showed him the order on hotel-engraved notepaper. "See, señor . . . it's written here. Suite one-twenty. Champagne and canapés."

Kruger took the slip of paper, examined it carefully, then handed it back.

The waiter shrugged. "If you don't want it, señor, I can take it back. It's no problem." He smiled affably. "It's a new complimentary service for our suite guests."

Kruger glanced again at the food trolley. He was thirsty and tired, and the suite was humid. The chilled champagne and the appetizers looked refreshingly tempting.

"Very well, you may come in."

Kruger stepped back, and the waiter wheeled the trolley slowly into the center of the room, close to the table where the others sat, several yards away.

As he began to undo the wire around the neck of the champagne, the man with the dark, greased hair said, "Leave it. We can attend to that ourselves."

The waiter nodded, a grateful look on his face. He patted the linen tablecloth, rearranged two of the glasses, coughed quietly.

Kruger took the hint, impatiently removed his wallet, and handed the waiter a single note.

"Muchas gracias."

Kruger noticed the scar on the young man's cheek. "Your name?"

"Ricardes, señor. Mario Ricardes."

"See that we are not disturbed again, Mario."

"Yes, señor. Of course, señor. If there is anything else you wish, please do not hesitate to call room service."

Kruger nodded impatiently.

Hernandez turned toward the door, away from the silver-haired man, toward the big blond with one hand behind his back. He took one last look around the suite and tried hard not to make it obvious as he smiled.

"Buenas tardes, señores."

He had his hand on the doorknob now as he bowed slightly, glimpsed the men at the table—the tired-looking man in the blue crumpled suit, then just a second's glance at the silver-haired man—before he closed the door after him, took three, four steps, then let out a long sigh.

Santa Maria . . .

He walked quickly back toward his room.

The three men were seated at the table again.

Meyer was still feeling the effects of dehydration after the long flight. He licked his parched lips. The iced champagne looked appealing, but it would have to wait. It was time to answer any questions.

The silver-haired man's tone was businesslike. "The shipment . . . ?"

Meyer nodded. "The cargo will be picked up from Genoa as arranged."

"And the Italian?"

"He will be eliminated, but I want to be certain we don't arouse suspicion concerning the cargo. It would be prudent to wait until Brandenburg becomes operational. Then he will be dealt with along with the others."

The silver-haired man nodded his agreement, then looked at Meyer intently. "Those who have pledged their loyalty . . . we must be certain of them."

Meyer said firmly, "I have had their assurances confirmed. And their pedigree is without question."

Kruger shifted restlessly in his chair as he looked at Meyer. "And the Turk?"

"I foresee no problems."

Kruger said, "The woman in Berlin . . . you're absolutely certain we can rely on her?"

"She won't fail us, I assure you." Meyer glanced over at the elderly man. "There are no changes to the names on the list?"

The man shook his head firmly. "They'll all be killed."

"Your travel arrangements?" Meyer inquired. "Everything has been organized?"

"We leave Paraguay on the sixth."

Meyer looked at the two men. "The schedule . . . perhaps I should go through it once more?"

Both men nodded.

Meyer ran a finger around the rim of his shirt collar. Even with the air-conditioning on, the heat was unbearably oppressive. Ninety percent humidity at least. He wished the meeting would end. A matter of no more than ten minutes now, he was certain. Kruger would want to go over the key points again. He licked his dry lips, glanced at the food trolley the waiter had brought, the neck of the champagne bottle visible in the ice bucket.

"It's quite warm in here. Perhaps I might have a glass of water?"

Kruger nodded.

Meyer stood and crossed to the side table, where a carafe of water and several glasses sat on a tray. He poured himself a glass of the tepid liquid, glancing at the iced champagne on the food trolley as he drank. He had barely eaten on the flight. The appetizers looked so appetizing. Meyer finished his glass of water and filled another. He would have to move the trolley out of sight; it was beginning to distract him, the sight of that delicious food and the chilled champagne nestled in the ice bucket.

When he leaned across and gently pushed the trolley away, he was surprised that it moved so smoothly on its wheels. He saw it slide away rapidly, glide across the carpet, and bump into the desk in the far corner, rocking the table lamp, almost knocking it over.

Meyer turned and saw Kruger glance up at him from his papers. Meyer returned to his seat, wishing the meeting would end.

Everything was going fine until Hernandez heard the click in the earphones.

He sat on the bed nervously smoking a cigarette. The dated Japanese tape recorder lay in front of him, the cores of the tape still turning smoothly.

The men had been speaking in German; Hernandez heard the voices clearly as the machine recorded their conversation.

In his childhood, his mother had spoken to him in both Spanish and German, sometimes in Guarani, that curious, expressive mixture of Indian-Spanish that the ordinary Paraguayan preferred to speak. But German was second nature to him, the language his Paraguayan father had hated but his mother persisted in using.

And then he heard the click in the earphones.

The voices became muted, more distant, and then nothing, only a faint buzzing sound.

Hernandez swore out loud. He turned up the volume quickly, pressed the earphones closer. Nothing. Dead. Torres had said the equipment was good, sensitive, could pick up the buzz of a mosquito at ten yards. Well, either it was picking up the buzz of a mosquito right now or the microphone had worked itself loose or been damaged . . .

Or the men had found it.

Hernandez wondered whether to leave, just go, get out now. No, better to stay, because the men wouldn't know which room he was in, wouldn't know where the receiver was situated. And from the room, he could always call the police.

Please, God, don't let them find the microphone.

Hernandez sat on the bed for another fifteen minutes, smoked two more cigarettes, listening to the faint buzzing in his ears. Then he heard a loud bang like a gunshot. Seconds later came the sudden sound of laughter in the earphones, the thin clink of glasses, the faint sound of voices.

"Prost."

"Prost."

"Prost."

A chorus of prosts.

Hernandez let out a loud sigh, began to relax, began to understand. The men were drinking the champagne. Thank heaven. They hadn't found the microphone.

The three men raised their glasses once more, in silence this time, the meeting concluded. Meyer looked at the silver-haired man, saw him sip the champagne. The man was pleased, very pleased, Meyer could tell. The meeting had gone well.

Finally Kruger put down his glass and said to Meyer, "We must take our leave of you. It's a long drive back north. The driver will take you to the safe house."

Meyer nodded. The silver-haired man placed his glass on the trolley and gripped Meyer's hand firmly in both of his, a warm handshake, Meyer feeling the pride, the pleasure, well up inside himself.

Kruger nodded to big Schmidt, who opened the door, stepped out into the corridor, eyes left, then right. He turned, nodded the all-clear.

Meyer and Kruger picked up their briefcases. The silver-haired man followed after Schmidt, then Meyer next, Kruger last, taking one last look around the room to make sure nothing had been left behind, before closing the door after him.

Schmidt led the way to the elevator.

Hernandez heard faintly the last words of the conversation in suite 120 and then silence. Curse Torres and his equipment.

But at least he had something on tape. If only he knew what the men were talking about.

He shivered inside, hearing the sentence in German again in his mind. "Sie werden alle umgebracht." They'll all be killed. Whom were they going to kill? And Brandenburg—what was Brandenburg? And what was the list? The pedigree? And who was the Turk? Their words made no sense.

A chill coursed through Hernandez's body like an electric shock. Most likely the men were big dealers from Europe. The ones who came over once or twice a year to renew narcotics contracts, to discuss prices. But there was something odd about the whole thing, something strange, a gut feeling he had that wouldn't go away. Two of the men spoke the accented German of immigrants, their vowels softened by the lisping Spanish. Only one spoke pure guttural German, the singsong German of Bavaria.

Hernandez shook his head, confused by it all.

"The driver will take you to the safe house," the voice had said. Where was the safe house? Right now it didn't matter; he just wanted to leave the hotel as quickly as possible. But first he had to retrieve Torres's equipment from the suite. If he worked fast, maybe he could follow the men to the house they spoke of. He picked up the telephone, punched in the number.

"Room service," said the answering voice.

"Ah, room service! My colleagues in suite one-twenty appear to have some difficulty in trying to contact you. They wish a food trolley removed from their suite. At once."

"Of course, señor. Pronto. Suite one-twenty."

Hernandez replaced the receiver, threw off the waiter's jacket, dark trousers, and tie, then dressed again hurriedly in the business suit and blue silk tie. No need for the dark glasses, he decided. He had everything inside the case within two minutes, ready to go, key card to the room in his pocket.

The spare tape lay on the bed and he stuffed it inside his jacket pocket. He was ready. He opened the door to his room a crack, listened, and waited for the room-service waiter to appear.

In the lobby, Kruger went ahead of the others and crossed to the reception desk. The man behind it looked up, flashed a white-toothed smile.

"Señor?"

"Suite one-twenty," said Kruger. "We are leaving now. The bill has been paid, I believe?"

The man consulted the computer. "That is correct, señor. In cash, when the suite was booked. Everything was to your satisfaction?"

"Yes, thank you. My compliments to the hotel. The champagne and canapés were excellent. Buenas tardes." Kruger went to turn but saw the receptionist stare strangely at him before quickly glancing down at his computer again. Kruger hesitated.

He saw the man look up again, a quizzical expression on his face. "Champagne? Canapés? We have no record of such an order, señor."

Kruger swallowed. "I beg your pardon?"

The receptionist said mildly, "There is no record of such an order on our computer. Obviously a mistake."

Kruger said nervously, "The bottle of champagne and canapés delivered to our suite . . . you're saying they were not compliments of the hotel?"

The man smiled broadly, as if Kruger were joking. "No, señor.

Of course not. But I can check to be absolutely certain. Perhaps an order was sent to your suite by mistake. However, I doubt it."

Kruger turned visibly pale. The receptionist was already reaching for the telephone beside him, dialing a number. A moment later he spoke into the receiver, rapidly, but Kruger wasn't listening to the man's conversation. Something was niggling at him, worrying him. He was a cautious man, a man who never overlooked minor details, a man who checked and double-checked facts before coming to a conclusion. But this was odd . . .

The man replaced the receiver and looked at Kruger. "Room service has no record of such an order sent to suite one-twenty, señor. It's most strange."

Kruger could feel the palms of his hands sweat. "The waiter . . . his name, I think, was Ricardes."

The man smiled again. "It was he I just spoke to."

"The young man was tall. A scar on his right cheek."

The receptionist scratched his head. "No. Ricardes is not tall. And a scar? No, certainly not. I don't understand, señor."

But Kruger did. Kruger understood. His mind was racing. And he tried to focus his cold fury. He waved a dismissive hand at the man behind the desk. "A misunderstanding, obviously." Then he stepped back a pace, as though remembering something. "Excuse me, but I think I've left something in the suite."

The man smiled. "Of course, señor. Gracias."

Kruger turned and crossed quickly to where Schmidt, the silver-haired man, and Meyer waited, the three men sensing his disquiet.

"I think," Kruger said in a voice as cold and icy as death, "I think we may have a problem."

Hernandez heard the room-service waiter pass by his door, saw the flash of the man's white coat, and glimpsed his face. It was a different waiter this time. He waited until the man had knocked several times, and, receiving no reply, had taken a plastic key card from his pocket and inserted it in the door. As he stepped inside, Hernandez moved forward, closed his door, and crossed the hallway quickly.

He followed the waiter into the suite; the bemused man turned to look at him.

"Señor?"

Hernandez pretended to search through his pockets as he smiled. "I was just about to leave, but I think I have left my glasses in the bathroom. Would you be so kind as to fetch them for me?"

"Of course." The waiter crossed to the bathroom, switched on the light, and stepped inside.

Hernandez knelt beside the trolley and fumbled for the tiny transmitter taped underneath.

In the lobby, Kruger wasted no time. He acted quickly. In such matters he had sole responsibility, and now he exercised it. He gripped Meyer's arm.

"Take the chief and go outside to the car. Tell Kurt he's to drive you both to Franz's place and wait there until you hear from me. Tell the other driver to stay with the second Mercedes and remain at the entrance to the lobby. Werner is to go to the rear of the hotel. If there's a fire exit, tell him to wait by it. Give Rotman and Werner a description of the waiter who came to our room. Tall, dark-haired, young, perhaps thirty. Scar on his right cheek. As soon as they see him, I want him killed. Tell them, Meyer. I want him killed."

Kruger saw the silver-haired man look grimly at him, an uncharacteristic fury in his voice.

"I want him found, Hans." The man's voice almost shook. "No matter what it takes."

Kruger gave a sharp nod of his head. The silver-haired man went past, Meyer beside him, and strode quickly toward the exit.

Kruger beckoned to Schmidt. Both men walked rapidly toward the elevator.

* * *

"I'm sorry, señor, I can't find your glasses. You're sure you left them in the bathroom?"

As the waiter came out of the bathroom, Hernandez smiled and stood up from the trolley. He held up the glasses in his hand, the microphone-receiver already in his pocket.

"How stupid of me. I must have dropped them . . . here they are. But thank you for your help."

"No problem, señor."

Hernandez allowed the waiter to pass with the trolley. "I'll just check that I left nothing else behind."

"Of course, señor." The man left, closing the door after him.

Hernandez examined the room. The men who had been here were professionals. They would have been careful not to leave anything behind. He checked nonetheless. Finding nothing, he stepped from the room, closed the door after him.

He crossed the corridor and went into his room. A minute later he had stepped outside again, dragging his suitcase after him. He closed the door, saw the elevator open.

As the two men stepped out, Hernandez froze. There was a split second of mutual recognition, in which he felt his heart stop and saw the two men hesitate and stare at him—the dark-haired man and the big, rugged, blond bodyguard from the suite. The blond reached inside his jacket, the butt of a pistol appearing.

Hernandez swore, turned, and ran back down the corridor toward the fire-exit doors.

"Halt!" A rush of feet came from behind him as the shout in German rang out.

Hernandez reached the doors and pushed through. He raced down the emergency stairwell, the suitcase banging against the walls, slowing him. He cursed its weight, hearing the racing footsteps behind him on the stairs.

"Alto! Alto!" The voice was shouting in Spanish now, but Hernandez was intent on reaching the safety of the car, taking two, three steps at a time as he descended the stairwell rapidly. He came to the ground-floor exit ten seconds later, his chest heaving. As he pushed open the emergency doors and burst out into the darkness, he hesitated.

No!

He heard the men racing down the stairwell behind him. If he didn't slow them quickly, he'd never reach the car. He scanned the area frantically, saw the row of metal garbage bins nearby. Thrusting out his free hand, he grasped one of the metal lids, turned in the same movement, placed the lid on the ground, and kicked, wedging the lid between the base of the metal doors and the concrete.

He raced toward the car, reached the Buick just as he heard the fists pounding madly on the doors behind him, the voice raised in frantic anger.

"Sind Sie da, Werner? *Werner!*"

Fists beat on the metal like a roll of mad drums, but the wedge held. Hernandez flung the suitcase into the car and climbed in, the voice from behind the door louder, more desperate.

"Werner! Schnell!"

Hernandez fumbled to insert the key in the ignition. The key found its mark, and he switched the car on.

The engine spluttered and died.

Hernandez felt every drop of blood drain from his body. "No! Please! Not now! Start, please start!"

He turned the key again, pumped the accelerator, turning at the same time that he heard the deafening noise behind him, the grating sound of metal scraping on concrete as the garbage lid gave way and the two men burst out through the emergency doors.

The Buick's engine suddenly exploded into life. Hernandez hit the accelerator hard and the car shot forward. As he swung out into the exit lane, he saw a figure come racing toward him out of the darkness.

A man. Hernandez saw him reach into his jacket, fumble for something.

Werner . . . the man must be Werner.

Hernandez pushed the accelerator right to the floor. As the Buick rocketed forward, he flicked on the headlights and switched to high beam, saw the man shield his face from the sudden glare as he raised a pistol in his right hand. It was only a split second, but it was enough. The man twisted to the left to avoid being hit, his body crashing into the hood of a nearby car, the headlight glare catching the terror on his face.

Hernandez swung the Buick between two parked cars and drove at high speed toward the Calle Chile.

It took Kruger and the men two frantic minutes to race to the front of the hotel, where the second Mercedes waited.

The driver was already gunning the engine, saying, "What's going on?"

Kruger was like a man possessed. He flung open the door and pulled the driver bodily from the car, climbed in, and found the phone in the glove compartment. He punched in the number desperately.

As the number dialed out on the crackling line, Kruger cursed. He heard the click, and the line was lifted at the other end.

"Sí?"

"Have we a clean line?" Kruger spoke rapidly.

"One moment." There was a long pause. "Go ahead."

"It's Kruger. I'm at the hotel. We have a problem. I think someone overheard us discussing Brandenburg."

8

ASUNCIÓN

It was dark, and the man and the two girls sat around the poolside table of the big house in the wealthy suburb of Asunción, sipping drinks the manservant had brought. There were lights on under the swimming pool, giving the smooth water a turquoise color.

Franz Lieber looked across at the two beautiful young girls sitting opposite.

They were both half-caste mestizos, and very young and very ravishing, no more than seventeen, and they looked like twins. They were voluptuous, as only young girls can be, their bronzed, silky flesh protruding in all the right places. Cheap jewelry dangled from their wrists and necks, and their short, tight summer skirts displayed generous portions of their legs.

Lieber smiled and said, "My friend will be here soon. In the meantime, relax, enjoy yourselves."

Lieber saw the girls smile. One of them leaned forward to sip her vodka, showing her figure to Lieber deliberately. *Only seventeen,* thought Lieber, *but already she knows how to use her body like a weapon.*

The wiser of the two said, "Madame Rosa says you are very generous, sí?"

Lieber grinned. "I'm always generous to girls who please me."

The girl laughed and said, "Then I will please you very much." She looked at her friend, and they both giggled. Lieber smiled back wolfishly. He was fifty, with thick gray hair swept back off his forehead. He was a big man and big-boned. He also had big appetites: in food and drink, as his generous belly testified, and especially in women.

Tonight he and Hans were going to enjoy themselves, spend some time with the girls. It was a favor Lieber extended to certain guests, a refreshing, stimulating end to an evening. Hans would be here soon. In the meantime, he would have some fun . . .

He smiled at the girl who had not spoken. She was fresh, not long in the business, Lieber guessed.

"What's your name?"

"Maria."

"Come here, Maria."

The girl glanced at her friend. Her friend nodded, and the girl stood up slowly, came around to stand in front of Lieber. She looked good enough to eat . . .

The mobile phone on the poolside table rang. Lieber answered, "Sí?"

He heard the voice, recognized the urgency in it, and said, "One moment."

He covered the telephone mouthpiece and turned sharply to look at the girl, then at the other. "I need to talk in private," he said curtly. "Go inside and wait." He gestured to the open French doors behind him, light spilling from a sumptuously furnished room beyond.

The two girls hesitated.

"Now!" Lieber roared.

The girls jumped at the sound of his voice, speaking in whispers as they crossed quickly to the open French doors. Lieber waited until they were safely inside and out of listening range, then pressed the button on the scrambling device clipped to the phone.

"Go ahead," he said.

Lieber listened to the frantic voice.

"It's Kruger. I'm at the hotel. We have a problem. I think someone overheard us discussing Brandenburg."

Hernandez's eyes flicked to the rearview mirror as he drove toward the center of the city, not knowing where to go, what to do, only that he needed to hide.

He swung the Buick left onto the Calle Chile, past the illuminated pink dome of the Pantheon on the Plaza de los Héroes. The traffic was thin, and Hernandez wove swiftly in and out of the lanes. His heart pounded with fear as he watched to see whether the twin beams of a car's headlights would appear rapidly behind him. But none did. No one was following him. Not yet.

The red Buick was a problem. Its color made it easily identifiable, and the men had seen the car. He needed somewhere to hide it. Hernandez knew now where to go. He swung past the brightly lit Plaza de la Constitución, and down toward the river, where the streets became narrower and darker.

The warrenlike riverside barrio of La Chacarita loomed ahead, a drowsy, dark place of tin-and-cardboard shacks built on river mudflats. He could smell the river now, the rotten smell of sulfur and silt and mud, the river low. A familiar fishy odor swept into the car through the open window. At the river's edge, he drove right and halted outside a shabby house of peeling white plaster.

Hernandez climbed out and pulled the suitcase after him. La Chacarita was for the poorest of the poor, a tough area that even the cops avoided. He locked the driver's door and checked the others before stepping up to the house and knocking softly on the door.

Nearby, a group of old men sat chatting on the stone steps outside an old shanty dwelling. They glanced up but otherwise paid him no attention. Hernandez looked toward the river; a full moon dotted the silvery water with *camelotes*—floating clumps of matted waterweeds that looked like malignant bumps on the river's surface.

He heard a scraping noise behind the door and turned back.

A girl's voice called out softly, "Who is there?"

"It's Rudi."

A metal bolt rattled and a moment later the door opened. A young woman stood there in the dimly lit hallway. She wore a plain white cotton dress, and her brown eyes sparkled at her visitor. A look of innocence lit up her beautiful brown face, a look that always brought out the tenderest feelings in Hernandez.

"How's my Graciella?" Hernandez smiled.

She smiled back shyly, her long brown hair falling about her shoulders as she looked down at the suitcase. A sudden expression of fear darkened her face. "You are going away, Rudi?"

Hernandez shook his head. "No, Graciella. But I need a place to stay until the morning."

She didn't ask why, simply nodded and led him inside and closed the door. She took Hernandez by the hand into a small room off to the left, with a single ancient wooden bed set against a peeling wall.

Above the bed a tiny red light flickered below a picture of the Virgin, the room frugal, but spotlessly clean.

"You sleep in my room, Rudi?" The girl looked up into his eyes. Her body was full, would have been undeniably tempting to any man, but Hernandez shook his head.

"I'll sleep on the kitchen floor, Graciella." He smiled fondly at her and cupped her face in his hand. "Now, be a good girl and make me some yerba mate."

The girl nodded and smiled back at him. As his hand came away from her face, she took hold of it silently and led him toward the kitchen.

It took Franz Lieber five minutes to make the necessary phone calls. When he had finished, he looked at the turquoise water of the swimming pool, its pale, icy-blue calm as smooth as a sheet of glass. In contrast, there was a rage inside Lieber.

He swore.

Just when everything was going smoothly, just when everything was coming together, some snooping Latino goes and screws it up. The man was dead once they found him, whoever he was, of that much Lieber was certain. There was no place in the city the man could hide.

How could anyone possibly have known about the meeting? Lieber ignored his drink and concentrated hard, searching for weak links, for flaws. But there were none, especially in South America, especially in Paraguay, not here, not on his territory. The only ones who knew about the meeting were top people, and they could all be trusted, of that Lieber was certain. So how?

He sighed heavily. The consequences of failure were too awesome to even contemplate. Years of planning destroyed, millions wasted. Millions. Lieber grimaced. He had invested heavily in this, in time and money, and now everything was in jeopardy.

The man would simply have to be found, no matter what resources it took. At least forty men were already scouring the city, watching the airport, the railway and bus stations, the main exit roads. Lieber hoped the man hadn't too much of a head start. Kruger's description of him was vague—tall, in his thirties, dark-haired, a noticeable scar on his right cheek—but the man's big, ancient, red American car, that was something. Not many of those in Asunción.

Lieber pushed himself up from the chair angrily. The Mercedes would be here soon. He would have to get rid of the young women.

"Norberto!"

The mestizo manservant scurried out from the house.

"Sí, señor?"

"Take a car from the garage and drop the women off at Rosa's." Lieber produced his wallet, handed the servant a wad of notes. "Give them this. Tell them I don't need them tonight."

"Sí, señor."

"Do it now. Pronto!"

Lieber stepped into the study, taking the phone with him. The room looked out onto the front driveway. He poured himself a generous measure of scotch and drank half of it in one swallow. As he went to stand by the window, the phone buzzed in his hand. It was Kruger.

Lieber switched on the scrambler and said, "I've got forty men out looking. I'm doing the coordinating."

"The airport, the railway station?"

"All being covered. Including the main roads out of the city. I've issued a description of the car and the man."

Kruger's stern voice came down the line. "The others should be with you any minute. We want this *Schwein,* no matter what it takes. I'm afraid of the consequences for all of us if he isn't found."

Lieber swallowed. "Don't worry, he'll be found."

The line clicked. As Lieber put the phone down by the window, he saw the headlights of a car sweep into the driveway and bear rapidly up the path. The Mercedes had arrived.

9

The young woman lay sleeping on a tattered mattress by the old blackened stove.

She was seventeen, and Hernandez loved her—not the way he did his other women, but in a special way, a protective way. Graciella Campos had a mind that would have fit more comfortably into the body of a ten-year-old. In the barrio, she could have been trodden on, used, abused.

When he first met her, the men were already queuing up to use her body for a handful of Guaranis at a time. He was writing an article on the orphans in the barrio when a woman had told him about Graciella. Could Hernandez help?

When he met her, he was struck by her incredible beauty and innocence. Her grandfather guardian had died; she was penniless, and Hernandez took pity on her. He had offered to pay for a place for her outside the shantytown, this little delicate flower living in the dung pile of La Chacarita. But the child in the woman's body had refused, was scared outside of her natural habitat. The barrio was home to her despite the grinding poverty.

So Hernandez became her guardian, gave her what he could afford each week, got her a job on the cleaning staff at the cathedral near the plaza. He'd arranged with the woman who introduced them to call on Graciella every day, attend to anything she couldn't manage. But somehow she always managed.

The men no longer bothered her. A friend of his, a tough, honest man who worked on the riverboats, acted as her guardian angel. Already her guardian had cut and bloodied the faces of several who had not respected his protection.

Graciella's shanty house had three tiny rooms. They were in the largest, the room that served as a kitchen, a room the girl had proudly decorated in a simple, clean way. Whenever Hernandez came by, he always made sure he brought her something—a plant, some candy, a cheap trinket—to please her, to see the smiling brown eyes look up at him with innocent gratitude. But not tonight.

It was after 3 a.m. now, and Hernandez sat restlessly at the rickety old kitchen table. Graciella refused to leave his side and sleep in her tiny bedroom, wanting to be near her protector. But Hernandez was not tired. Too much was going through his mind. Graciella had proudly made them a supper before she fell asleep on the mattress on the floor.

The tape machine lay on the table, and he had the earphones on. Having listened to the tape so many times in the last seven hours, he knew the words the way an actor knows his script, every word engraved in his memory, every inflection noted. Graciella had been mildly intrigued. When she saw Hernandez with the tape machine, she had smiled and said, "Music, Rudi?"

Hernandez smiled back and shook his head. "No, something more important than music, Graciella." She hadn't comprehended and turned back to her cooking. It would have been pointless trying to explain; she never would have understood.

Now he looked again at the tape. What was on there wasn't much, certainly not as much as he had hoped for, though at least it was something. But what?

He rewound the tape, pressed the PLAY button.

"The shipment . . . ?"

"The cargo will be picked up from Genoa as arranged."

"And the Italian?"

"He will be eliminated, but I want to be certain we don't arouse suspicion concerning the cargo. It would be prudent to wait until Brandenburg becomes operational. Then he will be dealt with along with the others."

Pause.

"Those who have pledged their loyalty . . . we must be certain of them."

"I have had their assurances confirmed. And their pedigree is without question."

"And the Turk?"

"I foresee no problems."

"The woman in Berlin . . . you're absolutely certain we can rely on her?"

"She won't fail us, I assure you." Pause. "There are no changes to the names on the list?"

"They'll all be killed."

"Your travel arrangements . . . everything has been organized?"

"We leave Paraguay on the sixth."

"The schedule . . . perhaps I should go through it once more?"

Hernandez pressed the PAUSE button, sighed.

What was the shipment the men talked of? The white powder Rodriguez mentioned? And the men, who were they? Buyers from Frankfurt? The men who came to South America to negotiate contracts? But Hernandez sensed that something didn't fit. Something was strange about the older man, the one with the silver hair, but he didn't know what. A shiver rippled down his spine. He replayed the last part of the conversation again.

"We must take our leave of you. It's a long drive back north. The driver will take you to the safe house."

He waited for a moment, then pressed the STOP button.

He made up his mind then that he would phone Sanchez, tell him everything he knew, ask his advice. But already the men would be changing their plans, surely. Hernandez shook his head. In a way, he had risked so much for so little: voices on a tape, discussing something he could not comprehend.

He glanced at his watch. Three-ten. Sanchez wouldn't be on duty until eight, maybe nine, in the morning. Hernandez cursed silently. He wanted Sanchez to hear the tape. Perhaps he could help decipher it.

He looked down at the angelic face of Graciella sleeping and felt a twinge of guilt. The men wouldn't find him in La Chacarita; he felt certain of that. But no matter how remote that possibility, he was putting her in unnecessary danger.

Hernandez pressed the machine's EJECT button, and the tape popped out. He held it between his fingers. Perhaps it would be better to put it in his safe place until he could speak with Sanchez. That way, he would have nothing incriminating on him if the men found him.

The spare, unused tape lay on the table where he had left it.

Hernandez stood. Graciella stirred, turned over, continued her sound sleep. He would leave the car. It wasn't far to walk to the station where he kept the rented locker. He could take the side streets and be back in twenty minutes once he safely hid the tape. He stepped quietly into the hallway, slipped back the bolt of the front door, and took the spare key from the nail on the wall where Graciella always left it.

The man was tired.

He had scoured the streets of Asunción all night, and now it was after three o'clock. There was a year's pay for the man who found the car or the driver, and the thought of all that money was the only thing keeping him awake. The description of the guy he was looking for was vague; really, he needed a photograph. But the car was a help. It was easier to find a car than a face, and an old red American model shouldn't be difficult. But so far, no luck. The same with the other men; they passed each other in their cars as they scoured the city.

He had met two of his comrades at a coffee stand near the Plaza de la Constitución. They didn't know what was going on, either. Only that the man or the car had to be found, on Franz Lieber's orders. The money was proof enough that this was important.

The man rubbed his aching eyes and turned his car onto the plaza. The dark streets of La Chacarita loomed beyond. Not the kind of area you ventured into unless you wanted to risk your life. Even the thieves here were legendary. They joked about it in Asunción: make sure that if you're driving in La Chacarita and you have to give hand signals that you're not wearing a wristwatch.

The man grinned to himself. He had a .45 automatic pistol in the glove compartment, and a knife under his seat. Anybody hassled him and he'd blow a hole in him the size of a fist.

He drove across the brightly lit Plaza, and the car rolled gently downhill into La Chacarita . . .

It took Hernandez ten minutes to walk to the old railway station. He wasn't afraid; many people knew him in the barrio. The maze of narrow streets was deserted, and he walked slowly.

Fifty yards from the station entrance, he froze. Parked across the street, facing the entrance, were two cars, a dark Mercedes and a white Ford. Two men stood beside the Mercedes, smoking, talking. Hernandez swallowed. Such a sight would not have troubled him normally, but there was something odd about the scene. No trains were due for another four hours at least. Why would men like these wait outside the station at this hour? Both men wore suits, looked European. Like the men at the hotel. Like businessmen. Hernandez stepped into the shadows.

He looked toward the entrance, caught a glimpse of two more men standing idly by. One was young and blond and wore a leather jacket and open-necked shirt; the second was middle-aged, burly, and casually dressed. These did not look like businessmen, but they were waiting for him, Hernandez felt certain. Covering the station in case he tried to leave the city.

He swore. What he did at the hotel must have set off alarm bells. *Relax. Take it easy.*

But what if there were more men inside the station? How could he get safely to the luggage box?

He waited in the shadows for several more minutes until a thought struck him. He smiled. Perhaps there was a way.

* * *

Hernandez reached the rear of the station minutes later. A double wooden gate served as a rear entrance, one the railway workers used.

It was unlocked and he stepped into a small yard. A uniformed station worker sat in a tiny, glass-fronted office reading a magazine. The man stared up at him for a moment, then continued reading. People living in the barrio took this shortcut all the time.

A minute later, he was on the nearest platform. An ancient diesel engine stood silently up against the buffers, the smell of grease and oil thick in the humid air. The area where Hernandez stood was deserted, but he could see the platforms nearest the station entrance clearly, perhaps sixty yards away.

Indians and peasants slept nearby. An old man selling water and pistachios was asleep at his stand, his head down, nestled in his arms. Women in colored shawls waited with their husbands and sleeping children for the early morning trains. But no burly men in business suits like those at the hotel. The locker area was tucked away behind the shuttered concession stands, thirty yards from where he stood.

He scanned the distant crowd again, but he could see nothing unusual, no men like the ones he had seen outside. Still, it would be prudent to be careful. Hernandez saw a railway official sleeping soundly on a nearby wooden bench. His uniform jacket lay on the back of the bench. Hernandez crossed to where the man lay, saw that no one was watching, took the jacket, tugged it on, and continued walking.

When he reached the locker, he inserted the key.

"Señor . . ."

Hernandez heard the voice behind him and froze. He turned his head slowly, felt the instant fear. He saw the elderly man standing there.

"Por favor, señor . . ."

The man's face was dark mahogany, his skin deeply wrinkled. He carried an old, battered suitcase. An unlit cigarette hung from his lips. He smiled at Hernandez and pointed to the cigarette.

It took Hernandez a moment to understand. Then he fumbled with shaking hands in his pockets, gave the old man the cheap plastic lighter, and said, "Keep it. I have another."

"Muchas gracias, señor." The man turned and shambled away. Hernandez exhaled. Quickly, he opened the locker door, placed the tape on top of the envelope containing the photographs, and locked the door again. He replaced the keys in his pocket, crossed back to where the sleeping official lay, and returned the jacket.

The man had decided to drive down to the river and work his way back up, zigzagging through the warren of dark streets. At the water's edge he stopped, wrinkling his nose at the smell of sulfur and rotting fish. He wondered whether to turn left or right. He decided to turn right. He had the doors locked, and the automatic pistol was out now, on the seat beside him.

After three hundred yards of driving slowly, eyes scouring the waterfront and the tiny alleyways that ran between the shanty homes, he glimpsed the flash of red. An old red Buick, its rear badge unmistakable, its chassis rusting, stood parked in front of a house with white peeling walls. His hand automatically reached for the gun as he pulled into the curb. He smiled and grabbed for the phone on the seat instead and punched in the number quickly.

The line clicked. A voice said, "Sí?"

"It's Dortmund . . . I think I've found the car."

Hernandez walked slowly back along the river, taking his time.

La Chacarita was a deserted place of shadows at this early hour. He would tell Sanchez about the tape tomorrow, tell him everything he knew, hope that he could help. Leaving the tape in the locker had been a wise decision, he reflected. Even if the men caught him, he could bide his time, perhaps do a deal if he was forced to. What the voices on the tape said must be important. The presence of the men at the station testified to that.

He was too nervous and excited to sleep. He stopped by the river and lit a cigarette, thinking, knowing that something was happening, something really big, worth killing for, remembering the faces of the men on the first floor as they came out of the elevator, knowing with certainty that they would have killed him. He would tell Sanchez all this; it was too dangerous for him to pursue this alone now.

Hernandez looked at his watch in the lunar light. It was time to get back to Graciella's place and try somehow to get some sleep. He flicked away the lighted cigarette, watched as it cartwheeled into the silvery water, then turned and started to walk back toward the house.

As he approached he saw that the front door was open.

He froze.

He had closed the door after him, he was certain. Or had he? His mind was in such turmoil . . .

Hernandez heard the click and wheeled around instantly, felt the blood draining from him, saw the two men armed with pistols lunge at him, their faces a blur because already there was a rough hand over his mouth, stifling his cry, another gripping his hair, jerking his head back, pushing him into the house. As the door burst in, he was propelled forward with an almighty force, into the kitchen now, lights blazing in the tiny room, crowded with men . . .

Hernandez felt a sharp punch in his side, the hand still on his mouth, stifling his scream. Figures crowded around him, more blows rained down, pulped his face, bruised his body until he could hardly stand, the salty taste of blood in his mouth. Rough hands threw him back against the wall, two quick, sharp blows to his kidneys making him want to throw up.

Two big men held Graciella, her tiny body like a rag doll's between them. A white towel gagged her mouth, and there was blood on her pretty face, terror in her eyes. The recording equipment lay on the kitchen table still. Two of the men from the hotel, the dark-haired one who had opened the door to him and the elderly, silver-haired man, they stared at Hernandez with contempt.

The hand that covered Hernandez's mouth came away for an instant, and the dark-haired man's fist smashed into his face. Hernandez felt a sharp crack of bone and reeled back in pain, the bridge of his nose shattered, his scream muffled by the hand again over his mouth. Another blow struck him across the neck, fists raining down on him. Someone gripped his hair and jerked his head up so that he was staring into the face of the dark-haired man.

The eyes were gray and cold, threatening. "You will answer my questions. If you lie, the girl dies. If you tell the truth, she lives. You understand?"

The man jerked his hand toward Graciella. The two men holding her yanked her head back savagely by the hair until the whites of her eyes showed. One of them ripped her dress. The other took a big silver knife from behind his back, pressed the tip of the blade against the girl's chest.

The dark-haired man said again, "You understand?"

Hernandez heard Graciella's muffled cries and wanted to vomit. He nodded quickly.

The man stared into his face. "How did you know we were at the Excelsior? Answer quickly now."

The hand on Hernandez's mouth came away.

Hernandez gasped, "I was at Tsarkin's house the day he killed himself . . . covering the story for *La Tarde* . . . a call came . . . from the Excelsior Hotel . . . I answered the telephone . . ."

The dark-haired man's eyes lit up, understanding. He wrenched at Hernandez's pockets, ripped out the wallet, and examined the contents. He plucked out the press identity card, scrutinized the photograph, then handed it to the silver-haired man, the one in charge, before he nodded for Hernandez to go on.

Hernandez's voice came in short gasps, thick with fear, as he told him about Rodriguez. What he had been told about the men. About the equipment. About his plan. The dark-haired man turned pale.

He turned to look at the older man, whose face was even paler, eyes glaring over at Hernandez.

The dark-haired man nodded toward the table. "The tape. We checked; it's blank." His tone demanded an explanation.

Hernandez sucked in air. His body was on fire with pain; the blows had almost crippled him.

"Answer!" the man screamed.

"The microphone . . . there was a problem with it . . ." Hernandez began quickly, but the man suddenly cut him short with a sharp wave of his hand, as if he knew, a sadistic smile on his face now, his hand coming up to seize Hernandez's jaws in a painful pincer grip. Hernandez wanted to scream: *No, the real tape is in a safe place, I can take you to it. We can deal.* But the man spoke quickly.

"Rodriguez . . . what he told you . . . who else did he tell?"

Hernandez tried to shake his head. The man's grip still held him. "He told no one else . . . Only me."

"You are certain? I want the truth."

"Yes."

"And did you tell anyone else?" Urgency in the man's voice now. His grip tightened.

"No. No one."

Pause. "Tell me . . . why did you leave this house?"

"To get some air. I . . . I couldn't sleep."

"Where did you go?"

"I . . . walked along the river."

The man's eyes searched Hernandez's face for the truth. "The cargo Rodriguez told you about . . . what do you think it was? Answer truthfully now. The girl's life depends on it."

Hernandez looked at him through bruised and bloodied eyes. "White powder. You're shipping cocaine." Saying it and not caring, knowing now that he was dead no matter what he said, knowing that Graciella was dead, only hoping for her sake it would be quick . . .

The man released his grip. Hernandez begged, "Please . . . the girl . . . knows nothing. She's only a child."

The dark-haired man was smiling now, laughing as if something had amused him. He turned toward the older man with the silver hair. The man nodded.

The dark-haired man turned back. He stared into Hernandez's eyes.

"You're one stupid Latino!"

Then he turned and clicked his fingers. It happened quickly. The man holding the knife in front of Graciella raised his hand. The blade flashed. Hernandez was about to scream, but a hand came over his mouth again. He watched in horror as the knife came down, sliced through her chest from the valley between her breasts to the navel of her stomach. Hernandez saw blood spurt in a fountain, the whites of her dying eyes looking to heaven, her body suddenly limp, engulfed in blood. He felt the vomit rise in his stomach.

And then the big, blond bodyguard he had seen in the hotel stepped forward out of nowhere.

Hernandez saw the flash of another blade as the man drew a jagged knife from under his coat. Hernandez tried vainly to scream, but the hand trapped the cry in his throat, other hands pinning him hard against the wall.

He watched in mute horror as the jagged metal arced and dug savagely into his chest like a hammer blow. An agonizing pain blossomed, and then he slid back against the wall, slid down into the dark, growing pool of his own blood.

PART TWO

PART TWO

10

A log fire blazed in one corner of the restaurant.

From where they sat by the window, Volkmann could see the ancient cathedral spire rise into the gray afternoon sky, the red-and-brown-slated rooftops of the medieval center of old Strasbourg stretching in jagged rows. A cold wind blew across the Place Gutenberg, needles of rain clawing at the window.

You could usually set your watch by Ferguson's appointments, but almost half an hour had gone by, they had ordered, and there was still no sign of him.

The head of British DSE hated German food, which was why when they had their weekly informal meeting, Ferguson always chose a French restaurant.

Volkmann stared toward the bronzed statue of Johannes Gutenberg. The cold Place named in his honor was almost void of pedestrians despite the nearness of Christmas. Across the street, a stout, red-faced little salesman was standing on a chair, struggling to hang coils of silvered decorations among a store's seasonal window display.

Tom Peters sat opposite, sipping a glass of Bordeaux. The section's number two, Peters was a stocky Welshman of medium height, with graying sandy hair and a ruddy face.

He smiled at Volkmann. "There was an article in *Le Monde* only last week. Some hack reckoned that soon it'll be like the bad old days of the Great Depression." Peters nodded toward the struggling salesman. "For that poor guy's sake, I hope all the work is worth it."

Volkmann swallowed a mouthful of wine. "Did Ferguson say what he wanted to talk about, Tom?"

"Yeah. Something to do with the bloody Krauts."

The worries Volkmann had discussed with Sally Thornton seemed to be looming. DSE wasn't really working. On the face of it, the organization seemed to be dying of boredom, but he knew the problems went much deeper than that.

The German Section seemed to be on a go slow. Even the people in the French and Italian sections were spending more time than usual lingering over coffee. The only lively presence was in his own department, the British, and that of the Dutch. Both sections were busily working at their desks as if nothing were amiss, incurable bureaucrats that they were.

Ferguson arrived. A tall, gaunt man, pasty-faced, pushing sixty, he dressed like an English squire in Donegal tweeds, checkered shirt, and woolen tie knotted thickly. He took a seat at the table, apologizing.

"I see you've started without me." Ferguson smiled when he saw the wine bottle, and accepted a glass from Peters. "Have you ordered? I better do the same."

Ferguson ordered the fillet of sole with lemon sauce. He sipped his wine and sat back.

"I thought I'd let you know I had a meeting with Hollrich; it's what delayed me. He's been in Germany for the past week, consulting with his masters."

"Anything that concerns us?" Peters asked.

"It's the people in Berlin and Bonn," Ferguson replied. "They're talking about money problems, fiscal cutbacks. Considering the economic circumstances prevailing just now, it's as good an excuse as any. The Germans want to scale down their involvement in security cooperation. Concentrate on the problems closer to home."

"Well, they would, wouldn't they?" Peters raised an eyebrow.

Ferguson swirled his wine. "They say it's mainly money problems. That the mandarins in Bonn are whining about the need for spending cutbacks. We can all understand that."

"But the whole operation is run on a shoestring. You made that point, sir?" Peters said.

There was a silence at the table for several moments as the waiter brought their orders. Ferguson waited until the man had left before replying.

"It's not that simple, Tom," he said. He cut his fish with measured care. "Hollrich's main concern right now is with the internal situation in Germany. The world's troubles, or the rest of Europe's, hardly matter. We all know the problems in Germany are pretty serious these days. You watch TV; you've seen the protest marches and the riots. The chancellor's in trouble with a minority government. He's too weak to take any kind of action.

"I know it increases the workload for everyone else, and we'll just have to carry on, but that's the situation we're stuck with for now. I'm seeing Hollrich again on Monday. Naturally, I pressed the importance of the Germans staying within DSE. He said he'd pass on that message to his superiors."

Volkmann asked, "Anything else?"

Ferguson hesitated. "There is, actually. Something I want you to look into. A favor for Pauli Graf of the German Section." Ferguson paused. "It's a difficult time, and I don't want to rock any boats. However, something's come up I think we need to check out."

Volkmann said, "Which area?"

"It looks to be some sort of smuggling thing. Perhaps narcotics. According to Graf, Hollrich wasn't remotely interested. He said they hadn't the time or the manpower."

Volkmann asked, "So what's the problem?"

"A woman in Frankfurt, an old acquaintance of Graf's, was in South America recently. She discussed something with Graf that may interest us."

"Us?" said Peters.

"DSE, obviously," replied Ferguson.

"Why can't Graf handle it himself?" Volkmann asked.

"As I say, his people don't seem to want to touch the woman's information." He spread his arms helplessly. "Who can figure the Germans right now? Graf is being posted back to Berlin as of tomorrow. He says his department wasn't really interested because the crime—if there was a crime—took place in South America, outside his jurisdiction." Ferguson looked up. "On top of that, the woman failed to go through proper channels—a definite no-no where Hollrich is concerned, he's such a darned bureaucrat. She didn't take her information to the German police, so he won't touch her."

"Any particular reason why she didn't?"

Ferguson shrugged. "None that I know of. After Graf told her he couldn't help, she asked to talk to DSE. Said she had information concerning a smuggling operation into Europe."

"Who do you want to handle it?" Peters asked.

"I had thought Joe." The head of British DSE looked to Volkmann. "You've got the language and the experience in the field. You know your way around. It may not amount to anything, but no harm checking it out."

"That's all we've got? There doesn't seem a heck of a lot to go on."

Ferguson looked mildly irritated. "I've told you everything I know, Joe. Graf has helped us often in the past. I'd like to return the favor."

Volkmann noticed the stout salesman across the street. Finished with his display, now he peered hopelessly out the window. "What about the woman?"

"Her name's Erica Kranz. Freelance journalist by profession." Ferguson removed a slip of paper from his pocket, handed it across to Volkmann. "I've written out her address and phone number. Pay her a visit, see what it's about. You could drive up to Frankfurt tomorrow. But give her a call first."

"Okay, if you say so."

"If I'm not around, you can report to Peters. I've already requested information on Erica Kranz from the German Section. The file should be delivered to you by tonight." Ferguson smiled. "Sometimes I despise the Germans for their bureaucracy, but sometimes I'm grateful for it. They've got files on everyone."

Volkmann noticed the salesman across the square was standing at the entrance to the shop, hands clasped behind his back, examining his work. The pavement was still bare of shoppers.

Volkmann saw Ferguson observing him, then his boss's eyes flicked to the salesman.

"I think I read somewhere recently that during the Depression it was just the same—everyone who was still in business chasing after what few pennies were in circulation. Every economy's a basket case right now. But thank heavens we can leave such problems in the incapable hands of our politicians." Ferguson grinned, pouring himself another glass of wine.

Peters glanced over at Volkmann and raised his eyebrows. Volkmann smiled and sipped his wine, and said nothing.

The Orangerie Park, with its exotic birds, miniature lake, and cascading waterfalls, its landscaped gardens and its pavilion built by Napoleon for Empress Josephine, lies within a short walking distance of the offices of the DSE.

Unlike the imposing headquarters of Interpol in Lyon, the offices of the Direction de Sécurité Européenne in Strasbourg are little known. Situated near the Parliament building on the Avenue de l'Europe, the six-story building houses an amalgam of all the main European intelligence agencies and specialized police forces, whose representatives pool and act on matters of mutual security within the European Community.

Whereas the target of Interpol is the international criminal, its actual powers are limited. Its officers are drawn from the police forces, are confined to providing mostly an information service, processing and disseminating information within three main criminal categories: criminals who operate in more than one country; criminals who do not travel at all, but whose criminal activities affect other countries; and criminals who commit a crime in one country and flee to another.

But since the nations of the world have differing criminal and legal procedures, Interpol's officers do not have power of arrest, despite popular portrayal to the contrary in books and films. The organization is limited to providing a clearinghouse of information on criminal activity.

The DSE has a function similar to Interpol, except its officers have powers of arrest within all the member states. Drawn from both the police forces and intelligence services of Europe, DSE concerns itself with four main categories of criminal and terrorist activity.

Category One covers terrorist activity, both indigenous terrorism and terrorists from outside Europe or who may use Europe as a base or as a target. Category Two is concerned with smuggling in all its forms. Category Three covers espionage, both national and industrial; Category Four, fraud and counterfeiting.

Each member state has its own representative section in the DSE Strasbourg headquarters and liaises with other national sections in areas of mutual concern and interest, and with a single function: to combat all four categories of criminal and terrorist activity and to maintain their shared database.

Volkmann's office in the British Section was on the third floor, which also housed the Dutch Section. Below the window was a small square, called simply the Platz, empty on this cold December afternoon. He arrived back from lunch at two and went straight to work, sifting through the reports. There were the usual subjects: narcotics, smuggling, terrorism; intelligence gathering, ready to be acted on or filed away.

When he finished more than three hours later, he found Ferguson's slip of paper and dialed the woman's number in Frankfurt. When Erica Kranz answered, he explained that he was a liaison officer with DSE, and that Pauli Graf had asked someone to have a talk with her.

"Can you tell me what this is about, Frau Kranz?"

The woman's voice sounded uneasy. Volkmann thought he detected a trace of fear. "I'd prefer not to discuss the matter over the telephone, Herr Volkmann. But it's pretty important. Could we meet?"

"Maybe I could drive up to Frankfurt tomorrow morning. Pauli Graf gave us your address. Unless you want to meet somewhere else?"

"No, my place is good. My apartment's on the top floor. Is midday okay?"

"Midday's fine. Talk to you then. Good afternoon, Frau Kranz."

Volkmann cleared away his desk, went down to the parking lot, and drove to his apartment. It was a modest place by Strasbourg's standards, a compact two-bedroom apartment in one of the old houses along the Quai Ernest, overlooking a small, paved courtyard.

It was after ten when Koller from the German Section appeared with the file, looking irritated. "Do you mind telling me why you want the woman's file?"

"Nothing special. Just routine."

Koller inquired no further. "Just make sure that the copy I've given you is returned."

When Koller left, Volkmann ran a hot bath and poured himself a large scotch. Afterward, he lay on the bed and read Erica Kranz's file.

It made interesting reading.

Born in Buenos Aires, Argentina, of German-born parents, Erica Kranz had one older sister, married to a Frenchman and living in Rennes. Her father died in South America when she was three, and the girls had returned to Germany with their mother in the same year.

A graduate of Heidelberg University, majoring in journalism, she had dabbled at the university with the Greens and other ecological-political organizations, but she had no known political affiliations or activities at present. Single. No known vices, no convictions. She worked as a freelance journalist and had frequent assignments from the popular German women's magazines.

All very straightforward, Volkmann thought. But then came a paragraph about her father that sent chills through his soul.

Manfred Kranz had been a young major in the Leibstandarte SS division during the last war. He had once been wanted in connection with war crimes committed in France and Russia. Twenty male inhabitants of a small village in southeastern France called Ronchamp had been publicly executed during the German retreat. Manfred Kranz was the unit commander responsible. And in Russia, he had been implicated in the execution of two hundred prisoners of war during the German assault on Kiev. He was never brought to trial, the Argentine authorities refusing to cooperate in his extradition.

Letting it all sink in, Volkmann crossed to the bedroom window.

It had stopped raining, and the clouds had long disappeared and darkness fallen. He could see the lights of Germany burning into the winter's night beyond the Rhine. He never took the trip across the border unless he had to. Ferguson knew he disliked dealing with the Germans. With few exceptions, he had avoided social contact with them even when he had worked in Berlin, that least German of cities.

He set the travel clock for seven, undressed, turned off the light, and lay in the bed. The paragraph about Manfred Kranz disturbed him, and he tossed restlessly for some time before he finally fell asleep. He dreamed about his father.

11

FRANKFURT, GERMANY. FRIDAY, DECEMBER 2

Volkmann found the apartment block with no difficulty, tucked away behind the Eiserner Steg on the south side of the river. The woman was waiting for him in the open doorway when he came out of the elevator.

She was tall and full-figured, with dusky skin and pale blue eyes. Her long legs were clad in tight blue jeans tucked into high leather boots, and she wore a loose black sweater. Her blond hair was tied up, emphasizing her high cheekbones. She wore little makeup and her face looked tense. Volkmann introduced himself and showed her his identification before they went inside.

In the background, he heard a Schubert string quartet playing softly on a mini sound system by the window.

"I was just going to make some coffee. Would you like some, Herr Volkmann?"

"A coffee would be fine."

"Take a seat, make yourself comfortable."

Volkmann watched her as she went into the kitchen. Her file said she was in her thirties. She would have passed for a female executive with one of the Frankfurt commercial banks.

The apartment was spotless and furnished in a modern style, large and airy, filled with potted plants and packed bookshelves and pale leather furniture.

When she returned with two cups of coffee, she sat opposite Volkmann on a white leather couch, her legs crossed. Her face appeared pale and drawn, and now that Volkmann looked closely, he saw that the blue eyes were red-ringed from crying.

"Perhaps you had better tell me what you told Pauli Graf."

"Are you German, Herr Volkmann?"

"British. Your people in the German Section of DSE weren't particularly interested in your case. Pauli Graf has been posted back to Berlin, and he passed you on to us unofficially." He smiled. "If it matters, I can ask your people again."

She shook her head. "No. I was just making an observation. Your accent, it's a little different, that's all." She brushed a strand of blond hair from her face and briefly looked toward the window. "Until last week, I was in Asunción in Paraguay on a week's holiday. I stayed with my cousin, Rudi Hernandez." She bit her lip. "I sensed that he was troubled by something during my stay. When I asked Rudi what it was, he told me he was working on a story. Something the newspaper he works for as a journalist knew nothing about."

When she hesitated, Volkmann asked, "What kind of story?"

"A pilot he knew in Asunción, a man named Rodriguez, told Rudi that certain people were smuggling cargoes out of South America into Europe. Just before I arrived in Paraguay, this pilot, Rodriguez, telephoned Rudi and asked him to meet. He told Rudi he had a favor to ask. He wanted Rudi to write a story, a newspaper article, but not to publish it, to hold it somewhere safe, with a lawyer perhaps. If Rodriguez was killed, Rudi was to print the story."

The woman hesitated again. "You see, Rodriguez once worked for these people who did the smuggling. They hired him and his aircraft to transport a number of cargoes. His business was smuggling. But now he was certain the men who had hired him wanted to kill him."

"Do you know what these cargoes were?"

She shook her head. "Rodriguez thought they were narcotics, but he wasn't sure. All he could say was that there had been several consignments, all delivered to Montevideo in Uruguay over a period of almost a year. The consignments were packed in sealed boxes. Rodriguez said he had been very well paid by these men. He also gave Rudi the name of the man who had hired him to do the work, Nicolas Tsarkin."

Volkmann gave her a questioning look.

"Rudi knew very little about him. Said he was a businessman, a German immigrant, no criminal connections that he could find."

Volkmann nodded. "Go on, please."

"Two days after Rodriguez delivered the last consignment, he noticed that he was being watched. That's when he became afraid and contacted Rudi. He told him he thought he had become involved in something over his head, something very big, and that these men meant to kill him. So Rudi agreed to go along with Rodriguez's request. I think he thought he might be onto a good story. But three days later, Rodriguez's body was found in a street in Asunción. He had been killed by a hit-and-run car. There were no witnesses.

Rudi was certain that Rodriguez was murdered by the people he worked for."

"What made him so certain?"

"The way Rodriguez died. And Rodriguez had told Rudi the men he worked for were very secretive. Their secrecy was almost obsessive. Rudi said they killed Rodriguez because they wanted no one to know what they were doing."

Volkmann put down his cup. "Did Hernandez inform the Asunción police about all of this?"

"No. He wanted solid evidence first. He wanted the names of the people involved, and he wanted to be sure what the cargoes contained. That what these people were doing was definitely illegal."

"I really don't see how this matter concerns DSE. You've got no solid proof."

"No, but Pauli Graf told me that DSE concerned itself with many areas . . ."

Volkmann shrugged. "Yes, but South America isn't exactly our territory."

"Then there's something else that might interest you."

"Tell me."

"Before I left Asunción, Rudi had asked me to check on something for him. He needed some information. Four days ago, I telephoned Rudi's apartment to tell him of my progress. There was no reply. So I telephoned his office. A reporter at the newspaper, he told me . . ." The woman's voice trailed off, her head bowed. Volkmann could hear the Schubert quartet, muted, barely audible, the music filling the silence.

"Told you what?"

"He told me Rudi was dead. The police found his body in a house in Asunción. The house of a young girl. They'd both been murdered."

Erica Kranz took a handkerchief from the sleeve of her sweater, wiped her eyes.

Volkmann asked, "How do these murders concern DSE?"

She looked at him steadily. "Before Rodriguez was killed, he took

Rudi to Tsarkin's house, a big estate on the outskirts of Asunción. They watched this house. Rudi wanted some photographs for the story. He had a telephoto lens fitted to the camera. Two men walked out into the grounds of the property. Rodriguez pointed out Tsarkin. But what interested Rudi was not Tsarkin, but the second man with him. You see, Rudi recognized him, had seen him before. In Europe, not in South America."

"I don't understand."

"Rudi met the man ten years before at a party at Heidelberg University, where I was a student. His name was Dieter Winter."

"Go on."

"Rudi stayed with my family at the time, and I had brought him along to the party. Dieter Winter had a heated argument with Rudi that almost came to blows. Rudi remembered him vividly. He said it was the first time he had ever wanted to hit someone. He showed me one of the photographs he took of the two men in the grounds of the Asunción house. An old man and a younger man strolling together. The old man was Tsarkin, Rudi told me. The younger man looked like Dieter Winter. I remembered him from campus. Rudi asked me to check up on him when I returned home, just to be certain.

"When I returned to Frankfurt, I discovered that Winter's body was found in a Berlin alleyway a week ago by the police. He'd been shot to death."

She reached across for a large buff envelope that lay on the coffee table, removed a newspaper clipping, and handed it to Volkmann. It was no more than a couple of paragraphs and described the discovery of a man's body in an alleyway near the Zoo U-Bahn in Berlin. The victim was shot five times at close range. No witnesses, and the man's identity was given as Dieter Winter. The police were requesting anyone with information to come forward.

"This man, Winter, what was so strange about his being in Paraguay?"

Erica Kranz shrugged. "It just seemed weird to Rudi that Winter should be there, so far from Germany. And the fact that he might have been involved with these smugglers who killed Rodriguez."

"Have you mentioned this matter to anyone else?"

"Only to Pauli Graf."

"Why didn't you go to the police?"

"I had the feeling that Pauli seemed to think it a matter for your people. And besides, the Bundespolizei are really only interested in what happens on German territory. But your people, Pauli told me, don't work only in Europe."

Volkmann put down his coffee. "What exactly do you want me to do?"

She looked at him intently. "I'd like to know why Rudi died and who killed him. I'm traveling to Paraguay again early next week. Rudi would have wanted someone to follow up his story. I'm a journalist; that's my profession. But my interest is also personal."

"You haven't answered my question."

"You have contacts in the police of other countries. Perhaps you could give me a letter of introduction, suggest someone I could talk with in Paraguay. Or even advise me."

"I advise you to leave it to the Paraguayan police. Use the proper channels and leave Pauli Graf out of it." Volkmann looked at her directly. "Tell the German police what you told me. They'll pass it on to their own people in DSE if they think it's important enough."

There was a hint of impatience in Erica Kranz's reply. "That's what Pauli Graf told me. But that takes time, and I'm leaving for Asunción the day after tomorrow." She looked at Volkmann steadily. "So I'd appreciate any help you could give me. It would make things easier. Besides, as I said, the German police don't normally concern themselves with a crime that happens on the other side of the world. But your people . . . your interests are wider. Unless I got it wrong?"

The Schubert rose and fell faintly in the background as she continued to look at him expectantly. Suddenly she looked very young, and Volkmann saw the pain in her eyes. On the other hand, he had little appetite to get tangled up in the German desk's problems.

"To be honest, I'm not sure this is DSE's territory."

"I understand. But thank you for listening."

Volkmann stood. "When does your flight to Asunción leave?"

"Sunday next. From Frankfurt. I've taken some time off work. I feel I owe it to Rudi to help investigate his death."

"I'll check with my people. I can't promise, but if there's anything I can do to help, I'll telephone before you leave."

"I appreciate it."

"Good afternoon, Frau Kranz."

Erica watched as Volkmann crossed the corridor to the elevator. She closed the door after her and went to stand by the window. The Rhine barges were having a bad day of it, the sturdy vessels tossing about in the gray swells. She saw Volkmann cross the street below and walk toward a parked car, his raincoat flapping about his legs.

So different from Rudi, who had always smiled, and yet the same soft, brown eyes. And there was something else, too. She had sensed an almost palpable dislike toward her in Volkmann's manner.

She watched as he walked away, then dismissed the thought from her mind as she went to wash the coffee cups.

It was after four when Volkmann arrived back in Strasbourg. Ferguson and Peters were both out, and he wrote his report and delivered a copy to Ferguson's secretary, along with a copy of the woman's file.

She told him Ferguson was in Paris and wasn't expected back until later that evening. Volkmann sent a security fax to the Bundespolizei headquarters in Berlin requesting information on Dieter Winter, giving what details he could about the man and requesting a photograph, if available.

Volkmann left the office two hours later, arriving at his apartment a little after six. At ten o'clock, Ferguson telephoned.

"I read your report. All very murky but interesting."

"Any reply to the request I sent to the BP?"

"It arrived this evening. Along with a photograph."

"What did they say about Winter?"

"Graduated from Heidelberg ten years ago, majoring in history. Involved in several right-wing groups during his student days, but no arrests. The BP has no idea why he was killed. The area where it happened is a stomping ground for petty drug dealers. They tried that tack, however, and came up with nothing."

"Had Winter any narcotic convictions?"

"None. But considering the area where the shooting happened, that's the angle the BP hinted at."

"Nothing else?"

"The weapon used in the Berlin shooting is the part that interests us. A Walther nine-millimeter, but South American–manufactured ammunition. The BP thinks it was the same weapon used in the killing of a German industrialist in a Hanover restaurant a year ago. One of our citizens, a British business colleague of his, was wounded in the same attack and died a couple of days later."

"What do you think, sir?"

"It could be anything, Joe. Personally, I think you ought to take the trip along with the woman. This journalist could have been onto something that may concern us. There are several bodies now. Someone had reason to kill. I'd be very interested in learning what that reason is."

"You really think it's necessary?"

"I think so. We can always bill the expenses to the Germans if it ends up in their court."

"So what do I tell her?"

"Just that we're probing. That Winter's death interests us. See Peters about tickets first thing tomorrow morning. I take it the woman won't have any objection?"

"I doubt it."

"Good. I'll make contact with the people in Asunción and send them a copy of her statement, translated, of course. Good night, Joe."

Volkmann heard the line click and put down the receiver. He sat on the bed, half undressed, before turning off the bedside light. His mind went over the meeting with Erica Kranz. He wondered about the sighting of Winter in Paraguay and the shooting in Berlin, the murders in Asunción. How did they all connect? Or did they connect? There were no answers, not yet, there couldn't be, only more questions, a pebble thrown into a pond, eddying in endless circles.

He had left the copy of the woman's file with his report. He recalled again the paragraph on the last page of her file, the information about her father's crimes. Though these happened a long time before the woman was born and her father was dead before she had a chance to really know him, he still shivered now in the darkness, remembering that single paragraph.

NORTHEASTERN CHACO, PARAGUAY. SUNDAY, DECEMBER 4

The silver-haired man sat in the cane chair on the veranda. Inside the house he heard the two servant boys, Emilio and Lopez, busy with their chores, tidying and sweeping.

The man stared out at the torrential rain. In a while the rain would stop; the dark, pregnant rain clouds over the nearby rain forest would deplete. And in the morning the sun would shine again, and the gardens and the trees would steam as the heat evaporated the rainwater.

"Nature's cycle," a tutor had told him once, when as a child he had noticed the phenomenon. Remembering the words, he smiled to himself.

Kruger appeared, and slumped into one of the cane chairs.

The silver-haired man cupped his wrinkled face in his hand and said, "You contacted Franz on the radio?"

Kruger nodded. "Nothing to worry about."

"You're absolutely certain, Hans?"

"The journalist was working alone. There's no question."

"And the tape?"

Kruger drew on his cigarette, blew out smoke. "Definitely blank. I had Franz have the tape and the equipment thoroughly checked.

The microphone was faulty. Apparently, the only sound that could be picked up was at extremely close range and even then only very faintly. But he recorded nothing."

"There's no doubt?"

"None. Franz's technician is an expert. According to him the equipment was highly sensitive. Handled without care it could be easily damaged. Franz had the equipment disposed of."

The silver-haired man gave a sigh of relief. He looked out at the jungle, beyond the rain falling in heavy sheets. "And the travel arrangements, are they all in order?"

"The helicopter arrives at nine. In Mexico City, Konrad will take us to Haider's place."

The silver-haired man thought a moment and said, "The journalist, I still want his background checked. But discreetly. Tell Franz. And no more hitches. The pilot and the journalist, they will be the last of our problems. What happened at the hotel must not happen again."

Although the man's voice was soft, the admonition was clear.

Kruger nodded in reply. There would be no more problems, of that he was certain. Franz's men had checked every avenue thoroughly.

"That will be all, Hans. Thank you."

Kruger left, his footsteps echoing on the wooden floorboards.

The silver-haired man remained seated, watched as Kruger crossed the veranda to the house. Alone now, he stared up at the rain forest beyond the sheeting wall of water.

He hesitated, then slowly removed his wallet from the inside pocket of his linen jacket, took out the copy of the photograph. The grainy old photograph of the blond young woman and the dark-haired man.

A moment later the servant boys appeared, Emilio carrying the silver tray, Lopez behind. The silver-haired man smiled over at them fondly, their faces full of adulation.

Then the boys stared at the photograph in the man's hands, before smiling up at him.

The man patted their heads in turn as the boys came to stand beside him.

As he pointed down at the photograph, the man said in Spanish, "You'd like to hear the story again?"

The boys nodded eagerly, their faces smiling up at the gentle blue eyes.

The silver-haired man carefully replaced the photograph in his wallet and began to speak.

12

ASUNCIÓN. MONDAY, DECEMBER 5

The detective who welcomed Volkmann and Erica Kranz in the arrivals area that Monday morning wore a crumpled white suit that seemed a size too large for his stocky body. His dark eyes looked tired. Introducing himself as Captain Vellares Sanchez, he led them to an unmarked police car and drove toward the center of the city.

A shimmering wave of heat hit them as they stepped from the terminal, hot enough to hurt their lungs. It was summer in Asunción, trees and flowers in bloom, eucalyptus and palm trees lining their route, palm fronds hanging limply in the scorching afternoon air.

Volkmann sat beside Erica in the rear, the windows rolled down but the heat still oppressive. The big detective mopped his face with a handkerchief as he drove. He barely spoke, except to inquire if they had had a pleasant flight.

Asunción was a riot of color and noise, a mixture of old and new: nineteenth-century façades and yellow-bricked adobes and tin-

and-wood shanties existing side by side with modern buildings and apartments. Ancient yellow trolley cars screeched noisily along the main avenues.

The detective's office was on the third floor of the Comisaría Céntrica, the Central Police Station, on Calle Chile. It was a drab, hot place with peeling gray walls and ancient furniture. An old rusting filing cabinet stood in one corner; an electric fan whirred overhead.

A young recruit brought them strong, aromatic Paraguayan tea. "Yerba mate," explained Sanchez. "You have been to Paraguay before, Señor Volkmann?"

"Never."

"The tea is an acquired taste. But as good as beer on a hot day." Sanchez removed his jacket, loosened his tie, and waited until the young recruit had left before he unlocked a drawer in his desk and produced two files: his own file and the one containing the report the *seguridad* received from Volkmann's headquarters, translated into Spanish.

Now he smiled briefly at Erica, remembering Hernandez talking about her, appreciating her beauty. Striking. Long legs. Like one of the women you saw on the cover of the glossy, gossipy American magazines. A figure that would bring an instant reaction from men.

He opened the files and looked up at Volkmann. The man could have been a cop, but Sanchez knew he wasn't. Something more than a cop. The seguridad had telephoned him late the previous day, sent him a copy of the report from Europe, asked him to cooperate, and if he needed a translator.

Sanchez told them he didn't: he spoke English and this was an opportunity to get some practice. He wondered, not for the first time, why the two had traveled together, wondered what more there was to the deaths of Rodriguez and Hernandez.

A map of Asunción City lay on his desk, a mark in red indelible pen to indicate the area where the bodies were found. He turned the map around so they could see it, indicated the street where the girl's house stood, and spoke slowly.

"We found the bodies here on the morning of the twenty-sixth, in a house in the district of La Chacarita, near the Paraguay river, a short distance from the main railway station. Rudi's car we found parked outside the house. The keys of the car we found in the grass outside, as if someone had thrown them there."

When the detective paused, Volkmann asked, "Who does the house belong to?"

"To the young woman whose body was found with Rudi Hernandez. Her name was Graciella Campos, age seventeen. But her mind, it was the mind of a child, you understand? She had no family alive. She rented the house."

Erica leaned forward, a look of pain in her blue eyes. "Did this girl know Rudi?"

"Sí. He gave her money. To pay for food and rent and clothes. It was a kindness, you understand. Not a payment for anything else. They were simply friends."

Erica Kranz's face was pale, not from the heat, but from hurting inside. She nodded.

Sanchez lowered his voice out of respect. "The girl and Rudi had both been killed with knives. A drunk old man who sometimes sleeps in an alley near the girl's house found the bodies. The girl usually gave him some hot tea in the mornings. When she didn't answer his knock, he tried the door. It was open. When he discovered the bodies, he told a local priest, who called the policía."

Volkmann asked, "How long had they been dead?"

"Not long. Maybe four, five hours."

Sanchez took several police photographs from the file and handed them to Volkmann. He looked at Erica Kranz. "Forgive me. But I would prefer you did not look at these, señorita. They are not pleasant."

There were five photographs, taken by forensics, all in vivid, horrific color. Volkmann examined them carefully. Two were of the body of Hernandez, two of the girl, one photograph of both bodies lying close together, faces up. The girl's brown face looked pitiful in death. The savagery of her wounds shocked him. The simple white frock she wore was ripped apart above the waist and drenched in blood.

He next studied the photograph of the body of Rudi Hernandez. The man had suffered much the same fate; the torso had been slit from chest to groin, his innards spilling out onto the bloodied floor.

Volkmann grimaced, saw Erica turn away as if to avoid seeing the photographs he handed back to Sanchez, who quickly replaced them in the file. "Señor Sanchez, did the forensic people find anything?" Volkmann asked.

Sanchez looked at him blankly. Erica translated into Spanish, *forense*. Sanchez remembered the word now.

"You speak Spanish very well, señorita."

"I was born in Buenos Aires," Erica answered quietly.

Sanchez nodded. Hernandez had not told him that. He looked at Volkmann again.

"The forensic people believe that different knives were used to kill the victims. Both blades were hunting knives. The one used to kill Rudi had a very big blade. Perhaps a bowie knife, they think. But other than that, nothing much. No fingerprints. Some faint footprints, but nothing they think would really help. There were bruises on the arms and faces of both bodies that suggest several people helped in the murders. But whoever they were, they were careful not to leave anything behind. No prints, no real clues. And a knife is not like a bullet. Sometimes it is more difficult to trace such a weapon. My men searched the area around the house and the barrio itself. No discarded knives or bloodied clothes. Nothing."

Sanchez saw Erica wince as he spoke, wondered if he should be so explicit. He took a pack of cigarettes from his pocket, offered them to her and Volkmann. When both refused, he lit one for himself and further loosened his tie as Erica leaned forward, her voice strained. "The place where the bodies were found. Did no one see or hear anything? Were there no witnesses? Surely someone must have heard *something*?"

Sanchez blew out smoke, shook his head. "The old man I spoke of saw and heard nothing. He had drunk a lot of cana the night before. I have spoken also to many people in the barrio, in La Chacarita. It is the same story. No one saw or heard anything. And believe me, they would have talked. The girl's death shocked them all. Some old men saw Rudi arrive at the house around seven-thirty in the evening before he died. They did not see him come out." He paused for a moment before going on. "There is one small thing, however, that may be important."

Sanchez hesitated again. "The day after Rudi and the young girl were murdered, *La Tarde* published a story about the deaths. There was a photograph of both on the front page. A night watchman at the central railway station on the Plaza Uruguaya came to see us. He said he saw a man who looked like Rudi come in the back of the station very early on the morning of the murders, maybe three o'clock. But he couldn't be certain. He was tired, had been on duty since the previous afternoon." Sanchez shrugged. "Perhaps Rudi was at the station, perhaps not. Perhaps he meant to leave Asunción, take the girl and go someplace if he thought he was in some kind of danger. But the ticket office was closed then. Or maybe, if it was Rudi, he simply had something on his mind and went for a walk, to get some air."

Sanchez addressed Volkmann. "Of course, the report your people sent changes matters, I believe, when we consider what Rudi said he was doing, writing this story. Also, there are two other things that are important."

The detective tapped his cigarette ash into a cracked glass ashtray on his desk. "Number one, Rudi's press card was missing. And also his wallet. Yet he still had money in his pocket. Not much. But enough. And a gold ring and a watch he wore were not taken."

Volkmann nodded. "You're saying whoever murdered Hernandez and the girl didn't intend to rob them?"

"Sí. I think we can forget about a simple robbery. And the girl was not sexually assaulted. Also, considering your report, it seems that Rudi and the girl may have been killed for other motives. A robber would have taken all the money, the ring, and the watch, unless he was disturbed at his work. I don't believe that happened. No one reported hearing any disturbance, and the bodies were not discovered until seven that morning. Also, these were not ordinary murders. To kill like that, brutally, with knives, you must be someone crazy. You understand? So I don't think the motive was to rob. I think it was to kill.

"There is a clue to this. Rudi borrowed some equipment from a friend he knew, a man named Torres. He is a technician with an electronics company. Torres went to the newspaper office when Rudi had not returned this equipment to him. When they told him Rudi had been murdered, he came to us."

"What sort of equipment are we talking about?"

Sanchez turned to Volkmann and drew on his cigarette, exhaled slowly. "Special electronic equipment that would allow a person to hear and record something spoken from a distance away. Japanese, and expensive. A small microphone-transmitter and a receiver. I am sure you have heard of such equipment. It was borrowed by Rudi the day before he was killed. We questioned Torres. He said Rudi told him he wanted the equipment for *trabajo clandestino* . . . undercover work."

Sanchez glanced at Erica, to make sure his words were correct, saw that she understood. He looked back at Volkmann as the man spoke.

"Is that all Rudi told Torres?"

"Sí. No more. Not where he was going or why exactly he needed the equipment. Only that he would return it safely the next day. We have not found the equipment. It was not in the girl's house, or in Rudi's car or apartment. Perhaps it is still lying around somewhere, wherever Rudi used it. Or perhaps the people who murdered him have it, or have destroyed it."

Sanchez paused, looked at Volkmann, speaking softly. "I believe Rudi used the equipment the day or night before he was killed." He tapped a file in front of him. "There's one other thing. In the report your people sent us, it says that Rudi Hernandez was observing the home of a man named Nicolas Tsarkin. According to our smuggler friend Rodriguez, Tsarkin was the man who originally hired him, no?"

"That's right," Erica answered.

"And that there is a connection to another dead man, named Winter, in Germany?" the detective asked.

"Yes," Erica replied.

"Interesting," he said. "Let me tell you a few things. First, Rudi and I were friends. We helped each other out when we could. Sometimes a tip. Sometimes more than that. Second, not long before he was killed, Rudi gave me a tip. Keep an eye on Señor Tsarkin, he said—though without going into the reason why. That was the way with his tips sometimes. But I was familiar enough with him to take what he said seriously."

"Did you find anything?" Volkmann asked.

"No, nothing." Sanchez paused dramatically. "But on November twenty-third, Señor Tsarkin put a gun in his mouth and blew his brains out. Another death. Interesting. That's the third thing. I called Rudi and asked him to join me at the scene of the suicide. I asked him then why he was interested in Tsarkin, but he wouldn't say. Perhaps he didn't know. But there was a phone call at the Tsarkin home that he answered."

Sanchez raised his eyes to heaven. "I have half a dozen men on the scene who are capable of lifting a telephone receiver. But a reporter grabs it, then stonewalls when I ask him about it, says it was a wrong number. Now, I'm not so sure Rudi was telling the truth. Maybe that phone call led him to use the tape equipment, who knows? But the people behind Señor Tsarkin, the ones who killed Rodriguez and Winter, as well as Rudi and Graciella, must have caught on to Rudi. And then they found him and killed him."

He waited for a moment to let all that sink in. "Now that we have your report, we are looking even more deeply into Señor Tsarkin, but nothing as yet has emerged."

Volkmann nodded and asked, "What can you tell us about this smuggler, Rodriguez?"

Sanchez sat back. "Norberto Rodriguez's body was found two weeks ago in the city. Our forensic people said he had been killed by a car. The car drove away, did not stop. There were no witnesses. We thought it was an accident that someone did not report, a drunk driver perhaps. Or even a fellow criminal. But my men would have heard whispers in the underworld. In Rodriguez's case, they heard nothing. But now I know from your report that something else is possible . . . that these people he worked for killed him."

"What kind of work did Rodriguez do exactly, Señor Sanchez?"

"He owned an old DC4. He flew cargoes mostly to the ports of Montevideo in Uruguay or Porto Alegre in Brazil, for shipping on to Europe and America."

"Are we talking narcotics?"

"Sí, narcotics of course. But also whatever made a good profit. Gold. Jewels. Leopard skins. Rodriguez was one of the best smugglers. Very, very good." Sanchez allowed himself a brief smile. "So good we never caught him."

Volkmann loosened his tie, the heat in the small room cloying even with the fan whirring away. "Rodriguez's friends, people who knew him, people who might have worked with him—have you talked with many of them?"

"Rodriguez nearly always worked alone. And concerning the people he did work for, he told no one. To tell would mean death." Sanchez paused. "However, there is a man he sometimes worked with, a man named Santander. A smuggler also. We are trying to find him, but so far we have had no luck." Sanchez shrugged. "Even if we find Santander, he may know nothing."

"Have you talked with Rudi's colleagues at the newspaper, his friends?" Erica asked. "Perhaps he confided in one of them about his story."

Sanchez nodded. "They knew nothing about any special story Rudi was working on. We also checked Rudi's desk and locker at the newspaper. Also his apartment. There was nothing in any of them that would suggest such a story. And no photographs like the ones mentioned in your report. Nothing that would help us."

"Rudi said that anything he had, he kept in a safe place."

"Sí, señorita, I read that in the report I received. I must tell you that I had every bank in Asunción contacted yesterday. Rudi Hernandez had an account in one, but no deposit box. I am also having the banks outside Asunción checked just in case. But that will take time." He looked intently at her. "Did Rudi tell you of any other information or evidence he had?"

"No."

"Did he suggest where this safe place might be?"

Erica shook her head. "All he said was that what he had was not much. But that it was in a safe place."

The detective nodded. "I will have a photograph of Rudi shown to the banks, in case another name was used. Do you remember if Rudi said *anything* else? No matter how unimportant it seems to you?"

"No. I'm certain."

Sanchez tapped the file containing Volkmann's report. It had helped, opened a door, even just a little.

He stubbed out his cigarette. There was nothing more to be said until his men turned something up, if they were lucky. The heat in the small, drab room had become unbearable. He went to close the file, the meeting at an end, then looked at Erica. "Rudi's parents are dead, sí?"

She nodded.

"His belongings," Sanchez said solemnly. "Rudi's things . . ."

He saw Erica nod once more. She understood. He removed a set of keys from an envelope in the file and handed them across to her.

"These are a copy of the keys to Rudi's apartment," Sanchez explained. "In case there is anything from it you wish. Something personal, photographs perhaps."

Erica accepted the keys. "Thank you."

Sanchez pushed himself up from the chair, grabbed his jacket.

"And now, señor, señorita, I will take you to your hotel." He spoke gently to the woman. "But perhaps I might speak with Señor Volkmann in private first? I have some police business to discuss."

Erica nodded and stepped out into the hallway. Sanchez watched her leave, then turned to Volkmann.

"The security police in my country, the seguridad, keep a file on certain citizens. Rudi Hernandez was a journalist. Journalists are, shall we say, a special case. Because of their work, you understand."

Volkmann nodded, and Sanchez crossed to behind his desk, removed a file from a drawer, came back, and handed it to Volkmann.

"This is a copy of the file. It's not much. Hernandez was not a troublemaker. There is nothing of much interest. But perhaps it may help you understand the man."

Volkmann took the folder. "Thanks, I appreciate it, Sanchez."

Sanchez said, "Please, call me Vellares. About the man named Winter that Rudi recognized with Tsarkin: my men are checking with the immigration people. I will let you know as soon as I have something." He pulled on his coat. "The report your people sent— you have nothing more to add?"

Volkmann shook his head. "Have you got a photograph of Winter?"

"Sí, I have one here."

He removed a photograph from a file on his desk. A head-and-shoulders shot, enlarged. The man in the picture was blond, sharp-featured, thin-lipped. Sanchez stared at the photograph, then looked up. "It is a difficult case, I think, Señor Volkmann. Strange. And Rudi was a good man. I want to tell you I will do everything I can. We were friends for many years."

"The bodies are still at the morgue?"

"No. The funerals were three days ago. Had I known the lady was coming, I would have delayed the burials. But the forensic people were finished with their work. And the police morgue is full. Tomorrow I will take her to the cemetery. She may wish to say a prayer."

"I'll tell her. Thank you."

"I will also take you to see the girl's house where the bodies were found. And we can talk with Mendoza, Rudi's editor, and with Torres, who loaned Rudi the equipment." The detective buttoned his coat. "And now I will take you to your hotel. Your people, they have made arrangements?"

"The Excelsior," said Volkmann.

Sanchez said, "It's a nice hotel."

13

ASUNCIÓN

Volkmann and Erica checked into the hotel, and after dinner, he ordered a taxi to take them to Rudi Hernandez's apartment.

It was a bachelor's place: a bedroom, kitchen, living room, and a tiny bathroom. On one of the bookshelves were photographs in small silver frames. Hernandez's family, Volkmann guessed. One of a blond woman and a Latin man, the man smiling broadly, the woman's face serious, unsmiling. There was a silver-framed photograph of Erica taken in a Bavarian inn, looking much younger, her hair long, laughing out at the camera and holding a stein of beer, her arm around a young, handsome, smiling man.

Volkmann looked at her now. The long flight and the seven-hour time difference between Frankfurt and Asunción were taking their toll. She picked up the photograph from the shelf and stared down at the image silently.

"Rudi?" Volkmann asked.

She nodded, faint smudges under the blue eyes. "I can't help thinking about the last time I was here and he was alive."

She replaced the photograph and Volkmann went to look around the apartment. The police had been untidy in their work; there were drawers open in the bedroom and clothes left in disarray. In the kitchen, all the cupboard doors were ajar.

When he came back into the living room, he found Erica staring out the window. The lights of the city twinkled beyond the glass, a clear view down to the Rio Paraguay, boats moving back and forth in the encroaching darkness.

As he moved closer, she turned, and he saw tears running down her cheeks.

"Forgive me. I . . . I kept remembering. What the detective said today . . . about the way Rudi died."

"It's been a difficult day. How about I pour us both a drink?"

The vodka and tonic bottles were on the coffee table, a bowl of ice between them.

"Tell me about Rudi," Volkmann said.

Grief strained Erica's face. "He was a good and kind man, and a good journalist. Rudi was always quick to laugh, no matter how black things were." She shrugged. "I really don't know what more to tell you, except that he loved life."

Volkmann had read Sanchez's file but there wasn't much: two pages in English, translated especially—personal details, political affiliations, age, family background. He wanted to hear from Erica if there was more: hidden things, private things, things that all men keep to themselves, or share with a woman. Some small clue, something that would open a door for him.

"Tell me about Rudi's background."

"You mean his family?"

"Sure, his family."

"Rudi's mother and mine were half sisters. After the war ended, they were brought as children to Argentina by my grandparents. Years later, Rudi's mother met a Paraguayan, a biologist who was studying at the university in Buenos Aires. When he graduated, they married and went to live in Asunción, where Rudi was born. He was their only child."

Erica toyed with her drink, looked up at the photographs on the shelf. "Rudi was very much like his father. He always laughed. His mother was sterner. She wasn't a happy woman."

Volkmann glanced at the picture of the pretty, smiling woman. "Why?"

Erica brushed a strand of hair from her face. "My mother told me a story once. She and her sister lived in Hamburg during the war, when they were small children. One night the city was being destroyed with firebombs. In the bomb shelters, people were praying and everyone was frightened. When a bomb fell nearby, the ground shook and the lights went out. People were crushed in the chaos. Rudi's mother was only a child and she was frightened. She ran out of the shelter, distraught. What she saw outside on the streets was even worse—burning buildings, corpses, the inferno of that terrible night. Childhood friends she knew, relatives, many were dead. She became withdrawn after that. Rudi said she relived that night every day of her life."

"How did Rudi's parents die?"

"My uncle often took his family with him when he worked on biological surveys. A light aircraft they were on crashed in the southern Amazon. Rudi was a passenger, too, but he survived. They found him four days later, badly shocked and bleeding. His face was permanently scarred. For a long time afterward, he was devastated. He began to visit us more often in Germany because we were his only relatives. But he couldn't live there, he said, even though he spoke the language. I think Rudi found the Germans too stern. The Paraguayans were his people."

She looked down at her empty glass. "May I have another drink?"

Volkmann considered bringing up what he knew about her father, but decided against it. He poured them each another drink, spooned in the ice cubes. "Can I ask you why your family returned to Germany?"

She sipped her drink, held the glass in both hands. "My mother had met my father and married him in Buenos Aires. He was a businessman, a German immigrant, and very much older than she. But he died when I was three, so I don't remember him. My grandparents had died also, so I guess my mother felt a little lost.

"She sold my father's business and decided to return home. She figured it was better for me to study in Germany. After I graduated, she married again and moved to Hamburg. We drifted apart after that. The whole family did. But Rudi and I always wrote. He was like an older brother."

Some instinct made Volkmann want to reach over and touch her, comfort her, but he suppressed it, didn't know how she might react. "I've been wondering about Dieter Winter. Did Rudi say what they talked about in Heidelberg?"

Erica frowned. "I asked Rudi that same question. It was just small talk, he said. Winter was very drunk when they met, but he seemed intrigued by Rudi's background, by the fact that he was half German and from South America. That's another thing Rudi thought strange when he told me he recognized Winter in Asunción. At the party, Winter asked Rudi if he socialized among the German colony in Paraguay. Rudi said no, they bored him. He preferred the easygoing Latins. He said Winter seemed to take the remark as a personal insult and became quite aggressive."

"Is that what made Rudi dislike him?"

She shrugged. "He found him pompous and a loudmouth. And Winter had said that if Rudi thought so little of Germans, he should go back where he belonged. Just like the immigrant workers in Germany, Winter said. Germany didn't need another *mischling*."

She put down her glass. "That word. I'm sure you know it's not a nice word. It's used to describe someone who is only half German, a half-caste."

"Sure, I know what it means, Erica."

Volkmann placed his empty glass on the table and stood. The heat that came and lingered in the small apartment was stifling, despite the air-conditioning. "Sanchez said he'd call tomorrow morning to take you to the cemetery to visit Rudi's grave. You think you could cope with that?"

"Will you come, too?"

"If you want."

She nodded. "Yes, I'd appreciate it, Herr Volkmann."

"Call me Joe." He gestured to the telephone nearby. "How about you call a taxi to take us back to the hotel?"

It was after eight when they returned to the Excelsior. A pre-Christmas party was in full swing in one of the hotel's ballrooms. In the lobby, tuxedoed men and beautiful, olive-skinned women in sleek dresses stood around an illuminated Christmas tree sipping drinks.

Erica looked tired in contrast, her mascara smudged. As the taxi had passed the offices of *La Tarde,* she had suddenly started crying. In the dim cab, Volkmann reached across and held her hand, felt her lean into his shoulder, smelled the scent of her perfume, her blond hair brushing his cheek, Erica holding on to his hand until they stepped from the taxi.

They exited the elevator on the fifth floor, near their adjoining rooms. Volkmann opened her door for her. "If you can't sleep or you want to talk, I'm in the next room."

"Thank you, Joe. Forgive me for crying, but I guess it's been a hard day."

He waited until she had closed her door, then went into his own room. The air-conditioning was on, but the room was still humid. He undressed slowly and lay on the bed in the cloying darkness.

He could still smell the scent of her perfume as he closed his eyes and fell asleep.

The telephone rang in his bedroom an hour later. He switched on the bedside lamp and picked up the receiver sleepily, hearing the stilted English, recognizing the voice.

"Sanchez here, Señor Volkmann. Did I wake you? My apologies . . . the jet lag . . . I remembered just as I rang."

"What's the problem, Vellares?"

"No problem. Something has turned up. The man you are interested in . . . the German."

"Winter."

"Sí, about him. And something else. Santander . . . the smuggler who sometimes worked with Rodriguez. The local police in San Ignacio picked him up late this afternoon. A place not far from the border with Argentina. He's being brought back to Asunción tonight. It could wait until tomorrow but I think you may be very interested to hear what he has to say. Do you want to come to my office tonight?"

"I'll call a taxi."

"No. Rest for now. My men have to check some things out first. I need a little time. I'll send a car to the hotel for you at midnight. Bring the woman if you wish."

"Midnight," repeated Volkmann.

"Sí. Rest, my friend," said Sanchez, and then the line clicked dead.

14

NORTHEASTERN CHACO, PARAGUAY

Kruger stood on the veranda smoking a cigarette, watching the men as they worked. Dusk, clouds obscuring the moon, the stars of the Southern Hemisphere barely visible, faint pinpricks of light beyond the brooding blackness of the rain forest.

The electric generators were on, and a flood of light circled the property. It spilled out onto the dark edge of the jungle, out beyond where the heavy truck and the small pickup stood parked, the light making the jade-green leaves of the jungle plants beyond the gravel driveway shine as if they had been polished brightly.

Rain no longer fell, but the air was humid again. Kruger's blue cotton shirt was open at the neck and patched with sweat.

Schmidt was supervising the three other men loading the truck and carrying the heavy boxes himself, two at a time, from the garage to the truck.

Kruger watched big Schmidt's muscled flesh bulging and straining beneath his blue overalls. The big bodyguard looked as if he had been hewn from rock. *You wind Schmidt up and point him in the right direction. Tell him to kill, and he kills. All brawn, no brain. But useful, very useful.*

Kruger glanced across at the garage. Light flooded out through the open doors, the garage filled with wooden and cardboard boxes. All the papers traveling separately to Mexico City in steel fireproof boxes. Everything was on schedule, and the house would be emptied by morning. His only worry was that the truck would not be large enough to transport everything, but Franz assured him that it would.

Kruger caught a sudden movement out of the corner of his eye. The curtain of the room nearest him moved. Then he saw the brown face of Lopez. A moment later the face of the second boy, Emilio, appeared.

Both were no more than fifteen, glad of a bed and food, diligent young workers once you watched over them. No one had told them what was happening, and they watched the loading of the boxes with curiosity, their soft faces like those of young girls: awed, innocent, interested, watching the men move back and forth to the garage in a steady rhythm. The boys themselves would never have asked what was happening, knew their place, too grateful for having a full belly ever to question anything. One of them, Emilio, turned toward Kruger and smiled. Kruger smiled back. The faces disappeared, and the curtain fell back into place.

Footsteps rattled the veranda. Kruger exhaled smoke and dropped the cigarette, ground it out with his shoe.

The silver-haired man appeared. He wore a light cotton dressing gown over his white pajamas, ready to retire.

Kruger said, "The men will have the truck loaded by midnight. Anything we're not taking with us Schmidt will burn."

The man nodded, then placed a hand on Kruger's shoulder a moment as he stared out at the jungle's edge.

"Are you glad to be leaving, Hans?"

Kruger smiled. "It's been a long time. Too long."

"But you won't miss this place?"

Kruger shook his head. "It's been a prison. When I was younger, perhaps it didn't seem so hellish and claustrophobic. But now, I'm just glad to be leaving. And you?"

"It holds memories, of course. Fond memories." The silver-haired man fell silent as he looked out toward where the men worked, dressed in blue overalls, moving smartly as they carried the metal and wooden boxes from garage to truck. Almost everything of importance he possessed was packed in the boxes: his personal belongings, his paperwork and files, years of hard work. "What about the boys?"

"Schmidt and I will take them up to the rain forest."

"Make it quick, Hans. I don't want them to suffer. No pain, you understand?"

"Of course. I'll make certain."

The man walked back across the veranda and entered the house.

Kruger waited until his footsteps had died, then he turned back to watch Schmidt.

NORTHEASTERN CHACO. MONDAY, DECEMBER 5, 11:57 P.M.

There was no traffic as the pickup truck bumped along the rutted jungle road. Not at this hour, not in this part of the Chaco, so remote, empty, vast. The rich, sweet smells of jungle and earth wafted in through the open window, a slight breeze cooling Kruger's face. The pickup traveled at no more than a bumpy thirty miles an hour, its headlights washing the rich green undergrowth ahead in silvery light.

Kruger sat in the passenger seat. Now and then he glimpsed the eyes of jungle creatures staring out at them, pinpricks of reflected light amid the silvery green, before they disappeared, scurrying off into the bushes.

As the truck came round a sharp bend, one of the boys laughed and pointed beyond the windshield. Kruger looked toward the headlights sweeping the road: a mongoose scurried across their path before disappearing into a clump of mango trees. The boys giggled.

Kruger smiled down at them in the darkness of the cab. The four of them were squashed into the pickup's cabin: Kruger, the boys, and big Schmidt, his granite face staring blankly ahead as he drove slowly along the narrow dirt track.

Kruger saw the gap in the jungle just ahead and tapped Schmidt on the shoulder. The man swung the pickup left, onto a narrow overgrown path, the engine whining as the truck moved up toward the mountain.

They were an hour from the house. This part of the jungle was remote, the path hardly ever used, furrows in the soil left by a truck or car during the rainy season months before. Kruger knew this terrain; it was the last place on earth anyone would look.

The truck bumped hard, dipped in and out of the rutted track, and Kruger heard the reciprocal thump of the wooden crates in the back as they lurched and then settled back down. The boys laughed again. Kruger could see their brown faces dimly, eyes bright, smiles of innocence. The trip was an outing, and they were enjoying themselves, no hint of fear.

"Are we there, señor?" Lopez's thin voice asked.

Kruger smiled. "Soon. Almost there."

The engine strained even more now, the last steep portion of the drive before they reached the clearing at the top. Schmidt changed gears. The vehicle bumped again. The boys laughed once more as the wooden boxes in the back jolted and slid.

The boxes had been Kruger's idea. They made the ride in the pickup seem all the more plausible. A chore for the boys to perform; he told them he needed their help in disposing of the wooden crates. The boys looked like the young, sweet boys you saw in church choirs, their frail bodies more suited to housekeeping and cleaning and waiting tables than manual labor. But they had jumped at the opportunity to travel in the truck.

They had been brought to the house three years before the old housekeeper had died. Kruger understood the reasons: the boys were illiterate, barely understood their own Indian language. They asked no questions and were happy in their own company.

Now the engine's whine receded and the vehicle began to level off its climb. Schmidt changed gear as Kruger stared ahead. The foliage became thinner in the higher atmosphere, and now the headlights suddenly illuminated an open space beyond. They reached the edge of a chasm. Stars sparkled, the night sky stretching out vastly before them.

Schmidt swung the steering wheel round, and the pickup truck turned in an arc and halted. The engine sputtered and died. Silence, then came the night shrieks and clicks of the humid jungle. The boys shifted restlessly in their seats.

"Here, señor?"

"Sí, here," replied Kruger.

"We carry boxes now?"

"Sí."

Schmidt and Kruger opened their doors and stepped out; it was a little cooler up here in the mountains. The chasm lay ten yards away. A deep rock cavity that seemed bottomless. No one went down there, only scurrying, foraging animals. Kruger took the heavy-duty flashlight from behind the passenger seat and switched it on, aimed the beam at the ground. He glanced at his watch. Midnight.

The light was good, even without the flashlight, the headlights of the pickup on dim, the sky above their heads awash with moonlight. He was tired, very tired. He could gladly have slept there and then, but this had to be done first, this last thing.

The two boys moved toward the back of the pickup, ready to unlock the pull-down at the rear.

Kruger nodded. Schmidt reached inside his overalls, took out the long, silenced pistol, and placed it behind his back. Kruger saw the hilt of the big bowie knife protruding from the man's overalls at the knee pocket.

He turned to look at the boys as they were about to unlock the pull-down, talking quietly between themselves in their Indian dialect. The faint babble of excited conversation could almost have been a final prayer.

At that moment Schmidt stepped up behind them. Kruger saw the silenced pistol appear, as it was aimed smartly at the back of the taller boy's head.

Phutt!

A split second, then the second boy's head, just as he turned, his mouth open in horror.

Phutt!

The two bodies pitched forward violently as the sounds of the pistol ruptured the silence. There was the faintest cry from the second boy as the bullet had smacked into the nape of his skull, then no sound, only the ceaseless noises of the jungle.

Kruger pointed the flashlight at the bodies. Blood flowed from the tiny wounds at the base of the boys' skulls. One of the bodies twitched in the light, a sharp spasm and then the brief sound of air expelled. Schmidt saw the movement, aimed instantly, and fired again. The tiny body bucked, fell still. Kruger again played the flashlight over the bodies. No sound, no movement this time.

"Strip them."

Schmidt placed the pistol on the hood of the pickup. Kruger turned away, took out a packet of cigarettes, and lit one. He heard Schmidt at work, grunting as he knelt over the bodies, removing the clothes.

By the time it was done, Kruger finished his cigarette. He stubbed it out in the pickup's ashtray. He was careful to leave nothing behind. So careful that he and Schmidt wore soft, flat sneakers. So careful that he would tell Franz to remove and burn the tires of the pickup once he had returned with the vehicle to Asunción.

Now the bloodied clothes were in a heap a yard from where Schmidt stood. Kruger crossed to where the thin bodies lay and examined them.

"You know what to do. Take your time. Do it properly."

Kruger watched as Schmidt set to work. He had to watch, had to make sure the job was done correctly. He had seen men killed, had killed men himself. But he had never seen a body stripped of its flesh before. The faces and the fingertips. Not that the boys' fingerprints had ever been taken, not that it was likely the bodies would ever be found, but Kruger was not prepared to take that chance, had to be certain no one could trace them back to the house.

He watched as Schmidt took the big jagged-edged bowie knife from the knee pocket of his overalls and set to work. He picked the body closest to him, turned it over. Emilio. The face looked up at the sky, eyes wide open. Kruger watched, fascinated and revolted at once.

Fifteen minutes later Schmidt had finished his work.

Kruger played the flashlight over the bodies. Mutilated beyond recognition. Bloodied hollow gore where the innocent brown faces had been, the whites of the skulls eerily visible, the hollow eye sockets gaping black.

Kruger helped Schmidt carry the corpses one at a time to the edge of the chasm and fling them into the void, heard the sounds of each body seconds later as it flailed against rock on its downward journey into the black pit of the crevice. Schmidt finished the job by tossing in the mutilated body parts: gory handfuls of skin and organs. Then Kruger shone the flashlight down into the chasm. Nothing visible, only a tangle of green and rock.

Blood stained Kruger's hands and overalls. He wiped his hands on the grass and saw Schmidt do the same. The blood would wash away with the first fall of rain. Schmidt packed the clothes into a black disposable bag, wiped the bloodied knife on his overalls, before removing them. The overalls went into the black disposable bag with Kruger's.

Schmidt stowed the bag in the back of the pickup and climbed into the driver's seat. As Kruger went to climb in beside him, he paused to shine the flashlight about the clearing. Nothing was left behind. The jungle animals and vermin that inhabited the chasm would finish their work. Pick the bodies clean of flesh.

He glanced at his watch: 1:00 a.m. Eight more hours, and he would be gone from this hellish country. He might still manage a couple of hours' sleep before the helicopter arrived. He ached all over now, limbs tired.

As he climbed wearily into the cab beside Schmidt, the engine throbbed to life. Then the pickup turned in an arc and drove back down the narrow track.

15

ASUNCIÓN. TUESDAY, DECEMBER 6, 1:02 A.M.

Sanchez was seated behind his desk.

There were dark rings beneath his eyes, and his face looked swollen from lack of sleep. A coffeepot stood on a tray beside him, three cups poured, a half-smoked cigarette lying in the glass ashtray on the desk. Volkmann and Erica sat opposite him.

Sanchez opened a fresh file and stared down at its contents, several sheets of handwritten paper in Spanish.

"First, let me explain what I've learned about Winter. He visited Paraguay eight times in the last three years. Each time at intervals of about four months, each time for a stay of only two or three days. The reasons on his immigration papers say 'company business.'"

Sanchez had already explained that Winter's date and place of birth as registered on the immigration papers matched the information Volkmann's people sent in their report.

"On each immigration paper a hotel address was given for the period of his stay. On each occasion that he flew into Paraguay, he landed in Asunción. Four times from Miami, three times from Rio de Janeiro. All were connecting flights from Frankfurt. The last time Winter visited Paraguay was three months ago. Then he stayed at the Excelsior Hotel. Before that, at the Hotel Guarani. Before that, the Excelsior. Before that, some other hotels, but mostly the Excelsior. I have details; you may see them if you wish."

Sanchez handed Volkmann a page, which he examined.

When Volkmann looked up, he said, "You've checked with all of the hotels?"

Sanchez shook his head. "So far, only the Excelsior and the Guarani. My men have still to check the others. It may take some time."

"The immigration papers Winter filled in before landing: was there a company name given on any of them?"

"No. None."

"So who paid Winter's hotel bills?"

"In the two hotels we've checked so far, Winter paid. Always in cash. And in each case, he used a suite, not a room, although he was the only guest registered."

"What about any telephone calls he made? Do the hotels keep a record?"

"Sí. They keep a record of all local and long-distance calls made by their guests; that is the law. But the hotels my men checked so far, the Excelsior and the Guarani, they have no record of any calls made by Winter. The only things on the bills were meals and drinks."

Sanchez picked up his coffee, sipped the black liquid. Seeing the still-lit cigarette, he puffed on it once more before crushing it in the ashtray.

"No company name," said Volkmann. "No telephone calls. What about the car-rental firms? You checked with them?"

"I have a list of all the car-rental firms in the city. They will be checked as soon as my men have time." Sanchez consulted the file again. "The photograph your people sent of Winter—I had my people ask at the hotel if any of the staff remembered him. But of course no one did." Sanchez shrugged again. "Big hotels, lots of new faces every day. My men are still checking the other hotels on the list."

Sanchez turned to Erica. "But at least we know now that Rudi was not mistaken about seeing Winter in Paraguay."

Volkmann said, "You mentioned Winter always hired a suite."

"Sí. Always." Sanchez consulted the file again. "On eight occasions."

"That suggests he meant to entertain, or impress. Or both."

"Perhaps. But we need more information." Sanchez shrugged.

Erica leaned forward in her chair. "What about this man who sometimes worked with Rodriguez?"

"Sí, Miguel Santander."

"Have you questioned him?"

"Sí. Before you arrived. He heard about Rodriguez's death. I told him we are now treating the case as murder. Santander thinks we consider him a suspect. He says Rodriguez's death had nothing to do with him. He claims he has been near the southern border for the last two weeks. Up to no good, of course. But he cannot come up with a good alibi." Sanchez smiled briefly. "That suits us. He is scared and has talked a little." He stood up wearily. "What he has to say is important. He is downstairs in one of the interview rooms. Come, I will take you."

The interview room had the same gray, peeling walls as Sanchez's office.

Volkmann saw a thin-faced man who looked to be about thirty seated at an ancient wooden table between two young, standing policía. The man was deeply tanned, unshaven, his stubble making his dark face appear even darker, his features more Indian than Spanish. His grubby hands fidgeted nervously.

Sanchez gestured to the two policía to indicate they should leave.

When the men withdrew, Sanchez offered two chairs to Volkmann and Erica. She accepted; Volkmann remained standing.

"This is Miguel Santander," Sanchez said. "He speaks a little English. Or if you prefer, I can translate."

Santander smiled weakly. "Please, I speak English. I like to practice." His smile broadened, showing stained, uneven teeth as he regarded Volkmann and Erica.

Sanchez did the introductions, explaining only that his two friends were interested in Rodriguez's death. He offered Santander a cigarette, lit it.

"I want you to tell my friends here what you told me. Slowly. So they can understand you. Comprende?"

"Sí." Santander scratched his jaw. "From where do I begin?"

"From when Rodriguez asked you to help him."

Santander drew on his cigarette nervously and glanced from Volkmann to Erica. "One month ago, Rodriguez come to me. He say he need to hire plane from friend of mine. His own plane is old, and he need part for an engine generator. So until he get part, he need to hire other plane."

Santander glanced at Sanchez, then back at Erica and Volkmann, as if making sure he was understood. "The work Rodriguez does, sometimes it can be dangerous. For my friend who owns the plane, I need to know it's going to be okay, that there are no problems. No big risk. Because if Rodriguez have trouble, my friend, his aircraft, maybe it is taken by the policía. So I need to know what kind of work Rodriguez is doing before he can hire the plane."

Santander looked at the faces around him and shrugged. "He tell me some people use him to fly cargo across the border. To Montevideo. Already he has done many trips. These people, always they want Rodriguez to work alone. And always he must fly at night."

Santander wiped his mouth with the back of his hand. "Each trip is always the same. Rodriguez, he fly plane to quiet place up north in the Chaco. There is no runway, just field. A field in the jungle with lights. He land there, and men are waiting. They put boxes on plane. Boxes made of wood and steel. He fly these boxes to Uruguay, near Montevideo. He fly low, at night, so the radar don't see him. In a field near Montevideo, it is the same. No runway, just field with lights. When he land, men are waiting to take boxes off plane. Rodriguez do this every two months in one year." Santander shook his head. "And no problems. Never any problems."

Santander paused, scratched his stubble nervously. "I trust Rodriguez. To me, he never tell lies. He say to me your friend's plane will be safe. He said he only had to do one last trip. A special cargo. Just one small box. Then he is finished working for these people."

Santander paused again, looked up at Volkmann. "Rodriguez, he's good pilot. So I say, okay, you got the plane. But then he phone and tell me he don't need it. He get the part for his generator."

Santander sat back, looked at Sanchez. "That's all I know. Rodriguez was a friend. Me, I would have no reason to kill him. I never kill person in my life." He glanced at Erica, then Volkmann, a plaintive look on his face. "This you must believe."

Sanchez said to Volkmann, "Do you have any questions for Señor Santander?"

"When was the last time you saw Rodriguez?"

The smuggler's dark, Indian eyes flicked up nervously at Volkmann. "One month ago. When he ask me about hiring the plane."

"Not afterward?"

"No, I swear. Two days later he phone to tell me he don't need the plane. I don't see or speak to him again."

"The name Rudi Hernandez. Did you ever hear Rodriguez mention that name?"

Santander thought for a moment, shook his head. "No, señor."

"Rudi Hernandez. You're certain?"

"Certain. I never hear him say that name."

"Did Rodriguez mention the names of those who hired him?"

Santander shook his head. "No names. Rodriguez never tell names. In such business, sometimes people you work for, they don't give you names. It is better that way, you understand?"

"The places Rodriguez picked up and dropped off the boxes. You know where they are?"

"Rodriguez did not say exactly. Only that they were quiet places with no towns, no villages. The place in the Chaco where he picked up the boxes, he did not say. When I ask Rodriguez, all he would say is that it is one of the old German *colonias* up north, señor."

"Did Rodriguez describe any of the men, or how many there were?"

Santander thought for a moment. "No. He say only that they work quickly. In ten, maybe fifteen minutes all the boxes are loaded. The same in Montevideo." Santander thought for another moment. "But I think Rodriguez say that in the colonia, there was an old guy in charge."

"A German?"

Santander shrugged. "I guess."

"Did Rodriguez know what the cargo was?"

Santander scratched his stubble again. "He did not tell me. I don't think he know. But the boxes are heavy, I think. Except the last one."

"Why do you think they were heavy?"

"Rodriguez say he need a lot of runway. A long field. To lift off. And also a lot of fuel in the tanks."

"He said nothing else?"

"No, señor. Nothing." Santander looked up at Sanchez. "I tell the truth. Believe me."

Volkmann sighed, feeling the tiredness taking hold of him. "How many boxes did Rodriguez carry on each flight, before the last one?"

"I don't know, señor."

"Big boxes, small boxes?"

Santander shook his head, shrugged. "Sorry, señor."

"These people Rodriguez worked for, how did they pay him?"

Santander shook his head again. "He tell me nothing about that.

But I think cash. After each trip. In such business, that is how it is done."

"How did Rodriguez meet them?"

"He never tell me."

"Is there anyone close to Rodriguez, someone maybe he might tell things to about his work? A woman, a friend maybe?"

"No, señor. Rodriguez always keep things to himself. Even when he was drunk, he did not talk about his work. To nobody. I am certain."

"Is there anything else you remember? I want you to think hard. Anything. No matter how small."

"Nothing. I swear it." Santander made the sign of the cross.

Sanchez said, "If I discover you are lying to me, amigo . . ."

"As the Lord is my judge. Rodriguez was a friend."

Sanchez grimaced, stubbed out his cigarette, looked toward Volkmann. "You have any more questions, señor?"

Volkmann shook his head.

The three of them were seated in Sanchez's office again. The detective had more coffee, fresh and hot, brought to them. It was after two, the room silent now except for the gentle whirr of the fan overhead.

Erica sipped her coffee. "You think Santander is telling us everything he knows?"

"Sí, I believe so. And he is not the type of man who kills. Just a petty smuggler." Sanchez picked up the coffee cup. "What he said about the old man in the German colony, it helps a little. But there are many German colonies in Paraguay. People who came here before and after the last war. Immigrants. What Santander said wasn't much, but it makes the picture just a little clearer."

Volkmann's thoughts were elsewhere. After a time, he said, "The electronic equipment Hernandez borrowed: what distance could it work over?"

Sanchez shrugged. "Not far, maybe a mile."

"Hernandez could have been anywhere the night he was killed."

"I agree. The only clue I have is the word of the night watchman, who claims he saw him at the railroad station." Sanchez shrugged. "Who knows what Rudi was doing there, if he was there? Maybe he used the recording equipment there, but I don't think so. The watchman says the man he saw carried nothing and was in the station for perhaps only five minutes. Torres's equipment, you would have needed something to carry it in. A bag, a small suitcase perhaps."

Volkmann considered. "Okay, let's say Hernandez was at the station. Why does a man go to a railway station in the early hours of the morning? And why enter through a rear entrance?" He was thinking aloud, but he asked the question.

"Perhaps it was the quickest way?" Sanchez frowned. "Rudi meant to buy a ticket on a train to someplace, leave Asunción? But the ticket office was closed until later in the morning."

"Wouldn't he have known that?"

Sanchez nodded. "I understand. It leaves a question. If Rudi did go to the station and stayed for only a short time, it suggests perhaps that he had a purpose. But what purpose? I don't know the answer. Why do people go to a train station in the early hours of the morning? To catch a train, or to meet one, if there is one. But neither is possible in this case."

Sanchez glanced at Erica. She met his eyes for a moment before looking away. She was listening to the conversation but not listening, preoccupied, her hands restless, a frown on her face. Sanchez thought, *She's still grieving.*

Volkmann said finally, "What about the other hotels on the list?"

"My men have not called in yet. I will have the communications desk call them up."

Sanchez shuffled the file pages on his desk before closing the folder. Erica looked at him, a strange expression on her face, her brow furrowed in concentration. In her right hand she fingered the keys to Rudi Hernandez's apartment and car. She was toying with them.

Now she spoke softly, in Spanish. "You asked why Rudi might have been at the railway station. At the station . . . are there boxes, or lockers . . . for luggage, for people to leave things?"

Sanchez raised an eyebrow. He looked down again at the bunch of keys in the woman's hand; she was holding one of them between thumb and forefinger. He answered her in Spanish.

"I believe so."

Erica hesitated. "Maybe Rudi had one of those boxes?"

Sanchez looked at her blankly.

Volkmann looked at them both, wondering what they were saying.

The railway station faced the Plaza Uruguaya.

Inside the main hall, a half-dozen drunks slept it off in quiet corners. Indians and mestizos with young families, their babies wrapped in colorful blankets, sat or slept under the concession shops. Poor people from the north and south waited for the early trains, soft, pitiful brown eyes and looks of bewildered innocence on their lost faces, too penniless even to afford one of the cheap hotels nearby.

Some of them watched sleepily as the three people walked briskly through the station. The smell of diesel oil hung in the humid air. Sanchez looked at the curious, waiting people and pitied them.

The left-luggage boxes were near the concession stands. They turned a corner and saw the serried rows of several dozen metal boxes set against a concrete wall, black numbers stenciled on their doors. Sanchez stopped, facing the middle row.

"The keys, señorita."

Erica handed him the keys.

Sanchez examined them again. Two of the keys had nothing to do with Hernandez's apartment or car or office desk or locker, Sanchez knew. He had wondered about those keys. The way Erica had wondered. He had asked her at the police station what had made her think Rudi might have kept a luggage box at the station. She had shrugged. A feeling. An intuition.

The Indians in his country had a word for it: *mon-ia-taah-ka*. A voice from the world beyond. Perhaps Erica was right. Perhaps Rudi had kept a box here. The safe place he had told her about.

Now Sanchez fingered the key that looked closest to the size of the keyhole in the nearest locker facing him. The number 27 was stenciled in big letters on its metal door. He inserted the key. It went all the way in. He tried to turn it. The key moved a little, but no more, Sanchez feeling the resistance of the lock levers.

He turned to Erica and Volkmann as he removed the key, saw the looks on their faces. Hope, urgency.

He pointed to the left, where the row of boxes began, and smiled faintly. "Perhaps we should start at the beginning. It is always a good place to start. Sí?"

16

ASUNCIÓN. TUESDAY, DECEMBER 6, 3:45 A.M.

The air in Sanchez's office was gray with cigarette smoke.

They found the tape and the six photographs in the station locker marked number 39.

Each photograph was of the same two men. One was Dieter Winter, the other Nicolas Tsarkin. Winter's blond hair and thin, sharp features were unmistakable when compared to the head-and-shoulders shot Sanchez received from Volkmann's people.

The pictures had been taken with a telephoto lens. The two men were walking on the grounds of Tsarkin's estate—the last place he saw Rudi Hernandez alive. *At last,* Sanchez thought, *proof of a connection between Winter and Tsarkin.*

If only the tape made sense . . .

They listened to it eight times. Erica translated the conversation for Sanchez, then transcribed it in Spanish, the detective reading her writing slowly, questioning the inflection of words in the hand-written script—like Volkmann, curious, perplexed—examining the cryptic words over and over, asking Erica to translate again from the German, making sure no nuance was ignored, no word overlooked.

"You want to hear the tape again?"

Volkmann nodded. Sanchez pressed the PLAY button on the player lying on his desk before lighting another cigarette and sitting back.

Deep, guttural voices filled the room once more, Volkmann almost knowing the words from memory.

"The shipment . . . ?"

"The cargo will be picked up from Genoa as arranged."

"And the Italian?"

"He will be eliminated, but I want to be certain we don't arouse suspicion concerning the cargo. It would be prudent to wait until Brandenburg becomes operational. Then he will be dealt with along with the others."

Pause.

"Those who have pledged their loyalty . . . we must be certain of them."

"I have had their assurances confirmed. And their pedigree is without question."

"And the Turk?"

"I foresee no problems."

"The woman in Berlin . . . you're absolutely certain we can rely on her?"

"She won't fail us, I assure you." Pause. "There are no changes to the names on the list?"

"They'll all be killed."

"Your travel arrangements? Everything has been organized?"

"We leave Paraguay on the sixth."

"The schedule . . . perhaps I should go through it once more?"

There was a long pause on the tape until Volkmann heard a voice speak again.

"It's quite warm in here. Perhaps I might have a glass of water?"

They all heard the clink of glass a few moments later, the sound of water poured, the long silence, then the click on the tape, followed by a faint buzzing noise.

Sanchez leaned across and pressed the FORWARD button, until the sound of voices came again, but this time very faintly, the words fuzzy, crackling, barely audible.

"Prost."

"Prost."

"Prost."

Another pause, then very faintly, "We must take our leave of you. It's a long drive back north. The driver will take you to the safe house."

Silence.

Sanchez waited to make sure the conversation had finished, with what sounded like the faint noise of a door being closed, then he switched off the machine.

Volkmann looked down at the transcript he had scribbled in his notebook. Sanchez asked what the word *Brandenburg* meant. Erica explained that it was the name of a city west of Berlin and was also the name of a German province that had once contained part of the state of Berlin. The famous Brandenburg Gate that stood near the Reichstag, the old German parliament building, was once the original entrance to the territory. Hearing the answer, Sanchez scratched his head. The explanation did not help.

"Brandenburg," he said thoughtfully, "is not a place. But obviously a code for something else."

Volkmann nodded. He had come to the same conclusion.

"But for what?" Erica asked.

"Exactly. For what?" Sanchez looked at each of them. "For drug movements? Possibly. But we'll have to dig deeper, won't we?" His shoulders drooped with exhaustion and helplessness.

"And what's 'the list'?" Volkmann added. "'They'll all be killed'?"

he quoted. "Who? Where? How many? And who's the Italian, the Turk, and the woman in Berlin?"

Volkmann tried to concentrate on the tape. Three different speakers, he decided, checking his notes.

"Your travel arrangements . . . Everything has been organized?"

"We leave Paraguay on the sixth."

The sixth. Today.

He asked Sanchez to rewind the tape on those lines. Listening again to the faint voice that had spoken the reply, Volkmann felt certain it was the same voice that later said, "We must take our leave of you. It's a long drive back north . . ." What was "north"? They had discussed that line also. To Sanchez, "north" in Paraguay meant a vast area of jungle and swamp and scrubland called the Chaco. The detective pointed to it on the nicotine-stained map on the wall.

"North" could even mean over the border . . . Brazil . . . Bolivia. Or simply a suburb far north of the city.

Volkmann said to Sanchez, "What about Tsarkin, the suicide case? He can't be a complete cipher. Tell me again everything you know about him."

Sanchez studied the file open on his desk, the coroner's report, the letter from the oncologist at the San Ignatio hospital.

"He was ninety-one, a retired businessman, a naturalized citizen of this country for many years, and a former director of many companies. On November twenty-third, in the San Ignatio hospital, he was given only days to live. He had stomach cancer. The bleeding had become very bad. The hospital doctors who treated him said he was in pain and very weak, despite drugs."

"You're certain it was suicide?"

Sanchez yawned, put a hand to his mouth, blinked several times. "There was no question, especially considering his poor health. But after I received your report the other day, I asked one of my people to find out more about Tsarkin. I will have his immigration file checked out."

"You said there was a safe open in the study where you found the body. And embers in the fireplace."

"Sí. But this sometimes happens when people kill themselves. Private letters, personal things, they destroy them beforehand." Sanchez shrugged. "Especially if they have something to hide. In Tsarkin's case, we know now that is most likely true. We found no papers left of any interest. One of my men is checking the calls made to and from Tsarkin's house recently, especially on the twenty-third. I mentioned that there was a call Rudi Hernandez answered. Perhaps we can find out who made it."

It was still dark beyond the office window. Sanchez could hardly keep his eyes open. He should have finished work at five the previous day. He had telephoned his wife, told her he would be late, how late he didn't know.

"How long before you get the information on Tsarkin's background?"

Sanchez looked up at Volkmann and shrugged. "The office of immigration records does not open until ten o'clock. Then we can check Tsarkin's past. When he came to Paraguay, and from where. Also, I will have Tsarkin's servants questioned again. Perhaps they can tell us about his business acquaintances. Friends. People he socialized with."

Sanchez looked at his watch. Almost four o'clock. He, too, remembered the words on the tape, the words the woman had transcribed: "We leave Paraguay on the sixth."

He pushed himself achingly up from the chair and stretched his arms. The smoky air in the office stung his eyes, yet he stubbed out his cigarette and lit another. He slowly shook his head. "A question. In the hotels Winter stayed at, he always hired a suite. You asked a question. Why does one person need to hire a suite?" He paused. "You suggested it might be to impress someone. Could it have been a business contact, or a woman perhaps?" He paused again. "A suite, it is also big enough to hold a meeting, sí?" Sanchez raised his eyebrows questioningly.

"A hotel would also be a suitable place for someone to hire a room and try to listen to what was being said in another room nearby, would it not?" He looked down, plucked the list of hotels from the relevant file, and shrugged heavily. "Perhaps it is worth investigating. Just now, it is all I can think of."

Volkmann said tiredly, "You could be right. But which hotel? Asunción's a big city."

Sanchez briefly examined the list. "The hotel Winter stayed in most often, your hotel, the Excelsior. Perhaps if we tried there first? Then the Hotel Guarani."

The receptionist insisted on calling the night-duty manager first.

The man appeared minutes later, tall and immaculately dressed in a dark suit, crisp white shirt, and gray silk tie.

Sanchez showed his identity card and stated his request. The manager offered no resistance, led them politely to his office around the corner from the lobby.

He pulled up chairs for all of them and asked Sanchez, "The date again?"

"November twenty-fifth."

The manager rummaged in a filing cabinet drawer. He removed several thick wads of registration cards held together with rubber bands, brought them over to the desk, and sat down.

"Is there a particular name you wish to check on?"

"Hernandez. Señor Rudi Hernandez. He may have been a guest here."

"Guest information is kept on the computer. However, the original registration cards are maintained in alphabetical order, so it should not be difficult to find."

The manager riffled through the first block of cards he picked. "Hernandez . . . Hernandez . . . yes." He looked up. "One Hernandez, but the first name is"—he consulted the card again—"Morites. Morites Hernandez."

Sanchez held out his hand; the manager passed him the registration. A commercial traveler, the card declared, from São Paulo.

Sanchez glanced at Erica's handbag and asked in English, "Señorita, do you have any correspondence from Rudi?"

"In my room . . . I have a letter in my suitcase."

"Would you be so kind as to bring it to me?"

Erica nodded silently and left. When she returned five minutes later, she handed the letter over, unfolding the pages first, Sanchez comparing the handwriting on the registration to the handwritten letter he placed beside it on the desk.

The writing sloped in different ways; the writing on the registration cramped, secretive; the writing on the letter Rudi had sent to Erica large, stylish, the letters fat, generous.

Sanchez looked up. "No. Not the Hernandez we are looking for."

The manager appeared slightly relieved. Sanchez said, "November twenty-fifth. How many people stayed at the hotel?"

The manager looked from Sanchez to Volkmann and Erica, this time switching to perfect English. "It was a busy night, I remember. We were full. There was a convention and several functions—"

"How many people?" asked Sanchez.

"Perhaps three hundred guests."

When Sanchez sighed, the manager shrugged. "I'm sorry I haven't been able to help you."

Sanchez sounded determined. "We will need to check all of these cards."

The man stared at him in disbelief. "All, señor?"

"Sí. All. And I will need a list, a computer list, of all the guests who stayed here on November twenty-fifth. Their names. Their passport numbers if they were foreigners. Who made their reservations. Who paid their bills. Your computer. It has all this information?"

The manager nodded, dumbly.

"Then please see to it at once," said Sanchez.

"Señor, you realize the hour? I have other duties. Perhaps when the day staff arrives—"

Sanchez interrupted sharply. "I need this information now. It cannot wait. So please do as I ask. Otherwise I will be forced to contact your superior." His voice softened a little. "I would be grateful for your cooperation, señor."

17

NORTHEASTERN CHACO. 5:40 A.M.

The sounds of the jungle awakened him.

He rose from the bed, drew away the mosquito net, and dressed slowly. As his eyes adjusted to the semidarkness, he took in the room, bare now except for the bed and suitcases and the clothes hung on the back of the door where one of the Lima boys had left them, freshly washed and pressed for the journey. He thought of the boys now as he buttoned the soft cotton shirt. Their deaths had been necessary to protect him.

When he finished dressing, he went downstairs to the kitchen. He found a tired-looking Kruger sitting at the pinewood table smoking a cigarette, a glass of water in front of him.

"We burned the remaining provisions," Kruger said. "If you wish to eat breakfast, there's only some bottled water and dried nuts."

The silver-haired man nodded. "Just water, Hans."

Kruger stubbed out his cigarette in an empty cigarette packet lying on the table, then crossed to the sink in the corner and unscrewed the cap on a plastic bottle of drinking water. He took one of the remaining glasses and rinsed it first with the tepid water before filling it almost to the brim and handing it across.

The silver-haired man took a sip, looked out beyond the open kitchen window at the dark mass of jungle rising up to the distant rain forest. Already the night sky was streaked with an aching blue. It would soon be light. The unceasing sounds of the jungle throbbed outside. A bird flew past, a banana flit, its yellow plumage discernible even in the twilight. He looked back at Kruger and said, "The boys . . . ?"

"It's done," Kruger responded. "Schmidt made sure it was as quick and painless as possible. And that no one could identify them." He saw a look of pain crease the man's face.

"We'll wait until first light to burn what's left in the house. Franz and his men should arrive in the next hour to pick up the vehicles. A few more items have to be loaded onto the truck. Half an hour's work, no more. Then we'll begin the final check and cleanup."

The tall, silver-haired man looked toward the corner of the old, wooden outhouse. A place where he had spent solitary hours in childhood, serving his sentence alone.

He put down the unfinished glass of water on the pine table. "I wish to take a walk before we leave. The men can stay here. I would prefer to be alone, Hans."

The silver-haired man saw the look of alarm on Kruger's face, and he smiled gently as he placed a hand reassuringly on his shoulder.

"I'll be perfectly safe, Hans. There's no danger, I promise you."

"As you wish."

The man crossed to the door and stepped outside.

Kruger watched him go, then glanced at his watch.

Six-ten.

Three more hours. Three more hours and he would finally be quit of this godforsaken place.

ASUNCIÓN. 5:55 A.M.

It took them almost an hour to find the hotel registration card.

Volkmann found it, the three of them sitting around the desk, a pile of cards and a page from Hernandez's letter in front of each of them. The signature on the card was in a different name, Roberto

Ferres, but the style was unmistakably the same: the sloped and dotted letters, the amplitude of the script, matching Hernandez's writing exactly.

Once they found the card, Sanchez requested a list of guests staying on the first and second floors. Now the information lay in front of him, several reams of folded computer printout sheets. Sanchez held the registration card in his hand and looked at the harassed manager.

"The room that Señor Ferres hired on the first floor: the bill was paid in advance?" The information was on the registration card, but Sanchez asked just the same. There was an amount included in the bill for a bottle of champagne and canapés. That had puzzled him.

"Yes, in cash," the manager replied, glancing at the card in Sanchez's hand.

"Was the room key returned?"

"There is no need for our guests to return keys. The locks are opened with plastic disposable key cards. For security, they are changed by computer each time a new guest checks in. You wish to see the room where this gentleman stayed? I believe it is unoccupied at present."

"Perhaps later." Sanchez knew it was pointless. By now, the room would have been cleaned a dozen times. He looked at his watch. Six-fifteen.

Sanchez asked, "If there was a disturbance in Señor Hernandez's . . . Señor Ferres's . . . room, would it have been reported?"

The manager looked slightly alarmed. "What kind of disturbance?"

Sanchez shrugged. "A fight. A disagreement. Excessive noise."

"My staff are very diligent. If anything unusual happened, they would have reported the matter, and it would have been recorded." The manager smiled briefly. "Sometimes it happens. Couples argue. Throw things. You think something happened in this gentleman's room?"

"Perhaps. Perhaps not."

"I can check the daybook for complaints on that floor if you wish."

"I would appreciate it. Also, if this gentleman left anything behind in the room. Perhaps personal belongings. You can check?"

The manager nodded, then left them once more.

Sanchez rubbed his eyes and said to Volkmann and Erica, "The champagne and food . . . I am puzzled. Why would Rudi want to order them?"

He unfolded the ream of computer printouts. The list started with the first room number on Hernandez's floor. Slowly, carefully, he read through the printout, eyes scanning the information presented. Room number. Guest. Bill charges.

After a while, he blinked several times, rubbed his bloodshot eyes, looked up.

"At last, a light shines in the darkness."

Volkmann and Erica stared at the detective.

"Someone booked a suite on the same floor as Rudi's room." Sanchez smiled broadly for the first time. "A Señor Nicolas Tsarkin."

The manager returned moments later carrying a thick ledger open in his hands. He informed Sanchez that no complaints were made about the first floor on November twenty-fifth or in the early hours of the following morning. And nothing was left in any of the rooms.

Volkmann said, "Any chance we could see the suite Tsarkin hired?"

"I'm sorry, it is occupied at present. But as soon as the guests check out this morning, I will arrange it." The manager shrugged. "I'm sorry I can be of no further help."

Sanchez nodded. "I am grateful for your assistance, señor."

There was a knock on the door. Volkmann saw a man enter and speak quietly to Sanchez in Spanish. Sanchez asked to be excused, crossed to the man, and both stepped outside the office.

Erica's exhaustion showed; she was restless, her eyes sleepy. Volkmann realized neither of them had slept for more than a couple of hours in the past twenty-four. A wisp of blond hair fell across her face; she brushed it away, smiled briefly at him.

He said, "How about you go up to your room and rest? I'll call you if anything comes up."

"I'll be fine, Joe."

Sanchez came back into the room. "That was Detective Cavales. He got a list of telephone calls made from Tsarkin's house in the last two weeks. There were two calls made to a radio-telephone link in northeastern Chaco."

Sanchez paused, let the information sink in. "We've got a name: Karl Schmeltz. And an address. It's in an area up in the Indian country. Just north of the Salgado River near the border with Brazil. A desolate place, with not many people. Jungle and scrubland. The kind of place where a man shoots himself for something to do."

"How far?" Volkmann asked.

Sanchez shrugged. "Four hundred miles, maybe more. It takes perhaps ten hours to reach by car. The roads are very bad. Jungle roads."

Volkmann checked his watch. Six-thirty. He needed sleep, to close his eyes, not to travel along rutted jungle roads. And by then, by then perhaps it would be too late.

"By helicopter," Sanchez said, "it takes two hours. Maybe a little less."

"You can arrange that?" Erica asked.

Sanchez nodded.

ASUNCIÓN. 6:41 A.M.

Volkmann stared down through the helicopter's Plexiglas as the buildings of Asunción shrank below him.

It was cramped in the cockpit, the sun ahead of them, the military pilot wearing sunglasses. The muted noise of the blades as they chopped the air filled the cabin.

There were five of them in the Dauphin helicopter apart from the pilot. Erica and Volkmann, Sanchez and Cavales, and another detective named Moringo.

Sanchez's two detectives were armed with pistols and pump-action shotguns. Two military M-16 rifles lay beside Sanchez, along with six spare clips of ammunition. The second rifle was for Volkmann, Sanchez keeping the weapon by his side until it was needed.

The Dauphin bumped a little as they climbed higher. They were over scrub forest and jungle already, adobes and huts of wood and straw and fields of sugarcane below. The Rio Paraguay flowed off to the right, a gray-green ribbon of water snaking through a patchwork of greens stretching as far as the distant horizon.

Volkmann could sense the tension and exhaustion in the cramped cabin.

Finally, the radio crackled and a metallic-sounding Spanish voice came over the speaker. The pilot switched to earphones, then spoke to Sanchez and Moringo in Spanish. Sanchez turned to Volkmann and Erica, his voice almost a shout to drown out the noise.

"That was Asunción on the radio. I requested the local policía to meet us near the house. They'll direct us to the property and assist us." He glanced at his watch. "We'll be in radio contact in under an hour. Moringo here knows the region, but not the exact place. He thinks it's very remote."

Volkmann nodded. He sat back, his body aching now for sleep as he stared down, mesmerized by the vast emerald sea of jungle below, the monotonous, rhythmic sound of the chopper blades almost sending him to sleep.

It was 7:00 a.m.

NORTHEASTERN CHACO. 8:25 A.M.

Kruger looked up at the sky as he stood on the veranda, scanning for the helicopter, for a glint of sun on Plexiglas, listening for the sound of the blades.

Nothing.

Franz Lieber had departed with his men an hour earlier, driving his own Mercedes back down the gravel path, his men transporting the other vehicles to Asunción.

It was warm already, humid and hazy, clouds obscuring the sun. The elderly, silver-haired man came out of the jungle fifty yards away, hands clasped behind his back as he strode up the narrow path that led to the river.

Kruger looked toward the side of the house where the ashes of Schmidt's fire still smoldered faintly. Schmidt had done a good job. Kruger already checked the house and the outhouses himself— nothing remained. He ran a hand through his hair, was about to look up at the sky again when he heard the noise and turned round. The man had stepped onto the veranda.

As he came to stand beside Kruger a flock of tiny yellow birds flew past them.

"Franz came," Kruger said, watching the streak of yellow disappear into the jungle. "He sends his regards and says he looks forward to joining us later."

The silver-haired man nodded in reply. Moments later they both heard a faint sound and looked up instinctively. One of the men in the house must have heard it, too, because he came out with a pair of powerful Zeiss binoculars, started to sweep the sky.

The distant sound increased, a faint throbbing now. Kruger scanned the hazy sky again and saw a brief glint of light off to the right, in the direction the man pointed the binoculars, then another glint as the sound became louder, an unmistakable chopping noise in the air.

Kruger glanced at his watch. Eight-forty. "The helicopter," he said calmly. "It's early."

The silver-haired man took one last look over at the small outhouse, then at where Schmidt had burned the remaining papers, even the old things he had kept since childhood.

All gone now, black ashes, smoldering still. His eyes swept over the jade green of the jungle. One last, lingering look before he turned finally to Kruger as the helicopter noise grew louder.

"Tell Schmidt to check and douse the fire. Ensure everything has been thoroughly burned. Then get the men together with the suitcases."

It was Volkmann who saw the vehicle first, the blue and white of the police car a mere speck, waiting on the ribbon of desolate road in the distance. The roads here were primitive, brown-red strips of dirt, looking like tape stuck onto the lush, green jungle.

Volkmann tapped Sanchez on the shoulder and pointed downward. Sanchez picked out the blue and white, pointed it out to the pilot. The Dauphin banked sharply, turned toward where the speck of color waited.

They had been in contact with the local policía on a special frequency for almost fifteen minutes, Sanchez translating the commentary for Volkmann. He looked exhausted but came awake now, staring out beyond the Plexiglas, talking rapidly into the microphone to the sergeant in the car below them.

Sanchez turned to Volkmann. "The sergeant says the property is straight ahead along the road another mile. They will follow us there."

There was a cry from Cavales as he pointed beyond the helicopter's Plexiglas. "There. To the left."

The pilot followed the line of his finger. The sky was hazy with clouds, but even Volkmann could see the house, less than a mile away. It stood alone in the midst of the jungle, painted off-white, very large, one of the largest haciendas they had flown over in the last half hour, a narrow, private road leading up to a clearing in front of the property.

As the tension rose in the small cabin, the helicopter began to bank sharply to the left. The pilot shouted something to Sanchez, who said to Volkmann, "The pilot says maybe he can land in front of the hacienda if there's a big enough clearing."

Volkmann saw the blue-and-white car race below them, moving fast along the narrow dirt road, plumes of russet dust in its wake.

The helicopter suddenly slowed, hovered, less than a quarter of a mile from the hacienda, the pilot shouting something to Sanchez.

"We go for the clearing, okay?" Sanchez said to Volkmann. "But two sweeps over the hacienda first, just in case there's trouble waiting."

Sanchez tapped the pilot's shoulder and spoke rapidly. The helicopter began to move forward fast, dropping height, going in low. Volkmann tensed. Sanchez clenched his teeth and grabbed one of the automatic rifles and three clips of ammunition. He handed them over.

"For you, in case there's trouble. But make sure the woman stays in the chopper, sí?"

Volkmann glanced up briefly at the hazy sky, saw something glinting in the far distance, a flash of white light, and then it was gone. He tensed, checked the rifle, then looked down as the helicopter began its sweep.

Volkmann knew after the first sweep that the house was empty.

The pilot kept the helicopter in a steady angle of bank, circling the property in a perfect circuit, then sweeping out, coming in low again, barely clearing the surrounding jungle.

There was a black stain on the landscape to the right side of the house, looking like an oil spill at first, but on the second sweep, Volkmann recognized the remains of a fire, the helicopter's blades causing the dark blot to lift and swirl as small black flakes rose and billowed into the air, eddying into a scattered mess.

The veranda was empty, the windows of the house bare of curtains, and a clutter of outbuildings stood at the rear, looking dilapidated and weathered, a small wooden outbuilding set off to the right of the house.

On the second pass, Volkmann glanced over at Sanchez, saw disappointment on his face but the eyes alert, awake, ready. But there was no need to be ready, Volkmann knew, seeing the blue-and-white police car speed along the private gravel track that led up to the white hacienda.

As the car came to a sudden halt, four policía scrambled out, wrenching guns from holsters, crouching as the helicopter began to descend on a flat clearing to the right of the driveway.

As soon as they landed, Sanchez stepped out, followed by his men, handguns and shotguns at the ready, Volkmann close behind carrying the rifle, Erica remaining with the pilot, who was closing down the engines.

The heat and humidity of the jungle hit them as they crouched low to keep their heads below the slowly dying blades. Then the swish of the rotors died, and it seemed to Volkmann that there was only utter silence and wilting heat, until seconds later, the clicking, shrieking sounds of the jungle erupted all around them.

Two uniformed policía from the car rushed forward, waving their guns, chattering loudly, pointing to the house.

Sanchez spoke to them briefly, then replaced his gun in his waist holster. He turned to Volkmann, the look of exhaustion on his face saying it all, knowing, as Volkmann knew, that they were too late.

He nodded toward the house. "Come, amigo. Let's take a look inside."

It became apparent to Volkmann that something was wrong. No one left a house this empty, this bare. No one picked a house this clean, leaving it like a corpse stripped of its flesh after the vultures had been at it.

Nicolas Tsarkin made his departure the same way, Volkmann reflected. Cleared away everything with equal thoroughness.

That is what the house, the property, suggested: a wooden skeleton. Echoing, hollow, the scrubbed floorboards inside creaking eerily underfoot, swept clean, swept of everything.

Erica joined them from the helicopter, only the pilot choosing to remain outside, indifferent, listening to a commercial radio station he had tuned in to the receiver on board, oblivious to the heat as he stalked the area around the Dauphin, chewing gum.

The house was large inside, thirteen rooms, Volkmann counted, each sanitized, each bare, nothing covering the floorboards, not even a thread of carpet remaining.

Sanchez ordered all the policía and his own men to go through the house room by room, checking for anything, for any clues. Then he went with Volkmann and Erica to look at the outbuildings.

There were three of them. Two had been garages, they guessed, big enough to accommodate a large car each, but nothing in either, nothing except faded, oil-stained patches on the ground.

The last was not much larger. It appeared to have been a storeroom, or a child's playhouse, built of wood. Again, nothing inside, only a number of very faint white paint marks on one of the walls. Volkmann and Sanchez moved closer, examined them. The marks had been painted a long time ago, and when they looked closely, they saw that they resembled faintly the pattern of a spiderweb, as if someone had started painting the interior and then changed his mind, or a child had been playing with a paintbrush.

None of them spoke as they examined the place, Sanchez smoking a cigarette, looking over the walls, the floors, until he seemed baffled and overcome by it all.

As they stepped out into the sunlight, Volkmann saw the remains of the fire. The ashes were scattered in small, irregular clusters by the wake of the helicopter's blades. He knelt down and touched the center of the largest cluster. The ashes were soggy, as if water had been poured on them. He found a stick in a nearby thicket and poked at the remains until he had sifted through all the black clusters scattered by the helicopter's blades.

Nothing.

The sun was out now from behind the clouds, the heat becoming unbearable. Volkmann looked at Erica, then at Sanchez. Small beads of sweat glistened on the detective's brow.

"Did the local sergeant tell you anything useful?" Volkmann asked.

"He's lived around here for most of his life," the detective answered. "The people here kept to themselves, he said. He scarcely knew of their existence."

"How far to the nearest town?"

"Twenty miles. The nearest house, ten."

Volkmann kicked a cluster of ashes, paused, then looked at Sanchez and said slowly, "What do you think, Vellares?"

Sanchez wiped his brow with the back of his hand, looked at him, shrugged. "The Indians in my country, they have a word . . ." Sanchez said it, a long, unfathomable word, a bewildered look on his sagging face. "It means . . . very strange. Very . . . weird." He stared at Volkmann. "You know what I'm saying?"

Volkmann knew. In both the house and the small outbuilding, he had sensed something. He had shivered stepping into both of them. Something inside him felt touched by something, Sanchez sensing it, too, and Erica, Volkmann could tell.

A feeling none of them could put into words.

There was a noise behind them. Volkmann turned, saw the helicopter pilot call Sanchez over, talking in Spanish.

Moments later, the detective returned holding something in his hand.

"The pilot found this lying in the bushes. The helicopter blades must have blown it from the fire."

Sanchez handed Volkmann a piece of glossy paper, the remains of a very old black-and-white photograph. Half of it was burned, the right side of the picture cracked and worn, but the image still discernible. The photograph was of a woman, a blond, young, pretty woman, smiling at the camera, with sky and snowcapped mountains behind her.

The young woman's right hand was linked through the arm of a companion, a man wearing some sort of uniform. Only the man's shoulder, his left arm, and part of his torso were still visible. The rest of the photograph was scorched, its black edges ragged, flaking with cinder. But what caught Volkmann's eye was the conspicuous dark band around the man's arm: a black Nazi swastika set in a white circle.

Volkmann stared down at the photograph for a long time until Sanchez said, "Turn it over."

He did as the detective asked. There was a date, in German, scrawled in the top right-hand corner in faded blue ink. "Elfter Juli, 1931": eleventh of July, 1931.

Volkmann looked up, shielded his eyes from the strong sun. He saw Erica and Sanchez stare over at the white house before both turned back to look at him.

"What does it mean?" Sanchez asked.

Volkmann flicked over the half-burned photograph, looked down again at the blond young woman in the picture, and wondered the same.

PART THREE

18

Franco Scali stood at the window of the harbor office and gripped the Zeiss binoculars tightly. She was two hours late, the *Maria Escobar,* and in those two long hours Franco thought he must have lost half a kilo in sweat. But now the ship was heading into the harbor. All twelve thousand tons of her. A beautiful sight.

"Franco?"

Scali put down the binoculars and smiled at the pretty, dark-haired young secretary seated behind her desk.

"What is it, sweetie?"

He was glad of the distraction now that the ship had finally arrived. The secretary wore black stockings and a short, thick, black woolen skirt, a glimpse of stocking top visible when she crossed her legs. Franco knew she did it to tease him, an unhappily married man with three growing children. He sighed inwardly. She was like that. A teaser.

The office above the warehouse had a sweeping view of the old port. But it was a drafty, cramped place, and Franco wore a heavy woolen sweater. He felt hot, despite the icy wind that whistled around the port. It was stress, Franco knew.

"The *Maria Escobar* . . . ," the secretary said finally.

"What about her?"

"The ship's load sheet. Don't forget to give me the copy."

"It's downstairs in the warehouse. I'll give it to you after the *Escobar*'s been unloaded."

The load sheet contained the original and the carbon copies, all part of the one form so there could be no mistakes, no alterations, as far as the ship's cargo was concerned.

"The things I do for you," Franco added with a smile. "And I don't even get a kiss."

The secretary gave Franco a flirting grin out of the side of her wide, sensual mouth. "Franco . . . you're a married man."

"They're the best kind. Didn't your mama ever tell you that?"

She giggled. "The copy load sheet, Franco . . ."

"When I'm through with the ship."

"Well, don't forget."

She was only a junior—Franco the senior clearance clerk, fifteen years older—but she talked to him as if she were his boss. Franco liked it. The secretary thought she had him in the palm of her hand, teasing him, wearing those short skirts and tight blouses. But she didn't: Franco was too clever for that, far too clever. Besides, Franco Scali had other plans.

He turned away as she began to polish her crimson nails, his eyes watching the *Maria Escobar* creep into the harbor. There was no need for the binoculars now, because the ship was only minutes from docking, the sprawling old city of Genoa off to the left, with its maze of jagged backstreets.

Franco put down the binoculars and winked. "Ciao, sweetie. I've got work to do."

He went down the stairs to the busy warehouse, picked up the paperwork from the tiny glass-fronted office at the entrance.

An icy wind blew in from the sea, and he pulled on a reefer jacket and crossed the yard apron. His eyes were drawn up to the crane cabin, where Aldo Celli waited to operate the grab. Franco gave the man a wave and then the thumbs-up sign. Seconds later he heard Aldo start up the crane's motor. "Aldo the Hawk," they called him. Because the man swooped down with the crane grab on the cargo containers as if they were prey.

Franco saw the *Maria Escobar* nudging stern-first into the harbor, the men on docks ready to tie her up. He looked around for the customs officer, saw no sign of him, but he'd be here, for sure.

Sometimes customs just checked the seals, or broke the previous port seal and looked inside the big steel cargo containers to satisfy themselves, or just to show their authority. But they had never caught Franco yet. He was always careful, and this one was a peach. There would be enough cash from this one job to buy a new car and plenty left over to spend on the girls in the smart clubs near the Piazza della Vittoria. And he needed money. Everybody needed money these days; things were going so crazy. Even his old man had said it was worse than the old days.

Franco licked his dry lips. The cargo was well hidden, he told himself, relaxing a little. The *Maria Escobar* almost docked now, Aldo up in the crane, itching to get going with the grab.

Franco ground out his cigarette and felt a nervous flutter in his chest. Coming fast across the yard apron was the fat, waddling figure of Paulo Bonefacio, the customs officer. Paulo the Pest, *Il Peste* for short, because he hassled you, wanted to check every freaking container, every nook and cranny, like the man was looking for a medal from the Italian Customs Service. What the devil was he doing here? It should have been his day off . . .

Il Peste came up to him, puffing and grunting. "Ciao, Franco."

"Ciao. I thought Vincenti was on today?"

"He's sick," answered Il Peste. "Why, you expecting an easy time?"

Franco forced himself to smile back, the *Escobar*'s gangway coming down. He could feel the tension returning . . . *Of all people, it has to be Il Peste checking the containers* . . .

"Come on, Franco, let's see what we can find, eh?"

Franco swallowed, not too hard, and tried to keep smiling. "Sure."

The fat customs official grunted and started across the harbor, to where Aldo would drop the containers before the conveyer took them farther along the port.

Franco Scali said a silent prayer, watching Aldo Celli swing the crane grab round and pick up one of the heavy metal containers off the ship as if it were a lightweight cardboard box. The one Franco was waiting for was a blue container with three gray-striped markings, and it hadn't come out of the hold yet. Only five containers lay on the dockyard apron where Aldo had dropped them. Forty containers this load, and knowing Il Peste, he'd want to check almost every one.

Franco pumped sweat as he helped the men maneuver the containers into place, Aldo swinging them up from the *Maria Escobar*'s hold and down onto the apron. *Let's get this over with,* thought Franco.

Il Peste examined the clipboard list of documents in his hands. Franco knew the man was totally incorruptible, got worked up like a bloodhound when he found something not right on the ship's manifest or contraband in the containers.

It didn't happen too often, but if Il Peste found anything like that, you were in the slammer. And no one would dare retaliate: the man's brother, Stefano, was a Carabiniere inspector. Franco tried to time it so that Il Peste wouldn't be around when he had something special coming in. Only it didn't always work out that way.

Like today.

Franco cursed under his breath now as another container swung out of the *Escobar*'s hold, Aldo enjoying himself up there in the crane's nest—twenty-five more to go—Franco sweating, as he looked over at the customs official. Il Peste stared at the neat line of containers laid out on the apron, waiting until the last one was out before starting work, like an athlete waiting for the crack of the starting pistol.

The wind whistled around the harbor. Franco watched as Aldo swung the crane grab up and into the hold again.

It was the last container. Blue, a band of three gray stripes around the sides. The one Franco was waiting for. Aldo lifted up the container, swung her across and down, landing her with a smack.

Go easy! What I got in there is worth a whole lot of money, you Genoese moron!

Franco heard the dying whirr of the crane's motor. Shouts from the men as they finished working and removed their leather gloves, waiting for Il Peste to start. He came up beside Franco, looking ready to do battle.

"Forty containers, right?"

"Yeah."

"You got all the documents?"

Franco handed them over. All the containers were sealed individually with a stamped customs seal from the last port, or from the port of origin. Franco's job was to clear his cargo and paperwork through customs as fast as he could. Mostly the customs guys didn't delay you, took a perfunctory look to cover themselves.

But not Il Peste. He was meticulous. And sometimes he used the duster, a brass knuckle-duster, to tap the insides of the big steel boxes, making sure there were no false bottoms or walls. That was the one fear Franco had today: if Il Peste used the duster.

The fat official looked up from the documents. "Okay. Everything looks in order."

"How many you want to do?" Franco asked. None, he hoped, but knew that was asking too much. One, two maybe. *But please, not the last, not number forty.*

Il Peste looked at his watch. "I gotta finish early today. I got a christening to go to. Stefano, my brother, his wife had a baby boy. I'm an uncle again."

"Congratulations!" Franco slapped Il Peste on the shoulder as he turned to the dockers. "Hey! What you think? Paulo is an uncle again. Stefano's wife just had a baby boy."

The men muttered their congratulations. Il Peste smiled, apparently warmed by their mumbled good wishes. It was good, thought Franco, a really good sign. Maybe his prayers had been answered. Maybe the man wasn't going to be too thorough today.

A chill wind whistled through the harbor as Franco smiled. "You got time afterward, I'd like to buy you a glass of vino to celebrate."

"Some other time, Franco. I got to be at the church by three."

"Sure, no problem."

Il Peste consulted the documents on his clipboard. "We just do . . . let me see . . . number three. The third one."

Franco beamed. "Okay by me."

"And then the last one. Number forty."

Franco tried hard not to show his apprehension, tried to stay cool, but felt his legs begin to tremble. "Sure . . ."

Il Peste turned toward the containers, laid out in aisles of ten, four deep, before looking back at Franco, staring into his face.

"What's wrong, Franco? You look pale. You feeling okay?"

Franco felt his bowels shiver, rubbed his stomach, grimaced weakly. "My wife cooked carbonara for dinner last night. It didn't taste too good."

Il Peste nodded, mildly sympathetic, then strode quickly toward where the rows of containers began.

Franco was sweating like a pig.

Come on, man, get it over with.

Number three container done, and no problems. The contents tallying with the customs manifest.

They were outside the last container now, number forty, Franco trying to control his fear as he watched Il Peste break the lead customs seal before two of the men opened the container doors for him.

Whatever you do, don't use the knuckle-duster, man . . . don't use the duster.

The official consulted the clipboard. "What's the port of origin?"

"Casablanca."

Il Peste studied the documents, shook his head. "No, it's not."

Franco glanced at the documents over Il Peste's shoulder. "Oh, sure . . . I forgot, it's . . ."

"Montevideo," corrected Il Peste. "Casablanca was first port of call."

"Yeah, Montevideo."

Containers from South America usually put the customs guys on guard. Narcotics were the big thing. Franco, sweating, stepped a little into the container, twenty-six boxes inside, twenty-six big and small, but still room for more, the big container not full.

"What's the manifest say?" Il Peste asked, but not waiting for a reply, looking down at the document himself on the clipboard. "Twenty-six boxes. All machine parts, except one box of medical supplies. Okay, let's have a look."

They stepped into the container, and Franco saw him take a flashlight from his pocket. He flicked it on and counted the boxes, checking that none had been tampered with. Il Peste finally grunted his satisfaction, ticked off one of the entries on his customs form, then suddenly he sniffed the air.

"You get a funny smell?"

Franco sniffed. "No . . . I don't smell nothing."

"The medical supplies . . . Which box?"

Franco moved several of the boxes aside, felt the sweat drip down his back, on his brow. He wiped his forehead with the back of his hand.

"I think I see it," Franco said.

Il Peste moved to where the box lay on top of another and picked it up, sniffed it, then put the box of medical supplies aside. "It's okay."

Franco almost sighed out loud. But Il Peste didn't put his flashlight away. Franco saw the man's right hand go into his coat pocket, the gold-colored knuckle-duster coming out. *No, man . . . not the duster!* Franco watched, horrified, as the man fitted the chunky brass metal into his fat fingers.

He smiled at Franco. "A couple of taps . . . for luck."

Franco smiled back, tried not to betray his unease, watching nervously as Il Peste went around the container tapping the sides, stopping, then tapping again, listening carefully to the sound, comparing it to the previous one, as if he were a piano tuner.

When he moved toward the right container wall, Franco felt his heart beat even faster, the pumping in his chest coming through his ears, through his whole body, feeling his pulse in the tips of his fingers.

Not the right wall . . .

The duster kept tapping . . .

Tap . . . tap . . . tap . . .

Tap . . . tap . . . tap . . .

Il Peste suddenly stopped.

Franco saw the man's head turn slightly to the right. *I don't believe it . . . he's found it!* Franco wanted to weep, felt the blood drain out of his body as Il Peste hit the spot again.

Tap . . . tap . . . tap. . . . The brass knuckle-duster smacked against the right side wall, down near the back of the container, Franco listening, hearing the slight difference in sound, just a touch.

Tap . . . tap . . . tap . . .

Franco wanted to throw up. Il Peste was now hitting a spot less than a yard away from the hidden compartment. "Hey, Franco . . ."

Franco looked up, startled, his heart beating in his ears like hammer blows.

"Yeah?" The question came out like a croak in his throat.

Il Peste looked up at him in the dim-lit back of the container, pointing the flashlight away. "You got the right time?"

"What . . . ?"

"The time . . . What's the time?"

Franco looked at his watch, hand trembling. "Two . . . two-thirty . . ."

"I've got to call my brother at the station. You mind if I use your telephone?" Franco shook his head dumbly and swallowed. Had the flashlight been shining on Franco's face, Il Peste would have seen its paleness.

"Why . . . what's up?" Franco asked quietly.

Il Peste tapped at his own watch. "My watch . . . it's stopped; that's what's up. I'm gonna be late for the christening. Let's wrap her up."

Franco sighed audibly, the sigh sounding like a small breeze. Il Peste heard it, shone the flashlight in Franco's face.

"Hey . . . You look sick, Franco. You okay?"

Franco belched with fear and smiled innocently. "It must have been the pasta."

It was raining on the Via Balbi when Franco parked his car across the street from the bar.

He saw the man as soon as he stepped inside. Blond, thin-lipped, sitting alone at the counter, in his mid-twenties and wearing glasses. He flicked a glance at Franco, removed his glasses, and wiped them with a handkerchief.

Franco ordered a vino rosso and lit a cigarette. The blond man's action was his signal. The cigarette was Franco's: no problems, he had the box. The blond stood, paid for his drink, and left the bar. Franco waited another couple of minutes, finishing his cigarette and wine, then paid the barkeeper.

He climbed into the Fiat and drove around the corner to the deserted parking lot opposite the Banco d'Italia.

A dark-colored Fiat was already waiting. The blond young man sat in the front with a passenger, a man whose face was partly hidden in shadow. Franco rolled down the window, the rain falling more softly now.

"You have the cargo?" the man said in good Italian.

"Sure. You have the cash?"

The man handed across a large envelope. Franco flicked through fresh banknotes in thin wads.

"The box," the man said.

Franco pressed the button underneath the dashboard, the lid flicking open. His own secret cubbyhole; he had fitted it himself and it was virtually undetectable. The smuggled box just about fit. It was so heavy Franco had to support it on the car's window frame. He wondered what it contained. Gold, must be, judging by the weight of it. Heavy, like all the others. But it wasn't any of his business what the Germans were smuggling. His business was to make sure he was paid. He hefted it out and handed it across through the window gingerly.

The man passed it carefully to his passenger.

"Don't forget our arrangement. Any problems, any inquiries, you contact us."

Franco said, "That was the last one?"

"Yes."

"Good."

The young man sensed Franco's change of tone. "Why? Was there a problem?"

"No. But there could have been. The customs guy today . . . He looked hard, you know what I mean?"

A slight edge of panic in the blond's voice. "But he found nothing. Suspected nothing?"

"You think I'd be here if he did?" Franco shook his head. "No . . . I'm getting out of this smuggling business. From now on, you want something delivered, you don't call Franco, okay?"

"I think that's a wise decision."

Franco started the car, said it aloud as he pulled away in the white Fiat: "So do I, amico. Ciao."

19

STRASBOURG, THURSDAY, DECEMBER 8

The flight from Asunción to Madrid had been delayed, and it was almost midday when they landed in Frankfurt.

Volkmann drove Erica to his apartment, then he left her and headed to the office to type up a preliminary report. He put a copy in Ferguson's mailbox with a note saying he'd be in the next morning before noon.

At five, he had an early dinner with Erica in a small restaurant near the Quai Ernest, and they walked back to his apartment. After he had unpacked, he made up the spare bedroom and poured two brandies.

The afternoon before, Sanchez drove them to a small cemetery on the outskirts of the city. Volkmann and the detective waited under a jacaranda tree while Erica said her prayer.

Later, Sanchez had taken them to the house in La Chacarita

where the bodies were discovered, and there were brief interviews with Mendoza and Torres, but neither man had been able to add to their statements. They visited Tsarkin's residence in the late afternoon, and Volkmann saw the manicured lawns, the paintings on the walls, the open safe in the study. Sanchez's men had searched the rooms again, top to bottom, but found nothing.

At the airport, Sanchez promised to get the report on Tsarkin's background to Strasbourg as quickly as possible. His men were still digging through the files at the immigration office.

"I hope to have some information within the next twenty-four hours," Sanchez said as he led them to departures. Erica thanked him, and the detective smiled and said to Volkmann, "Look after her, amigo. Take care, and good luck."

On the flight back, Volkmann explained that he wanted her in Strasbourg should Ferguson need to talk with her. When they landed she was exhausted, and she had accepted his suggestion that she use the spare room in his place instead of booking into a hotel. They could arrange that next day if Ferguson needed her for longer.

After Erica went to bed, Volkmann poured himself another brandy. Darkness had fallen beyond the window, the spire of the Gothic cathedral illuminated in the distance. No heat here, just a cold, chill wind rattling the windows.

As he sat sipping the brandy, feeling the aching tiredness take hold, he heard Erica tossing restlessly in her sleep. He thought of the white house and the photograph of the woman taken a long time ago.

He wondered what the heck Ferguson and Peters would make of it all.

FRIDAY, DECEMBER 9

The three men sat quietly in the warm office.

The tape machine on Ferguson's desk was on. When it finished playing, Ferguson switched it off and shook his head.

Three photographs lay faceup on the desk, copies made by the police in Asunción, and he stared down at them with interest. Faces to go with the story. One was a shot of Dieter Winter and Nicolas Tsarkin, taken with a telephoto lens. Another of Tsarkin himself, head and shoulders only, that looked like a copy from a passport. Hard eyes, a narrow mouth, and a face that was thin and secretive. The third was a black-and-white photograph of the woman, her right hand linked through a man's arm. The Nazi armband was a curiosity, Ferguson reflected.

He adjusted his glasses and picked up the photograph of the pretty blond woman and stared at it again. Volkmann had paper-clipped a note to the snapshot, mentioning the date on the back of the original photograph: July 11, 1931.

Ferguson penciled small asterisks and question marks in the margins of the report, points to be clarified by Volkmann.

Now Ferguson scanned through the document once again. It made interesting reading. Volkmann spared no detail in describing the scene at the remote Chaco house.

"The remains of the bonfire were analyzed, Joe?"

Volkmann nodded, tired, but his eyes alert. "Sanchez's people did a preliminary analysis of the remains. Papers and photographs mostly. And wood and cardboard. But also some food traces, dried provisions. Nothing was left in the house or outhouses. Every room stripped clean. Whoever these people were, they wanted every trace of their presence completely destroyed." He shook his head. "I've never seen anything like it before. Like the whole property had been sanitized, scrubbed clean."

Ferguson paused before replying. "Leaving the question of the Chaco property aside for now, where's the connection to Winter? What's it all got to do with his death?"

Peters leaned forward in his chair. "Might I make a suggestion, sir?"

"By all means."

"We know Winter was in South America not just once, but on at least eight occasions."

"Go on," Ferguson prompted.

"We know the ammunition used in both the Winter shooting and the killing of the businessmen in Hamburg a year ago was South American. We also know a lot of terrorist groups have been getting their supplies from there, since the Russians stopped supplying them." Peters hesitated, glanced at Volkmann. "And then there are the cargoes flown to Montevideo. There are countless possibilities, sure. But it could be weapons and munitions. It's a plausible reason why Winter was in South America."

Ferguson sighed, then stood and crossed to the window. "Plausible, yes. But speculative. And it doesn't explain why Winter was killed in Berlin." Ferguson turned and raised an eyebrow, looked at Volkmann. "What do you think the cargoes are, Joe?"

Volkmann hesitated. "Difficult to say. Weapons or narcotics seem likely. Or even precious metals. But if it was narcotics Rodriguez transported for these people, then the Chaco house wasn't used. The chemical agents used in the processing would have left behind trace elements." He shook his head. "But there were none of those on the property."

"What about the land it's on? Was it checked?"

"Sanchez had the local police check the land within a three-mile radius. There was a field that looked like it could have been used as a temporary airstrip two miles from the house. It had some deep tire marks on the surface and faint oil stains in the soil. I'm guessing it could have been the place where Rodriguez landed."

"Was the aircraft Rodriguez used examined for narcotics traces?"

"The DC4 was impounded at Asunción. Sanchez had his lab people go over it."

"And?"

"There were minute cocaine traces in the aft cargo area." Volkmann shook his head at Ferguson. "But it proves nothing. Rodriguez could have made dozens of runs in between for other customers, ferrying narcotics."

Ferguson sighed, crossed back slowly to pick up a file from his desk. Inside were the original and two copies of the faxed report he received from Asunción.

"I received this from Paraguay an hour ago. It's in English. I delayed showing it to you both because I wanted to discuss Joe's report first. You had both better read it now before we go any further. I've got copies for each of you. It deepens the mystery, I'm afraid."

Ferguson handed them each a copy of the report Sanchez promised. Volkmann took the three sheets and read slowly.

To: Head, British DSE
From: Captain Vellares Sanchez, Policía Civil, Paraguay
Subject: Visit of your officer, J. Volkmann, and his
         investigation
Status: Highly Confidential

After recent investigation the following can be reported:

1. The Chaco property your officer visited occupies a
    tract of land some 400 acres in size and was bought
    and registered in the name of Erhard Schmeltz in
    December 1931, one month after Señor Schmeltz, his
    wife, Inge, and their son Karl emigrated to Paraguay.
    Records reveal that Erhard Schmeltz was born in
    Hamburg in 1880, his wife one year later. According to
    his immigration records, Schmeltz served in the First
    World War in the German Army. His financial status
    upon arrival in Paraguay was five thousand U.S. dol-
    lars.

    The Chaco property was used for the production
    of quebraco wood until 1949. Señor Erhard Schmeltz
    died in an automobile accident in Asunción in 1943.

    Police file sources disclose that from December
    1931 to January 1933, he was in receipt of considerable
    sums of money sent from Germany. From February

1933 onward, money was sent to him in Asunción via
the official German Reichsbank at exact six-month
intervals, using bank drafts. Each draft was for the
sum of five thousand U.S. dollars. After his death,
Schmeltz's wife became the recipient. The drafts finally
ceased in February 1945.

No further information exists on the recent occupants of the Chaco property. Señor Schmeltz's wife
died in 1949. The property register then recorded a
change of ownership to the Schmeltzes' son, Karl, born
in Germany in July 1931. No specific town or city of
birth was given in the immigration records, and there
are no photographs recorded in civil offices of Karl
Schmeltz. His present whereabouts are unknown.

2. Regarding Señor Nicolas Tsarkin, the following information has been confirmed:

He arrived in Asunción from Rio de Janeiro on
November 8, 1946, and applied for Paraguayan citizenship two days later.

His immigration application stated his place of
birth as Riga, in Latvia. On arrival in Paraguay he had
the considerable sum of twenty thousand U.S. dollars.
Señor Tsarkin stated on his application form he was a
war refugee and businessman. Paraguayan citizenship
was granted one week after his application.

For your information, many refugees came to South
America after the war. The Paraguayan government of
the time had pro-German sympathies: thus, ex-Nazis
were admitted, particularly those with foreign currency or gold in their possession.

In Señor Nicolas Tsarkin's case, a security police
file exists. I have seen the file but am not permitted
to transmit a copy. However, the following facts were
recorded:

- Nicolas Tsarkin was born in Berlin, not Riga.
- Tsarkin's real name was Heinrich Reimer.
- He was a major in the Leibstandarte (SS) division when the war ended in 1945.
- According to then-reliable sources named in the file, Tsarkin was wanted for a number of war crimes on the Russian and Allied fronts. It should be pointed out that at no time during his life in Paraguay was Tsarkin ever in trouble with the police. Nor were there any applications for his extradition, overt or otherwise. He apparently led an exemplary and successful business life and covered up his past successfully.
- Tsarkin prospered in Paraguay, starting a number of businesses, importing farm machinery and mechanical parts. He was unmarried. No business connection has been discovered between Tsarkin and the Schmeltz property.

One further interesting detail. A military radar installation at Bahia Negra, northeast of the Chaco, registered an unfiled flight thought to be a light aircraft or helicopter shortly after our arrival at the Chaco property.

The unidentified aircraft was vectored proceeding northeast to the Brazilian border toward Corumba and was then lost from radar contact. This is being investigated further.

ENDS. Sanchez

Ferguson looked perplexed. "As I say, it rather deepens the mystery."

"You think there's a link to Winter's death in all this?" Peters asked. "To the photograph of the woman? To what happened to the journalist and the young girl?"

"It's possible." Ferguson stared down at the photographs, at the one of the blond young woman. "You say Tsarkin was responsible for booking the hotel suite, Joe?"

"That and every hotel suite used by Winter in the last two years during his visits to Paraguay. But it tells us nothing. Except that maybe he was some sort of organizer."

Ferguson made a steeple of his fingers. "I'll have a copy of the taped voices sent to the laboratory in Beaconsfield for analysis. See if it offers any clue about the speakers. Did any of you notice the one curious but connecting strand in all of this?"

Ferguson held up the young woman's photograph. "This man, Erhard Schmeltz, mentioned in the report—the money he received from Germany commenced the same year the photograph was taken, if the date on the reverse is to be believed." Ferguson paused as he placed the photograph back on top of the file. "Erhard Schmeltz seems a pretty curious character. He arrives in Paraguay in 1931 from a depressed Germany with five thousand American dollars in his possession. That must have been quite a small fortune back then."

Volkmann was troubled by another connecting strand in Sanchez's report. Both Tsarkin and Erica Kranz's father had been officers in the Leibstandarte SS. A coincidence, maybe, but still it bothered him. He wondered if the others had noticed, but neither made any comment.

Ferguson said finally, "With all the uncertainty about just now, I'm not sure the Germans would pursue this with much vigor. So for now, it's in our court."

"What do you want me to do, sir?"

"The shipment the Italian talked about on the tape—it may be worth asking the Italian desk to double-check their port entries for consignments from Montevideo after the twenty-fifth." Ferguson considered. "Anyone got any suggestions?"

Volkmann said, "Maybe Erica Kranz knew students who were close to Winter at Heidelberg. People at the same university who might have known him."

"It's worth a try," Ferguson replied.

"You want me to go it alone?" Volkmann asked.

"For the moment, yes. Take the woman along, if she's got no objections; she may be helpful, considering her contacts at the university and her press connections. What about her work commitments?"

"She's taken some time off."

"You better explain that this is still a security operation. Right now she's an informant we need to protect. If you need any help, let me know."

Volkmann stood. "The photographs . . . I'd like copies."

"I'll have the lab get them."

"What about Erhard Schmeltz?"

Ferguson looked up. "What about him?"

"Could we have his background checked? The fact that he was receiving money from the German Reichsbank may tell us something about the occupants of the house."

Ferguson nodded. "All a long time ago, but very well, I'll have Tom send a request to the Documentation Center in Berlin. Schmeltz would have left Germany before the Nazis came to power, but who knows? Because of this Reichsbank business, the Document Center may have him on file. I'll also request information on Reimer, alias Tsarkin. If what Sanchez says is true, they ought to have his file. Leibstandarte SS—the same SS division as Erica Kranz's father, if I remember from her file. You noticed?"

"Yes, sir."

"Do you trust her?"

"In what way?"

"The fact that she knew this Winter at the university. And that her father and Tsarkin were in the same SS division. One connection I could accept, but two I have questions about. And there's a third."

"What's that?"

"She's been to South America, and she knew the journalist. Do you think she's telling you everything she knows?"

Volkmann shrugged. "I couldn't say. They were cousins," he

reminded Ferguson. "It seems they were close. And she knew something about the story he was working on . . ." He left the thought unfinished.

"So you believe her?" Ferguson asked quietly.

"Probably, but I'm still not sure why she chose to come to us in the first place, out of the blue. So there's always the possibility of some kind of deception . . ."

Ferguson nodded. "Okay, let's leave it at that for now. Good luck, Joe. Keep in touch."

After Volkmann left the office, Ferguson turned to Peters. "You think Joe will be able to handle it?"

"Sir?"

"You know how he dislikes the Germans. By the way, Erica Kranz is staying at his place."

Peters raised his eyebrows. "Who suggested that?"

"Joe did." Ferguson smiled. "He'll want to stick close to her to find out all he can. In case she's covering something up, not telling us the full story."

"Very wise."

"I'm still curious as to why she insisted on dealing with DSE and not the German police." Ferguson looked at Peters. "I can't put my finger on it but something's not quite right about all this, and it bothers me. What's she like?"

"Kranz? A bit of a stunner. The kind you'd crawl over broken glass to get a date with."

Ferguson smiled. "That'll be all for now, Tom."

The Oriental Restaurant in Petite France was empty except for the two of them.

Erica's blond hair fell loosely about her shoulders, and she had put on makeup. She wore a pale blue sweater and a navy skirt, legs smooth in sheer stockings.

A waiter hovered, serving them attentively. Crisp beef and vegetables. A bottle of dry white wine, ice-cold.

Volkmann had told her about the report from Sanchez, stipulating that it was confidential. He saw her puzzlement as he explained about the owner of the Chaco property, Erhard Schmeltz, and about Tsarkin's background.

"But the Reichsbank business with Schmeltz happened so long ago."

"We still need to check it out. The date on the back of the photograph and the first bank drafts being sent to Schmeltz happened in the same year. They may be connected. Besides, it may tell us something about Schmeltz's son. Because apart from his name, we've pretty much nothing to go on."

Erica put down her glass. "You mean records are kept that far back?"

"There are two German agencies that kept records of former Nazis and SS personnel like Reimer. The first is the Document Center in Zehlendorf in Berlin. It's originally an American institution, and a repository of Nazi Party organization documents."

He explained that in 1945, American troops had captured almost the entire records of SS personnel and the Nazi Party and its organizations in various locations throughout Germany. Those and other party records were later stored in Berlin in special underground vaults, to aid in the prosecution of war criminals.

"The second agency is run solely by the German government. It's known as the Z-Commission and located in Württemberg. Its staff consists of a small number of operatives and attorneys whose function it is to investigate, and prosecute if necessary, known war criminals." He told Erica that whereas the Berlin Document Center was a repository of Nazi organization documents, the Z-Commission had actually hunted down Nazis and SS guilty of war crimes and mass murder, and most of the documented files it kept were copies of the ones in Berlin. But because many of those wanted for war crimes were either dead or had been prosecuted, government funds had gradually diminished as the Z-Commission was wound down.

He took a sip of wine. "So the files and records of most former Nazis or SS will still be documented, but Berlin has all the original documents, so that's our best bet. They may have no record of Erhard Schmeltz, because he left Germany before the Nazis came to power in 1933, but it's worth a try."

Erica considered. "Sanchez mentioned an aircraft in his report. Could he find out where it landed?"

"If it was anywhere other than a regular airport, I doubt it. It could have been another helicopter. In that case, it could have landed anyplace there was a clearing big enough. And we're assuming it was the people from the Chaco house. We could be wrong."

Erica put down her glass. "So we really have nothing to go on."

"We've got Winter's old friends at Heidelberg University. People he associated with. Did you know any of them?"

"I moved in a different crowd. But there were a few I knew in Winter's circle. Why?"

"Anyone close to him?"

She hesitated for a moment. "Actually, there was Wolfgang Lubsch from Baden-Baden. You may have heard of him—the terrorist?"

"I know of him," Volkmann acknowledged. "Last I heard, he was wanted by the German police and leading an offshoot of the Red Army Faction. But I can't say I know much about him or the organization he runs. I haven't had much to do with German terrorists, thankfully. They can be pretty nasty people."

"Back when I knew him, Lubsch was terribly passionate and intense. I'm not surprised he's become so extreme." She caught Volkmann's eye. "Anyhow, I used to see Lubsch and Winter together now and again. It was kind of a funny relationship. Lubsch was very far to the left, and Winter was extreme right. I guess they liked to spar."

"Terrific. The one man who might give us a line on Winter turns out to be a terrorist and probably unreachable."

Erica said, "Maybe not. I knew his girlfriend, Karen Holfeld. We roomed together one year. I think she's living in Mainz somewhere."

"You think you could find her?"

"I could telephone some old friends who might know. She may have lost contact with Lubsch. But if I do find her, what do I say?"

He thought for a moment. "How about telling her you want to write a story with a colleague from one of your magazines . . . a human-interest piece about those involved in left-wing politics? Tell her you want to talk with Lubsch in confidence. And that you won't use his name. Maybe he'll bite at the chance of some positive publicity. Your old school ties may help. But keep it low-key. And if you can't find this Karen through your own friends, I'll put my people on it."

He fell silent, then said, "I'd like to ask you a question. Did you sense anything strange about the Chaco house?"

"In what way strange?"

"Apart from the way it was left. A feeling. Like an atmosphere."

She put down her fork. "I sensed something. But I'm not sure what. The small house, the one next to the hacienda . . . I remember that I shivered when I stepped inside, even though it was a hot day." Erica shrugged. "It was kind of like the feeling you get when you step into a house in which someone has died." She looked at him. "Is that what you mean?"

"Maybe. I'm not sure. All I know is that it felt kind of weird."

When the waiter took away the dishes, Erica reached across and touched his hand. "Thanks, Joe. Thanks for your help."

Volkmann looked over at the blue eyes and the pretty face and wondered if she meant it, or if she was just a good actress.

He was awakened by the telephone ringing in the next room. It was midnight, the bedroom curtains lifting and falling in a soft breeze. He dressed and went into the living room.

Erica was sitting by the telephone, a notepad open beside her.

"I've made a lot of calls. I think I've managed to trace Wolfgang Lubsch."

"How?"

"Someone I knew in Heidelberg . . . she gave me Karen's phone number." She caught Volkmann's eye. "When I called her, she seemed wary about talking to me."

"That shouldn't come as a surprise—especially if she and Lubsch are still friends."

"I asked her if Lubsch was open to an interview. She told me he wasn't eager to talk to reporters these days. So I tried the approach you suggested—with a few embellishments. I said I wouldn't use Lubsch's name but that the article was very important to me. She seemed to think Lubsch might be interested in a story like that. She told me she'd phone and ask him. She called back just now and said it was okay."

"Good work. So when do we get to meet him?"

"Tomorrow afternoon we're to be in a bar called the Weisses Rossl at four o'clock. It's in an old wine town on the Rhine called Rüdesheim, about an hour's drive from Frankfurt. Karen asked me not to involve anyone else, apart from us. I assured her she could trust me."

He waited until Erica had gone, watching her retreat into the spare bedroom before he telephoned the night-duty officer, Jan de Vries, and requested the files for Wolfgang Lubsch of Baden-Baden, a graduate of Heidelberg. De Vries promised to get back to him by eight that morning.

After Volkmann replaced the receiver, he crossed to the bookshelves. He found the *Times Atlas* and flicked the pages. He traced with a finger to the place on the border between Paraguay and Brazil named Bahia Negra, where Sanchez had said the radar picked up the aircraft signal. From the map, it looked like a small, insignificant town straddling the border on the banks of the Rio Paraguay. He wondered if Sanchez had made any further progress, but knew the man would make contact if he did.

He replaced the atlas on the shelves, then went back into the bedroom and found the Beretta 9 mm service pistol, removed it from the holster, and checked the action. There was a full clip of shells and a spare magazine. He read through Hernandez's tape transcript again. When he finished, it was cold outside and raining now, fine needles scratching at the glass. He lit a cigarette, inhaling slowly.

20

RÜDESHEIM. SATURDAY, DECEMBER 10, 3:00 P.M.

The town faced the riverfront, a maze of cozy inns and narrow, cobbled streets.

In summer, the pretty wine town would have been flooded with visitors, the Rhine banks awash with the floating hotels and tourist barges. But in winter, the visitors trickled to a few hardy weekenders.

Volkmann drove through the town to get his bearings, then made his way down toward the waterfront and parked the Ford. He left the Beretta and his DSE identity card tucked under the driver's seat; Facilities had provided him with a press ID card.

A couple of squat tourist ferries were tied up for the winter season. It didn't feel like Christmas, but decorations hung in shop windows, and in the central platz colored lights winked in the fading afternoon light.

They walked through the cobbled alleyways toward the center of the old town. Most of the *weinstuben* were closed, but they found a café open and ordered coffee and pastries.

Erica's blond hair was tied back and she wore hardly any makeup, but her face was still strikingly pretty. Volkmann said, "You better describe Lubsch to me. If I'm going to meet a dangerous, wanted terrorist, I want to know as much as I can."

Erica sipped her coffee. "He wasn't the kind of guy most women would find attractive. Small. Thinly built. Glasses and red hair. But he looked kind of vulnerable and at the same time arrogant, if you know what I mean. A dreamer. But very bright. Does that help?"

He smiled. "It's enough. Does your friend Karen still have a relationship with him?"

"Your guess is as good as mine. But Karen always had a reputation as a man-eater. Even though she's married now."

"Tell me more."

"She and her husband run a business together. It's in the center of Mainz. And her name's no longer Holfeld, but Gries."

"What kind of business?"

"A sports boutique. You know, high-end athletic shoes, designer active wear. Very fashionable. Very chic. Business is booming, Karen claims."

"Which department was she in on campus?"

"Politics, the same as Lubsch."

"So how did she get into sportswear?"

"Apart from politics, Karen was very physical—into running, swimming, hiking, climbing. At university, she always had lots of boyfriends."

"What about you?"

"What do you mean?" she answered, coloring a little.

"At the university. Did you have lots of male friends?"

"A few," she said carefully.

"You don't like to talk about that part of your life?"

She shrugged. "Not to someone I've just met."

"Fair enough," he said with a slight smile. "Tell me about the right-wing groups Winter belonged to."

She paused for a moment to collect her memories. "I don't think they were particularly organized. Just guys who got together to drink and tell each other how brilliant and deep they were and—what's the expression in your language—to throw the bull?"

He laughed. "Close enough."

"They'd throw the bull about the state Germany was in," she went on. "They liked to scapegoat immigrants. In their view, Germany had become a half-breed state because of its five million immigrants. When they were drunk, they might shout insults at foreign-looking students. There were fights, too, a few times, but nothing serious."

She paused. "And when they were very drunk, they'd beat their beer mugs against the tables and chant, 'Germany for the Germans.' I saw a Nazi salute or two now and again. But most of us just thought that these guys were being stupid and silly."

"After they graduated, what became of them? Did they stay involved in extremist politics?"

Erica shook her head. "I really can't say. I didn't pay them a lot of attention—except when I was in the same beer hall or at a party and couldn't avoid them." She looked at him. "You know, Joseph Volkmann, you're a very strange man."

"Tell me why you think so," he said softly.

"You make me want to fill the silence by answering your questions. To confide in you. I'm the journalist. And that's supposed to be my strategy. It's rather absurd."

"What is?"

"I spend the night in a man's apartment about whom I know nothing. It's not the kind of thing that usually happens, Joe."

"And what does usually happen?"

"Nothing to write home about, I assure you. I have my work. I listen to my music. I go out with friends. But mainly my work. I'm afraid I'm not *hausfrau* material."

"You have a boyfriend, Erica?"

She shook her head. "There's no one special right now." She looked across at him. "Don't I get a chance to ask some personal questions?"

He smiled. "What would you like to know?"

"Do you like your work?"

"It's what I'm trained to do."

She smiled again. "Was that a yes or a no?"

"I guess it's a yes."

Dusk was falling. Lights coming on in the cobbled street outside.

He said, "I had Lubsch checked out. No surprises. His group's been involved in at least two kidnappings and the murder of an industrialist. He also likes making withdrawals from German banks without having an account. All in the name of freeing the downtrodden and protecting the defenseless, no doubt."

He looked hard at her. "But he's no ivory-tower intellectual, Erica. He's a dangerous, wanted man. Maybe even a killer. If you decide you'd rather not go with me . . ."

"If it means finding the people who killed Rudi, I want to meet him."

"Good. Just remember, he can't know that I'm with DSE." Volkmann produced his press ID. "It's genuine. So what you told Karen ought to hold up. No matter what happens, stick to our cover story."

"What about when we have to ask Lubsch about Winter?"

"Leave that to me. You're sure you can go through with it, Erica?"

"Yes."

"Okay, let's go find this bar and pray we're not walking into big trouble."

They reached it five minutes later, an ancient *bierkeller* near the waterfront, all dark wooden beams and smelling of smoked sausage and candle wax.

They were the only customers, and Volkmann chose a table at the back next to a fire exit and ordered two glasses of schnapps.

The waitress who served them had hardly left their drinks when a clean-shaven, dark-haired young man came in wearing a gray plastic Windbreaker. He ordered a beer and sat at the bar as he unfolded a newspaper.

Five minutes passed, and Volkmann was conscious of the young man observing them. He didn't resemble Erica's description of Lubsch, but as soon as the waitress moved into the kitchen, the young man stood and crossed to their table. One hand remained inside his pocket.

He looked at Erica and said sharply, "Your name's Erica Kranz?"

"Yes."

"You're Volkmann?"

When Volkmann nodded, the young man said to Erica, "Wolfgang wants me to check you both out." He half smiled. "You understand, it's simply a precaution."

The man's eyes flicked momentarily toward the kitchen, where the waitress had gone.

"There's an alleyway behind here, directly to the right. Finish your drinks and meet me there in two minutes. When you approach me, keep your hands out of your pockets and by your sides, and don't attempt to do anything foolish. All I want to see in your hands are your identity papers. Got that?"

Erica began to speak, but the man barely raised his hand. "Just do as I say. Otherwise, the meeting's off."

The man turned back toward the bar. He finished his drink and folded his newspaper. He went out the front, veered to the right, and disappeared.

Volkmann said, "Okay, finish your drink, and let's do as the man says. You've got ID?"

Erica fumbled for her press ID.

"Keep it in your hand, like he said." They finished their drinks, and Volkmann led the way.

The alleyway behind the bierkeller was narrow, and poorly lit. Another laneway led off to a cobbled street. The young man was waiting, hands in the pockets of his Windbreaker.

"To the right, quickly. Hands up against the wall. And don't speak." He said to Erica, "I'm going to have to search you, too, for weapons."

The man's hands moved expertly over them. When he finished, he told them to turn around.

"Your identity papers."

They handed them over, and he scrutinized them, turning the photographs toward the light, looking from photographs to faces. He handed them back and looked at Volkmann.

"You came by car?"

"Yes."

"Did you see anyone following you?"

"No."

"You're certain?"

"I guess so."

"I asked if you were certain, Volkmann."

"So far as we could tell, no one followed us."

"Okay. Follow me. And no questions." The man turned abruptly and led the way down the laneway behind him.

As they stepped through into a narrow, deserted street, the young man raised his hand, and the dull growl of an engine filled the growing darkness.

A big gray Mercedes delivery van suddenly pulled across their path. A man with pockmarked skin and wearing green overalls sat behind the wheel, gunning the motor.

The side doors of the van opened with a roll of metallic thunder, and two young men jumped out. One of them held a Glock pistol in his hand and gestured with it for Volkmann and Erica to get inside.

The men pushed them into the Mercedes, and they were forced down roughly onto the floor and then the door banged shut.

"Put these on."

One of the men thrust two black balaclavas at Volkmann and Erica. Each was eyeless, a small slit at the mouth to breathe through.

When Volkmann hesitated, the man kicked out viciously, his boot slamming painfully into Volkmann's thigh.

"Do it! Now!"

As Volkmann pulled on the balaclava, he saw Erica do the same, and then the blackness took over as the young man spoke again.

"Try to move or talk, either of you, and you're both dead."

The big diesel engine gave a deep, noisy roar, and the van lurched and moved forward.

21

The Mercedes van turned off the mountain road and into a heavily wooded valley in darkness.

The driver halted outside a mountain cabin. As he switched off the engine, the side door slid open, and the two men in the back jumped out.

Volkmann felt a hand grip his arm, and he was yanked out. He could smell the woods, heavy and pine-scented, and hear the sounds of feet crunching on gravel. Seconds later he was being pushed through a doorway.

Now the smells were different: dry must, rotting wood, rancid food. Wooden floorboards shook under his feet. A hand yanked the eyeless balaclava from his head, and in the sudden flood of light that followed, he was momentarily blinded.

Erica stood beside him. She glanced at him briefly before she looked over at a man wearing wire-rimmed glasses who stood by a shattered window.

He wore a dark, padded Windbreaker, blue jeans, and scuffed white sneakers. He was small and wiry, with red hair, and his face had several days' growth of red stubble. His features didn't look German except for the eyes, which were very blue and sharp, like the small eyes of a nervous animal, but with a hint of arrogance. His jacket was unzipped, and a Glock pistol was tucked into his trouser belt.

Volkmann figured from the look on Erica's face that the red-haired man was Wolfgang Lubsch. He guessed that the room was part of a mountain cabin. A traditional *Berghütte,* one of the thousands that dotted the German hills and valleys, used by hunters and woodsmen and holidaying families. A kerosene lamp hung from a meat hook embedded in a ceiling beam.

The two young men from the Mercedes stood nearby. One was tall and blond and carried an AK-47 slung over his shoulder. The second was smaller and ruggedly built. He seemed like a man who relished physical contact, and he held a leather truncheon in his right hand as if to prove it.

Volkmann's wallet lay on the table, the contents scattered. The photograph from the Chaco of the blond young woman lay beside a clutter of paper money, his French driver's license and press ID, and the contents of Erica's handbag were spilled out next to them.

The man with the truncheon pointed silently to the chairs.

When Volkmann and Erica sat, the red-haired man wearing glasses stepped forward. His fingers probed among the items scattered on the table before he examined Volkmann's license, then tossed it back down.

He took a pack of cigarettes from the pocket of his jacket and lit one with a Zippo lighter. As he inhaled, his nervous blue eyes settled on Erica.

"It's been a long time. You look as pretty as ever, Erica."

"Wolfgang . . ."

"Forgive the dramatics in bringing you here like this, but I'm sure you realize that someone in my situation has to tread carefully." Lubsch grinned. "But then, I'm presuming you know why I've been cautious?"

Erica glanced for a moment at the man brandishing the AK-47, then back at Lubsch. "Because you're a terrorist."

"That's a question of perspective, surely. If the British had captured George Washington, he would have been hanged or shot, no? An eighteenth-century terrorist. And the terrorist founders of the state of Israel are now honored statesmen and Nobel Peace Prize winners." Lubsch removed his glasses and rubbed his eyes. "So, tell me. What do you want from me? I'm very interested in this article you want to write."

Erica slipped a quick glance at Volkmann, who nodded almost imperceptibly; then she looked back at Lubsch. "Joe and I are working on a story. But it's not exactly the one I told Karen about."

"Oh?" Lubsch said, his eyes intent and curious. "And what's the real story?"

"A man was murdered in Berlin ten days ago. Someone you knew at Heidelberg."

"Who?"

"Dieter Winter."

Lubsch paused, but his face showed no reaction. "I read about it in the papers. What's it got to do with me?"

"We're trying to find who killed Winter and why."

"And why are you so interested in Winter's death?"

Erica hesitated. "Because we think his death is connected to other murders."

"Really. And what murders might these be?"

She told him about Rudi Hernandez and about what they had found in Paraguay.

Lubsch inhaled on his cigarette, then shrugged. "So what's this got to do with me?"

"The German connection," she answered. "The men in Paraguay are Germans. And Winter was killed in Germany. The police don't know who killed Winter or why. They think there may be a drug connection, but they're really in the dark. You knew Winter at Heidelberg. I hoped you could help us. That maybe with your connections you knew people we could talk with. Anyone who might know what Winter was involved in, or who his friends were."

Lubsch smiled. "Interesting. Do you know what these cargoes from South America were?"

"No."

Lubsch stared at Volkmann. "And what part do you play in all of this?"

"We're working on the story together."

Lubsch glanced down at the table. "You carry a French driver's license, Volkmann. But you're not French, or German, are you? Your German is rather excellent, but your accent"—Lubsch shook his head as he looked back up—"a vowel here and there betrays you."

"I'm British."

The small blue eyes stared suspiciously. "Is there any other reason you're both so interested in Winter, besides what you told me?"

"Should there be?"

"I asked the question, Volkmann. Answer it."

"There's no other reason."

Lubsch nodded his head, the merest of gestures.

The scar-faced man lifted a hand, and the leather truncheon swished through the air and struck the left side of Volkmann's face. The force sent him flying backward. The man with the truncheon caught the chair and pushed it back again. Erica screamed, and a hand went over her mouth.

Volkmann felt the cutting sting the truncheon left on his face, and when his hand went to touch his jaw, he felt a painful welt.

Lubsch gripped Volkmann's hair savagely and yanked his head back. "Are you sure there's no other reason, Volkmann?"

"I told you . . ."

Lubsch stared into Volkmann's eyes. "Then listen to me, Volkmann. Listen to me, both of you. Number one, I don't help smart reporters who set me up for a meeting on the pretext of some stupid story. Number two, I take a very poor view of people wasting my time and putting me at risk meeting them. Do you understand?"

Lubsch waited for an answer. When Volkmann didn't reply, the terrorist roughly pulled Volkmann's hair back again. "I asked you a question, Volkmann. Do you understand?"

"Yes."

"Good."

Lubsch released his grip and turned to Erica as the hand covering her mouth came away.

"And you. Don't contact Karen again. What Volkmann got was a friendly warning. Next time, there won't be one. For either of you. And understand something else. You're on dangerous ground sniffing around Winter's friends. If you want to stay alive, I'd forget about him and your story."

Lubsch nodded to the man with the truncheon, who turned and went out. Moments later came the sound of the Mercedes starting up.

The man with the AK-47 slipped outside. Then came the rumble of the van door sliding open.

Lubsch grabbed the kerosene lamp from the hook in the wooden beam and crossed to the door. He looked back at Volkmann and Erica. "Remember what I said. And be grateful you're both still alive."

Lubsch extinguished the lamp, and the small cabin plunged into darkness. Footsteps crunched on the gravel outside and a door slammed shut.

The van moved off down the track. Its engine noise faded, and then there was only silence and the squalid smells of the cabin.

They followed the track through the forest, and it took them half an hour to reach the village. The road sign said KIEDRICH. It was pitch dark, and when Volkmann and Erica stepped into the first inn they saw open, the half-dozen customers inside looked at them warily.

Erica was pale and her lips trembled. Their clothes were covered in mud after the walk through the woods, and they tried to ignore the stares.

Volkmann dabbed his jaw. "Not a pretty sight, are we? Order us a couple of drinks while I see to this, will you?"

He went into the men's room, threw cold water on his face, and dabbed it with some bathroom tissue. The welt had swollen painfully and it hurt when he touched his skin, but the flesh hadn't been cut.

When he came out, Erica had ordered two brandies, and he asked the innkeeper for some ice. He put a couple of ice cubes in a handkerchief and pressed it to his face.

The innkeeper inquired, "Is everything all right?"

"Wonderful. Our car broke down and I bumped into a tree in the darkness. I know we're in Kiedrich, but where exactly is that?"

"Twenty miles from Rüdesheim. There's a breakdown service in the next town, if you need to get your car."

"A taxi would be better. Can you call us one?"

"Of course. Enjoy your drinks."

When the taxi came it took half an hour to reach Rüdesheim. The Ford was still parked near the station, and they drove back to Erica's apartment, arriving just after ten.

Erica looked at his swollen face and came back from the kitchen with some ice cubes wrapped in a cloth and a bottle of schnapps. She poured two large measures and handed one to Volkmann.

He dabbed his face, tried to smile, but winced in pain. "Now that's what I call an entertaining evening, even if I didn't exactly enjoy the experience."

"Are you okay, Joe?"

"I've felt better. You?"

Erica's hands were trembling as she sipped her drink. "I really thought Lubsch was going to kill us. Do you think he meant what he said?"

"You better believe it. He's a nut case. Worse, he's a nut case with a cause, which makes him even more dangerous."

"Do you think Lubsch knows something?"

He put down the cool cloth. "You can bet on it. Otherwise he wouldn't have warned us about Dieter Winter and his friends."

"Why do you think he wanted to warn us off?"

"I don't know, Erica. Only he can tell us that. But I'd like to know why he asked if we were interested in Winter for any other reason besides the one you gave him."

"You're not going to try to contact him again, are you?"

He shook his head. "People like Lubsch don't give second warnings. If I did that, he'd kill me."

She seemed genuinely afraid. "So what now?"

Volkmann thought. "I want you to drive down to my place in the morning and wait for me there. I'll give you a key. I think it's better after what's happened that you stay out of Frankfurt for now." He looked at her. "You've got a car?"

"Yes, it's down in the parking lot. You're sure? About me staying in your place?"

"It's for your own safety, Erica. If Lubsch is in contact with Winter's friends, they may come looking for us both."

He crossed to the window and cautiously pulled back the curtain. It was a clear, calm night, the Rhine barges moving slowly back and forth on the water. Across the street by the river he saw a group of youths with shaved heads drinking from cans of beer as they strolled toward the Eisener Steg, their harsh, guttural voices carrying in the darkness.

When he turned back, Erica asked, "Do you want me to get some more ice for your jaw?"

Volkmann tried to smile. "No, but another drink wouldn't go amiss."

She made dinner for them and afterward they sat on the couch. "I'm still trembling after meeting Lubsch. Doesn't anything frighten you, Joe?"

"The same things as most people."

"Tell me about yourself."

"What do you want to know?"

"Anything. Everything." Erica hesitated and smiled. "You're a stranger to me."

"There isn't much to tell."

"Are you married, Joe?"

"Divorced."

"You had children?"

"No, no kids. Maybe my one regret."

"Tell me about your family. In your apartment there was a photograph. Of you as a small boy, I think. The couple were your parents?"

He nodded. "The photograph was taken by the sea in Cornwall, in the southwest of England. It's where we spent our summers when I was a child."

"What did your father do?"

"He was a college lecturer."

"Do you see him often?"

"He died six months ago."

"I'm sorry." She was silent for a moment. "You didn't want to be like him and teach?"

"I guess it wasn't for me. I joined the army as an officer cadet. Later, the intelligence service."

"Was your father proud of you?"

"My father hated uniforms, Erica. But I had my mind made up."

"Tell me more about your family, Joe. I'd like to hear."

"My mother used to be a concert pianist, but she doesn't play professionally anymore."

"Of course, I know of her." She colored a little. "I never made the connection. She was pretty famous. Who are you more like, your mother or father?"

Volkmann smiled and his jaw hurt. "My father, probably. Though I guess he'd never have thought it."

"He didn't look like an Englishman."

"And how are Englishmen supposed to look?"

"I meant that he looked more middle European. Tall and dark."

"He was a refugee, Erica, he and my mother both. They went to England after the war. My mother was from Hungary; my father's family came from the Sudetenland."

"With a name like Volkmann, they must have been Germans."

"Yes, they were Sudeten Germans. Jews. Volkmann isn't exclusively a Jewish name, but that's what they were." He saw a look of surprise on Erica's face, and she blushed. "That's how I learned my

German. For a long time it was the only language my father spoke. He always spoke English badly."

She said quietly, "And your mother's family? They were Jewish also?"

"Hungarian and Catholic. So I guess that makes me half Jewish."

"Do you go to the synagogue?"

"No. Because my mother isn't Jewish, I'm not. And my father's family were Jews in name only. When I was a child, my father took me only once to the synagogue, just to satisfy my curiosity."

Erica was silent; then she said, "The war must have been terrible for your father."

"He was in a camp, if that's what you mean. That's where he first met my mother. They were both just kids. They used to meet at the wire separating the men's compound from the women's. When the camp was liberated, they lost each other. They met again in London many years later and married."

"I don't understand. Why was your mother there? She wasn't Jewish."

"Not only Jews were sent to the camps. Intellectuals, homosexuals, vagrants, Gypsies. Even respectable, middle-class, ordinary people like my mother's family. Anyone the Nazis considered a threat to the Reich, however feeble the reasons. Surely you knew that?"

He saw the look on her face then, and she said, "It was a terrible time . . . for Jews, for Germany, for everyone. You must hate Germans."

Volkmann said, "Not hate, but distrust. And not individuals. No people are more intellectual than the Germans; they're rational and philosophical. And yet no people became as brutal as they did during the Nazi period. I simply can't understand it—how your countrymen could let it all happen. I worked in Berlin for three years. I used to wake nights, thinking of what had happened here in this country of yours. To my parents and people like them."

She was silent for several moments. "Does that mean you don't trust me, Joe? Because I'm German."

"To be honest, it makes it difficult."

She nodded. "Then I'll have to work on that problem, won't I?"

He didn't answer her.

"You said your father hated uniforms. But you chose to wear one. Why?"

"Because maybe I always wanted to protect him."

"From what?"

"From anyone who might try to hurt him again."

"I'm sorry, forgive me, Joe. I shouldn't have been so inquisitive."

"How in heaven's name did we get into that?" Volkmann stood. "How about some coffee?"

He was standing over the sink rinsing a cup when she came to him moments later.

"Joe?"

He turned. She looked into his eyes. "When you came to my apartment at first, I thought you were distant. Maybe even rude and arrogant. And that you didn't like me. Maybe that feeling was even mutual. But in Asunción when I cried, I felt that you cared. I felt that you knew what pain was." The blue eyes looked into his face. "Something bad once happened to your father, didn't it, Joe?"

He didn't reply but stood looking into her face.

She said, "Would it sound terrible if I asked to kiss you, Joe?"

She was standing close to him. Her fingers gently touched his face, her lips meeting his mouth softly at first, then more fiercely as they kissed.

When they finally drew apart, she looked up at him and said, "I think maybe I've wanted to do that since Asunción."

The long-ago nightmare came to Volkmann that night as he slept . . . He could see the sweat on Felder's fleshy face and almost smell the man's fear as they stood in the woods. Spring was in the cold dawn air, and Volkmann remembered how absurd it was: the trees budding into life and Felder about to die.

The big East German had his hands tied behind his back, and he was shaking as his eyes flicked nervously from Ivan Molke to Volkmann. They both trained the silenced Berettas on Felder, and he was trembling as soon as they emerged from the car.

Molke said quietly, "Turn around and look away, Felder. It'll be easier."

Suddenly Felder seemed to break, anger taking over. "Anything I did was on orders, I swear it."

Ivan Molke shook his head. "You want to know something, Felder? Your people in East Berlin will think we've done them a favor."

Sweat beaded Felder's brow. "Yes, I killed two of your people. But I did it on orders. I swear."

"That's not what your people are saying. You acted alone."

"It's a lie!"

A sudden noise came from behind. A pigeon flew out of the low branches, its wings beating furiously in the silence of the forest.

Felder saw his opportunity and made a run for the trees.

Volkmann raised the Beretta and fired.

The first shot hit Felder in the back of the head. When it did, his body punched forward; the second hit him in the shoulder as he stumbled. The big man groaned, and rolled over on his back, just as Molke ran forward and pumped another shot into Felder's barrel chest. He lay on the ground, blood pumping from his wounds, a gurgling sound coming from his lips.

Molke looked at Volkmann and said hoarsely, "Get the shovels from the car. Joe. We haven't got all bloody day. We'll bury him here."

Volkmann had killed and seen men killed before, but never so close that he could hear their dying breath. He was aware of the cold sweat on his forehead and the nausea in the pit of his stomach as he hurried back toward the car.

As he removed the shovels from the trunk, he heard the faint crack of Molke's Beretta.

He came back, and Molke said, "Are you okay?"

"Sure." Volkmann looked down at the body. There was a trickle of blood at Felder's right temple where Molke had given him the coup de grâce.

Molke said, "Even his Stasi and KGB friends were shocked by what he did to our two men. There are unwritten rules, Joe, and Felder broke them. No one's going to grieve for him, not even his own people."

Volkmann started to dig. The earth was soft and moist, the sweet humus of the forest rising up to their nostrils. He felt a sharp crack as the shovel hit something hard, and Ivan Molke suddenly stopped digging and stared down at the soil, a look of horror on his face.

"What the devil!"

Volkmann saw the top of the muddied skull in the fresh soil. As Molke's shovel turned it over, there was another skull revealed beneath.

Molke paled as he knelt down, took out his gloves, and pulled one on. He picked up the skull, placed it beside him, then the other, before he clawed at the earth with his gloved fingers. In the raw soil was a tangle of bones, and it looked to Volkmann as if they had been there for a long time. Neat holes drilled the back of each skull. Molke turned away and vomited.

"Cover it up again."

"But . . ."

Molke wiped his mouth with the back of his hand. "Just do it. Cover it up. We'll bury Felder someplace else."

Molke's face was drenched in sweat, and Volkmann thought it absurd that Molke could be so calm at seeing Felder's bloodied corpse while the skeletal remains deeply affected him.

They drove back toward the city and Molke pulled up outside a café off the autobahn. "Let's have a drink. I need one after that."

His hands were shaking, and Volkmann followed him inside; they found a quiet table away from the groups of noisy truck drivers. Molke ordered them each a double schnapps and swallowed his own drink in one gulp.

"What do we do about the remains we found?"

Molke shook his head. "Nothing. Whoever they were, they've been dead a long time. I just didn't want a killer like Felder buried beside them."

"I don't get it."

Molke looked at him. "The bodies have been there since the war."

"How can you be so sure?"

"Joe, I was born in Berlin. My father, too. The Gestapo and SS used to take people out to the Grunewald and put a bullet in the back of their skulls. Communists. Socialists. Jews. People they didn't want to bother sending to the camps or to prison. They simply took them out into the woods and shot them." He considered, the irony striking him. "Just like we did with Felder. Except, these people were not like him. They were just ordinary people."

"How can you know?"

"About the bodies? My father was in Flossenbürg, Joe."

"He was Jewish?"

"No, he was anti-Nazi. He managed to hide out until '44. Then one night the Gestapo raided the house where he was in hiding. They took him away. My uncle, his wife, their two young boys, they took to the Grunewald. They sent my father to the camps. Ravensbrück first, then Flossenbürg."

"Your father died there?"

Molke shook his head. "He survived. He lived in Hamburg in an old folks' home until his death five years ago. I guess Berlin had too many memories for him." Molke looked away, toward the window and the cold spring morning and the passing traffic. "When he came home after the war, he was in limbo. Flossenbürg finished him. He was never the same. My mother and father split. She said she couldn't live with a ghost. That's what he was, a ghost."

A look of grief ravaged Molke's face. "You know what the strange thing was? The day he died, one of the SS camp guards at Flossenbürg was in a Munich courtroom. He'd killed men with his bare hands. But the jury took pity on him because he was an old man and near death and gave him a suspended sentence. One year."

Molke gritted his teeth. "A week after I buried my father, there was a picture in the newspapers of the old SS guy coming out of court with a smile on his face and waving to his friends and family. He didn't look near death to me. You know what his defense attorney said? 'Justice has been done.'" Molke shook his head. "The longer I live in this world, the more I realize there's no such thing as justice. Not real justice. There's an old saying: 'Every sin has its own avenging angel.' But it never works out that way. You know what I mean?" Molke hesitated, looked at Volkmann. "What about your father? He's alive, Joe?"

"Yes."

"You see him much?"

Volkmann wanted to tell Molke. But not here. Another time.

"Sure."

"You're lucky, Joe. Sons need fathers as much as fathers need sons."

22

Erica left at ten the following morning. Soon after that, he looked around her apartment, starting with the living room. He didn't know what he was looking for and he disliked having to search through her personal belongings, but he knew it had to be done.

Next to the computer terminal sat a neat stack of papers and a small wooden filing cabinet. He searched through the papers first, then the unlocked filing cabinet. Mostly rough drafts of magazine articles and correspondence from editors.

He was aware of the scent of Erica's perfume as he went through the closet and drawers in her bedroom. Her clothes and underwear were put away neatly, and under some panties he saw a bundle of old letters addressed to her bearing Paraguayan stamps. All were in Spanish, and were signed by Rudi Hernandez. He looked through the other drawers.

He came across two slim photograph albums on a shelf in the mirrored sliding wardrobe. One contained mostly photographs from Erica's childhood, snapshots of her and her mother and sister that appeared to have been taken in Argentina.

The second album contained mostly photographs of Erica in her teens and twenties, taken with friends at Heidelberg, and a couple of pictures with Rudi Hernandez.

On the wardrobe floor were some boxes containing jewelry. He examined them and the rods of clothes, searching in pockets, but he found nothing of interest. He tried the bathroom. Perfumes and makeup and some pills and herbals in plastic bottles.

He crossed back into the kitchen and sat on the couch. He knew that he had to make contact with Lubsch again, despite the danger. He thought about how he'd do it, then picked up the commercial directory by the telephone.

He found the name and address in Mainz where Karen Gries had her shop.

STOCKHOLM, SWEDEN. MONDAY, DECEMBER 12, 7:30 P.M.

The restaurant was ten miles from Stockholm along the north coast, an intimate place of log fires and pine tables. Only half a dozen other customers were dining that evening, and with typical Scandinavian respect for privacy they ignored Shaeffer and his companion.

The food was excellent, Shaeffer thought, as he chewed a delicious mouthful of fried Baltic herring, then washed it down with a sip of ice-cold beer. It was a pity about the company.

The Turk had hardly spoken. He was tall and handsome, with a haunted look in his brown eyes. His thinning black hair was brushed back off his face and he wore a cheap, ill-fitting suit. He regarded Shaeffer with wary detachment, and when he did speak he spoke good German.

Shaeffer couldn't fail to notice the thick pink scars on the backs of the man's hands. "I take it the meal is to your satisfaction?"

Kefir Ozalid sipped his mineral water and spoke quietly. "Yes, thank you."

Polite but distant. As if the man disliked Shaeffer. The Turk irritated him from the beginning of the meeting. Had it not been for the excellent smorgasbord, Shaeffer considered, the evening would have been a washout.

An hour later, they stepped out onto the cold, snowy street, wearing their overcoats.

A wooden promenade overlooked the glassy, freezing Baltic Sea across the street, a harbor nearby. Shaeffer could understand why the Turk had chosen such a place; in winter the harbor town was desolate. Anyone following them would have been easy to spot.

The Turk pulled up the collar of his frayed overcoat and tugged on his woolen gloves, then gestured for Shaeffer to follow him across to the promenade.

"There have been no changes to the plan?" Ozalid asked.

"None. And you, there are no last-minute doubts?"

The young man shook his head. "None." There was a finality in the Turk's reply. "Your people will keep to your agreement?"

"Of course," Shaeffer replied. "I've been authorized to transfer the money to the account once you've kept your part of the bargain."

The Turk turned toward the cold, dark sea, as if the money were of no importance. Shaeffer removed an envelope from his pocket.

"All the necessary details are inside. Destroy them once you memorize everything. The airline ticket is in the name on your false passport. The money in the envelope will more than cover your expenses."

"There's no change concerning my identity?"

Shaeffer shook his head. "None. You're a businessman trading with a Berlin electronics company. Any questions?"

The Turk shook his head and tucked the envelope in his pocket.

Shaeffer added, "Once you reach the safe house, our people will give you secure passage to Switzerland. After that you're on your own."

The Turk flashed a rare smile, but no humor there. "Presuming I live, of course?"

And with that, he turned and walked back across the snowy street.

Snow was falling as the Turk entered the drab apartment building near Stockholm's Skansen district.

He went up in the creaking elevator to the eighth floor. Graffiti was on the walls; the noisy, overcrowded apartment block was bursting at the seams with immigrants. Ethnic music blared on every floor the elevator passed, and children cried out in a babble of tongues.

The Tower of Babel, the tenants called it. Africans. Arabs. Vietnamese. Turks. Kurds. Refugees who had dreamed of a better life but traded their dignity for a nightmare.

Despite the shabbiness of the building, the apartment offered a panoramic view of Stockholm. He switched on the lights, removed his overcoat, and went to stand by the window. The city winked beyond the thick fall of snow. Like the snow that fell on the blue mountains in Izmir in winter. For a brief moment it made him think of home and Layla.

He tried to ignore the thought as he took the envelope from his pocket, ripped it open, and studied the contents. Half an hour later he put the pages back in the envelope, then lit a cigarette from a packet of Turkish he kept on the scratched pine coffee table.

Something bothered him about the meeting. Something bothered him about the whole thing. Something not quite right. He sensed it from the start.

Not about the crime he intended to commit, but about the people and the plan. Yet he accepted it knowingly because he so wanted to kill the man who had allowed his life to be flooded with grief. And if his own life was forfeit, then so be it. He had resigned himself to that.

For Layla.

Allah was with him; he sensed it in his bones. He glanced down at the thick pink scars that ran in ugly puckered waves along his hands and arms. He thought again of Layla. Of the big, dark brown eyes lifting to his face, the sweet clean smell of her hair, and the taste of her breath like honey on his lips, seeing her for the first time all those years ago in his father's village in the mountains. A young, innocent girl in bare feet. Far too beautiful for him.

He looked up at the photograph of Layla above the unlit fireplace and he wanted to cry, no matter how long ago the pain.

He stubbed out his cigarette, tried to push away the thoughts creeping in on him: the fire consuming flesh, the sadistic grins on the faces of the men with shaved heads, laughing as fires raged around their victims. And Layla, her body bloated with their love, unable to move.

Hate made him want to do this. Hate made him want to kill. And it was only hate that kept him alive.

Minutes later, he unrolled the blue woolen prayer mat, placed it facing the window.

When he had said his prayers, when he had prayed for Layla, he rolled up the prayer mat and kissed it as if he were kissing her again, then placed the mat on the shelf beside the fire.

23

MAINZ. MONDAY, DECEMBER 12

Volkmann took the A66 autobahn to Wiesbaden and across the Rhine into Mainz, arriving just after ten.

He parked the Ford in a twenty-four-hour underground garage near the cathedral and walked to Karen Gries's address.

The markets area was busy with Christmas shoppers. A maze of alleyways and shopping malls branched off from the street, and Karen Gries's shop was on the first floor above a modern art gallery. Volkmann spent half an hour checking out the nearby streets.

As he walked toward the cathedral, he tried to figure out his plan.

A bar stood almost directly opposite. The name overhead said ZUM DORTMUNDER. Maybe seventy yards away was a shopping mall. On the mall's first floor was a smart café whose panoramic window looked down onto the street, and Volkmann reckoned there was a clear view back to Karen Gries's premises.

He bought a copy of the *Frankfurter Zeitung* and went up to the café, sat by the window, and ordered a coffee. He watched the street below, the view unobstructed, and he could see Karen Gries's place on the opposite side of the street. When the waitress came with his coffee, he asked her what time the café stayed open to, and the girl told him they stopped serving fifteen minutes before the mall closed at eight.

Volkmann familiarized himself with the street layout, then tucked the newspaper in his pocket. He went downstairs to the mall and crossed the road.

An alleyway veered off near Karen Gries's shop. It led to the back of a bakery and then onto a public parking lot. For his plan to work, a lot depended on luck and timing, even assuming that Karen Gries would take the bait.

A narrow flight of stairs led up to a landing and a glass-fronted door. The sign on the frosted glass said, in English, SWEATSHOP, BRUNO & KAREN GRIES.

Just as Erica said, it contained fashionable athletic wear, tastefully displayed. He saw a balding, middle-aged man fitting a woman with hiking boots.

Behind the man was a glass-fronted office, where a woman with tight-cropped blond hair and wearing a leather jumpsuit sat talking with an Asian woman. Volkmann guessed that the woman with the cropped blond hair was Karen Gries and the man was probably her husband.

The blond kissed the Asian woman on the cheek and handed her a plastic shopping bag, then came over to Volkmann.

"Can I help you?" she smiled.

She could have been pretty, Volkmann thought, but she wore too much makeup. It made her look a bit trashy. "Karen Gries?"

"Yes."

"My name's Volkmann. I'm a colleague of Erica Kranz's."

Her smile faded instantly. "What the devil do you want?"

"It's about Wolfgang Lubsch. Is there somewhere quiet where we can discuss it?"

"What did you say your name was?"

"Volkmann. Joseph Volkmann." He flashed the press ID.

"Why did you come here?"

"Your friend Lubsch had a chat with Erica and me yesterday. Only it wasn't very helpful. I need to talk with Lubsch again."

Karen Gries flushed angrily. "You're wasting your time coming here, Volkmann. Lubsch isn't a friend; he's someone I knew a long time ago. Erica asked if I could help find him because she wanted to talk with him. But that's as far as I was prepared to go. So if you don't mind . . ."

She turned away impatiently, toward the balding man, who was finishing a sale. He half smiled and stared at Volkmann warily before turning back to his customer.

Volkmann said, "We can do this one of two ways, Frau Gries."

"What do you mean?"

"Either you do as I ask, or I call the police and tell them what a bad girl you've been. I'm sure they'd be interested to learn that you're associating with a wanted terrorist. Before you know it, the antiterrorist squad will be crawling all over this place. Your customers can read about it in the newspapers."

The woman's eyes blazed. "Are you threatening me, Volkmann?"

"I'm asking for your help. I could also tell your husband you're still seeing Wolfgang Lubsch."

Karen Gries's mouth tightened with rage. "Who do you think you are, making an accusation like that?"

"You do still see him, don't you?"

The balding man went to open the door for his customer. Volkmann saw him stare across before he came to join them, as if he sensed something was wrong.

"Is everything all right, Karen? Can I be of any assistance?"

Karen Gries turned to him quickly and said, "Bruno, this is Herr Volkmann. A colleague of a friend of mine. I'd like to talk in private. Can you be a sweet and look after things here?"

The man shook Volkmann's hand. "Glad to meet you." He looked at his wife, and his hand touched her waist. "You're sure everything's okay?"

"Of course, Bruno." Karen Gries smiled. "You better look after the store." She turned back to Volkmann and said in a businesslike manner, "We'll use the office, Herr Volkmann."

Volkmann followed her into a small, cluttered office. When she closed the door, Karen Gries sat stiffly behind the desk. "What do you mean by coming here?"

"Do you know where Lubsch is?"

"No, I don't."

"But you can get in touch with him?"

She placed her manicured hands on the desk. "Listen to me. Lubsch isn't the kind you mess around with. By coming here and threatening me you could get hurt. Badly hurt." She looked at his face. "And I'm not just talking about a bruised jaw. That goes for Erica as well as you. You call the police, and Lubsch won't take it lightly. Understand me?"

"I want you to contact Lubsch. Tell him to meet me again."

"Are you crazy? Go, Volkmann, get out of here."

As Karen Gries stood up, Volkmann looked at his watch. "It's eleven-fifteen. I want Lubsch to meet me at seven this evening. That ought to give you enough time to get in touch. Otherwise, I make my call."

"Volkmann, you're crazy. I want you to leave. Now, this minute."

"You want to know how crazy I am?" Volkmann picked up the

phone on the desk and punched in a number as Karen Gries stared at him.

They both heard the line click, and Volkmann said, "Police?"

Karen Gries's eyes opened wide as her hand slammed down hard on the cradle.

"I never should have listened to Erica."

Volkmann put down the receiver. "Seven o'clock. If Lubsch is a minute late, I make my call."

Her face was still flushed. "Where?"

"In the bar across the street. Tell him to meet me inside at seven exactly. Tell him I want to talk with him alone. Just talk. There's no need for any rough stuff, understand? And don't try to contact Erica; she's no longer in the country."

"I just hope you realize what kind of fire you're playing with, Volkmann."

Volkmann walked back to the underground garage and drove over the Rhine Bridge and past Wiesbaden.

He still had almost eight hours to kill, and after half an hour he reached the Taunus Nature Park.

In summer the big park would have been busy with tourists and campers, but in winter it was a vast, desolate place, wind whipping through the banks of pine and fir trees. It was bitter cold. He saw a sign that pointed toward the lake.

He climbed out of the car, locked the door, and walked along the path through the trees until he reached the water.

The lakeside was choppy and deserted. A wooden pier jutted out into the gray shore. The water was deep at the end of the walkway, and Volkmann stood looking at the scene, going over possible scenarios in his mind. If his plan worked out, the lake was remote enough for him not to be disturbed.

If the plan worked.

He drove back into Wiesbaden and found a hardware store on the outskirts. He purchased a twenty-yard length of orange-colored nylon rope, a rubber-wrapped flashlight, and four spare batteries. Volkmann put his purchases in the glove compartment, then drove back to the apartment in Frankfurt.

When he went up, the windows in the front room were closed, but the air smelled of fresh lavender. He poured himself a scotch from the bottle in the kitchen.

He stared at his reflection in the wall mirror and raised an eyebrow as he said to himself, "You must have a death wish to attempt what you're about to do, Volkmann."

He checked his watch. Two-fifteen. He'd have time to rest for a couple of hours before he risked meeting Lubsch for the second time.

He drove back into Mainz, arriving just after five.

He didn't know whether he would need the Ford or not; it depended on how many men Lubsch would have with him and what kind of transportation they had. He had no doubt Lubsch would make an appearance, but he guessed that the terrorist wouldn't come alone and would certainly be armed.

He had dealt with people like Lubsch before; they wouldn't think twice about shooting in a crowded street, and Volkmann knew that for his plan to work, he'd have to act quickly.

He decided to use the same underground parking garage again, near Karen Gries's place. He checked the Beretta before he got out of the car, making sure the weapon was cocked and the safety was on, then he slipped it into his pocket. He placed the flashlight and spare batteries in his other pocket and put the nylon rope in the pouch inside his overcoat.

Darkness had fallen, and Christmas lights were strung across the buildings. He walked along the illuminated one-way street, mingling with the shoppers. If he guessed right, Lubsch and his people would arrive early. He thought maybe in an hour, but just to be certain, ninety minutes. He guessed Lubsch would send a runner to watch the bar long before Volkmann was due. Lubsch or his people wouldn't expect him to be armed, and they wouldn't expect him to go on the offensive.

He walked back to the café where he had sat that morning. He ordered coffee and unfolded his newspaper, keeping his eyes on the road outside, looking down only to check his watch.

It was 5:31.

It wasn't the Mercedes van this time, but a dark blue Opel sedan.

It trundled down the one-way street, then disappeared around the corner. It did the same thing three times before it pulled up fifty yards away on the same side of the street as Karen Gries's premises. Two men sat in front and one in the back.

Volkmann recognized Lubsch in the driver's seat, his face illuminated by a string of colored Christmas lights above the street. The little red-haired man wore the same padded dark Windbreaker. Volkmann couldn't see the faces of the other two men from where he sat.

Five minutes later, the man in the rear of the Opel stepped out and closed his door, then walked toward Gries's shop. Next to the art gallery was a pharmacy, its neon sign lit up overhead, and the man went to stand in the alcove. He pulled out a newspaper and began to browse through it. Volkmann recognized him as one of the men from the Mercedes. He was going to watch the bar from across the street, and Volkmann guessed the guy had a walkie-talkie.

Volkmann felt his heart pounding in his chest and his palms sweated. The street below was still crowded with shoppers, which would give him cover, but it was also dangerous. If Lubsch or his men started firing, there was a real danger a passerby could get shot.

Volkmann rechecked his watch. There was still more than an hour to go before the meeting. He knew he had to make his move before Lubsch left the car or drove around the block again.

The man in the passenger seat beside Lubsch would be a problem. And his luck would depend on whether the terrorist who was watching the bar across the street had left the rear door of the car unlocked.

He saw Lubsch's face peer out through the glass and then look away impatiently. The third terrorist, standing in the alcove, stared over at the bar from behind his newspaper every few moments. A Christmas tree illuminated the pharmacy window, its lights winking; the lurid colors tinted the man's face and fogging breath as he watched the Zum Dortmunder bar.

Volkmann's body tensed. He folded his newspaper and paid for his coffee.

It was time to go.

He stepped out onto the street and crossed over. He was ten yards behind the Opel, and as he walked toward it, he strained his eyes to see if the door lock in the rear was up. Five yards from the car, he saw that it was.

The guy sitting in the passenger seat was wiping the side window with the sleeve of his coat, and Volkmann got a glimpse of his profile. It was the same man who had wielded the truncheon, and he was grinning as he spoke with Lubsch.

Volkmann turned and went back down the street. The alleyway behind the bakery was empty, and as he entered it, he unfolded his newspaper, slipped the Beretta under the fold in the pages, and flicked off the safety.

He went back out onto the crowded street, toward the blue Opel. The man in the passenger seat was still wiping the side window; Volkmann saw his companion standing in the alcove glance toward the Opel, then step back out of view.

Volkmann came up alongside the car from behind, wrenched open the door, and clambered into the backseat, the Beretta already out. The two men in the front turned, and Volkmann saw the surprise on their faces as Lubsch said, "What the—?"

Lubsch was reaching frantically in his jacket, and the passenger was doing the same.

Volkmann's fist smacked twice into the passenger's face hard, and the man's head cracked against the window.

As Lubsch struggled to remove his gun, Volkmann pressed the Beretta firmly into the terrorist's neck. "Don't."

Lubsch turned chalk-white.

"Slip the gun out of your pocket. Hand it to me, slowly, grip-first, or I take your head off."

"Volkmann, you're dead . . ."

"Do it, or you'll be keeping the devil company."

Lubsch slowly removed a Glock from his jacket and handed it over.

Volkmann said, "Face front. Keep your mouth shut, and start the car. Drive to the end of the street, then turn right. And don't try anything as we go past your friend."

"Volkmann, when this is over—"

Volkmann yanked Lubsch's collar tight, and pulled him back, pressing the Beretta harder into the terrorist's neck. "Are you deaf? Behave yourself, and you and your friend here walk away from this alive. You don't, and I drop you both. Get it? Now start the car. Drive."

He let go of Lubsch, who leaned forward and started the Opel. Volkmann's free hand was already moving over the passenger. The man was out cold, and Volkmann found a Walther PPK in his right pocket and a walkie-talkie in the other. He put them on the floor beside Lubsch's weapon.

As the Opel pulled out from the curb and picked up speed, Volkmann kept the Beretta steady.

He saw Lubsch's man in the alcove stare at the Opel in disbelief as it went past the pharmacy, and then suddenly the man dropped his newspaper and was running after them.

Volkmann said to Lubsch, "Keep driving. Move it!"

As the car picked up more speed, the third man caught up beside them, running fast. Volkmann put down the safety locks just as he reached the car and began wrenching at the door handle. The man's face was up against the window, and when he couldn't open the door, his fists hammered madly on the glass, his face convulsed in confusion and anger.

Volkmann pressed the Beretta into Lubsch's neck and said, "What's your friend's name?"

Lubsch answered through clenched teeth. "Hartig."

Volkmann smiled out at the running man. "Happy Christmas, Hartig."

And then the car picked up even more speed and rounded the corner, and the face was gone from the window.

24

Thirty minutes later, Volkmann told Lubsch to take the turnoff for the Taunus Nature Park.

The passenger started to come around. Volkmann slid his thumb into the concavity behind the man's left ear, his other four fingers sliding around the man's neck and locking in a vise. He applied the pressure quickly and heard a small cry as the man's body sagged.

Lubsch's eyes flicked angrily at Volkmann, who kept the Beretta aimed at the terrorist and said, "Keep your eyes on the road."

As the passenger slumped back in the seat, Volkmann heard the man's breathing, heavy at first, then slow and regular. He felt for a pulse. It was slow. The amount of pressure he used would keep the passenger out for a couple of hours. From the crack of bone when he had hit the man, Volkmann guessed he had broken the man's nose.

Lubsch asked, "Who the devil are you?"

"Keep driving and shut up."

The half-moon night sky was patchy with black clouds. Twenty yards from the lakeshore, Volkmann ordered Lubsch to halt and get out of the car.

Trees at the edge of the forest tossed furiously in the wind, and as Volkmann stepped out, he flicked on the flashlight and told Lubsch to move down to the jetty. Moonlight silvered the choppy lake and Volkmann shone the flashlight ahead.

As they approached the boardwalk Lubsch suddenly made a frantic run for it. Volkmann sprinted after him, dropped the flashlight, and gripped the terrorist's shoulder. As Lubsch spun around, his small, wiry frame crashed into Volkmann in the darkness.

The terrorist grappled for the weapon in Volkmann's hand and tried to wrench it free but he locked the little man's neck in a vise. Volkmann heard his gurgle as he fought for breath, and moments later, Lubsch's body sagged and slid to the ground.

He retrieved the flashlight and shone it in Lubsch's face. The man wasn't unconscious but his eyes were dilated from lack of oxygen, and as his hands massaged his neck, he started to cough violently on the grass.

His voice was hoarse with pain. "When this is through, you're dead, Volkmann. Dead."

Volkmann jerked the Beretta. "Get up, Lubsch. Walk down to the pier."

Lubsch struggled to stand, and when they came down to the water, Volkmann said, "Now tie your shoelaces together."

"What?"

"You heard me. Tie them."

Lubsch did as he was ordered. When he finished, Volkmann flashed the light and checked them. He told Lubsch to take off his belt and then lie down on his stomach. When Lubsch hesitated, Volkmann forced him down. Once the terrorist had removed his belt, Volkmann used it to tie the man's hands behind his back, then he pulled Lubsch up into a sitting position. A bitter cold wind coming in off the black water clawed at their faces.

"We can do this the easy way or the hard way, Lubsch. The easy way is for you to tell me what I need to know. The hard way is for me to deliver you and your buddy to the nearest police station."

Anger blazed in Lubsch's face. "You think you'll get away with it, Volkmann? My men would hunt you down and find you. Who are you? Police?"

Volkmann ignored the question. "Think about it. A high-security prison for maybe twenty years. That's if the judge is in a good mood. Guards watching your every movement. No visits except from your lawyer, if you were lucky enough to find one who'd take your case." Volkmann slipped the Beretta into his pocket, removed the nylon rope, and held it in front of Lubsch's face. "So what's it to be? I wrap you and your friend up like a Christmas present for the cops, or you talk?"

Volkmann shone the flashlight in Lubsch's face; the terrorist blinked and looked away. The icy-cold wind was lapping the dark water with ragged gusts.

Lubsch shivered, his skin raw from the cold. "And if I talk, what's in it for me?"

"I let you and your friend go."

Lubsch spat his reply. "What do you want to know?"

"What I wanted to know the last time we met. About Dieter Winter and his friends."

"How do I know you'll keep your word, Volkmann?"

"You'll have to trust me. But if I find out you lied to me or didn't tell me everything, I can promise you that your friend Karen will get a visit from the police."

Lubsch's face strained with rage. "You really are crazy, aren't you? Just like Karen said you were—"

Before the terrorist could finish his sentence, Volkmann reached over and gripped Lubsch's collar and dragged him over to the edge of the jetty. He grabbed a handful of Lubsch's hair and pushed his face into the freezing-cold water. Lubsch bucked and squirmed, his legs kicking wildly in the air.

Volkmann saw the air bubbles rise before he pulled Lubsch's head back up. The terrorist gulped in deep breaths as his lungs fought for air.

". . . Okay, okay. I'll tell you."

Volkmann dragged him back into the middle of the pier and Lubsch caught his breath. His hair was plastered over his forehead, water dripped from his face, and he shivered violently.

Volkmann said, "I want to hear it from the beginning. From how you first met Winter. Leave nothing out. Got that?"

Lubsch coughed and spat. "I first met Winter at Heidelberg. He was in the history faculty."

"You were friends?"

"No, just acquaintances. We used to meet sometimes to drink and talk."

"Tell me everything."

Lubsch sniffed, then spat into the water. "Winter and I had different political views. He was a right-wing fanatic; I leaned the other way. But he was always a convincing speaker. For a time, he even managed to convince me that we had something in common."

"Like what?"

Lubsch looked up at Volkmann, then turned his head away again. "The future of Germany."

"What's that supposed to mean?"

"It was a pet topic with Winter. He and his friends had this idea that they could change the country."

"And who were his friends?"

"Fellow students. Others who shared his views." Lubsch hesitated, then said, "What's this got to do with me, Volkmann? The murders you spoke about, or something else?"

"Just carry on talking until I tell you to stop. What about Winter's friends?"

"Six months into our second year at the university, I'd gotten to know Winter pretty well. He was a drinker and a talker, and sometimes we'd have a beer together and argue about politics. We held opposing views, but our discussions were always good fun. Then one day Winter asked me to join him and a group of his friends for a weekend on Lüneburg Heath. There were to be seven of us. Some were students, but others came from different parts of Germany and from different backgrounds, most of them working-class. Toughs, a couple of them, and out of their depth intellectually. We stayed in a rented house in the forest and drank in the local inns. We walked and talked day and night. About politics. Philosophy. History."

"The others, they all knew Winter?"

Lubsch looked up. "Sure. It was like a fraternity. They all knew each other pretty well."

"Who were these people?"

"I told you, Winter asked them along. I'd never met them before."

"I want names, Lubsch."

"I remember only one. A science student. His name was Lothar Kesser. He was about my age, and he came from Bavaria."

"Where in Bavaria?"

Lubsch shook his head. "Some hick town, I don't remember where."

"You said the group was like a fraternity. What did you mean?"

Lubsch shrugged. "It was like they had some bond between them. It was kind of weird. Like a secret society. Don't ask me to explain it, Volkmann, because I can't. But it was like I was outside the circle, not one of them. I was there only because Winter asked me. I guess they liked me because I was an intellectual who wasn't afraid of action. And because I liked to spend time talking with Winter, maybe they thought they could convert me."

"Go on."

"One night after everyone's gone to bed, this guy Kesser suggests we go for a walk in the forest. Just him and me. It's dark and gloomy outside, and we've had a few drinks. Kesser said he wanted to talk with me in private.

"So we walked together and Kesser talked about Germany's past. Not the bad things. The good things. How Germany had always come through in times of great suffering and upheaval. Overcome all obstacles. Created order out of chaos. That sort of bull. Like Kesser was giving me some sort of political speech. He said that Germany would go through a phase of disorder again. There were definitely going to be problems in the future. Not only in Germany, but in all of Europe, in the world. Politically. Economically. Socially. But there were also going to be opportunities. And that we were all Germans together and that when that time came, we should strive together to seize the opportunity to create a better Fatherland. I was pretty drunk, but I thought Kesser was talking garbage, and told him so."

"How did he respond?"

"He got annoyed and said that when the right time came, he and the others who supported his beliefs would have financial support for their cause. He said he knew I was involved with the Red Army Faction. That he didn't see me and my friends as terrorists, merely as disenchanted Germans who sought a different Germany. He said we could join him if we wished."

"And what did you say?"

"I said it was kind of him, but he was wrong. I wasn't involved with any group. I was drunk, Volkmann, but I was careful. I didn't know if Kesser was playing some kind of trick. Maybe he and Winter were police plants. They do that, you know. Send their brightest cadets into German universities to spy on extremist undergraduates. Lead them along, and then trap them."

"How did he react?"

Lubsch shrugged. "He said I was making a grave mistake, and that was the end of our conversation."

The wind gusted across the lake and Lubsch shivered.

Volkmann asked, "When did you see either of them again?"

Lubsch said, "That's when it got weird. Winter phoned me a week later. He said he wanted me to listen to an important proposition, but not over the phone. I was curious, so I agreed to meet near the Black Forest. I took along a couple of men to check out the location first. Winter and Kesser were there alone. We drove up into the mountains. Kesser did all the talking. He said he had a proposition for me and my group."

"What sort of proposition?"

"He said he could offer us weapons and explosives. Whatever we needed."

Volkmann paused. "Did Kesser say where he got the weapons?"

"No, only that the offer was genuine."

"And what did you think?"

Lubsch smiled grimly. "I thought it was crazy. A right-wing radical supplying a left-wing terror group with weapons. Where's the sense in that?"

"You didn't accept?"

"Of course I did. I might have thought Kesser was crazy, but I wasn't. We always needed weapons. The Russians stopped supplying groups like ours after the Wall came down."

"What kind of weapons did Kesser's people deliver?" When Lubsch hesitated, Volkmann prodded him with his shoe. "I asked what kind, Lubsch?"

"Small arms and explosives mostly. Machine pistols, assault rifles, handguns. Grenades and Semtex. And once a rocket launcher we needed to take out a politician's car."

Volkmann looked down at the terrorist. "You've been a bad boy. Didn't your people question Winter's motives?"

Lubsch shook his head and laughed quietly. "Volkmann, we would have taken weapons from the devil himself, as long as they were reliable and shot straight. But there was a condition. Every time we'd get a supply, we'd get a request. A favor to do in return. They'd suggest we hit certain targets."

"What sort of targets?"

"Those American and Allied bases still on German soil. Banks. State property and institutions. Some of the hits fit in with our scheme of things, and we were happy to oblige. But then about six months ago, Kesser's requests became more outrageous. He wanted us to start bombing immigrant hostels. And he wanted us to hit some people. He gave me three names he wanted killed. He didn't say why, just that they were part of the deal."

"Who were the people?"

"One of the names on the list was a liberal politician I knew in Berlin, and I wouldn't go along with it. I told Kesser it wasn't our style. We'd only hit targets we thought deserved to be hit. Big businessmen who corrupt this country. Politicians who support them. But we wouldn't do the names on the list."

"What did Kesser say?"

"He just smiled and said he'd handle it himself. But after that, things were strained between us, and then the weapons stopped."

"Who did Kesser want dead?"

Lubsch paused. "A guy in East Berlin. His name was Rauscher, Herbert Rauscher. Another was a woman in Friedrichshafen, near the Swiss border."

"Her name?"

"I can't remember."

"Think, Lubsch."

"Hedda something. Pohl or Puhl. I'm not sure."

"Who was she?"

"A nobody. The widow of a businessman."

"And the man in East Berlin, Rauscher?"

"A small-time businessman. Another nobody."

"Your people checked their backgrounds?"

"Of course. We weren't going to kill just for the sake of it, Volkmann."

"Who was the politician in Berlin?"

"His name's Walter Massow." Lubsch looked out at the cold lake and his teeth chattered. "He's not a political animal, just a good and honest man trying to do his best for the downtrodden in this country. That's why I told Kesser, 'No way. If Massow was hit, I'd take it personally.'" The terrorist looked back. "And after that, I told you, the supplies halted."

"Did you ask why they wanted you to carry out the attacks on the immigrant hostels?"

"Kesser was a right-wing fanatic. It was the sort of thing you'd expect from someone of his background."

"What do you mean?"

"That time on Lüneburg Heath, I overheard him talk about his father. He was some big-shot SS man during the war. I heard him say the old man had helped draft the Brandenburg Testament for Adolf Hitler, whatever that was. But Kesser said it like a boast, as if it were proof enough of his pedigree."

Volkmann remembered the words on the tape. And there was that other word as well, *pedigree.*

"The Brandenburg Testament. What is it?"

"I just told you. I have no idea."

"The politician, Massow, what happened to him?"

Lubsch shook his head. "Nothing. He was left alone."

"And the others?"

"I've no idea." Lubsch shivered as a gust of icy wind blew in off the lake.

Volkmann said, "Why do you think Massow wasn't killed?"

Lubsch shrugged. "Maybe Winter thought it more tactful to let Massow live after he heard my views. I don't know, Volkmann. Either way, I was out of the game."

Volkmann stepped down to the edge of the jetty, felt the icy wind slash at his face.

"What you've told me, none of it makes any sense, Lubsch. What was in it for Winter and his buddies? Why did they want you to play hit man? They could have done it themselves. They had the weapons."

Lubsch smiled bitterly. "I have a theory. Maybe it makes sense."

"Tell me."

"Maybe the plan was to spread anarchy. Blame the left wing for hits like that, and the right-wing groups gain more support. But whoever was behind Winter, they sure had money and good organization to buy and ship arms and supplies in such quantities."

"Did your people kill Winter?"

"No."

"Who did?"

"I don't know. Winter had a big mouth, especially when he was drunk." Lubsch shrugged. "Maybe he talked too much and somebody didn't like it."

"How do I find Kesser?"

The terrorist looked up, his face blue and cold. "I've no idea but I'll give you some advice, Volkmann. The advice I gave you before. Keep away from him and his friends. Unless you and Erica want to end up dead."

"Do the names Karl Schmeltz or Nicolas Tsarkin mean anything to you? Were they ever mentioned?"

"No."

"You're sure?"

"I've never heard those names." Lubsch's teeth chattered again. "I've told you everything. Are you going to untie me now, Volkmann? Or am I going to sit here all night and freeze to death?"

Volkmann shone the flashlight slightly to the right so it didn't shine in the terrorist's eyes, but so that he could still see the man's reaction. "One more question. Erica Kranz."

"What about her?"

"How well did she know Winter at Heidelberg?"

"What are you asking me for, Volkmann? Ask her yourself."

"Just answer the question."

Lubsch shrugged. "I saw them talking together at parties a few times." The terrorist's face looked frozen. "Why? I thought she was a friend of yours."

Volkmann ignored the question and stood. "I enjoyed our talk."

"Don't push it, Volkmann."

He saw the rage in Lubsch's eyes. As he moved away, Volkmann hesitated, shone the light in Lubsch's face.

"I did you a favor tonight, Lubsch. By rights, you ought to be behind bars for the rest of your life. But if I learn you've been lying to me, or if you try to come after me, the police will pay your friend Karen a visit. One more thing: keep away from Erica Kranz."

Volkmann flicked off the flashlight, and the wooden walkway plunged into darkness.

"You'll find the car somewhere near Karen's place. I'll leave your friend behind to keep you company."

As he walked back toward the Opel, he heard the wind raging across the lake in the freezing darkness, and Lubsch grunting as he struggled with the belt on the pier.

25

When he let himself into the apartment, it was almost midnight and Erica was asleep in the spare bedroom.

He telephoned Peters's home number and told him what had happened with Lubsch.

"You took a big risk, Joe. You want me to pass Karen Gries's name to the German counterterrorist people?"

"Not for now. If Lubsch tries to come back at me, we'll do it then."

"You think he told you the truth?"

"Maybe, but I'll have to check it out."

"Okay. I thought you'd want to hear—we got some information about Erhard Schmeltz from the Document Center in Berlin."

"What did they say?"

"They've got records of the Nazi Party going back to 1925. There's an Erhard Johann Schmeltz, born in Hamburg and listed as party number six-eight-nine-six. His party application was made in Munich in late November of 1929, and his year of birth is the same as in Sanchez's report. Considering the date he applied and the fact that the party had over ten million members in Germany at its peak, Schmeltz would have joined pretty much at the start."

"What else did they say?"

"They have his original application and his file and photograph from the master files of the Nazi Party. He was also a registered member of the Brownshirts. But there's the interesting thing—Schmeltz didn't quit the Nazi Party when he went to South America. His party dues were paid in absentia until his death in 1944."

"How can they know that for certain?"

"The Nazis had something called the Gau Ausland. The best way to describe it is as a department that dealt with party members in foreign regions, people who had left Germany but still kept up their party membership. Committed Nazis. Schmeltz was registered with the Gau Ausland from November of 1931." Peters hesitated. "There's something else. The Document Center said Erhard Schmeltz's party application had a recommendation attached to it."

"What do you mean?"

"Apparently every application for party membership had to be recommended by the local leadership. But in Schmeltz's case, there was a letter sent from Prinz-Albrecht-Strasse in Berlin, the SS headquarters. It was signed by Heinrich Himmler, and it recommended Schmeltz's immediate acceptance. It suggests that maybe Schmeltz had contacts pretty high up in the party."

Volkmann let the news sink in. "Anything else?"

"The information on Tsarkin, alias Reimer. The Document Center had him on its list of SS officers. But there's really nothing much more in their files that could help us. I'll have their information on your desk tomorrow. You need anything else?"

"Lothar Kesser, scientist from Bavaria. I want him checked out. And I'll need a return ticket to Zurich, first available flight tomorrow morning."

"Why Zurich?"

"Remember Ted Birken?"

Peters laughed. "I thought they put that wily old fox out to grass years ago."

"They did. But he may be able to help."

"Okay. I'll organize the ticket. Keep in touch. Good night, Joe."

When he put down the telephone, Volkmann heard a sound and saw Erica standing in the doorway. She wore a dressing gown, and her eyes had a hint of anger.

"I heard you talking on the phone. You said you wouldn't contact Lubsch or Karen. Is that where you went today?"

Volkmann said nothing, and she looked at him accusingly. "You know what kind of man Lubsch is. What he's capable of. Why do it, Joe? Why put us both in danger?"

"He won't come back at you, Erica. I've made sure of that. If he does, I tell the police about Karen."

"I think there's something that worries me more, Joe."

"What?"

"That you didn't trust me enough to tell me what you were going to do."

When Volkmann didn't reply, she sat down. "Tell me what Lubsch said."

He told her, and she watched his face. "Do you trust him?"

"Trust him, no. Believe him, yes."

Erica shook her head. "Don't you think he could have been trying to mislead you? Why would Winter's people want Lubsch to carry out racist attacks on immigrants? To attack state institutions? The targets seem so diverse. There's no sense to it."

"Maybe. But I don't think the guy lied. You want to find the people who killed Rudi. Getting Lubsch to talk was the only way."

She looked away. The anger had subsided, but she didn't speak. Volkmann said, "Do you have access to any newspaper libraries?"

"The one at the *Frankfurter Zeitung*. Why?"

"I've got a job for you. Could you look through the files there? The people Winter wanted killed. Rauscher, and the woman Hedda Pohl or Puhl. See what you come up with."

"Can't your people check on that?"

"It would mean going through the German desk. And I'd prefer we kept it to ourselves for now." He paused. "The politician in Berlin—Massow. See if you can arrange a meeting for me."

"What do you want to talk with him about?"

"If what Lubsch said is true, there must have been a reason Winter's people wanted Massow dead. Maybe Massow knows why. I'll give you a number where you can reach me. If I'm not there, you can contact Peters or leave a message."

"You won't be in Strasbourg?"

He shook his head. "We know almost nothing about Erhard Schmeltz, or his son. But the information Sanchez sent—about the money transferred from the Reichsbank to Schmeltz in Paraguay—there's someone I'd like to talk to about it in Zurich. Someone who may be able to help."

He told her Peters's news and a frown creased Erica's face.

"You really think Schmeltz's past has anything to do with all of this? But it's such a long time ago."

"I know, Erica. But he's a big piece of the puzzle, so let's see what I can turn up in Zurich tomorrow."

ZURICH, SWITZERLAND. TUESDAY, DECEMBER 13

He made the telephone call to Ted Birken early that morning, and Peters arranged a ticket for the first flight out of Strasbourg to Zurich.

The plane was full, and when it landed, Volkmann took a taxi out to the house overlooking the Zürichsee. It was bitter cold but the sky was clear, and in the distance he could see the snowcapped mountains beyond the lake.

The house was pretty and neat and set in its own tidy gardens. Volkmann saw Ted Birken come out to the front door and wave a greeting.

The old man's shoulders were hunched beneath a loose-fitting cardigan, and he had aged. Volkmann realized it had been more than ten years since they last met, when Birken had guest-lectured at the house in Devon.

The blue eyes twinkled as he shook Volkmann's hand. "Good to see you again, Joe. Come inside."

The house was warm, and in the study Birken had set out a small wooden tray with glasses and a bottle of cherry kirsch. A fire blazed in the hearth and the window looked out onto the lake.

Ted Birken had been an intelligence officer for most of his adult life. A Jewish refugee from Germany, as a child he had escaped with his family to Switzerland in 1940. After the war Birken emigrated to England, where his unique talents—he spoke German fluently and had connections through his father, a once-prominent banker, with many major Swiss banks—were put to use by the British intelligence service.

Thus began a career that for several years saw Birken track down and interrogate senior Nazis who had secretly helped to dispose of many millions in gold and currency from the German Reichsbank and death camps in the last months of the war. When his work came to an end, Birken became a senior intelligence figure before retiring to Switzerland.

Volkmann saw the elderly man puff on his meerschaum and fill the two glasses with kirsch before the sparkling blue eyes swiveled to look at him. Birken was a businesslike man; he got straight down to it.

"You had three questions when you rang, one about the money that was sent to South America by the Nazi Reichsbank. The other concerning these men, Schmeltz and Reimer, and the Leibstandarte SS. Let's start with the first, shall we?" He took a sip of his drink, then sat back, puffing on his pipe before speaking.

"First, perhaps I had better explain the background behind Nazi funds so you get a fix on things. At the end of the war in May of 1945, the equivalent of almost ten billion dollars in today's terms had gone missing. That included lots of valuable art objects, too, but mainly gold and silver bullion, the so-called property of the Reichsbank. Some of it—quite a lot, actually—had been plundered from invaded countries." Birken paused to smile. "There was enough to equip another German army, and I think that was the vague intention of the Nazis when the plans to hide the caches were first discussed. But of course as the war situation became more hopeless, that idea was quickly forgotten, and many of the people whose job it was to hide the caches actually started working for themselves."

Volkmann sipped his drink. "So what happened to the bullion and money, Ted?"

"Some of it we located. But a lot of it vanished. It ended up in Switzerland or South America, and some in the Arab countries that had been favorably disposed toward Hitler. A few unscrupulous Americans helped themselves to some of the gold or did deals with the Nazis they apprehended, but it was small scale and to be expected. Quite a number of Nazis escaped to South America, as I'm sure you know. And quite a lot of the bullion and currency went with them. The people involved ranged from lowly privates up to high-ranking SS and Gestapo. They slipped out of ports all over Europe, but mainly from Italy. We tried tracking both them and the caches down in South America, but it proved a rather hopeless exercise. Most of the South American countries still had pro-Nazi sympathies at the time and did nothing to help us."

"What were the reasons behind taking the gold and currency to South America?"

Birken smiled. "It was considered a relatively safe and distant place. Some countries there with large German colonies were openly supportive of the Nazis. Paraguay is a good example. General Stroessner was the military dictator there for quite some time. He was part German himself, and pro-Nazi. Most of the loot that ended up in South America lined private pockets, though a considerable portion of it was controlled by Die Spinne—the Spider—the secret organization of former SS who set up down there. Otherwise known as the Kameradenwerk, and before that, as Odessa. There was a rather loose plan to regroup and eventually finance another Nazi Party in Germany when the time was ripe once again, but of course it came to nothing."

Birken paused, and the watery blue eyes looked at Volkmann. "Die Spinne, you're familiar with its original function?"

"No."

"Well, it had quite a few, actually. But the primary ones were to protect former SS men from prosecution and to help establish those same former Nazis and their families in commerce and industry. And, of course, to continue to propagandize the ideals of the Third Reich."

Volkmann looked out toward the gray, choppy lake and considered. "Did you ever hear of funds being sent back to Germany with that purpose in mind, Ted?"

"In what respect?"

"To finance extremists. Neo-Nazis."

Birken relit his pipe and said, "Mossad had a theory that some of the neo-Nazi resurgences in Germany over many decades were financed in part from Die Spinne funds, but there was never any solid evidence. Of course, Die Spinne was notoriously secretive and defied any attempts to infiltrate it. The Israelis tried to on a number of occasions, but their people involved on such missions usually disappeared, never to be heard of again."

The blue eyes regarded Volkmann keenly. "I presume this has something to do with these men, Schmeltz and Reimer, you asked me to check on?"

"It sure does."

"Do you mind my asking why?"

Volkmann told him the story. When he finished, Birken leaned forward.

"Do you have the photograph of the young woman with you?"

Volkmann removed the snapshot from his wallet. Birken studied it for a long time, then handed it back and shook his head.

"I'm afraid I don't recognize her. Of course, that date would have been long before my time. And the young woman could have been anyone. A public figure or simply an anonymous girlfriend of some Nazi officer."

"What about Schmeltz and Reimer?"

Birken nodded. "After you called, I had a look back through my diaries. I kept copious notes when I was tracking down the missing Nazi gold. As I told you once many years ago, the team I was involved with after the war had to go right back through the books, back to 1933, to try to figure out where most of the money and bullion had come from. What part was party funds, what part belonged to the German people, what part had been spoils of war, and so on." Birken smiled. "I hoped to write a book one day, but somehow I never seemed to get around to it. That's the reason I kept copies of almost all the major accounts serviced over the twelve years of the Nazi regime."

Volkmann nodded. "That's why I contacted you, Ted."

"The bad news is that I found nothing on this man Reimer, alias Tsarkin. He wasn't one of the people we were chasing. The twenty thousand American dollars you say he had when he arrived in Paraguay could have been a little nest egg he had stashed away during the years of the war, or it quite possibly could have been paid to him from Die Spinne funds."

"What about the owner of the Chaco property, Erhard Schmeltz?"

Birken again shook his head. "I found no record of money being sent to any Schmeltz in Paraguay. Not that I expected to. That's not to say that the Reichsbank didn't send him the funds. The account could have been serviced secretly. But the amounts sent to Schmeltz would have been small beer by comparison to some of the accounts the Reichsbank serviced abroad. Those were mainly for espionage work, for propaganda purposes. The real question is, why was Schmeltz sent money *before* the war? And why did the cash continue to be sent to his wife after his death?"

"Any ideas, Ted?"

Birken tapped his pipe. "Heaven only knows. It could have been for anything. Some Nazis set up slush funds through German immigrants in South America in the belief, I suppose, that one day they'd need them. There were always quite a number of German colonies in Paraguay, and most of them were fervently pro-Nazi." Birken shrugged. "Maybe the Schmeltz couple was simply playing bank manager for someone."

"What about the fact that Schmeltz's Nazi membership was endorsed by Himmler himself?"

Birken smiled again. "Now that is interesting. But I'm afraid I still can't give you an answer. It suggests that Schmeltz was a close acquaintance of Himmler's or some high-ranking Nazi, obviously." Birken raised an eyebrow. "But if some top Nazi was using this man Schmeltz to hoard cash for the future, I'm sure the amounts would have been much, much larger."

Birken paused. "Perhaps Schmeltz did someone a favor or kindness. Perhaps he was being repaid for it. It's the only explanation I can think of when you consider that Schmeltz retained his party membership despite being thousands of miles away. Either that or he was being used to set up a slush fund for some Nazi. Blackmail's another possible reason for the drafts, of course. But it's unlikely that Schmeltz would have remained in the party if that were the case. And I can only assume that the reason the monies ceased in February of 1945 was because by then, the Reichsbank was finding it increasingly difficult to transfer funds out of Germany, even through its Swiss accounts."

"What was the gold bullion that made its way to Die Spinne actually used for?"

Birken looked out toward the view beyond the window for a few moments, then turned back. "I think I'd have to agree with Mossad's theory, at least in part. I'm sure some of it was used to finance neo-Nazi movements over the years. And not only in Germany, but all over Europe, and in America and South Africa in particular. But until now, Germany's been too prosperous a country to have its keel unsettled by that kind of thing." Birken shrugged. "I imagine a lot of the money sent to South America kept quite a number of old Nazis and their families in considerable comfort."

"Are we talking millions here, Ted, or what?"

"Oh, much more than that, my boy. Probably as much as a quarter of the original amount that disappeared. Especially when you consider that the capital would have been put to work."

"How?"

"In business ventures mainly, and land purchase. Much of it in South America." Birken paused. "That's where your last question comes in. What do you know about the Leibstandarte SS Division, Joe?"

"Very little. Just that they were an elite within the SS, and Hitler's personal bodyguard."

Birken nodded. "That's right. They were first formed after the Night of the Long Knives, by Sepp Dietrich, a fanatical and dedicated Nazi officer. The SS men were all handpicked, hardened Nazis, fanatically loyal to Hitler. They were also instrumental in setting up Die Spinne and moving much of the Nazi gold to South America." Birken smiled. "It's interesting, but there is a slim connection between this fellow Erhard Schmeltz and Reimer."

"What kind of connection?"

"Reimer was Leibstandarte SS. Erhard Schmeltz was SA. A Brownshirt."

When Volkmann nodded, Birken went on. "Well, the Brownshirt SA was initially set up as Hitler's bodyguard. But after the Night of the Long Knives in 1934, when they were purged, some of their members ardently loyal to Hitler were inducted into the ranks of the Leibstandarte SS." Birken shrugged. "It's a small connection, but a connection nonetheless."

Volkmann glanced at his watch. "I'm booked on the twelve-thirty flight back, Ted. Do you mind if I use your phone to call a taxi?"

"Not at all. Let me do it for you."

Ten minutes later they saw the cab pull up on the gravel path outside. Volkmann finished his drink, and Birken stood up shakily.

"One last question, Ted. Did you ever hear of the Brandenburg Testament?"

The old man thought for a moment, rubbed his chin. "No, I'm afraid not. What is it?"

Volkmann shook his head, smiled. "I've no idea. Thanks for your help, Ted."

"Sorry I couldn't be more useful." Birken paused. "There may be one way I could try to get a fix on Schmeltz."

"How?"

"So many of the old Nazis are dead, of course. But there are still a few of them alive. I have a contact in the German Federal Archives Office in Koblenz. I could ask him to see if he can come up with some numbers close to Schmeltz's party membership number and check them with the WASt."

"What's that?"

"It's an acronym for the Wehrmacht Auskunftstelle. That's the German Army Information Agency. It's in north Berlin, and it's one of the main German military-personnel records offices. The WASt keeps information on all former German Army personnel, going back to before the last war. That includes the SS, which was actually part of the army. Whenever former German military personnel claimed a pension, at retirement age, they had to apply through the WASt. Only when their military service records were confirmed could the pensions be paid."

"You mean former members of the SS were paid pensions?"

"Lousy as that seems, yes."

"How can the WASt help?"

"Well, if we can get a list of Nazi Party membership numbers and names that were close to Schmeltz's, and those people served in the German military during the war and are still alive, they ought to be receiving pensions. The WASt will have a record of their addresses. But there really can't be too many of the old boys still alive, especially those whose party numbers were close to Schmeltz's and who knew him. That's your big problem But leave it with me and I'll see what I can come up with."

"Thanks, Ted. I appreciate your help."

"Not at all, my boy."

Birken led him to the front door, and the blue eyes sparkled as he gripped Volkmann's hand. "I'll be in touch if anything turns up." He smiled. "Do call again sometime. It's so seldom I get visitors these days."

It was almost noon when the taxi pulled up outside the departures terminal. As Volkmann paid the driver, he noticed the dark green Citroën pull up across from the terminal—he had spotted the same car in the rearview mirror on the way in from the lake road.

It was too far away for him to get a good look at the two passengers inside without making it obvious, but when he went to check in, he noticed the blond young man with the newspaper standing by the Hertz desk. He wore a long, dark winter overcoat, and his hair was cropped close to his skull. Volkmann felt certain he'd seen him that morning at the airport, standing by the information desk as he came out of arrivals.

When he was handed back his boarding pass, Volkmann walked back out to the departures entrance and stepped outside. The green Citroën had disappeared, and there was no sign of the young man with the newspaper.

He waited another ten minutes, going through the old routines, but he noticed no one watching him and he was certain he wasn't followed as he walked back toward the boarding gate.

26

STRASBOURG. TUESDAY, DECEMBER 13

He arrived back at DSE headquarters at three. Peters had left early but there was a message for Volkmann from the duty officer, and when he was put through, Jan de Vries came on the line.

"A message came through the Italian desk," the Dutchman said. "They say they're rechecking all seaport cargo manifests that arrived from South America within the last month. If they come across anything, they'll get back to you." De Vries paused. "Also, a voice-analysis report just came in from your place in Beaconsfield."

"I'll pick it up, Jan. Thanks."

There was some correspondence on his desk, but he ignored it for now. He felt certain that the blond young man at the airport in Zurich had been watching him and that the two men in the green Citroën had followed him out from the Zürichsee. But why? And who were they? It made him feel uneasy. Apart from Peters, only Erica knew he was traveling to Zurich.

He signed for the two-page voice-analysis report, then went back up to his office.

The report determined that there were three male voices on Hernandez's tape.

The first was in his late forties approximately. The man was a nonsmoker, heavily built.

Like the two other voices the German he spoke was a softer version of *plattdeutsch*. But the analysis suggested that all three men were bilingual, their voices softened by a Latinate tongue, most likely Spanish.

Of those two other voices, one was of a speaker roughly in his middle thirties, a smoker, likely of stocky build. And the other was of a much older man, in his late seventies or eighties. Possibly thin to medium build, and a nonsmoker.

The German they spoke was regionalized to nonethnic German colonies within either Paraguay or Argentina.

Volkmann made two copies of the report and left one each marked for the attention of Ferguson and Peters.

When he went through the correspondence on his desk, he found a large envelope from Peters, containing photocopied material from the Berlin Document Center.

Two manila folders inside each contained a sheaf of pages. A note was paper-clipped to the front of one of the folders. It explained that one set of original copies was from Heinrich Reimer's file and the second from Erhard Schmeltz's.

Volkmann picked Reimer's first.

All the relevant information was in the file. SS number, Nazi Party number. In Reimer's case there were notes concerning his education, medical history, his officer-training courses, his transfers and promotions, up to October 1944. Included was a four-page copy of Reimer's family tree, dating back to 1800, to show the Aryan purity of his background.

The third page contained three black-and-white photographs of Reimer. Two were head-and-shoulders shots, one front and one side profile. The third was a full-length photograph in the black SS uniform. The photographs showed a solemn-looking young man with cropped blond hair and a sharp face.

Volkmann put the file aside and opened the folder on Erhard Schmeltz.

The four pages inside contained a copy of Schmeltz's original Nazi Party application form. At the top of the application it read: NATIONALSOZIALISTISCHE DEUTSCHE ARBEITERPARTEI.

There was a line for the applicant's signature, and it contained Erhard Schmeltz's, the letters firm and bold. For "Profession" or "Occupation," the words "Fabrik Werkmeister," Factory Foreman, were written in Schmeltz's handwriting. The place and date of birth were given as Hamburg. In a box in the top right-hand corner was stamped the number 6896.

Schmeltz's address was given as 23 Brennerallee in Schwabing, and the date of application was November 6, 1929.

When he looked at the next page, Volkmann saw a copy of a letter headed Prinz-Albrecht-Strasse, Berlin, the headquarters of the SS.

A terse message simply said, "I recommend immediate acceptance of party applicant Erhard Johann Schmeltz into Gau Munich. Any queries, contact me personally." The letter was signed *H. Himmler, Der Reichsführer SS.*

The photocopies of Schmeltz's original master file card from Nazi Party records contained very little information: name and address, party membership number, date of entry into the party. But there was a head-and-shoulders photograph of Schmeltz.

It was of a plain, middle-aged man with a peasant's face and a thick, bullish neck. His dark hair had partly receded and was combed over his scalp. He wore an ill-fitting suit. Dark, bushy eyebrows were knit together as he stared at the camera.

Volkmann studied the image, wondering again what made Schmeltz leave Germany and travel to South America with his wife and child. And why he received such large sums of money.

Finally he put the folders back in the envelope, tidied up his desk, and drove to his apartment.

It was after five and dark when he let himself in, and Erica had set the table.

She poured him a glass of wine. "You're just in time for dinner. I went shopping in Petite France and bought fresh fish and vegetables and some bottles of Sauterne."

She looked good in jeans and a tight sweater, and her hair was down and fell about her shoulders. Over the meal he told her about the voice-analysis report and his visit to Zurich, but he made no mention of the man at the airport who had followed him.

"Did your friend in Zurich have any idea why Erhard Schmeltz received the money?"

He told her what Ted Birken had said. "But he was just speculating, Erica. So anything's possible. What about you?"

"I spent the day at the office, going through the library newspaper files on the murders."

"And?"

She handed him a black plastic file. "I put it all together in there. Lubsch must have told you the truth. At least about the two people Kesser wanted him to kill."

Volkmann flicked through the file. "Why?"

"A man named Herbert Rauscher was murdered in East Berlin five months ago. It's got to be the same man. The Berlin papers ran stories, and they were picked up by the major dailies."

"Tell me."

"Rauscher was shot dead at his apartment. Two bullet wounds in the head. According to the newspapers, there were no witnesses, and the Berlin homicide had no leads. I telephoned their office, but they wouldn't give me any information other than that the case is still under investigation."

Volkmann looked up from the file. "What about the woman?"

"Her name was Hedda Pohl, and she was murdered, too."

"Where?"

"Friedrichshafen in southern Germany, where she came from. As you probably know, it's near the Swiss border, beside Lake Konstanz. She was shot dead in a wood outside the town, a week before Rauscher. I rang the local paper in Friedrichshafen and spoke to one of the reporters. She gave me what few details she could. Hedda Pohl was in her late sixties, the widow of a businessman, and had two grown children. The police found no motive for the murder, and don't seem to be making much progress."

"Did you contact the local police in Friedrichshafen?"

Erica shook her head. "No, I thought you'd want to do that. But I've put a file together with all the newspaper stories I could get on the murders."

"What about Rauscher's background? Did the news articles say?"

"Just that he was a businessman, that's all."

Volkmann sighed and thought for a moment. "Did you have any luck with the politician, Massow?"

Erica brushed a strand of blond hair from her face. "He's still very much alive. He's got an office in Berlin's Kreuzberg district, a place where mostly poor immigrants live. I phoned his secretary and she penciled you in for an appointment in two days' time. Ten o'clock in Massow's office."

He wondered whether to mention the man at the Zurich airport, but decided not to. He smiled. "Good. Now, how about some more wine?"

She opened another bottle after dinner, and he spent a half hour reading through the file again. When he finished he crossed to the window and looked down. Erica said, "What do you think?"

"There's a detective I know with the Berlin homicide unit who might be able to help me look into Rauscher's murder. I'll call him tomorrow. Good work on the file."

"Thanks."

Volkmann looked down at the parking lot and the street opposite, but he saw nothing suspicious; if he was being watched, whoever was doing the watching was good.

He went to sit beside Erica on the couch, saw the soft nape of her neck as she leaned forward to refill their glasses. He thought she looked very beautiful. When she sat back, she noticed him staring at her.

"What are you looking at, Joe?"

"You."

She didn't blush, but turned away. When she looked back, Volkmann said, "You cared very much for Rudi, didn't you?"

There was a look like pain on her face and she closed her eyes, then opened them again before she answered the question.

"It was more than that. There were times in my life when Rudi was the only person I could turn to. There were certain things I had to face up to, unpleasant things, and he was always there when I needed to talk. Even if only on the telephone. He had a way of lightening everything, of making me laugh."

"What were the times you turned to him?"

"There was a time when I felt ashamed. Ashamed of certain things in my family's past."

"You mean about your father?"

The blue eyes turned to him again, but this time he saw the startled look on her face.

"How did you know?"

"Erica, the German police keep files on most of your country's citizens; you must know that."

"You mean especially on the children of war criminals? Tell me what you know."

He didn't repeat all the details in the file, but there was no need to. "Your father served in the Leibstandarte SS Division. The same division as Heinrich Reimer."

"What else?"

"At the end of the war, as a young man, he escaped to South America. The war-crimes people eventually tracked him down to Buenos Aires, but he died before he could be extradited."

Erica said nothing for several moments. Then finally she said, "The first day I met you, did you know about my father?"

"Yes." He looked at her as she spoke.

"That first time we met, I sensed that you found it difficult being near me. It was in your manner, in the way you looked at me. That maybe you hated me a little. Did you hate me a little, Joe?"

He shook his head. "No, I didn't hate you, Erica. *Hate's* too strong a word."

"But you disliked me, because I was the daughter of an SS officer? Because of what happened to your parents? And now you must distrust me even more because my father was in the same SS division as this man Reimer."

He didn't speak and she looked at his face. "Is that the reason you've been hesitant with me, Joe? Because of who my father was?"

"Yes."

She shook her head. "You know, it's a terrible thing that hate or distrust can be carried from one generation to another. That it can be passed from father to son. Because if that's so, there's no hope for any of us, not ever. Don't you see? You're blaming me for my father's sins."

"I'm not blaming you for anything, Erica."

"Oh, but you are, Joe. I'll tell you something. When I was a little girl, my father was everything to me. But I didn't know what he had done. Killed people in cold blood. Men, women, children. I didn't know that the hands I had held had inflicted so much suffering and death. I trusted him. And when he died, I felt I had lost someone that I had looked up to. I was sixteen when I first heard the rumors. And it was a year later before my mother finally told me the truth. From that moment on, he was no longer the papa I had loved, but a beast. He had let me love him and trust him when he didn't deserve my trust or love. But no, your files will never tell you that. They will never tell you of the pain and suffering and the humiliation of the families and children of these people who shamed Germany so. Do you think every child of every Nazi is proud of his parents' past? Do you, Joe? Some, maybe, but they are sick people. Decent people, ordinary people, they suffered because of what their parents did. I carry a scar around as much as you."

"Tell me."

The blue eyes looked at him intently. "We are both victims. You a victim of your father's past, I of mine. But you cannot see that, Joe. You think all Germans are untrustworthy and barbarians."

"I never said that."

"You don't have to. It's in your eyes. Just like now. You still don't trust me, do you, Joe?"

Volkmann said nothing. Finally he looked at her. "I'll be gone tomorrow for a day or two at most." She didn't ask him where, and then he added, "I was followed in Zurich today."

"What do you mean?"

"Two men in a green Citroën followed me."

"What are you saying?"

"Apart from my office, you were the only one who knew I'd be in Zurich."

He saw Erica's face turn red, and her eyes blazed back at him. "You think I told someone?" When Volkmann didn't reply, she said, "Who could I have told, Joe?"

"I don't know, Erica."

She shook her head. "You can't trust anyone, can you? I won't even dignify your question by telling you what I think of it."

He saw the wet eyes and the struggle to keep back tears, and he wondered if she was genuine. "I'm tired. Good night, Joe."

Not knowing what to say, or whether to believe her, he watched her leave the room.

He slept fitfully, and awakened at two. He crossed to the hallway and opened the door to Erica's room. The bedside lamp was still on, but she was asleep. He could see her bare tanned shoulders, and her blond hair lay strewn about the pillow.

A car hooted in the distance and distracted him. He looked at Erica's sleeping face one last time before he flicked off the lamp and crossed over to the window and pulled back the curtain. The window looked out toward Strasbourg, and the lights of the city peppered the darkness. He thought briefly of the voice-analysis report. Three voices. Three men. A little more substance to go with the shadow, but still things were moving too slowly.

Sie werden alle umgebracht. They'll all be killed.

He went through the taped conversation again in his mind, trying to unravel what he had learned in the last few days, trying to find threads that connected. There were two separate but perhaps parallel lines: what was happening now and what had happened in the past. The people from the Chaco house and what they were doing now. And Tsarkin, and Schmeltz and his past, and the photograph of the young woman taken in 1931, and how they related to the present.

How and why did they connect?

What was the link?

He heard the soft rustle of sheets and turned around, saw her sit up and look at him sleepily in the light washing through the window.

"Joe?"

"It's me. Go back to sleep."

"Some of the things I said . . . I'm sorry, Joe. Can you forgive me?"

Her voice was husky with tiredness, and he could smell the scent of her body as he went to sit on the edge of the bed.

"Maybe it was my fault. Maybe you were right."

She said quietly, "I don't know why I like you, but I do. I think maybe you like me, too. And that maybe the reasons go even deeper than both of us can understand. Rudi told me how the Indians in his country say that God always tries to find a way to take away the stone in our heart, to heal our hurt."

"What do you mean?"

"We're opposites when it comes to our pasts, but really we're two sides of the same coin. My father did terrible wrongs. He and those like him destroyed so many lives, and brought such grief to people like your parents. I'd never met a victim of my father's evil. But now that I know you, I feel I want to help mend that pain. To prove that good can overcome evil, that sins can be redeemed. Does that make sense?"

"I think so."

"Then will you do something for me?"

"What?"

"Try to trust me, Joe."

He placed a hand on her face. She pushed her cheek into his open palm and then kissed his fingers. It seemed to happen so naturally, and as she pulled him toward her, he found her mouth and kissed her. For a long time afterward they lay there, her head on his chest.

Her voice came to him out of the darkness. "Tell me about your father, Joe. Tell me what happened to him."

"Why do you want to know?"

"Because I want to know everything about you."

He looked away, toward darkness, toward nothingness. "When the Germans came to the Sudetenland, my father's family moved to Poland, to a village near Cracow. He and his parents and his young sister. Then the war came and the Einsatzgrüppen were moving through the villages, rounding up and killing Jews. They were the special groups of mobile killing squads the Nazis used before they organized the extermination camps. One day my father's parents went out to get some food. He never saw them again.

"My father was thirteen. His sister was six. On the fifth day when his parents didn't come back, he learned they'd been rounded up and killed. He decided to try to reach Budapest, where his mother had relatives. He got some food and wrapped up his little sister in warm clothes, and they set off.

"On the third day, near the border, one of the killing squads caught up with them. They took them into a forest clearing with a group of other Jews and made them stand in front of a shallow pit. My father knew what was going to happen. His sister was trembling and crying, and so was he. When she reached out to her brother for comfort, an SS guard tore her hand away, and told her not to move. But she was just a child, confused and distraught with fear, and when she reached out again, this time the SS man shot her in cold blood.

"After that, they made my father kneel down in front of the pit. The guards were drunk. The one who shot my father in the face wounded him but didn't kill him. My father lay in the pit with his sister's body, pretending to be dead.

"When the killers covered all the bodies with clay and left, my father lay there, bleeding, too shocked to move, barely able to breathe. When it was dark, he managed to free himself from the pit and the tangle of corpses. He buried his sister in a shallow grave and wandered the mountains for days with a bullet in his face. This time he made it to Budapest and his relatives.

"Then the Germans came again. His relatives were taken away. My father was caught in a roundup, and they sent him to Dachau, then to Belsen. The others were sent to the ovens. My father survived, but he could never forget what had happened to his parents and sister."

He lay silent in the darkness, and he could hear Erica breathing. He couldn't tell if she was crying, and he didn't speak or make a sound. It was such a long-ago pain that he couldn't cry, and all he could do was think of his father.

It seemed the silence went on forever in the darkness, and it was a long time before her hand came to touch his face. But Erica said nothing. There was nothing to say.

27

ASUNCIÓN. SUNDAY, DECEMBER 18, 2:45 P.M.

Thick, juicy steaks and fat sausages sizzled on the charcoal barbecue, and sunlight washed the garden.

Vellares Sanchez gazed down with no appetite at one of the slabs of meat as he speared it with a fork, turned it over to reveal the pink and bloodied rare underneath. Many things were bothering him. Many things, but all connected to one thing.

The face of Rudi Hernandez flashed before his eyes. Lying on the morgue slab, white sheet pulled back, wounds uncovered.

Sanchez grimaced and looked away from the unappetizing meat toward the sunlit garden. Clusters of neighbors, friends, and relatives stood chatting, drinks in hand. A special day. Maria, his youngest daughter, had made her Communion.

Innocent girls in white Communion frocks and boys in ill-fitting suits sipped lemonade and ate chocolate cake and traipsed about the lawn, bored now that the ceremony was over. He saw Maria wave at him and smile. Sanchez waved and smiled back.

The girl was very pretty, a tribute to her mother's good looks. One day the boys would be falling over themselves to catch her eye. But not yet. Innocence was to be savored.

The girl came up to him, flouncing her white frock. "Is the food ready yet, Papa? I'm hungry."

Sanchez patted her head of dark, curly hair. "Not yet, my sweet." He saw his wife, Rosario, coming toward him from the patio. She had a frown on her face.

He tapped his daughter's shoulder. "Do Papa a favor, precious. Go see if everyone is okay for drinks."

The girl nodded and skipped away.

Rosario came up beside him, still frowning. "I thought this was your day off."

"It is."

"Is everything okay?"

He nodded. "The food's almost ready."

"I didn't mean the food. Detective Cavales is inside. I asked him to join us, but he said no. He'd rather speak to you in private."

"Then I had better see him. Do me a favor. Take care of the steaks."

His wife knit her brow. "And I thought you were going to be free today."

"So did I." He kissed her cheek. "A policeman's lot is not a happy one."

"Nor his wife's. But you should have told me that before you asked me to marry you."

"And risk losing such a beautiful woman?"

She smiled back at him, picked up two cans of beer from the buffet table, and handed them to her husband.

"Take one in to Cavales. He looks as though he could do with a drink."

He took the beers, crossed to the patio, and stepped inside. The house was cool after the heat of the garden. He crossed to where the detective stood and handed him the beer.

"Compliments of Rosario. She said you looked like you needed one."

Cavales nodded. "It's hot." He looked toward the lawn. "Nice day for a barbecue."

"Maria's Communion," Sanchez explained. Cavales was single. No ties. No responsibilities. But a good cop. Ambitious, in a quiet way. And thorough.

"So," Sanchez said finally, "what brings you to this neck of the woods on my one day off? It's not a social call."

Cavales shook his head. He appeared tired. Like Sanchez, he had been working hard. Days and late evenings working on the case.

"I've been over at Tsarkin's house again."

Sanchez sipped the cold beer. "Go on."

"I know we searched it three, maybe four times and found nothing."

Sanchez smiled. "But you wanted to pick over the bones?"

Cavales nodded. "Something like that."

"So what did you find that the rest of us couldn't?"

"What makes you think I found something?"

"You see enough of my face at the office. And I'm not such an attractive man."

Cavales smiled. "You're right."

"So, tell me."

"I went through all the rooms again. Top to bottom. Just in case we missed something." Cavales paused. "We did."

"And what did we miss?"

"Photographs."

Sanchez blinked. "Explain."

"Photographs. Everybody keeps them. Albums. Of friends. Acquaintances. Relatives."

Sanchez shook his head. "There were none. I remember. Except one. A photograph of Tsarkin himself. On a dressing table in his bedroom."

"That's what I mean. There were no other photographs besides the one in the bedroom," Cavales said quietly. "Old people. They always got photographs."

Sanchez smiled. The man had a perceptive mind. "Go on."

"I spoke to Tsarkin's butler about it. He was very uncomfortable when I mentioned the photographs. Like he had something to hide."

"And did he?"

"You bet." Cavales put down his beer and lit a cigarette, offered one to Sanchez, who accepted. "I told him if there was anything he hadn't told us, he could be in big trouble. I told him I'd take him down to the station. He got upset. Said he'd done nothing wrong."

"But what had he done?"

"He said the day after Tsarkin committed suicide, and before we thoroughly searched the property, a man came to the house. An acquaintance of Tsarkin's, a businessman. He asked what the police had done and wanted to know if there were any papers left behind by Tsarkin. When the butler said no, he said he wanted to look just in case. The butler protested, but the man persuaded him it might be better if he cooperated."

"This man threatened him?"

Cavales shrugged. "Implied, rather than outright."

"Continue."

"He searched the house, then took away some photograph albums Tsarkin kept."

"And?"

"That's it. He also ordered the butler to tell no one what he'd done."

Sanchez sighed, sat on the edge of the chair by the window. "Did you get a name?"

Cavales smiled and nodded. "After a little friendly persuasion."

"The name?"

"Franz Lieber."

"Who is he?"

"All I know right now is that he was an acquaintance of Tsarkin's. But the name's obviously German."

Sanchez glanced toward the sunlit gardens and the cheerful knots of visitors. Maria was comparing dresses with another girl. His wife stood among a circle of female friends, laughing. He loved that woman, loved her to distraction. Many times he wished he weren't a cop, had chosen a different vocation so that he could spend more time with his family.

He turned to Cavales. "Give me an hour. I'll meet you at the office. I want Lieber's address and information on his background."

"I'm checking already. Two of the day shift are working on it."

Sanchez nodded. "An hour then."

Cavales left quietly without finishing his beer; Sanchez moved closer to the window.

Sunshine swamped the lawn. The sound of laughter reached him. A day to enjoy. Rosario wouldn't like it if he left, but he had work to do. He checked his watch; half an hour, then he'd drive to the office.

He stubbed out his cigarette and went to rejoin his guests.

4:35 P.M.

The pickup bar wasn't far from the Plaza Uruguaya.

Despite its shabby exterior, inside the décor was sumptuous. Coral-blue stucco walls, expensive cotton-print drapes. Upstairs were private rooms with silk-sheeted beds. Saunas and steaming showers for clients.

The women were equally attractive, reputedly the prettiest in Asunción. And the most expensive.

Lieber and his male companion sipped their champagne as they enjoyed the array of gorgeous women seated around the bar. Two dusky-skinned beauties approached.

Lieber found his wallet, peeled off some notes. "Not now, later, after we've discussed our business."

The women smiled, took the money, blowing departing kisses as they left their customers in peace, for now.

"Well, Pablo . . . happy?"

The man opposite Lieber was small, wiry, and seedy-looking. His name was Pablo Arcades. For ten of his thirty-five years he had been a police officer, an invaluable acquaintance of Lieber's. Especially since the man had two universal vices: money and women. As vices, they were weaknesses to be exploited.

Arcades grinned, his weasel eyes fixed on the women's curvy, retreating figures.

"You know me. I could hang out in places like this all day. You brought the money?"

"Afterward. First, let's talk."

6:02 P.M.

Lieber drove back through the darkening Asunción streets.

He slammed shut his mobile phone after he made the call. He remembered the woman's name from the list. He verified that. Yes. She was one of those in the web. She would need to be contacted as a matter of urgency, of that much Lieber was certain. And decisions would need to be made: take her out of the web or keep her in.

The rest of Arcades's information he would pass on. It would have to be acted on at once, Volkmann and Sanchez dealt with. Volkmann's part he couldn't understand: a British DSE officer, and not German. If anything, it should have been German. Lieber shook his head in confusion; the woman would be able to explain. He didn't understand why she hadn't been contacted before now. What was she up to?

In his mind he went through the checklist of what needed to be done. First contact security, then Kruger in Mexico City, to fill them in. There was business to be discussed with old Haider and the Brazilian, Ernesto. And there would be visitors, old faces calling to pay their respects, and offering their advice for the days ahead.

Lieber turned the Mercedes into the driveway of his house, tires skewing the gravel.

Out of the corner of his eye he caught sight of two men standing behind the open gates. Lieber, startled by their presence, was about to slam on the brakes when he saw the lights were on in the porch. Two more men stood there, a white car parked outside the front door.

Panic gripped him as he came to a sharp halt in front of the car.

Lieber climbed out warily as the two men came quickly forward.

"What's going on? Who are you?" Lieber demanded.

One of the two was a large, hulking man, his grubby suit loose on his oversized body.

"Señor Lieber, I presume?"

Lieber said nothing.

The big man smiled thinly. "My name's Sanchez. Captain Vellares Sanchez."

28

ASUNCIÓN. 6:32 P.M.

Every light inside the house appeared to be on, the mestizo butler nowhere to be seen.

They were in the study. The two detectives and Lieber. The big detective smoked a cigarette as his companion sifted through the contents of Lieber's walnut desk. The locks had been forced; papers and documents lay scattered on the floor.

Lieber looked at the big detective palely. "You have no right . . ."

"Señor, I have every right."

"May I remind you that I am a personal friend of the police commissioner's . . ."

"And might I remind you that my search warrant is in order."

Lieber examined the warrant, signed by a magistrate. "If you'd only tell me what it is you're looking for . . . ?"

"I told you already."

"I don't know what photographs you're talking about. All I know is that my property has been damaged. And that this is a flagrant abuse of—"

"Please, señor. Spare me." The hooded, sleepy eyes regarded Lieber carefully. "If you simply tell us where the photograph albums are, it would help matters."

"I really don't know what you're talking about."

Sanchez ignored the faked innocence on Lieber's face. "As I explained already, they were taken from the house of a friend of yours the day after he killed himself. Tsarkin's butler already told us. Really, señor, you're wasting my time."

Lieber swallowed. "I refuse to speak until I've contacted my lawyer."

"As you wish. You have a safe in the house?"

"A safe?"

"A safe for personal belongings. Businessmen usually have one, and you own several businesses in Asunción, señor. An import-export agency. A property-development company." Sanchez paused, letting Lieber know he'd done his homework, saw the man's eyebrows rise. "So, do you have a safe here in the house?"

"That's none of your business."

"Señor, you can be agreeable and cooperate. To do otherwise will certainly not help your situation."

"And what is my situation?"

The big man scratched his ear. "If I'm unsatisfied with your replies, I will arrest you on suspicion of being an accessory to the murder of one Rudi Hernandez, journalist. And two other murders also."

"That's quite ridiculous," Lieber said hoarsely. "I don't know what you're talking about."

The detective ignored Lieber's words. "You haven't answered my question. You have a safe?"

Lieber considered, then slowly took a set of keys from his pocket. "In the bedroom upstairs facing onto the driveway, you'll find a painting. A Vermeer copy. Behind it you will—"

Sanchez took the keys. "I know."

He handed them to the detectives. The men left. Lieber heard their footsteps ascend the stairs.

Left alone with the big man, Lieber glanced around, said amicably, "Amigo, there must be some mistake. You know, I have friends in high places, people who could—"

The detective raised his hand to silence Lieber. "Please. Spare me." He sat down, produced a cigarette, lit it. "My men will search the rest of the house again. This may take some time."

"My lawyer—"

"I suggest you remain silent," Sanchez interrupted, smiling thinly. "I'm sure you are quite happy to do that."

Lieber pursed his lips and said nothing.

It took almost an hour of waiting, yet he felt strangely confident. There wasn't a shred in the house to incriminate him. Nothing to connect him to the journalist and the woman.

He saw the two detectives come into the room as he sipped a scotch. One of them carried an album of photographs. Lieber frowned. It was an old album he kept in his bedroom. It hadn't been added to in years.

He saw Sanchez flick through the cellophaned leaves. He pursed his lips and looked up, walked over to where Lieber stood.

Sanchez held up the album. "This is yours?"

Lieber hesitated, then said, "Yes, it belongs to me."

Sanchez pointed to a photograph in the album. Lieber swallowed. "This snapshot," Sanchez said. "Where was it taken?"

The picture was of a white house. Three men together, Lieber one of them. Jungle cutting in on the right of the frame.

"I can't remember," he said hoarsely.

"Think. In the Chaco perhaps?"

"I told you. I can't remember. It's an old photograph."

The detective saw the look on Lieber's fleshy face and pointed again to the photograph. "The man on the left is you. The other two . . . who are they?"

Lieber shook his head as he saw the detective's finger point out the men in the photograph, taken many years before, one stocky, dark-haired, and young, the other older, tall, silver-haired, handsome.

"I told you. It was taken a long time ago. I don't recall."

Lieber saw the detective stare at him, frustration on his face. The man was unsure of himself, Lieber could tell. Searching. But lost.

"Señor, on the evening of November twenty-fifth and the early morning of November twenty-sixth, where were you?"

Lieber frowned. "I was at home, attending to important paperwork."

"Alone?"

"Apart from one of my staff, yes."

"No doubt your staff will attest to this if necessary?"

"No doubt, yes."

Sanchez glared at the man.

One of the detectives to whom Sanchez had given the keys to the safe returned, shook his head as he handed them back. Sanchez grimaced, placed the keys on the coffee table in front of Lieber.

Lieber said, "Have your men finished?"

"For now. Sí."

"You intend on arresting me?"

"No."

"Then I want you and your people off my property." Lieber stood to his full height, towering over the other man. "Your commissioner will hear about this intrusion of my privacy. Now leave. At once."

Sanchez put down the album on the study desk. "Señor, I will be back. Again and again, if necessary. I wish to assure you of that."

"That's harassment."

"No, señor." Sanchez smiled grimly. "I prefer to call it thoroughness."

Lieber felt the anger rise in him. "Be assured, your commissioner will hear from me."

Sanchez's smile broadened. "Yes, I'm certain he will. But you see, señor, there is a certain matter of a tape. A tape recording of a conversation in a certain hotel. I'm sure you know what I'm talking about. So be assured, you will see me again."

The smugness vanished. Perplexed, Lieber felt the blood rise uncontrollably to his cheeks, saw the detective's hooded eyes stare at him, search for a reaction.

He checked himself, then said hoarsely, "Go."

Forty minutes later, Lieber was on the Plaza del Héroes. He parked the Mercedes and observed the street. So far as he could tell, he wasn't being followed. He decided a public phone would be safer.

He found one in a hotel near the plaza. He made two calls, listened to the incredulous voices as he sweated in the hot kiosk. He kept the conversations as short as possible, all the time his eyes searching the hotel lobby to make sure he wasn't being watched. He told them his plans and received their immediate approval.

The third call he made to an unlisted number on the outskirts of the city. Lieber told the man what he wanted done, then put down the telephone and waited for the reply call.

It came less than five minutes later. He listened to the voice and noted the instructions. A minute later, he stepped from the hotel and walked back toward his car. His eyes scanned the busy streets for anyone following him.

No one did.

Sanchez stood at the office window looking down at the fronds of the palm trees along the *calle*, a mug of steaming coffee in one hand, a cigarette in the other.

Almost nine o'clock. Traffic streaked below, the blue-and-whites pulling up outside every now and then, disgorging their nightly cargo. Hookers. Pimps. Thieves.

He heard the door open loudly and turned. Cavales came in.

Sanchez said, "Well?"

"It was just like you said, he went to make a call. I had four teams following him. Twenty minutes after we left, he drove to the Plaza del Héroes and went into a small hotel, the Riva. We think he made just a couple of telephone calls, but we can't be sure. The woman watching him said he was pretty uncomfortable, so she didn't push it."

"Go on."

"He drove back home, stayed half an hour. Then he had his man-servant drive him to the outskirts. He walked for five minutes, then hailed a taxi. He changed taxis twice. The second took him to the airport, where he picked up a suitcase at the left luggage. We tailed the servant, too. He drove to the airport after he dropped Lieber off and stashed the suitcase in the left luggage, where Lieber picked it up."

"You managed to check the suitcase?"

Cavales nodded. "It contained a couple of shirts and a suit. Underwear and toiletries. The usual stuff. Nothing interesting." Cavales paused. "But there's something else."

Sanchez raised his eyebrows but said nothing.

"He picked up a package at the information desk, along with the ticket for his luggage. Two of our people followed him to the departure area."

"They didn't stop him?"

"There was something much more interesting to consider."

"Tell me."

"He had a passport in a different name and checked onto a flight for São Paulo, with the first connection to Mexico City tomorrow night. I guess the passport was the package he picked up. He must be running scared."

"The name he used?"

"Monck. Julius Monck."

Sanchez blinked.

Cavales said, "You want me to get immigration in São Paulo

to pick him up?" He checked his watch. "The flight doesn't land for another hour. Possession of an illegal passport is one thing. Using it is another. On that alone, he's got some questions to answer."

Sanchez's eyebrows knit closely together, as if the act of thinking was painful. "Bring me the map from the wall."

Cavales unhooked the large hanging map of South America, placed it on Sanchez's desk.

The big detective stared down at the multicolored patterns on the laminated, nicotine-stained cardboard, then traced a finger from the northeast, Chaco, to the Brazilian border.

"The report from the radar people at Bahia Negra. They said the flight they vectored disappeared toward Corumba, over the border."

"Sí."

Sanchez's finger traced a line on the map. "It's only a short distance from there to Campo Grande. There's an airport at Campo Grande. With a shuttle service to São Paulo, I believe."

Cavales scratched his chin. "I don't see the point."

"From Paulo there's a connecting flight to Mexico City. Lieber's destination. Maybe the people from the Chaco house took that route. Maybe they went to Mexico City also. Now Lieber's worried. He needs to talk to them. In person."

Cavales smiled. "Either that or Lieber's running for good."

Sanchez shrugged. "He's pretty scared about something. You saw the look on his face when I mentioned the taped conversation—it really worried him." Sanchez thought for a moment, then said, "Get onto Chief Inspector Eduardo Gonzales in Mexico City. Inform him of Lieber's likely arrival there in the name of Monck."

"Is Gonzales a friend of yours?"

Sanchez nodded. "We met at a police conference in Caracas. Have a photograph of Lieber wired to him. Lieber's connecting tickets are in the name of Monck, but just in case he has another passport, they should be able to identify him from the photo. And get onto São

Paulo, too. Ask them to watch Lieber when he arrives, make sure he makes the connecting flight he's booked on. Ask them to use their best undercover people. I don't want it blown."

"You want this Gonzales to pick up Lieber?"

"No. Simply followed. I want to know where he goes. Who he meets."

Cavales nodded, went to leave.

"And Cavales—"

"Sí?"

"The first available connecting flight to Mexico City. Book two seats." Sanchez smiled thinly. "But not the same route as Lieber, obviously."

Cavales smiled back, and left.

Sanchez opened his wallet and stared down at the photograph. It was the one he had removed from the album in Lieber's house. He had pocketed it deftly. Theft, but justifiable. He doubted that Lieber had noticed; the man had been too distracted.

Now he placed the picture on his desk and blinked. He studied the two men flanking Lieber. From the cut of the clothes, he guessed Lieber hadn't lied; the photograph was taken a long time ago. Ten years at least, but difficult to say. He saw a veranda behind the three men, painted white like the house in the Chaco jungle. His gut told him it was the same house.

He ran a hand through his thinning hair and sighed now as he thought of the work ahead. He would telephone his wife and tell her of his plans. No more than a day or two in Mexico City, if he was lucky. He stared down at the photograph of the three men once more as he picked up the receiver and went to dial his home number.

Rosario would understand.

This one was for Rudi Hernandez.

This one was personal.

29

Volkmann telephoned Jakob Fischer at Berlin homicide, but the policeman who answered said that Fischer was out of the office and wouldn't return until late that afternoon. Volkmann left a message saying he would call back later.

That afternoon he got a seat on the Lufthansa flight to Berlin. It was after four and growing dark when he landed at Tegel airport. Half an hour later when he made the call, Jakob Fischer came on the line.

"It's been a long time, Joe. I got your message. How are you, my friend?"

"Good. And you?"

"Six months from retirement and I can't wait to throw off the harness."

"I need a favor, Jakob."

Volkmann explained about Herbert Rauscher, and when he had finished, Fischer said, "Tell me exactly what you want, Joe."

"I'd like to know what your people have on Rauscher's death. And whatever background information you've got on him. I'd prefer to keep it unofficial and low-key for now."

"You think this Rauscher was involved in any criminal activity?"

"I don't know."

"Okay. It's out of my area, Joe, but I'll try to get a look at the file anyway. We keep most stuff on computer, so I may be able to get access."

"I'd appreciate it, Jakob."

It was almost two hours later when Fischer called back.

"I'm afraid I only got limited access to the file on the computer,

Joe. But I spoke to one of the homicide detectives at the station working the case, and he told me what he could."

"You want to tell me over the line?"

"I think it's best we meet. How about a beer?"

The main bar in the Schweizerhof was almost empty. Detective Jakob Fischer was in his sixties, but his walk was still brisk, his blue eyes bright. He shook hands with Volkmann and slumped into one of the big armchairs opposite.

They ordered club sandwiches and beer as they chatted about old times, and when Fischer finished his sandwich, he wiped his mouth and said, "What's this case about, Joe?"

Volkmann told him the bare facts and Fischer said, "Okay, let me tell you what I've got. Background first, just to fill you in. Herbert Rauscher was born in Leipzig. Sixty-eight years old at his last birthday. Moved to Berlin twenty years ago. Single, never married, respectable but a bit of a playboy with an eye for the ladies. Ran a small publishing firm that published tourist guides. Never in any trouble with the law."

The detective paused. "Then six months ago, someone murdered him. It happened late at night, about eleven. Two shots to the head. A close hit, according to the detective I spoke to."

"What did forensics say?"

"A silenced nine-mil weapon was used. That's all I've got."

"Where was he killed?"

"At his apartment near the Pergamon Museum. His girlfriend came home and found him. The file says she was checked out but came up clean."

"Where's the girlfriend now? Any idea?"

"I'm trying to find out. Her name's Monika Worch. That's all I know."

"I'd like to talk with her if you find her. Did your guys turn up anything else?"

The detective shook his head. "They tried the usual angles. People in the same business as Rauscher, but that led nowhere. But Rauscher may have known his killer, because there was no sign of anyone breaking into his apartment and it happened in the front room. A janitor on duty in the building said he heard nothing and saw nothing. Same with the neighbors."

"Was Rauscher political?"

Fischer frowned and shook his head. "Not that our people know of. He seemed more interested in making money than in politics. Why, do you think Rauscher's death was political?"

"I don't know, Jakob. Is Rauscher's apartment still unoccupied?"

"I believe so."

"Can I take a look?"

Fischer smiled. "I guessed you'd want to. My car's outside. Finish your beer, and then I'll drive you over. We'll see if my ID can get us in."

The apartment was in one of the luxury modern blocks the Soviets once built for their personnel in East Berlin decades ago. It was still well kept, with a neat garden at the entrance.

Jakob Fischer ignored the intercom system and banged authoritatively on the glass doors like a true policeman. When the night porter appeared, Fischer flashed his ID and told the man he wanted to see Herbert Rauscher's apartment. The man was intimidated by the authority of Fischer's voice and badge, and scurried off to find the keys.

When he came back with them, Fischer told him that he and his companion would go up to the apartment by themselves. The creaking elevator took them to the penthouse on the eighth floor.

A sign pasted on the door by the Berlin police forbade anyone to enter the apartment, and a third lock had been fitted on the door. It took Fischer almost ten minutes to open the third lock with a filed key he kept on a metal ring.

When they stepped inside, Volkmann was surprised by the lavishness of the apartment. There was a panoramic view of the granite

Pergamon Museum, and in the distance they saw the illuminated top of the Brandenburg Gate.

The apartment was expensively furnished with black leather furniture. There was a Sony TV and DVD player in a corner and an expensive Bang & Olufsen sound system by the window.

Volkmann saw the ruby-red bloodstain near the coffee table. A big, dark patch, and it looked as if someone had once spilled red wine there. The police hadn't left the rooms in disarray, and he had a good look around the apartment.

The bedroom closets were full of expensive suits and monogrammed silk shirts. He guessed Rauscher's girlfriend had cleared out all her belongings. Nothing hinted that Rauscher had any involvement in politics, and the only books were glossy coffee-table types.

"Nothing much here that helps, is there?"

Jakob Fischer shook his head, then checked his watch. "I guess not, Joe. It's getting late. How about I drive you back to your hotel? I'll be in touch as soon as I've got a bead on Rauscher's girlfriend."

30

BERLIN. THURSDAY. DECEMBER 15

He took a taxi to Walter Massow's office in Kreuzberg the next morning.

It was in a drab, prewar building right in the middle of a block of neglected tenements that teemed with Turkish and Asian immigrants. The entrance was daubed with painted slogans that someone had painted over again, and the windows on the first two floors were boarded up.

A young man was seated behind a desk on the ground floor. He cautiously checked Volkmann's identity card, then he pressed a button under his desk, and a door sprang open that led upstairs.

Four flights up, a young secretary went to fetch Massow. He was in his late fifties. Big, powerfully built, wearing glasses, and his gentle manner and soft voice belied his physique.

"I'm Walter Massow."

He shook Volkmann's hand firmly and led the way into a cluttered office with a row of filing cabinets set against the peeling walls. The window overlooked a small park, several blocks of run-down apartments opposite.

The secretary brought them coffee, and when she had left, Massow selected a toothpick from a small cup on the desk and played it around in his mouth as he looked across.

"May I ask what this is about, Herr Volkmann?"

Volkmann kept it to a minimum. He told Massow he was investigating the murder of a right-wing extremist named Dieter Winter and that his inquiries had revealed a connection with a threat to Massow's life.

Massow didn't seem worried as he sat back farther in his chair, and it creaked under his weight.

"May I ask why a British DSE officer is investigating this case? Surely it would be an internal matter for our police."

"The weapon that killed Winter was used in the shooting of a British-born businessman in Hamburg."

"I see."

"Have you ever heard of Dieter Winter before, Herr Massow?"

The big man shook his head firmly. "No, I haven't."

"Do you have any idea why Winter might have wanted you killed?"

Massow smiled as he chewed on the toothpick. "You say he was a right-wing extremist?"

"That's right."

"If I had a cent for every death threat or hate letter I received from people like that, by now I'd be on the rich list, living the good life and smoking Havanas." Massow suddenly stood up. "Let me show you something."

The politician crossed to a filing cabinet and removed a file. He flicked through a thick sheaf of papers and crossed back to his desk, where he spread the papers out.

"Letters," explained Massow. "Rather unpleasant letters. These are copies—the police have the originals—not that it means much. They never find these people."

Massow selected one and handed it across. The single-sheet copy page had been constructed from cutout newspaper-headline type. Across the top of the page a single line said: JEW LOVER. WE'RE WATCHING YOU.

Volkmann looked at it, and Massow handed across another. A single page but handwritten, the letters big and bold and threatening: IMMIGRANTS OUT! MASSOW, YOU'RE DEAD!

Massow said, "Those are some of the milder threats. There are others much worse." He smiled. "It comes with the territory, as they say."

Massow sat back again and gestured to the window. "This area I represent, Herr Volkmann, the people here are mainly of immigrant stock. Turks. Poles. Slavs. Asians. Greeks. People from the African countries. I do my best for them. But there are those, as there are in every country, who think people like my constituents should be sent back to wherever they or their parents came from. No matter that they have perhaps been born here and are as good citizens as the next."

Massow shook his head. "It happens in every country you care to mention. France. Germany. England. The United States. And no doubt, if the extremists and racists had the chance, they would send people like me back with them." He shrugged his big shoulders. "Now and then the thugs who call themselves Germans throw a pipe bomb through our windows or paint graffiti on our building. I'm not saying such things don't worry us, but we've become used to it."

Volkmann gestured to the letters. "Who are the people who send you these?"

"People like your friend Winter, I imagine. Extremists. Neo-Nazis. Immigrant haters. People haters. Lunatics." Massow shrugged, smiled. "I hope I haven't left anyone out."

"Have you ever heard of a man called Wolfgang Lubsch?"

Massow frowned. "The terrorist?"

"Yes."

"Yes, I've heard of him."

"How well do you know him?"

Massow smiled guardedly. "Herr Volkmann, the man is a wanted terrorist. Years ago when he was a student, I met him briefly at an immigrant rally. He's not a friend, if that's what you're implying. And on that subject, I'll say no more."

"And the death threat I spoke about?"

"What about it?"

"Do you have any idea who might have been behind it?"

"No, I don't. Except the kind of lunatic fringe I just talked about. Like I said, I receive so many threats." Massow smiled. "In fact, if they stopped, I might get worried that the racists and bigots have come to like me. And that would really frighten me."

"Why would these people want you dead?"

"Because to the extremists and racists, I'm a thorn in their side."

Massow stood up, took a step closer to the window. In the bright winter sunshine, his clothes appeared shabby, his big, kindly face creased with worry lines.

"Do you have any idea how immigrants are treated in this country, Volkmann? There are five million people of immigrant stock in Germany. In France, in Italy, there's a similar problem, but my real concern is Germany. Many of them came here in the years after the war, when there was a labor shortage. They came as laborers and did the dirty work most Germans refused. They settled here and had families and made a life for themselves. Now they are almost seven percent of the population, a figure greater than the Jews before the last war. But unlike the majority of Jews of that time, many are caught in a poverty trap.

"The laws demand that every worker be treated equally, but the reality is different. Wages among immigrants are lower than average, and unemployment runs at twenty-five percent. So they live in ghettos and immigrant hostels. The problem, then, is real and troubling. But even more troubling is Germany's response. When the racists and neo-Nazis provoked violence, it caused not only indignation, but demands for a limit to the number of foreigners entering this country. As if the victims were at fault and not those people persecuting them."

Massow frowned. "Now, when there is racist terror, the politicians say they don't have enough police. Yet when the terrorists rack this country, the police manage to guard almost every important businessman and executive in the land."

Massow looked out at the bright sunlight, then back at Volkmann. "When you leave this office, take a walk through the streets. Look at the living conditions. Look at the faces of the people living in this neighborhood. Really look. They are frightened people. Frightened of the shaved-headed toughs who attack their homes. Frightened of the future. What you see outside is a tinderbox waiting to be ignited. Because someday these people are going to raise their voices and organize themselves and fight back. And then this whole country will be set ablaze."

Massow shook his head ruefully. "Sometimes I wonder if things have really changed in this country."

"What do you mean?"

"Before the last war, the rally call of the Nazis was *Judenfrei*: free of Jews. These days, it's *Ausländerfrei*: free of foreigners. Today there are hardly any Jews left in Germany. But there are immigrants who might become the nation's next scapegoats. And the same undercurrents are there. Because these people are not Aryans with blond hair and blue eyes, they are not considered Germans." Massow sat forward. "Let me give you an example. One ultraright party used a simple anti-immigrant slogan during the last elections here. 'The Boat Is Full,' they said. And for that, they gained six more seats in Parliament."

Massow sat down again and said, "Forgive me, this isn't what you came to talk about. You asked about this man Winter, and I ended up giving you a lecture on what's wrong with this country."

"You're certain you never heard of Dieter Winter?"

"Never."

He walked back through the streets to the U-Bahn station.

The suburb was a busy maze of narrow streets, and as he walked, he did what Massow had suggested. Berlin's Kreuzberg had been a working-class area since before the last war and the immigrant tenements he passed were derelict and shabby.

Near the station he bought a bratwurst from a Turkish vendor, and as he stood eating and waiting for the train, he noticed the station walls daubed with racist slogans, and here and there, the hastily painted swastikas.

The people on the platform had the same dark, haunted brown eyes of his father, and for a moment Volkmann thought of the faces in the old black-and-white photographs of the ghettos at Warsaw and Cracow.

He pushed the thought from his mind as the train pulled into the station, the doors opened, and he stepped on board.

When he got back to the hotel there was a message from Jakob Fischer to call him. He did so and heard Fischer's voice.

"I found Rauscher's girlfriend, Joe."

"Where is she?"

"Still in Berlin."

"You've got a telephone number, Jakob?"

"Sure. I rang her. She didn't want to talk about her boyfriend's murder. But I told her I just wanted a friendly chat at her place, that otherwise I'd have to bring her to the station."

"What did she say?"

"She'll talk to us. She'll be at home by eight. Can I pick you up about then?"

"Sure. I'll be in the foyer."

The apartment was south of the city and when they came out of the elevator on the third floor, Fischer rang the buzzer.

She was about forty, with long blond hair, and very good-looking. She wore tight black ski pants and flat shoes, her white T-shirt tucked tightly into her pants.

Jakob Fischer showed the woman his ID, but she didn't pay much attention to it and she hardly looked at Volkmann before she led them into the living room.

"I told you on the telephone: I told your people everything I know. Don't you get it?"

"I understand, Frau Worch, but my colleague would like to ask you a few questions. We won't take up much of your time."

Volkmann addressed the woman, who looked back at him indifferently. "How long did you know your boyfriend?"

"Two years."

Volkmann looked at her eyes. "Did you ever hear of a man named Dieter Winter?"

"No."

"Are you sure your boyfriend didn't know of anyone with that name?"

She shrugged. "I really don't know."

Volkmann went through the other names, but the woman just shook her head. "I didn't know any of Herbert's acquaintances. Only a couple of the people he worked with."

The woman looked back at him steadily and Volkmann guessed she was telling the truth.

"Was he involved with any political group?"

"What do you mean?"

"Did he ever express any political opinions to you?"

The woman frowned, then shrugged. "Not to me he didn't."

"Was he ever racist in his remarks? Did he ever say how he felt about the immigrants in this country?"

She stared at Fischer. "What is this?"

"Please just answer the questions."

She looked back at Volkmann. "No."

"Did he have any friends or enemies who were extremists, neo-Nazis, or terrorists?"

The woman laughed. "Is this some kind of joke?"

Jakob Fischer said, "Just answer the question."

"Herbert didn't mix with anyone like that."

"What about his background? Did he ever talk about his past? His parents? His family?"

"Once or twice, sure. But he didn't say much."

"Tell me what he did say."

"His mother died when he was twenty. His father he never knew."

"Why?"

The woman shrugged again. "He died in some camp."

"A concentration camp?"

She grinned. "No. One of those places in Siberia the Russians sent our soldiers to after the war."

"Why was Rauscher's father sent there?"

"He was some kind of Nazi officer. Herbert only mentioned it when he was drunk."

"What did he say?"

"That his father was wounded in Berlin at the end of the war and captured by the Russians. That they sent him to one of their camps in Siberia."

"Do you remember anything else he said about his father?"

"No. He didn't really talk much about his past." The woman sighed impatiently at Volkmann. "Look, is this going to take much longer?"

"One more question. Do you have any idea why your boyfriend was murdered?"

"No, I don't. And I told your people that a hundred times already."

Volkmann looked at Jakob Fischer and nodded. Fischer stood up and said, "Thanks for your time."

He had one drink in the hotel bar with Fischer, then he walked him to the foyer.

"I appreciate your help, Jakob."

"I wish it was more constructive. What about Rauscher's father, Joe? You going to check up on his background?"

"There's not much point. There could have been hundreds of officers named Rauscher but I'd need a date of birth and a Christian name to take it further."

"Anyhow, let me know how it works out."

"Sure. I'll call you. And thanks again, Jakob."

"It's been good seeing you again, Joe."

He watched Fischer go, and then he went up to his room and poured himself a scotch. He opened the window and stood at the cold balcony.

None of it made any sense to him. If it was true about Rauscher's father being a Nazi officer, then Rauscher would have been the least likely target for Winter's people. Besides, Herbert Rauscher would have been a child when his father had been captured by the Russians and probably never knew the man.

He phoned Erica at the apartment before he undressed for bed and told her about his lack of progress. "What about the woman, Hedda Pohl, Joe?"

"We can drive down to Lake Konstanz tomorrow, see if we can turn up anything."

"When will you be back?"

"I'm taking the first flight tomorrow."

There was a pause, then Erica said, "Joe . . . ?"

"Yes?"

"I miss you."

31

Volkmann could see the snowcapped mountains of Switzerland across Lake Konstanz as they drove into the pretty lakeside town of Friedrichshafen. He parked the Ford, and they walked along the lakefront toward the police station. Christmas trees twinkled in the windows of the old Bavarian-style houses, a dusting of snow falling.

"How do you want to handle this?" Erica asked.

He smiled and flashed the press ID. "The same way we did with Lubsch. We're a couple of journalists on a case. Just be yourself, working a story."

Two officers were on duty at the desk. Volkmann showed his ID and asked to speak with one of the senior detectives on duty. It was ten minutes before a middle-aged man appeared from one of the offices. He was big and ruddy-faced, his beer belly protruding over his belted trousers. He introduced himself as Detective Heinz Steiner. When they showed him their press IDs and asked to speak in private, Steiner led them back to a small office down the hall.

"What can I do for you two?"

Erica said, "We're working on a series of articles on unsolved homicides for a popular German magazine and wanted to talk with you about the murder of a local woman named Hedda Pohl five months ago. We thought it would interest the readers."

Steiner's eyes flickered with curiosity, but he didn't move in his chair.

"What do you want to know exactly?"

Volkmann smiled. "About the woman's background. The newspapers didn't go into much detail at the time. And if you have any idea of why she was killed or by whom, I'd be grateful. Sometimes an article can help a case. Jog someone's memory and get you a lead."

Steiner considered, and seemed to relax, his tone less formal. "We've no idea why she was killed or by whom, but the case is still wide open, I assure you."

Erica took a notebook and pen from her handbag. "Can you tell me how the woman was murdered?"

Steiner lit a slim cigar and blew smoke up to the ceiling. "Three shots, one in the chest, two to the back of the head at close range. Nine-millimeter slugs. She went out one night in her car, told her son she was going for a walk on the promenade. But she didn't go to the promenade so far as we know. And she didn't come back. Her body was found by a hiker two days later in a forest two miles inland. Her purse had been rifled through and some money stolen." Steiner frowned and his ruddy face creased with lines. "But the murder was very strange."

"In what way?"

"You're the journalists. You ought to know that kind of crime isn't prevalent in this area. And Hedda Pohl wasn't your typical victim for that kind of death."

"Tell us," Volkmann said, opening his own notebook and scribbling.

"Lots of reasons. The style of murder was more like a gangland killing. Hedda Pohl was an elderly widow. Well-off, but not rich. No vices. Absolutely no criminal past or convictions. She hadn't ever got a parking ticket, in fact. A very upstanding lady, involved in her church." Steiner drew on his slim cigar. "Something else. We found her car nearby in the woods. It was like she went to meet someone she knew. But her family knew of no prearranged meeting."

Volkmann jotted a few notes. "Was she active politically?"

Steiner's eyebrows rose. "No, definitely not. Why do you ask that?"

"No reason, just trying to get a fix on the lady. How well did you know her, Detective Steiner?"

Steiner leaned back in his chair. "Quite well."

Volkmann looked up with interest. "That helps. Is there anything else about her background you can think of?"

"Her husband used to be a respected businessman. He passed away years ago."

"What about him—did he have any criminal background?"

Steiner laughed. "He was as clean-living as a Lutheran minister. Very decent."

"What about her family?"

"All upstanding. And as I said, she was a good woman and well liked locally." Steiner shrugged. "As to the murder, the only scenario we can think of that makes sense is that she picked up a hitchhiker. Some crazy who decided to rob and kill her."

"What about clues?"

Steiner shook his head. "No fingerprints. No clues. Whoever did it was very careful. A professional criminal, perhaps. Or someone who had killed before. We checked all the usual angles: family, friends, acquaintances. But nothing gave off a whiff of suspicion."

Volkmann looked at his watch, then said, "Thanks for your help, Detective. I'm sure you're a very busy man, so I won't take up any more of your valuable time."

"You're welcome, Volkmann. You'll send me a copy of your article?"

"You bet."

The snow had stopped as they walked along the promenade.

Erica slipped her arm through his, and when they sat on one of the benches that faced out toward Lake Konstanz, she said, "There's no obvious reason why Winter's people would want to kill her. She had no terrorist connections. No criminal past."

"There has to be a connection somewhere, Erica. We just can't see it."

"So what happens now?"

He looked out at the gray choppy waters. A small boat with a blue sail was being tossed in the swell, and as it tried to hug the lakeshore, the image seemed fitting. He felt hopelessly lost. "There's only one other thing I could do."

"What?"

"Talk to the Landesamt in Berlin."

The Landesamt was the German equivalent of MI5 or CIA and was responsible for keeping track of terrorist and extremist organizations. "It's the only hope we have of turning up more information on Kesser and Winter. If there's anything of significance in either man's past, they ought to have it in their files."

"You know someone who could help?"

"A guy called Werner Bargel. He's the assistant director. If he can't help us, then nobody can."

32

BERLIN, SATURDAY, DECEMBER 17

Werner Bargel sat in his office in the leafy suburb of Dahlem and waved to the chair opposite.

"Sit down, Joe."

At forty-two, Bargel was one of the youngest men ever to hold the position of assistant director of the Landesamt für Verfassungsschutz in Berlin, the state office for the Protection of the Constitution, otherwise known as Lf V.

Tall, thin, and boyishly fresh-faced, Werner Bargel looked more like a young, bespectacled accountant than a senior intelligence officer.

"Well, Joe, what brings you to Berlin?" He looked across and smiled. "It must be at least a couple of years since we last met."

"I'd like to pick your brains, Werner. And ask a favor."

Bargel raised his eyebrows. "Is this something you're working on that directly concerns my people?"

"It's too early to say."

"What kind of information are you looking for?"

"Have you been getting much trouble from the extremist groups recently?"

Werner Bargel sat back in his seat, placed his hands behind his neck. "Whenever you get a recession, you always get an upsurge in left- and right-wing activity—you know that, Joe. You get our reports?"

"Sure."

"There's a piece in this month's report about a percentage rise."

"Any new groups?"

"None that have caused us much grief. But the old ones have been pretty active of late. The usual stuff. Last month in Berlin another refugee center was evacuated after a three-day siege by right-wing gangs. Two black street vendors were stabbed in Leipzig a week later. A Turkish boy was tossed from a second-floor window in Essen and died from his injuries the same day. I could go on. But it's all in the report I told you about."

"Are your people worried?"

Bargel smiled thinly. "That kind of thing always worries us. We try to keep it under control. But there's always going to be that fringe element in every country, isn't there?" Bargel stared at him. "Is that the only reason for your visit?"

"A few weeks ago, a young man named Dieter Winter was shot to death in Berlin. You recall the case?"

Bargel thought for a moment. "The shooting was at the Zoo Station?"

"That's the one. I'd like to know if you kept a file on Winter."

"I can have it checked. Anything else?"

"I'm flying to Munich tomorrow. Winter had an address there. If it's okay with your people I'd like to take a look at Winter's place. Also, a guy named Lothar Kesser. Comes from somewhere in

Bavaria. Graduated from Munich University in computer science. If you've got a file on him and a photograph, I'd like to see them, too."

"That shouldn't be a problem. Was Winter involved with a right-wing group?"

"That's what I'm trying to find out. The murder weapon was also used in the shooting of a British industrialist in Hamburg. That's why Ferguson is interested."

"What about this other guy, Kesser?"

"I'm only fishing at this stage. There may be no connection."

"But you'll keep me informed if anything comes up that we ought to look into, Joe?"

"Sure."

"I'll get you a copy of last month's report. And a preview of the next." Bargel stood up. "You're staying in Berlin tonight?"

"At the Schweizerhof. I appreciate your help, Werner."

"No problem. I can have my secretary book a table for us this evening at Le Bou Bou, if that's okay with you."

"Why not? We can have a chat about old times."

The restaurant was almost empty but the service superb, as always.

Bargel brought along the reports and the files he promised but he didn't discuss them, except to say that he had arranged for Volkmann to be met in Munich and taken to Winter's last known address. They spent more than an hour talking about the old days in Berlin, and when they had finished their meal, Bargel walked with Volkmann back to the hotel.

"Do you ever see Ivan Molke now, Joe?"

Volkmann shook his head and said, "You know he took early retirement. Before he did, we used to talk now and again, but we've been out of touch for the last couple of years."

Bargel nodded. "Right." He caught Volkmann's eye. "I hear he's in Munich. Maybe you should call him up when you go south. I suspect he could be useful to you. I can give you his number."

Volkmann brightened, liking the idea. "Sounds good. You could be right."

"You and he were pretty close."

"Sure. When I was only a rookie posted to Berlin years ago, Ivan often took me under his wing. I feel bad that we've gotten out of touch. But you know how it is."

"Can I ask you a personal question, Joe?"

"Sure."

"What did you and Ivan do with Felder?"

"I thought you knew." When he saw Bargel shake his head, Volkmann said, "We took him out to the Grunewald."

"I always wondered. That animal deserved what he got." He looked at Volkmann and said, "He was a brutal killer. But then it was a lousy business in those days. We were up against the scum of the Stasi and KGB."

Volkmann asked, "Where do your own police and armed forces stand when it comes to right-wing activity?"

Bargel shrugged. "They're apolitical, or supposed to be. What they think personally, of course, is quite another matter. I guess some might sympathize with fascist groups. But there's nothing we can do about that, so long as it doesn't interfere with their work." The intelligent eyes regarded Volkmann carefully. "Why do you ask, Joe?"

"The number of neo-Nazi attacks is increasing. But your people don't seem to be having much success putting a stop to them."

Bargel said, "It's a difficult area. You've got the usual calls to put all these extremists away. But if you started doing that, you'd get the bleeding-heart liberals who oppose them, saying we're becoming a police state again, putting people in concentration camps. And for us Germans, that's a touchy subject." Bargel shook his head. "There's no easy solution."

"Do the neo-Nazis have much support?"

"Some, but they wouldn't appeal to the majority of Germans; that goes without saying."

"What kind of numbers are we talking about?"

"In Germany? A conservative figure would be over a hundred thousand."

"Hard-line neo-Nazis?"

"Pretty much hard-line. You could probably triple that figure with softer supporters."

"That's a lot of support, Werner."

Bargel regarded him keenly. "What you're really wondering is, could it happen again? Could a Nazi Party ever come to power again in Germany? Are you asking me that, Joe?"

"If I remember my history, the Nazis had fewer than five thousand supporters when Hitler led the Beer Hall Putsch in 1923. When he started his campaign to become chancellor of Germany, the party had fewer than a quarter of a million members."

Bargel shook his head fiercely. "It couldn't happen again, Joe. Surely you know that. Only those parties that conform to the Constitution are admitted to the political system. And then there's the five percent barrier. That means any party polling less than five percent of the vote in an election can't enter Parliament, which effectively excludes extremists. But besides all that, people are wiser; Germany would never tolerate another Nazi Party or anything like it.

"Sure, we have a problem with extremists. There's a neo-Nazi riot in the streets of a German city, and the world's press prints banner headlines that suggest the Fourth Reich is imminent. But in Germany, these groups have never had great support. And the people who do support them are cranks and misfits. The shaved-headed thugs who beat up immigrants and desecrate Jewish graves are not well organized. It's a fringe element."

Volkmann looked across. "But there are similarities, Werner. The street riots. Immigrants being attacked instead of Jews. The call to have foreigners expelled. All the social and economic problems you had in the past when the Nazis came to power."

Bargel nodded. "Sure, you can draw parallels in any situation. But another Nazi Party in power? Joe, it's not possible. You may say we allowed it in 1933. But Germany was different then. And besides, every day we see reminders, on television, in the press, of the sins committed in our name, and the vast majority of this nation has no wish to repeat those sins." Bargel shook his head vigorously. "That another Nazi Party would ever come to power in Germany? Joe, I could never see that happening. Besides, the problems with neo-Nazis is going to be resolved."

"How?"

"You know of Konrad Weber?"

"The vice chancellor? Sure."

"He's also the interior minister, responsible for federal security. He's a good man, Joe. Tough, conservative, responsible. Between you and me, I hear that Weber wants to bring in some tough changes in the law to put a brake on these extremists for good."

"What's he going to do?"

Bargel smiled. "Even if I knew, I couldn't tell you that. But my ears in the Interior Ministry tell me Weber's going to crack the whip pretty hard and put a stop to it for good."

They reached the hotel, and Bargel handed across the large envelope containing the files and reports. "You'll destroy the file copies when you're through with them?"

"For sure. Thanks, Werner."

As Bargel turned to go, he touched Volkmann's arm, and the sharp eyes looked at him. "And don't forget, Joe, if anything comes up that concerns me, let me know."

He read the reports in his hotel room at the Schweizerhof.

There was nothing much new in Winter's file except that he had been brought up in a Catholic orphanage near Baden-Baden. Judging from his institutional background, Winter was a classic joiner: a loner who needed to identify with a cause.

Kesser's file contained very little: a head-and-shoulders photograph of a handsome young man with thinning fair hair and high cheekbones. Graduating from Munich University the same year as Winter, he once worked as a programmer for a military research establishment on a two-year contract before moving to a commercial bank in Nuremberg.

No mention of his ever having been a member of any right-wing party, and his address was given in Munich's Schwabing district. Volkmann guessed the file had been deliberately kept brief because of Kesser's involvement in military research and that the file was probably classified.

When he finished reading he poured himself a scotch from the minibar. He stood by the cold balcony, wondering what Erica was doing at that moment.

As darkness fell he could see the Brandenburg Gate, and the winged statue on the gilded Victory Column, lit up so clearly they could be seen for miles.

He remembered the news pictures that flashed across the world that night the Wall came down in 1989, and the happy crowds waving the German flag; the young men climbing on top of the Wall in a rush of fervent nationalism, the looks of joy and energy on their faces as they sang "Deutschland über Alles."

As he closed the window, he took one last look at the illuminated Brandenburg Gate and the Reichstag building, then he locked the window and went to bed.

33

MUNICH. MONDAY, DECEMBER 19

Munich was bitterly cold, and it was almost 10:00 a.m. when the Landesamt man delegated to meet him at the airport pulled up outside Winter's address. It was a modest apartment building, and Winter's rooms were on the second floor.

When the man unlocked the door and stepped inside, he handed Volkmann the key. "I'll wait for you outside. Take all the time you want. Can I drop you someplace afterward?"

"The Penta Hotel. Your people searched the apartment?"

The driver nodded as he went to go. "Sure. But it looked as though someone beat us to it. Most of the belongings appeared to have been taken. It looked like a professional job. The police didn't find anything of interest, either."

Volkmann wandered through the studio apartment. It smelled musty, and a colony of spiders dangled on silken threads from webs in the ceiling fixture. In the tiny kitchen, in a filthy cupboard under the sink, were three empty Bushmills whiskey bottles and a couple of unopened cans of Dutch beer.

Bookshelves ran along the bedroom wall. The mattress had been tossed and he guessed the police had searched the place thoroughly. Among the books he noticed a tattered copy of *Mein Kampf,* which was standard reading for German history students like Winter. The rest were paperback thrillers. No photographs on the shelves and no inscriptions in any of the books.

He spent half an hour looking through the apartment before closing the door and stepping down into the cold street to join the driver.

At the Penta, Volkmann checked in and telephoned Ivan Molke. He got no answer and he left a message. He showered, unpacked his overnight case, and called the local Hertz office to hire a car.

The address off the Leopoldstrasse in Schwabing turned out to be a fairly prosperous-looking block, and Volkmann found Kesser's name on the intercom outside.

He found an office-supplies store in a mall around the corner and bought a plastic clipboard and large notepad. When he walked back to the apartment block, he wrote down the names of all the residents on the intercom on his pad and then pressed all the intercom buttons except Kesser's. During the barrage of questions that followed, the door lock buzzed and sprang open. Someone expecting someone.

As he stepped inside, an elderly woman appeared and looked at him quizzically, her eyes going to the clipboard.

Volkmann smiled and said, "Block management. A problem with the plumbing."

The woman nodded and went back into her apartment.

He climbed the stairs to the second floor and knocked on Kesser's door. When there was no reply the second time, he removed the locksmith's set from his pocket and probed the lock. He stepped into Kesser's apartment and closed the door after him.

He checked the bedroom first. In one of the drawers he found several parcels of new baby clothes still in their cellophane wrappers. He checked in the kitchen and bathroom, searching the living room last.

On the windowsill was a photograph of Kesser and a pretty young blond woman.

A couple of dozen books lined the shelves, computer-programming titles mostly, including a Bundeswehr signal-operations codebook marked *Geheim*—Secret—and some books on Ada, the military programming language. An album on one of the shelves contained photographs from Kesser's university days, and in one of them Volkmann saw a picture of Kesser and Winter together, taken in a beer hall, the two young men smiling at the camera.

He leafed back toward the front of the album, and saw a photograph of an older man who resembled Kesser. But it was a snapshot taken long ago in black-and-white, and the man was in the uniform of a Leibstandarte SS colonel, posed beside a burned-out Russian tank. He looked young for a colonel, and there was a written inscription at the bottom of the photograph: "To Hildegard with love. Manfred. October 1943."

Volkmann saw another picture of the same man, this time in color, and the man much older, a young boy on his knee, and he guessed from the resemblance that the boy was Lothar Kesser as a child, the features unmistakably similar.

He heard the faint sound of a car pulling up in the parking lot below. Volkmann closed the album and replaced it on the shelf. He crossed to the window. A man stepped out of a gray Volkswagen, and as he locked the door, a blond woman, attractive and obviously pregnant, stepped out of the passenger side, her stomach bulging under a floral maternity smock.

Volkmann recognized Kesser and her from the album photographs.

He took a note of the telephone number and then stepped out into the hallway and closed the door. He passed Kesser and the woman on the first-floor landing, the couple ignoring him as they juggled flimsy plastic bags of groceries. He noticed that neither wore a wedding ring.

In the parking lot, he took the Volkswagen's registration number and drove back to the Penta. He poured himself a scotch from the minibar and thought about the photograph in Kesser's apartment of the man in uniform. The Leibstandarte SS colonel was surely Kesser's father—the family resemblance was unmistakable.

The beer cellar was in the Markets area.

When he stepped down into the warm bar, he heard a group of young people singing in the corner. He had almost forgotten it was less than a week until Christmas, and then he saw Ivan Molke sitting alone at the end of the bar, hunched over a beer.

He looked older, his hair graying at the temples, and he wore a gray business suit. He smiled as he recognized Volkmann and beckoned to him.

"Hey, it's good to see you, Joe." Molke shook his hand firmly. "There's a room in the back where we can talk."

He ordered a beer for Volkmann, and when it came, he led the way into the small room. They sat facing each other across a trestle table.

"I heard about your father, Joe. I was sorry to learn of his death." Molke paused. "I presumed when you rang me that this wasn't going to be a social call. So maybe you better tell me what it's about."

"I need your help, Ivan. You're still in the business?"

Molke half smiled. "You know what they say: once in, never out. I quit officially two years ago and came south. But then, you would have heard." He paused to sip his drink. "I'm in partnership in an agency in the city. Countering industrial espionage." He smiled. "Not as exciting as the old days in Berlin, but it pays the bills."

"But you're still in?"

"The Interior Ministry uses me on a consultancy basis maybe once or twice a year." Molke paused. "So what's this about, Joe?"

Volkmann filled him in, and when he showed the copy of the black-and-white photograph taken of the woman in the Chaco, Molke stared at it before frowning.

"Interesting. But what's the connection between the past and the present? Between South America and Germany?"

"That's what I need to find out, Ivan."

"Can you discover who the young woman in the photograph might be?"

Volkmann shook his head. "I haven't had any luck. It was such a long time ago. Besides, she may have been no one important, not even related to Schmeltz. But the man in the photograph may be a clue."

Molke thought for a moment. "Many years ago, when Willy Brandt got tough on our institutions in Germany responsible for hunting down wanted Nazis, they used several experts to verify identities from photographs. Mostly academics who specialized in the Nazi period, and some ex-Nazis themselves. I can ask around if you like. If the woman in the photograph was somebody important, they may be able to help identify her."

"Thanks, Ivan."

"This guy Kesser whose apartment you checked. What do you intend doing?"

"I'd like to tag him for a few days. Maybe it'll turn up something. I'll see you get paid your going rate."

Molke smiled and waved dismissively. "When do you want to start?"

"Tonight, if that suits you?"

"No sweat, Joe. You want to use two cars or one?"

"Two."

"I'll bring along a couple of talkies in case we need them. They're long-range. The latest stuff."

It was eight-thirty when they pulled up in their cars around the corner from Kesser's apartment. The light was on in Kesser's living room, the Volkswagen parked in the lot out front.

They drove Molke's green BMW back around and pulled in across the street by the park, from where they could see the apartment block. Molke gave Volkmann one of the two-way radios, and Volkmann showed him the head-and-shoulders photograph of Kesser.

They sat in the BMW until well after midnight, when the lights in Kesser's apartment went out. A little after one, they decided to call it a night and arranged to meet back at the park at five-thirty.

34

MUNICH. MONDAY, DECEMBER 19

Volkmann slept until five, then showered and shaved.

As he pulled up outside the park half an hour later, it was still pitch dark, but Molke's BMW was already there. The light was on in Kesser's living room, and Volkmann could see a shadow move back and forth behind the drawn shades.

He climbed in beside Molke, who said, "The light went on ten minutes ago, just after I got here. Looks like he's getting ready to move. You want to do first tag?"

"Sure."

"Don't forget to keep the radio on. We can change tag every ten minutes. The traffic's going to be pretty thin while he's driving."

"Okay, Ivan."

As Volkmann climbed out of the BMW, Molke grinned and said, "Let's hope Kesser's not just taking an early morning jog in the park. I'd hate to have got up this early for nothing."

Kesser came out of the apartment half an hour later wearing a blue rainproof anorak and carrying a briefcase.

It started to rain heavily, and when Kesser's Volkswagen pulled out of the parking lot, Volkmann gave him a fifty-yard start before following, seeing Molke's lights behind him.

Fifteen minutes later, the Volkswagen pulled up at a filling-station restaurant on the Munich ring road, and Kesser took half an hour over breakfast and read a newspaper before filling his tank and taking the road south.

The traffic was already busy by seven-thirty, and it was more than an hour later when Kesser turned off from the Tergen See road and the Volkswagen began to climb into the mountains. The traffic was light, and several times both Molke and Volkmann had to drop back until they saw the gray Volkswagen turn off to the right and climb up a steep, narrow mountain track.

Volkmann halted the Opel a hundred yards farther on. The narrow mountain road Kesser took wasn't signposted, but a notice said that the property beyond that point was private.

Molke pulled up, climbed out of the BMW, and moments later slid in beside Volkmann. He rubbed the fogged window. A thick forest of pines rose up to the top of the mountain, smothered in a halo of low rain cloud, the woods patchy with snow.

"What do you think, Joe? You want to risk going up after him?"

Volkmann hesitated. "You know what that mountain is called?"

"I saw a sign a mile back that said the Kaalberg was this way." Molke smiled. "There's got to be something up that mountain for

Kesser to drive all this way. You want to risk playing lost tourist? The last town we passed through had a hunting shop. I could go and get us a couple of walking canes and waterproofs. A little exercise might do us both good."

"Sure, why not?"

Molke smiled as he climbed out of the Opel into the drizzle. "If Kesser appears again, give me a buzz on the radio. I'll be as quick as I can."

Volkmann moved the Opel just off the road's shoulder. Below lay a deep, wooded valley, the quaint wooden houses of a Tyrolean village barely visible in the rain.

The green BMW returned half an hour later. Ivan Molke climbed out carrying two sturdy mountain walking sticks and olive-green waterproof capes. He removed a pair of powerful Zeiss binoculars from the trunk before joining Volkmann.

They decided to keep off the dirt track Kesser took and instead climbed up through the thick pines. The rain softened to a light drizzle and in the forest, Molke tapped Volkmann's arm and pointed through the trees.

With the powerful Zeiss, Volkmann could make out a wooden sentry hut and two guards standing in front of a metal security barrier. Both wore civilian clothes and had Heckler & Kochs draped across their chests, one of the men smoking a cigarette.

Past the barrier, they saw the sloped, high roof of a large traditional *berghaus*. It had a jutting balcony and the mountain that rose behind was covered in low cloud. Nearby was a drab-looking concrete building, maybe twenty yards square.

Fifteen minutes later, they had moved back down through the forest and were sitting in Ivan Molke's BMW.

"What do you make of it, Joe?"

Volkmann shook his head. "Has the government got any top-secret research establishments in this part of Germany?"

"Why do you ask?"

"Kesser worked for a government research unit a couple of years back. And those guys at the sentry box wore no uniforms, but they carried machine pistols."

"There're a couple of hush-hush places in Bavaria, sure. But where, I couldn't say. You want me to check it out for you?"

"Discreetly, Ivan. I don't want anyone coming down on Ferguson for playing off-pitch."

"Okay. If it gets too hairy, I'll back off quietly. You want to call it a day?"

Volkmann nodded. "But I'd like to have Kesser watched for the next couple of days. A record of his movements kept. Who he talks to, who he visits."

Molke said, "I'll use a couple of the men from my agency; it shouldn't be a problem." He paused. "What about a bug on Kesser's phone?"

"You think you could do that?"

Molke smiled. "If his girlfriend stays out of the way long enough, sure."

"Okay, but warn your people to be careful, in case Kesser is armed."

"I'll start the watch tonight."

Volkmann checked out of the hotel and returned the rental car. Molke drove him to the airport and as they passed the signpost for Dachau, a white-and-green tour bus was turning off toward the concentration camp road.

The old camp at Dachau had been preserved after the war and lay a couple of miles to the north, a place the tourists and the curious came to see and one of the few remaining legacies of the Third Reich preserved for posterity. He had visited it after his last term at Cambridge, and stood on the infamous *Appellplatz,* where his father would have stood on cold winter mornings waiting for the five o'clock roll call, the barbed-wire perimeter and the watchtowers and the gas chamber and the ovens all grim reminders of his father's nightmare.

Beyond the rain-streaked glass of the tour bus he saw the faces of the passengers. Young faces pressing somberly against the damp glass. Several of them wore skull caps, and a sign against the glass proclaimed that they were a student tour group from Tel Aviv University.

As they overtook the bus, Volkmann noted the grim look on Ivan Molke's face, but neither man spoke.

It was after seven when he arrived back in Strasbourg and checked his desk. He had no messages, and neither Peters nor Ferguson was in his office. Two Italian officers were still on duty, and they stood by the coffeemaker talking with Jan de Vries. Volkmann lingered with them for ten minutes before he telephoned Erica and drove over to the apartment.

She seemed glad to see him, and he realized he had missed her in the past forty-eight hours. He booked a restaurant in Petite France, and over dinner she asked him what he had been doing in the last two days. He didn't go into detail and he didn't tell her what had happened with Kesser, just that he had got more information on him and Winter but that for now, it was classified. She didn't question him, and she didn't ask him what the information was, although he could see the curiosity in her eyes.

After dinner, they walked back through Petite France. The old town with its pretty period houses and its narrow, cobbled streets and babbling river was deserted, and at one of the weirs Volkmann stopped to look down at the water. He was aware of her looking at him, and when he turned to look back, he saw the blue eyes linger on his face.

Before he could speak, she had stepped closer, and as her lips brushed his cheek, he could smell her perfume.

She slid her arm through his, and they turned and walked back through the empty cobbled streets.

He looked back twice, but could see nobody following them.

35

On Tuesday morning, Volkmann went into the office at ten and found two telephone messages on his desk. One was from Ted Birken in Zurich, asking to be called back, and the second was from Ivan Molke, urging him to contact him right away.

He tried Molke's number first, but the voice mail kicked in and he left a message to say he returned the call.

When he telephoned Ted Birken's number in Zurich, he heard the polite, cheerful voice of Birken reply.

"I've made a little headway, Joe. Have you got a pen and paper ready?"

"Is it good news?"

"Hard to say. The director of Berlin Document Center, a chap named Maxwell, is an old friend. I asked him to check back through the early Nazi Party numbers and try to come up with a list of anyone close to Erhard Schmeltz's.

"Maxwell wanted to know what it was about. I told him the story, that you needed to find anyone still living who had had a number close to Schmeltz's. He agreed to have his people go through the files of a hundred numbers: fifty numbers above Schmeltz's party number and fifty below.

"Then I checked with the WASt. Out of the hundred names, only two are still alive. The first is a man named Otto Klagen, born in Berlin in 1910. He was a young man when he joined the party. His membership application was dated November 1, 1929."

"Where's Klagen now?"

Ted Birken sighed at the other end. "That's the problem. He's in an old folks' home in Düsseldorf. I telephoned the home, and they said

Klagen had a stroke months ago and his mind's not the best, so I doubt he'd be of much use to you even if he has heard of Erhard Schmeltz."

Volkmann said, "What about the second man?"

"Wilhelm Busch. He'll be pretty old by now. Like Schmeltz, his place of application was given as Munich. He joined the party as a youth."

"Have you got an address?"

Ted Birken gave Volkmann an address in Munich's northern suburb of Dachau. "I hope he's in better shape than Klagen. Otherwise you'll be completely wasting your time."

"Have you got a telephone number for Busch?"

"I'm afraid not. But you'd probably be best just calling cold and catching him unawares; otherwise he might not even consider talking to you."

"What was his war record like, Ted, any idea?"

"According to Maxwell, Busch ended up in military intelligence—the Abwehr. He wasn't wanted for any war crimes, and his rank in 1945 was *Hauptmann*—captain."

"What's his background after 1945?"

"Busch spent ten years in the Gehlen Organization, the forerunner of the German security services. It was riddled with ex-Nazis, as you probably know, so his credentials would have served him well. But he's a very old man now, long retired and living on his pension. If you need any more help from the Berlin Document Center, you can mention my name."

"Thanks, Ted, I appreciate your help."

"Not at all, my boy. It's been good talking with you."

Five minutes later Volkmann's telephone buzzed. It was Ivan Molke returning his call.

"We need to meet and talk, Joe."

He heard the urgency in Molke's voice. "Is there a problem, Ivan?"

"I think you could say that. I've pulled off my men watching Kesser."

"What the devil's wrong?"

"I'd rather not talk about this over the line, Joe. Can we meet? There's something I think you ought to see."

"I could drive down to Munich, be there after lunch."

"Let's meet in Augsburg. It'll shorten your journey, and besides, I need to get out of the office. You know where the main railway station is in Augsburg?"

"No, but I'll find it."

"Two-thirty, in the main bar. Do me a favor."

"What?"

"When you drive down, check your tail."

Volkmann frowned. "What's up, Ivan?"

"I'll tell you when I see you, but just do as I ask," answered Molke, and then the line clicked dead.

Volkmann stepped into Augsburg's main railway station. It was almost two-thirty.

On the drive down, he watched in his rearview mirror but no cars were tailing him, and he had stopped at half a dozen filling stations en route to be certain.

He saw Ivan Molke hunched over a cup of coffee and smoking a cigarette in a corner of the bar. He appeared tired, his face tense. Volkmann joined him, ordered a beer.

Dark rings stained Molke's eyes. "No tails on the way down?"

"Clear all the way. What's up, Ivan?"

Molke stubbed out his cigarette. "You came clean to me on Lothar Kesser, Joe? You told me everything I needed to know?"

"Sure, why?"

"I put two of my men on Kesser. One of them managed to get into the guy's apartment yesterday evening. Kesser's girlfriend's name is Ingrid, and she's his live-in. By the look of her, she's about six months pregnant."

"Go on."

"My man had maybe ten minutes in the place before Kesser arrives back. The second man kept watch and alerted him. My guy in the apartment hadn't much time, but he managed to find a note-book belonging to Kesser and a spare set of keys to the apartment. He didn't have time to plant a bug on the landline, but he photo-graphed a couple of the notebook pages and got out just before Kesser came up the stairs. My men gave me a mold of the keys and the photo prints they took of the pages in Kesser's notebook."

Molke quickly lit another cigarette. "Then, in the middle of the night, I get two calls within the space of ten minutes. It's the two guys I put on Kesser. One of them says his wife wakes up about three o'clock and goes downstairs for a glass of water. She sees the door to the study is open. She flicks on the light, and there's this guy search-ing through her husband's briefcase. She screams. The guy pulls a gun and points it at her like he's going to blow her head off. By the time her husband gets down the stairs, the intruder's gone, and his wife's fainted."

Molke registered the look on Volkmann's face, before he went on. "The next time the phone rings, it's Pieber, the second man. He's at his girlfriend's place, and he leaves late. He notices he's being fol-lowed home. Two guys in a dark-colored Volkswagen. When he gets to his apartment, he goes to his bedroom and checks the window but sees no one below. But half an hour later, he hears whispered voices outside the apartment door. He puts on the TV, walks around the apartment, making noise like he's very much awake, then he calls me. I get there ten minutes later, but there's no one outside the apartment. But someone's been at the door lock, no question."

Volkmann said, "You're certain this has something to do with watching Kesser?"

"Joe, there's nothing my men are working on at present that would involve guns."

"What do you want to do?"

"My men are off Kesser. Your people have authority, and they carry weapons. My boys can't, and it's getting too dangerous." Molke crushed his cigarette in the ashtray. "I just won't risk them getting hurt, Joe. You understand?"

Volkmann nodded. "You think Kesser knew your men had been in his apartment?"

"That's the funny thing. I asked them the very same question. They said they were sure Kesser suspected nothing, didn't know he was being watched. But obviously my men were."

Ivan Molke removed a notebook from his pocket, flicked it open. "I've got a record of Kesser's movements. Twice he's driven up to Kaalberg Mountain. Yesterday and the day before, he drove up there about seven in the morning, and left about noon."

"Did your men see any other activity there?"

"No one came or left apart from Kesser, and the armed guards are still there."

"What about checking out the place like I asked?"

"I talked with a few guys I know at the ministry. They say that there's maybe a dozen places in Bavaria used for military research. But they didn't want to talk in detail. So I went back to the village where I bought the mountain gear and asked around."

"And?"

"Nobody I spoke with seemed to know anything except that there's a lot of private land up there. Maybe a couple of square miles. There's a big mountain house, the one we saw. And a flat, concrete building directly behind the house that could be a laboratory. Someone bought the site a couple of years back, but none of the locals seem to know who it belongs to now or what goes on. They say the site's been marked off with 'Entrance Forbidden' and 'Private' signs all over the place."

"What do you think?"

Molke shrugged. "You said there were some books in Kesser's place, military communications stuff, so it's possible he might be involved on some government hush-hush project when you consider his background. And after what happened to my two men, I'd say it's likely. I can't stick my nose in there, Joe. I could have my license pulled."

Volkmann considered. "It doesn't make sense."

"What do you mean?"

"Why would Werner Bargel let me see Kesser's file if the man's a government employee working on a secret project?"

Molke shrugged. "Unless Bargel suspected that your people were onto something. Did he ask you to get back to him if you came up with anything?"

"Yes."

"Then maybe that's it." Molke hesitated. "Though something's pretty weird. The pages in the notebook my men found in Kesser's apartment. There were maybe a couple of dozen pages of lists of names and what looked like some pages of diagrams of some sort. But my men only had time to photograph a couple."

The lady serving behind the bar came to replace the ashtray with a fresh one and wipe the table, and when she had gone, Ivan Molke took out an envelope and shoved it across.

"Maybe you ought to take a look at the photographs."

Volkmann slid out the envelope contents. Inside were two enlargements of narrow, faint-ruled pages. One of the pages had two names with an X marked beside each. The second contained what appeared to be a roughly drawn map of some sort of building. Beside it was another map, this one giving directions, and underlined were the names of several towns. On closer examination, Volkmann saw what looked like the word *Kloster* circled in ink above the drawing. The German word for "monastery." Volkmann looked at the names again.

Horst Klee.

Jürgen Trautman.

He looked up at Molke. "Any idea who they are?"

"None. And like I said, there were lots more names. My man only had time to shoot one of the pages with names on it."

"What about the map?"

"I checked it out this morning."

"And?"

"The directions were clear enough. It's an old deserted monastery near Salzburg, over an hour's drive from Munich. There's no one there, check it yourself. I've drawn you a proper map with directions on how to get there." Molke tore a page from his notebook and wrote on it.

Volkmann accepted the page. "Who owns the monastery? Do you know?"

"After the religious order moved out ten years ago, the German government bought it, but it hasn't been put to any use since." Molke shrugged. "If Kesser's still working for them, it could be someplace they're planning to set up and use. So I'd tread carefully, Joe."

Volkmann tapped the photographed pages from Kesser's notebook. "Mind if I keep these, Ivan?"

"On one condition."

"What's that?"

"If state security comes knocking on my door, I want your word you'll explain that I was working for you."

"You have it, Ivan."

Molke reached into his pocket, slid across a set of keys. "They're for Kesser's apartment. I had them made from the molds."

Volkmann slipped the keys into his pocket. "Thanks for your help."

"One more thing. The photograph of the woman. The one you found in the Chaco."

"What about it?"

"I checked up on the specialist people our government used during the Nazi trials." Molke paused. "There was a historian. She specialized in the Nazi period and pretty much knew all the players. She just may be able to help with the photograph, or know someone who can." Molke shrugged. "It's all I can come up with, Joe."

"What's her name?"

"Hanah Richter. She was on the history faculty of Stuttgart University. But that was over twenty years ago and she wasn't young even then, so I'd say she's well retired by now. And I'm assuming she's still alive."

"Okay, I'll have my people check on her."

* * *

Volkmann walked back to the underground garage.

The streets were crowded with Christmas shoppers but no one was tailing him, and when he reached the car, he sat there for ten minutes, thinking over what Ivan Molke had told him. None of it made any sense, none at all.

All the clues seemed to suggest that Kesser was still involved in government research work and there was little to implicate the man.

He decided the best thing to do was to concentrate on the information he had: the two names Ted Birken had come up with, whose Nazi Party numbers had been close to Schmeltz's—Otto Klagen and Wilhelm Busch—and the sketch Ivan Molke had given him from Kesser's notebook.

Next, he called Erica at his apartment. He explained about Ted Birken's information, but he made no mention of what Ivan Molke had told him. She said, "What about this old man, Busch, who was close to Schmeltz's party membership number?"

"That's where I'm headed. He lives not far from Dachau."

"When will you be back?"

"That depends on whether I can locate Busch or not. And even if I do, he may not even want to talk. You're sure you'll be okay on your own?"

"I'm going to take a long walk in the Orangerie and then come back and drink your wine and watch television. Isn't there anything I can do?"

Volkmann smiled. "Keep your fingers crossed that Busch is alive and kicking. Talk to you soon."

It was almost four when he reached the old town of Dachau. Dominated by an ancient castle, it looked a picture of Bavarian rural charm. It seemed somehow absurd to Volkmann that the place that had once lent its name to the infamous concentration camp should be lit up with glittering seasonal lights.

He found the address in a street of prewar detached houses, a ten-minute walk from the road that led down to the old concentration camp. As Volkmann went to ring the doorbell a young woman pulled up in the driveway in a white Audi. She carried several shopping bags up to the door, and Volkmann went to help her.

"Danke schön." The young woman smiled as she reached in her purse for her key. "I'm sorry, I don't think we've met before."

"I'm looking for Wilhelm Busch. I believe he lives here."

"Are you a friend of my grandfather's?"

"No, we've never met." Volkmann produced his ID, and the woman stared at it for a moment.

She turned suddenly pale. "Are you with the police? My grandfather isn't in any sort of trouble, is he?"

Volkmann smiled. "No trouble at all, I assure you. May I speak with him?"

"He's not here. My boyfriend's driven him to Salzburg to visit a relative. My aunt hasn't been well."

"When will he be back?"

"Sometime tomorrow. Perhaps you can call back. Can I tell him what this is about?"

"It's a private matter. I'd really rather discuss it with him."

The woman shrugged. "Very well, I'll tell him you called."

And with that, she turned the key in the door and stepped inside.

He found a small hotel opposite the park near the S-Bahn station and checked in for one night. His room overlooked the park facing the station, and when he had shaved and showered, he phoned the duty officer in Strasbourg.

It was a young French officer named Delon who came on the line, and Volkmann explained that he wanted two names checked. He read out the names from Kesser's notebook.

"You've got addresses or descriptions?"

"Sorry, André. But see if either name comes up on our files. And if there's any connection between the two men."

"Which area—criminal?"

"I don't know, so you better leave it open."

The Frenchman sighed. "If you're trying to link them, that means we will have to do a random check on the names first. It may take some time."

"If you have no luck, ask the German desk to help. It's more than likely their territory, anyway, judging by the names. But there's a chance the three are government research employees, so if the Germans say their files are restricted, back off and don't explain."

He paused. "One more thing. A historian, Hanah Richter, who used to work on the faculty at Stuttgart University. She's long retired but see if you can locate her."

"Okay. This ought to keep me busy for the shift."

"Be good, André."

He took a walk through Dachau town to get some air, aware of his restlessness, and wondering if Sanchez had made any progress. He hoped so; he still felt he was floundering.

The old castle on the hill was lit up, and Volkmann realized that there was nothing to suggest to the casual visitor the brutality that had taken place in the nearby camp.

A small town in Germany like so many others, with young people in good spirits filling the streets and inns in the days before Christmas. He looked at them as he passed the crowded bars, their glasses raised, their voices loud and harsh and full of confidence.

It was almost midnight when he got back to the hotel. As he lay in bed in the darkness, he could hear the voices in the street below as the bars emptied. They carried up to his window, some of them shouting drunkenly. Then they faded, and a little after midnight a train rumbled past in the station across the street.

MEXICO CITY. 1:02 A.M.

Kruger stood beside the shimmering turquoise water of the swimming pool in the darkness as he smoked a cigarette, thinking of the telephone call from Asunción. He ran a hand through his dark hair and sighed.

Disturbing. Most disturbing.

So close.

And now this.

He would have to wait until Lieber arrived to hear the full story, but what he had heard had unsettled him. Unsettled all of them. Haider said Brandt had left saying they would be back for the meeting with Lieber. The others had gone to bed, leaving Kruger alone.

He stubbed out the cigarette in the ashtray on the poolside table, then walked through the villa to the rear gardens.

Five rooms through to the kitchen, then he stepped outside onto the back lawn. He checked his watch, noted the time, and then began to walk across the moonlit grass at a smart pace.

Balmy. The sound of crickets and the smell of eucalyptus. But Kruger's mind was on security. Once Lieber arrived in Mexico City, he would have him checked for tails before he brought him here. He couldn't take any chances.

Kruger reached the clump of trees at the end of the back lawn and checked his watch again, holding the face up to the moonlight.

Two minutes exactly.

Already he had timed how long it took to cross the expansive rear lawn to the old concrete garage behind the clump of trees, but he wanted to be certain. He passed one of the armed guards halfway across, acknowledging the man's nod.

He reached the old garage and stepped inside. Darkness. The smell of grease and oil. The large double wooden doors at the end were bolted.

He crossed to the doors, past the dark form of the vehicle, and pulled back the bolt, swung the doors out and open. An unlit alleyway lay outside, overgrown with weeds.

Haider had told him about the garage exit. A hundred yards from the villa proper, half hidden behind a clump of eucalyptus trees, the alleyway cut down to the maze of back roads in

Chapultepec. Unlikely that it would be needed, but it was an ideal emergency exit.

He bolted shut the garage doors again, then flicked a wall switch. A blaze of light flooded the room, and the dark, anonymous Ford stood waiting in the center of the garage.

A full tank of gas and a fresh battery. He made sure Schmidt took the car for a daily run since their arrival. All part of the contingency plan.

Kruger took one last look about the room, then switched off the light, closed the door, and walked back across the lawn toward the villa, counting his steps.

36

MEXICO CITY. TUESDAY, DECEMBER 20, 3:15 P.M.

Chief Inspector Eduardo Gonzales was a thin, energetic man of fifty with the gnarled face of a tough street fighter.

His office overlooked the Plaza de San Fernando and had an excellent view of sprawling Mexico City. On his desk were two ashtrays to assist his three-pack-a-day habit. One of the ashtrays was made of glass; the other a beautiful, ornate affair of quebraco wood in the shape of a half-cut coconut shell, carved by the Indians in Paraguay's Chaco. A present from his friend, Captain Vellares Sanchez.

Ugly, brooding faces were cut into the dark quebraco; the receptacle clasped by a perfectly carved wooden hand that was so in contrast to the ugly carved faces that it resembled on first sight some hedonistic chalice. The faces looked like the shrunken heads of

Amazonians one saw in the museums. But not frightening. Rather, they served to remind that evil had to be held in check by a strong hand.

According to the Indians.

So Sanchez had told him when he presented the gift in Caracas years ago.

Now strong December sunlight poured into the office. Hot, despite the season. A freakish warm front in from the Gulf of Mexico. An air-conditioning vent in a wall below the ceiling blew out a faint stream of chilled air.

A metal tray cluttered with bottles of sparkling water and a jug of fresh, iced lime juice and four glasses lay on Gonzales's desk. Despite the heat, they had remained untouched since a young policía had brought them in fifteen minutes before.

Four men sat around the desk. Gonzales and his senior detective, named Juales, a rugged, short-necked man with a squat body and bushy eyebrows, sat on one side, Sanchez and Cavales on the other.

Eduardo Gonzales inhaled on a cigarette, coughed throatily, then looked across at his two visitors. Both men were tired, their eyes red-raw after their long journey.

A police car had taken them directly from the airport, siren blaring, lights flashing. The formalities had been dispensed with, the greetings and well-wishings over. Sanchez briefly explained his reasons for wanting Franz Lieber, alias Julius Monck, followed.

Gonzales listened, his brow furrowed in concentration while Sanchez spoke. Now it was Gonzales's turn. He coughed, nodded to his detective, Juales. "Okay. Let's tell our visitors what's been happening."

Juales leaned forward. He wore a shirt and tie, and a portable phone was clipped to his belt, near his holstered Smith & Wesson. Juales spoke slowly as he read from written notes.

"The subject, Julius Monck, alias Franz Lieber, arrived in Mexico City two hours ago. One-sixteen local. I had six men watching him in the arrivals terminal, another two on the airport ramp, dressed as airport staff so we could identify him as soon as he stepped off the plane, from the photograph you sent." Juales glanced at Sanchez, then back at his notes.

"Once he collected his luggage, he went straight through customs. I'd briefed one of the customs men to stop him, and he checked the luggage thoroughly. Nothing of interest. There's a list of the contents of the single suitcase, if you want it."

Sanchez waved his hand in reply. "Later, please go on."

Juales looked down at his notes again. "The subject went to the exchange counter, changed U.S. bills into pesos. Then he made one call from a public kiosk at one-forty-seven. The officers said the call lasted just under one minute. Lieber seemed anxious. Soon as he finished the call, he went to a taco stand outside the terminal and bought a glass of fresh fruit juice, drank it, then went to the taxi stand. At one-fifty-seven, he took a taxi to the City Sheraton, arrived there at two-forty, and booked in straightaway under the name of Julius Monck." Juales looked up from his notes. "He was still there as of fifteen minutes ago. Room two-fifteen."

"And now?" Sanchez asked.

Juales tapped the portable phone clipped to his belt. "I've got six undercover men at the Sheraton. If Lieber goes in or out, gets visitors, or makes a call, my men will let me know—"

Gonzales interrupted. "The call Lieber made, you've got something on that yet?"

Juales shook his head. "Not yet." He turned to Sanchez and Cavales. "After Lieber made the call at the airport, I had one of my men wait by the telephone until a colleague from the technical division came. They hit the REDIAL button and recorded the digital dialing pips. They can play it back and decode it in the tech lab and find the number. Then we can trace to wherever it was called." Juales glanced at his wristwatch. "We ought to have that soon."

Sanchez nodded, saw Gonzales smile through stained-yellow teeth.

"Technology," said Gonzales, waving his cigarette. "It's beyond

an old policeman like me. These young guys in the basement lab
are like Einsteins. They play with computers all day. Me, I'd go nuts
down there." He smiled.

Sanchez nodded his head and smiled faintly. His bones ached to
the marrow, the city's high altitude making his chest hurt when he
breathed, and fogging his brain. He glanced at Cavales. The detective stared ahead blankly, then rubbed his raw eyes. *He must be feeling the same*, Sanchez thought. A bed would be welcome; a cold
shower first, then sleep. But there was no time for that. Not yet.

He turned to look at Gonzales. "The passport Lieber used—did
he ever use it to visit Mexico before?"

Gonzales went into a fit of coughing, pounded his chest with his
fist before he replied. "We checked, Vellares. The answer's no. Never.
No Julius Monck with that number passport."

Sanchez addressed Juales. "How many nights did Lieber book at
the Sheraton?"

"He told the desk clerk one, possibly two. He couldn't be certain."

"Is the hotel being cooperative?"

"We spoke with the manager," Juales replied. "No problem. He's
been very discreet. Even gave us a room two doors away. We've got
two men there. If Lieber comes out, we've got a copy key card. We
can plant a bug in his room in case he entertains visitors."

"What about his telephone?"

Juales said, "We've got that covered already. We're going to wire
into the hotel telephone system. The manager wanted to see our
permission first. Chief Inspector Gonzales has organized it." Juales
glanced at his watch. "Our people are on their way and should be
patched into Lieber's telephone within the next half hour."

Sanchez inclined his head gratefully at Gonzales. "My thanks,
Eduardo."

Gonzales smiled, coughed again, and looked at the carved ashtray as he ground out his cigarette, the dark, ghoulish faces staring
up at him. "It's the only way we beat the devils of this world. No?"

Gonzales stood up, hitched his trousers farther up his thin waist, glanced at the liquid refreshments still untouched on his desk. The atmosphere in the office felt charged. Expectant. Like worried fathers outside a maternity ward.

Gonzales said, "There's nothing more we can do until Lieber makes a move. We've got a hospitality room for visitors down the hall. I'll have some tacos and fresh drinks sent up, and you can rest yourselves." He looked down at Sanchez and smiled. "Besides, it will give us a chance to catch up on gossip since Caracas. Okay?"

4:40 P.M.

Franz Lieber stood at the window on the Sheraton's fifth floor. He swallowed his second scotch-and-soda, gripped the empty glass tightly in his big hand as he stared down at the city below. The air-conditioning was on, the hum distracting.

Tiredness racked his body, pains arcing intermittently across his chest in spasms, like tiny jolts of electricity. Rivulets of sweat ran down his back despite the air-conditioning.

Stress.

Lieber ran the back of his hand across his damp forehead.

The flights had been bad enough. Asunción to São Paulo. An overnight in Paulo, then the long haul to Mexico City. Throughout his long journey, anxiety gnawed like a rodent inside his skull. He took deep breaths, let them out slowly, trying to relax, but knew it was useless.

Mexico City out there and beyond—a ragged, noisy, dirty sprawl. Cities like this drained him. Claustrophobic, chaotic, orderless.

A woman would help relieve the tension. But Kruger had expressly forbidden visitors or phone calls.

Just wait. For the return call.

The hotel would be checked first. To make sure he had no tails, no one watching him. Lieber tried to tell Kruger it was okay when he had phoned him from the airport, that he had been careful, but Kruger refused to accept his assurance.

"Just stay in your room. I'll get back to you."

"How long?"

"As long as it takes; just wait for my call," Kruger snapped back, before he hung up.

Lieber shook his head and swore to himself, felt the trickles of sweat licking his spine. The waiting wasn't helping his stress.

How long before they checked him out? He'd been in the room almost two hours now. As he went to pour himself another scotch from the minibar, the telephone rang. Startled, he felt as if a shock of electricity had jolted his body.

He rushed to pick up the receiver.

Sanchez sat quietly in the small hospitality room. White walls. Thick, deep-pile carpet the same gray-blue color as Gonzales's uniform.

For ten minutes he and Gonzales had chatted, until tiredness overcame Sanchez. Now he sat sipping iced, freshly squeezed orange juice from a paper cup. A half-eaten taco and a hot chili sauce dip lay in front of him on a paper plate.

The others sat and talked. Mainly Gonzales. Stories about the old days in Mexico City, the problems, the interesting cases.

Juales sat there nodding occasionally at his boss, his neck lost in his shirt so that it looked as if he had no neck at all. Sanchez guessed he was very capable. His boss had chosen well.

"You think Asunción's bad," Gonzales was saying to Cavales, each man puffing on a cigarette, "you ought to try a month here. Twenty-three million people, amigo. Like a cross between a zoo and a luna-tic asylum, without walls."

Sanchez closed his eyes tightly, eyelids aching, opened them again. The view beyond the panoramic window was stupendous, as far as the high Sierras surrounding the city. The high altitude had a dizzying effect, making the effort of thinking and talking a slow process.

But something was happening.

He could sense it.

The next move was Lieber's.

He wondered what it would be.

Sanchez looked up, heard a soft click as the door behind opened. A good-looking young man in a cream-colored linen suit stood in the open doorway. He clutched a sheaf of papers, smiled warily at the two visitors and Gonzales before his eyes shifted to Juales.

"Captain . . . may I speak with you?"

Juales crossed to the man, and they stepped out into the hallway together. After a few moments of huddled conversation, Juales returned, holding a single sheet of paper.

"We traced the call made at the airport."

"And?" Gonzales prompted.

"It was to an address in Lomas de Chapultepec."

"An expensive area," commented Gonzales. "Did you get the name of the occupant?"

Juales shook his head. "Not yet. But my man did a little quick checking. The property's owned by a company called Cancún Enterprises. It's run by a man named Josef Haider. He's a businessman. Old guy. Very wealthy."

"I know who he is," Gonzales said quickly. He looked at Sanchez and Cavales as both men stood up.

Gonzales drew on his cigarette, blew out thick smoke. "Haider is German-born. Rich. A retired businessman. Owns a lot of property in the city." He coughed and smiled. "Maybe this fits in with what you told me about this other old guy . . ."

"Tsarkin?"

"Sí."

"Tell me."

Gonzales sighed. "Haider came here from Brazil maybe forty years ago. He must be very old now. But lots of powerful friends. I remember him because there was a problem once with an extradition warrant from France when I worked in headquarters. They said Haider was wanted for war crimes there. Claimed he was in the Gestapo. Long time ago, I know, but Haider must have greased a lot of palms, because the charges were refuted by our people. The French got nowhere." Gonzales smiled. "Simple when you have money, sí?"

Sanchez nodded. "And this is one of his properties?"

"It would appear so," said Gonzales. "It's in a wealthy area up in the Chapultepec Hills. Huge mansions and villas in the middle of landscaped parks and rocky ravines. Where only the very rich live." He smiled. "And maybe a few corrupt police chiefs and judges as well."

"Can you make a check on the occupants? Get some of your people to watch the place? I would appreciate it, Eduardo."

Gonzales nodded. "No problem, amigo. Straightaway."

A shrill sound startled them as Juales's phone buzzed. The man flicked it on, listened.

Sanchez heard nothing, only Juales's sharp replies as he frowned.

"When? You got the number? Put out an all-cars alert. But tell them don't approach. Just observe and report their position. Understood?"

Juales let his hand fall, looked at Gonzales. "Lieber got a call in his room three minutes ago."

"Our men were tapped into his phone?"

Juales shook his head. "No. The technicians were still working on it. They missed the call. By the time they got to the operator, Lieber had put down the phone."

"No! Of all the lousy luck."

"That's not all. Lieber left the Sheraton two minutes ago. Went down to the lobby, crossed the street, and bought a newspaper. A car came by, Lieber climbed in, and the car moved off like a bat out of hell."

"The car was a taxi?"

"Not a taxi. A civvy. Volkswagen Beetle."

"Our men followed?"

"Sí."

"And?"

Juales swallowed. "As of twenty seconds ago, we lost him."

37

CHAPULTEPEC, TUESDAY, DECEMBER 20, 5:14 P.M.

Lieber sat in the front seat of the white Volkswagen as it wove through the chaos of traffic.

Lunatic Mexican drivers, chili and pepper smells, and all the time the pressing, claustrophobic sensation of sweaty bodies. Everywhere. Millions of them.

Sweat still poured through his shirt, a fresh one he had hastily dragged on before he left the hotel. He was clear, according to Kruger. Two of Haider's men checked out the hotel and lobby for almost two hours. No cops or plainclothes so far as they could tell.

If he had been watched, the watchers were very good. But Lieber doubted that. He had moved too quickly, too carefully. Still, the cop, Sanchez, was not one to underestimate.

The cramped, whining Volkswagen felt claustrophobic, despite the open windows. The man in the driver's seat was one of Haider's people. He wore a sweatshirt and tennis shorts, and his forehead was creased as he concentrated on the traffic.

Outside the windows of the tiny Volkswagen, darkness fell, lights coming on, the traffic thickening—if it could get any thicker—a scene of utter chaos. But the driver knew the city, wove down side streets and alleyways, ignoring the irate screams and cries of street vendors whose barrows got in the way, the whiny-engined Volkswagen climbing up into the hills. The car was well chosen. Mexico City thronged with Volkswagens.

Now whitewashed adobes and filthy colonias were replaced by splendid villas with walled gardens. Armed, uniformed guards, some with leashed guard dogs, stood behind gates. Lieber was no stranger to Mexico City: Chapultepec was a place for the rich and elite.

Suddenly the Volkswagen turned into a quiet avenue and halted outside a double wrought-iron gate. A man appeared beyond the gate and peered into the car. Moments later, he opened the gates manually and let them through.

The Volkswagen strained up a winding gravel road to a white villa, set amid lush gardens full of jacaranda trees and thick-clumped flower beds of poinsettias and *cempazúchitl*. The flower of death, old Haider had once told him it was called.

Sulfur-yellow light washed over the vast lawns dotted with palm trees, and lights blazed in windows. The big villa was lavish. Private. Secure.

Lieber saw the swimming pool, a kidney-shaped shimmering of turquoise light. Next to it a patio and French windows at the side of the house. And then he saw the guards, Werner and Rotman. They wore shorts and sneakers and light rainproof jogger jackets as they patrolled the gardens, carrying Heckler & Koch MP 5K machine pistols.

He glimpsed big Schmidt nearby, a pistol in a shoulder harness across his chest, no sign of the sheathed bowie knife, but Lieber knew the man went nowhere without it.

Inside the lit windows he saw the figures waiting for him. Four men. The tall, silver-haired man and Kruger standing; old Haider seated in a comfortable armchair, lost in the leather, an inhaler clutched in one hand. Wrinkled, wheezy old Haider, face like a dried prune. They said he had killed men with his bare hands in the old days: strangled them, gouged out eyes, raped. But to look at him now, he could have been a grumpy, harmless old grandfather near the end of his days. But still part of the web.

The fourth man, Lieber knew, was Ernesto Brandt. A mischling. German father, Brazilian mother. Thinning hair, brown eyes, metal-framed glasses with thick lenses, and a high forehead that made him look like an eccentric professor. Maybe fifty, but youthful-looking. The man was important, had been one of the vital keys to the plan.

Lieber looked around as the Volkswagen came to a sudden halt in front of the porch.

5:20 P.M.

The piercing scream of the flashing blue siren tore into the growing darkness like a banshee. Traffic separated, horns honked.

Gonzales, in the front passenger seat of the unmarked squad car, said, "Take the next left."

Juales swung the car down a one-way street of two-lane traffic. He let out an uncharacteristic whoop as he nudged onto the pavement, the car tilting, driving for thirty yards like this, children and passersby staring.

"The only way to travel," Gonzales remarked above the siren's wail.

The news had come over the radio minutes before, and Juales had repeated it aloud, a look of triumph on his face: "They caught sight of the Volkswagen, heading up to the Chapultepec Hills. We're in luck."

Now Sanchez said, "What happens when we get there?"

Gonzales swiveled around in his seat. "We look and watch." He paused. "There's a couple of pump-actions in the back in case we need them. You both know how to use those things? I don't want my backside ending up like a colander."

Sanchez and Cavales smiled, said yes, they knew how to use the shotguns. The car began to climb, the streets less crowded, the houses less shabby. Gonzales switched off the siren.

Juales's phone buzzed on his lap, and he picked it up. He listened, then answered, "Good. We'll be with you in ten minutes."

He turned to the others. "The Volkswagen just turned in through the front gates of the address in Chapultepec. There's a guard at the gate. My men are parked and waiting a hundred yards down the street."

Gonzales smiled at Sanchez. "You think the people you want will be there, waiting for Lieber?"

"I hope so."

"You understand, Vellares, I can't go in without a warrant. And this place is full of rich people. The rich protect themselves. And someone like Haider's got lots of friends in high places, you can count on it. So we better do it strictly by the book."

"What do you suggest?"

"Well, we need a search warrant, to protect my butt." Gonzales hesitated. "There's a judge named Manza. He often helps me. Law-and-order type. I think he's my best bet."

"What about the periphery of the property?"

"The area's all hills and winding streets. Difficult sometimes to know where one property begins and another ends. But I'll have one of the cars take a quick run around. Have a look for rear exits and find a good vantage point where we can observe the place. But let's talk to the judge first."

Gonzales picked up the mobile. "Control. This is Chief Inspector Gonzales. I want you to patch me through to Judge Ricardo Manza . . ."

The avenue was well lit, and Juales parked the car in the shadows between two streetlights. They were on a hill overlooking the villa, under a clump of sweet-smelling eucalyptus. A perfect vantage point in the moonlight: the property lay two hundred yards below, the walled perimeter, the gates, the path leading up to the villa itself clearly visible.

The windows of the car were rolled down. The smell of eucalyptus and poinsettias. Big houses all around.

Sanchez listened while Gonzales spoke with the judge, arguing his case. The conversation was heated, but the judge finally agreed to sign the search warrant.

"Don't compromise me, Gonzi. Don't mess me up," Sanchez heard the judge say over the mobile.

"You have my word on it," Gonzales replied, then said his polite good-bye, turned to the others. "One of my men is picking up the warrant. He should be here in ten minutes."

"What happens then, Eduardo?"

Gonzales looked back at Sanchez. "It's best if one of my men climbs over the wall just before Juales hits the guy on the gate with the warrant. With one of our men inside, he'll make sure the guard doesn't alert the villa. It's risky, I know. They could have armed guards patrolling the grounds, and they might start shooting in any confusion. But it's the only way to surprise them. Just pray they don't have guard dogs loose on the lawns, or an electrified perimeter. Or else whoever goes over the wall could get chewed or crisped."

"What then?"

"Our man lets us through the gate, and we speed up to the house with another car behind us. Put the sirens and lights on at the last moment. That way, there can be no mistake. They'll know it's police, but they won't have time to think. And if they run, they run like scared rabbits." Gonzales paused. "But leave any talking to me once we're inside, okay? After that, you can have Lieber and whoever else you want for questioning."

Cavales said, "The people inside, they may be heavily armed."

Gonzales shrugged. "Up here in Chapultepec, everyone's heavily armed, amigo. They're probably legally held weapons. But once they know we're police, they'd be crazy to open fire. Unless they want to escape this place pretty bad."

A tap came on the car roof and everyone started. A man stood outside, and Sanchez realized it was one of the plainclothes policemen.

"What's the problem?" Juales said.

"There's some movement around by the side of the villa. A group of men just came out onto the patio. They're sitting at a table by the pool. Looks like they're having a meeting." The man paused and held up a night scope. "You want to take a look, sir? You can see them pretty well if you move up the rise."

Juales took the scope and handed it across to Gonzales, who said to the man, "You've found the rear entrance?"

"I believe so, sir. I've got a car there, with three men."

"Good. You've got another scope?"

"Yes, sir, Barca has one."

"Then we'll hold on to this one. Thanks, Madera."

The man turned and walked away into the shadows.

Juales drove up the rise for twenty yards and halted. They could see the side of the villa now, and the turquoise shape of the swimming pool. Gonzales looked through the scope across the narrow valley, then handed it to Sanchez.

"You can't see too good, Vellares. Just a bunch of people. No faces, just blurry green blobs."

Sanchez peered through the scope. The swimming pool looked bright green, and when he swung the scope a little to the left, he saw a group of static figures seated at a white table beside it. But too far away to get a clear view, the images hazy. Very little movement: a figure shaking its head, another leaning forward.

A sound came from behind and the same detective who had given them the scope handed Gonzales a folded sheet of paper, explaining it was the authorized warrant. Gonzales flicked on the interior light, scrutinized the sheet.

"Thanks, Madera. The bad news is, I want you to go over the wall just before Juales serves the warrant. Try not to look so unhappy about it. You got a pair of thick gloves in the car?"

"No, sir."

"Well, get a pair from one of the others. And quick. Someone's got to have a pair. Try one of the uniforms. Put them on before you go over the wall, because if you don't and it's electrified, you end up with stumps. And tell the others to prepare to move, but wait for my call."

Madera moved off into the darkness at a jogging pace.

Gonzales said, "Okay, we've got five cars. Three men to each car, except this one. Sixteen men in total. Six uniformed." He paused, lit a cigarette. "The three other cars stay outside, two covering the front and one the rear. So that leaves us and one more car to go through the gates. We head straight for the pool area. Any questions before we go?"

Nobody spoke. Gonzales nodded to Juales. "Hand out the pump-actions."

Juales went to the back and unlocked the trunk, then came back with two pump-action Remington shotguns and two boxes of cartridges. He handed a weapon each to Sanchez and Cavales and a box each of cartridges as well.

They stepped out and loaded the weapons, then climbed into the backseat again. Gonzales took the night scope once more, made one last check on the figures by the pool, then turned around in his seat. He looked at Sanchez. "There are a couple of guys wandering around the lawns. But it's difficult to see them clearly."

"They look like they're armed?"

Gonzales shrugged. "I can't tell, Vellares. But we'll have to risk it. Everyone ready?"

They nodded.

Gonzales slid his own Smith & Wesson from its holster and placed it on his lap, then picked up the mobile and pressed the TRANSMIT button.

"One to Nightwatch units . . ."

6:02 P.M.

On Gonzales's command, Juales stepped quickly from the car, unholstered his gun, and began to move down the hill at a jogging pace. Sanchez saw him raise his Smith & Wesson to chest height as he moved toward the villa's gates.

At the same time the detective, Madera, came out of the shadows where the other police car was parked twenty yards away. The man wore a pair of white gloves.

As Gonzales slipped across into the driver's seat, Sanchez saw Juales slow his pace, the white warrant visible in his hand. Ten yards from the gates, Juales pushed himself back against the wall, and waited.

Madera joined him. Juales laid down the gun and warrant, cupped his hands, and then Madera slid his foot into them. Juales lifted him up. It took three attempts before Madera gripped the top of the wall. He pulled himself up, and seconds later he disappeared over the top.

Juales retrieved his gun and warrant and began to move toward the gate. Sanchez noticed a police car a hundred yards down the street move slowly out of shadows, ready to follow Gonzales's car through the gates. He looked back to Juales where he waited next to the wall.

There was a sudden loud explosion, a gun discharging, followed by another shot, and Gonzales said, "What the devil—"

Everyone in the car tensed, and they saw Juales race to the gate, his weapon raised and clutched in both hands. Then the gate swung open, and Madera appeared.

Gonzales let out a sigh as they saw Juales slip inside, his gun raised in his right hand and waving the warrant at them frantically.

At that moment, Gonzales said, "Okay, amigos. Let's go."

He hit the accelerator, and the unmarked police car raced toward the entrance gates.

The five men sat around the poolside table.

Turquoise water shimmered under lights. Two butlers served them drinks by the pool at Haider's request, his wheezy old chest unable to stand the cloying air inside the villa.

Lieber told his story while the others remained silent. Told his story and waited for the reaction.

Old Haider wheezed and sucked on his inhaler, took a deep breath. Everyone around the table looked at him. Very slowly he rose from his sunken position in the chair. He was a small man, smaller still with the weight of years on his buckled old shoulders.

Spittle frothed on his lips as he spoke to Lieber. "How, Franz? How could there have been another tape?" Haider's voice sounded like a whispered, throaty death rattle.

Lieber sighed deeply. "Either we destroyed the wrong tape or there were two tapes. There's no other explanation."

Silence descended on the table. Haider's wrinkled claw of a hand went to his brow, massaged the flesh there, thinking hard.

"Is your police source certain about the information?"

"Absolutely."

Haider looked across at Ernesto Brandt, then at the silver-haired man. He was about to speak further when they all heard the crack of a gunshot somewhere in the distance, then another.

Kruger sat bolt upright, then jumped to his feet, his eyes fixed on something over Haider's shoulder. Haider turned, saw one of the guards come running across the lawns, machine pistol in hand, the big man's body pounding hard across the grass.

Kruger was already moving toward the man, meeting him on the lawn ten yards away. The man spoke rapidly, and Kruger turned and raced back just as everyone around the table heard the whine of car motors straining in the distance.

Kruger reached them, his face deathly pale, urgency in his voice. "We've got company. Two cars just coming in through the gates." He turned back smartly, called out to the guards. "Rotman . . . Werner . . . cover us!"

Just as Kruger wrenched the Walther from its shoulder holster, there was a sudden shriek of sirens, a ghostly flashing of blue light visible through the shrubbery and trees, and then the growling nose of a car screamed around the gravel driveway and bumped onto the lawn. Sixty yards away, heading straight toward the poolside, lights blazing.

"Everyone! Inside!" Kruger screamed at the top of his voice. As they moved toward the patio, he saw the first car, then the second, racing toward them, sirens wailing.

The guards were already reacting. Werner raised his machine pistol, and the weapon stuttered in his hands.

Kruger saw the windshield of the first car shatter, heard the thumping report of lead ripping through metal. The car careened across the lawn and scudded into a tree, its blue light suddenly dying, its siren fading like a dying wheeze.

The second car was thirty yards away now, weapons prickling from its windows. A blaze of fire erupted from the vehicle, guns exploding in the darkness. Werner was blasted in the chest, his big body flung backward.

Kruger swore, reached the patio doors just as a blast of lead pellet peppered the wall to his right. He saw the looks of alarm on the faces of the others as they moved into the villa through the French windows, saw the sudden paleness on the face of the silver-haired man as he called out to Kruger, "The back way, Hans. Quickly now!"

Schmidt, clutching his Magnum, aimed at the oncoming car, then squeezed the trigger twice.

The explosions rang around the lawns, echoed about the patio.

Kruger roared, "Inside!" He pushed them in through the patio doors, looked back to see Rotman fire a long burst at the second car, puncturing the vehicle, screams erupting from the vehicle, the windshield shattering, figures inside trying to shield their faces as the car wove aimlessly across the lawn, shot halfway across the turquoise pool, and nosed into the water.

As the guard fumbled for a fresh magazine, Kruger roared: "Keep us covered, Rotman!"

The guard didn't even look behind, simply raised his hand as he went to slam another magazine into the Heckler & Koch and moved for cover.

Suddenly Kruger glimpsed a movement to the left of the first car, saw a figure crawl out of the wreckage where it had hit the tree.

Kruger aimed the Walther, fired three quick shots, then turned and disappeared into the villa.

38

Sanchez lay on the grass and watched the man disappear into the house.

The car had come to a halt in a thicket of shrubbery, the left side of the vehicle embedded in the trunk of a eucalyptus tree. When Sanchez tried to move, he felt a jolt of pain shoot down his right leg.

He had flung himself from the car at the last moment, landed hard on the grass. Now his right hip was on fire, excruciating when he moved. The car was five yards away. He couldn't see inside, the windshield shattered by bullet holes.

Sanchez still had the shotgun, gripped in both hands, and he ignored the pain in his hip, grimacing as he called out, "Gonzales! Cavales!"

After a few seconds of silence, he heard a groan before an answer came back—Gonzales's voice—pain in the reply.

"Over here . . . !"

Before Sanchez could answer, he heard a movement off to the right and turned. A man crouched near the pool, a machine pistol in his hands. A blaze of light erupted from his weapon, and a rake of fire razed the grass beside the big detective.

Sanchez rolled to the right, into shrubbery, then aimed at the moving figure. The pump-action exploded in his hands and the recoil shook his body, but the man by the pool had moved out of sight and into the shadows of a clump of palm trees.

Rear guard. To slow them, Sanchez guessed.

The shrubbery Sanchez found himself in was poor cover. Twenty yards away, the second car sank in the turquoise pool, its blue light still flashing but no sound from the siren, bubbles rising like froth, crimson patches here and there in the pale water. The left rear-passenger door was open and riddled with holes, one of the bodies of the men hanging half in, half out. Sanchez could make out a head thrown back in the driver's seat, mouth open in death.

He suddenly thought of Cavales and Juales. Dead or still alive?

He heard Gonzales swear from behind the car wreckage by the tree. Sanchez called out, "Stay where you are."

Suddenly another burst erupted from near the pool, fire raging across the grass, raking the car. Then the firing stopped. Gonzales swore again.

Sanchez whispered, "Are you okay?"

"I'm alive," came the reply. "Can you see the guy with the machine gun?"

"Thirty yards away, by the pool. Can you cover me?"

"I'll try. But take it easy, amigo."

Sanchez rolled deeper into the shrubbery, ignoring the pains that shot through his hip, conscious of the urgency to move into the villa after the men. He crawled quickly on his belly through the thorny undergrowth, the pain making him wince. He came out ten yards away, at the base of another eucalyptus tree, eyes trying to pick out any movement in the darkness.

Nothing.

If he was going to pursue Lieber and his people, he would have to move quickly.

Suddenly a movement off to the left caught his eye, and he heard a faint rustling of bushes. He strained his eyes, then saw the man crouched low among the shrubbery, caught in a shaft of moonlight. Sanchez inched forward slowly, came to within a dozen yards of the man before he saw him turn, a startled look on his face as he saw the detective.

The pump-action in Sanchez's hands rose and exploded. The blast hit the man in the chest, a muted cry as his body was hurled back into the shrubbery.

At that moment Sanchez heard sirens wailing in the distance.

He turned, moved quickly back to Gonzales, ignoring the terrible pain in his hip as he knelt down beside him. In the wash of light from the house he saw sweat glistening on Gonzales's brow. A patch of dark below the right elbow where a bullet had penetrated flesh.

"Your arm . . ."

"We're getting too old for this, amigo. Let's stick to conferences. You got the gringo with the machine gun?"

Sanchez nodded and examined Gonzales's forearm. A bullet had rutted the flesh, chipped bone. Nothing serious, but painful.

Gonzales tried to push himself up. "The others . . . ?"

Sanchez looked back into the silent, bullet-riddled car, saw the frosted glass and ruptured metal punctured with holes, aware of his heart beating wildly as he moved forward to look. Bile in his stomach, anger in his head like a wild thing, knowing what to expect.

Even in the poor light he could see the bodies. Juales in the front passenger seat, his head to one side, mouth open, a slash of red across his chest, blood everywhere below the torso and waist. Sanchez put a hand to the man's mouth. A faint breath.

But in Cavales's case, there was no doubt: the top of the man's skull was torn apart, a gaping hole where the handsome face had once been. Sanchez wanted to vomit, held it, fury welling up inside him, wanting to rush into the villa after Lieber's people, blow them away.

He heard a sound behind him, looked around. Gonzales was standing now, a hand on the hood of the car as he stared at the scene inside.

Sanchez said, "Juales is barely alive; see if you can help him."

"Where are you going, Vellares?"

But Sanchez wasn't listening. The shotgun gripped in both hands, he was faintly aware of the wail of police sirens, coming closer.

"I'm going in after them, Eduardo. Tell your men."

"Are you crazy? Wait . . . my men are coming."

Sanchez didn't reply. His eyes were fixed on the patio door and the darkened room beyond, and he cocked the pump-action as he moved toward the villa.

6:08 P.M.

As they moved through the rooms, Kruger was in control, covering the rear, the emergency plan clear in his mind: quickly move to the garage, across the open space of the lawn first—a problem, too vulnerable—then drive down through the overgrown back alleyway to get away and reach the safe house. Speed was vital.

Keep moving.

Five rooms to the exit that led to the lawn and the escape route. They were in the third room. No more than two minutes to the garage. But already things were not going according to plan. Kruger swore. Haider was the problem. The old man was moving too slowly, joints buckled and gnarled.

He ordered Lieber and Brandt to carry Haider between them, and now the six men moved through the house more quickly, old Haider, feet dangling in midair between Lieber and Brandt.

Schmidt held the .357 Magnum in his right hand, eyes watchful. The house was lit up. Kruger extinguished the light as they left each room. It would slow anyone who followed.

Suddenly up ahead, a butler stepped out of a room, face pale, eyes wide. Everyone startled.

Schmidt raised his Magnum and fired. The explosive force of the bullet sent the butler sprawling against a wall, blood erupting on his white jacket.

They stepped past the crumpled body.

Schmidt opened another door, moved quickly into the deserted kitchen. Stainless steel, copper, dark wood. The door at the end led outside, to the garden, darkness beyond, and Kruger saw through the windows the vast stretch of silvered lawn.

Vulnerable. Too open. Sixty seconds to cross it at a trot. But they could make it.

Keep moving.

Schmidt slowly opened the kitchen back door, peered left, right, ahead, toward the vast silvered lawn, then turned back and nodded the all-clear.

Schmidt stepped out, the others following, old Haider wheezing and groaning.

Kruger was the last to step out; he saw the light switch by the door and hesitated. He heard a noise behind him, coming from somewhere back in the house. A door opening?

This time he left the light on, then followed after the others.

He was moving backward across the lawn ten seconds later, still covering the rear, the Walther ready in his hand, when he saw the kitchen door move a fraction.

Kruger had left the kitchen light on deliberately, knowing that if anyone came through, they would be at an immediate disadvantage: light looking into dark.

But Kruger would be able to see and respond.

And Kruger definitely saw the movement. Seconds later, the door burst open, a figure appearing, but only for a glimpse, and then the figure disappeared from view.

Kruger swore, went to fire, but knew the shot would be wasted. They were maybe twenty yards across the grass, moving fast—as fast as Haider would allow—Lieber and Brandt grunting under the weight of the old man as they carried him between them, another forty yards to go, breaths gasping, hearts pounding.

"Keep moving!"

Kruger knelt, raised the Walther, aimed toward the lighted kitchen, waiting to see the figure again . . . eyes scanning the room for movement, counting the seconds . . . and then a shotgun blast erupted and the kitchen light went out.

Kruger cursed.

The man was clever, knocking out the light, guessing his strategy. Dark looking into light so easy, dark into dark difficult, leveling the odds.

Kruger waited . . . eyes straining desperately to see into the silvery darkness . . .

A faint movement, to the left?

Kruger fired off three rapid shots . . . heard the crack of lead smack into glass, plaster, heard the kitchen window to the left shatter.

Then nothing.

A shout from behind him. "Kruger!" Leiber's voice. "It's Haider! Something's wrong!"

"Keep moving!" Kruger shouted back, not turning.

But he heard Haider's wheezing gasps, and his eyes darted back; the others almost at the garage, but Lieber and Brandt slowing, holding the sagging, ancient body of Haider between them, something up with the old man, his heart probably not able to take the strain. Kruger wiped sweat from his brow, tried to control his breathing as his eyes went back to the kitchen.

A movement. To the right.

Kruger fired three more quick shots in a short arc, heard the smacks as the lead hit glass, then concrete, wood, concrete.

And then suddenly he saw the figure.

Moving out of shadow: a large man in a light suit moving out onto the silvered lawn like a specter, the long barrel of a weapon held at waist height as he advanced steadily toward them.

Kruger aimed and fired three quick shots at the ghostly figure, saw the man buck and then spin.

Kruger went to fire again, but the hammer clicked. Empty. He tore out the spent magazine, slammed home a fresh one from his pocket.

He focused on the man again. The cop was still coming, his body listing to one side.

Kruger aimed the Walther, squeezed off one round, was about to squeeze the trigger again when the man's shotgun swung up, the weapon exploding and a blast of air whistling past Kruger's left like a hurricane, then another, and another . . .

Kruger cursed.

Screams erupted in the night. Something stung Kruger's left shoulder and he was spun around, the Walther wrenched from his hand. He saw Brandt and Lieber were hit, flung back onto the grass, hands flailing, old Haider collapsed between them.

Kruger searched frantically on the grass for the pistol, but couldn't find it . . . a numbing pain in his left forearm . . . He heard a groan from the tangle of bodies on the grass, then silence.

Forget the weapon . . . the man fifteen yards away . . . halting, loading again in the darkness, calmly . . . like it was no big deal.

Kruger saw the moment and seized it.

He scrambled backward, past the pile of bodies—Lieber, Brandt, old Haider—oblivious to his pain, not caring whether the three men on the grass were dead or alive, as he ran toward the garage where the others had entered.

As he ran, gulping deep mouthfuls of air, he waited for the shotgun blast to hit him in the back.

It never came.

Panting, he reached the garage door and stepped into darkness.

Sanchez stood in the middle of the lawn reloading the shotgun.

He saw the man run toward the building at the end of the lawn, half hidden behind a clump of trees. Too far away now to get a good shot.

He felt a numbing sensation in his right shoulder where two bullets had hit him with the force of sledgehammers, sending him reeling. No pain there, not yet, but it would come.

He loaded five shells and cocked the pump, stepped forward, his hip on fire.

The man on the lawn had given him no choice but to shoot. He had missed, the shotgun blast hitting the group of men instead as they moved across the lawn.

Sanchez swore.

These were the men; these were the people. No doubt in his mind. And he had wanted them alive, hoped they still were.

As he approached the bodies on the grass, he held the shotgun at the ready. He saw Franz Lieber's dead face in the moonlight. A gaping wound in his back from the pump-action. Sanchez grimaced; he had especially wanted Lieber alive.

He heard a groan. Another body, a man with glasses, big forehead. This one was still alive. A gurgling sound came from the man's throat, his face screwed up with agony, a bloody patch on his left shoulder.

Sanchez saw a third figure between the two men, lying facedown. Bloodstains on the man's pale suit where the shot blasted him. Sanchez bent, turned him over. A small, wizened old man. Sanchez stared at the face. Not one of the faces in Lieber's photograph. Nor the man lying on the grass near him, the one still alive. The man groaned again. Sanchez ignored him. Gonzales's men would deal with it.

Behind him came muted noises. Gonzales's men, somewhere in the house. Sanchez turned back toward the building. The man who escaped had gone inside after the others.

Sweat drenched the back of his neck, images burning in his skull. Rudi Hernandez and the young girl, the savage wounds inflicted on their bodies. Cavales, face blown away.

The images drove him on, desperate to find the men trying to escape.

Ten yards from the building, Sanchez saw lunar light washing on the wooden door. He approached cautiously and raised the shotgun. He squeezed the trigger twice: the blasts shattering silence, fragmenting wood, sending what remained of the door smacking back against the inside wall, where it bounced and shuddered off concrete.

The noise died.

Darkness inside. Sanchez saw a crack where the door abutted the frame. He peered in, listened. No sound. But if the men were inside, they could be waiting. His eyes narrowed, trying to discern shapes in the blackness.

The smell of oil. And gasoline. A garage? He could make out the shape of a big car parked in the center, a dull glint of polished metal, a sheen of glass reflected. He was certain he saw another door, ajar, at the end of the building, a thin crack of silver moonlight shining through. Had the men escaped there? Or were they waiting for him?

He listened carefully.

Still nothing.

He couldn't wait forever.

He took a deep breath, felt the sweat coursing down his face as he leveled the shotgun, swung around from the wall, moved inside. And then . . .

A light suddenly went on overhead and blinded him.

Sanchez barely heard the barked command: "Schmidt!"

In the sudden, blinding light, he saw the form of a huge man lunge at him from behind the car—big, blond, a crazy look on his face like a wild animal, a jagged knife in his hand.

Sanchez swung round the pump-action and squeezed the trigger. The deafening roar that followed raged through the garage like a sonic boom.

Sanchez saw the look on the man's face: ugly, snarling, his body like some boulder of granite bearing down on him as the shotgun exploded a yard from the man's chest.

The force of the blast halted his body in midair—his chest exploding, a cavernous hole appearing in the center of his huge torso, guts spilling out and a wave of gushing blood.

The man collapsed on top of Sanchez, pinned him against the wooden wall, the crushing weight knocking his breath out, the face up against Sanchez's own, eyes open wide.

Sanchez smelled the wheezing, foul breath.

The man was still alive.

Sanchez struggled frantically to push the man off, but the weapon was wedged between them. The terrible weight pressed down on him, making him helpless.

Two others appeared: a young, dark-haired man carrying a big Magnum pistol, and another older man, tall, silver-haired, coming toward him out of nowhere, Sanchez recognizing the faces from the photograph in Lieber's house.

Sanchez made a supreme effort, pushed with all his strength. The huge blond moved, and Sanchez saw the knife swing up. Sanchez found the pump-grip, reloaded, pulled the trigger just as the jagged knife thrust into his shoulder, cut through bone and flesh, pinned him to the wall.

Sanchez screamed in pain, and the shotgun exploded again. This time the man's face and head disintegrated, his body flung backward, as shotgun pellets deflected back, prickled Sanchez's body.

And then everything seemed to happen at once.

The two men came forward.

The younger man held the big Magnum in his hand, rage on his face, Sanchez realizing that the dead man had been expendable, a diversion. The man pointed the gun at Sanchez's temple, his other hand reaching to grasp the pump-action, wrench it away.

The silver-haired man stepped forward. His tall frame towered over Sanchez. Kind, soft blue eyes, but something in them Sanchez couldn't fathom.

Did it matter now?

The man's voice whispered something to his companion, but Sanchez didn't hear. Voices—Gonzales's men—coming from outside now, distant, too distant to save him, muted, carrying across the lawn.

The distant voices had decided his fate.

The man holding the Magnum pressed the big pistol hard against Sanchez's head.

It exploded.

6:20 P.M.

The moonlit lawns were awash with uniforms and flashing blue lights.

Ambulances came and went. A little later, a detective took a dazed Gonzales to the old garage, past the bodies on the grass.

When they showed him the body of Sanchez, he wanted to weep.

He looked at the corpse for a long time: the pitiful, lifeless corpse pinned against the wall, the jagged blade driven through his shoulder into the wooden wall, the powder-burned hole drilled through his forehead, the floor awash with blood.

Then he looked at the body of the big blond man. What was left of it. A stench of human excrement drenched the air. Both bodies had defecated after death. Normal.

Sanchez had taken four of them with him. It was little consolation. None really. Besides, there was no pistol near the body of the blond man; someone else had done this. A detective told him that roadblocks were being set up around the perimeter of Chapultepec. But it was a big area. Some hope.

When he finally stepped outside, Gonzales threw up on the lawn. In the silver light, a detective lit him a cigarette, and he took it, wiped his mouth, inhaled deeply.

Gonzales gripped the man's arm.

"Did Juales make it?"

The detective shook his head. "Dead before they got him to the ambulance."

Gonzales closed his eyes a moment in grief, said in a dazed voice, "How many others dead?"

"Four of our own men. The two friends of yours from Asunción. Six from the villa. That includes Haider and their man on the gate who got it from Madera when he tried to pull a gun." The detective paused. "I'm having roadblocks set up all the way to the city. A rookie says he thought he heard a car move off just after he heard the last gunshot. In the confusion and noise, he's not exactly sure. But the garage doors were open." He nodded back toward Haider's villa. "It's possible some of them got away."

"I want the roadblocks tight. You understand?" Gonzales sighed impatiently. "What about the one you found alive on the lawn?"

"He's wounded, not badly, but he's lost a lot of blood. Two of our men went with him in the ambulance. We'll make him talk just as soon as he's patched up."

"And the staff from the villa? Anyone alive?"

"A butler. We found him hiding in the basement. Another butler's dead. I didn't count him. Shot in the chest. He must have got in the way of their escape. That makes thirteen dead in all. The butler who's alive is too shocked to make sense. He took some pills to calm down."

Gonzales jabbed a finger at the detective. "Make him make sense. Find out how many people were here. Get descriptions, names. I want answers."

The man nodded, walked away.

Gonzales drew on his cigarette; his hands trembled. He looked back toward the scene of the carnage, shook his head, and spoke aloud. "Thirteen men dead . . . I don't believe it."

All for what? Who were these people? What the devil was going on?

The sound of an ambulance wailing up the driveway distracted him. Too late now. Sanchez never had a chance. To do what he did was *loco*. Stupid. He must have wanted these people from the villa badly.

Footsteps approached, a soft voice saying, "Sir?"

He turned, in a daze.

A young cop stood there awkwardly. "Sir, there's a man out front who says his name's Cortes. Judge Felipe Cortes." The young man put the emphasis on "Judge," hesitated, looked pleadingly at Gonzales.

"What does he want?"

"He says he wants to talk to the officer in charge. He seems pretty angry. Wants an explanation for all the noise and shooting. He asked if we knew where we were." The cop swallowed nervously. "He said this was a respectable area, not some tin-and-cardboard barrio."

Gonzales knew the judge: a pompous idiot who lived in a big house with servants and a fat wife. As corrupt as many of his neighborhood friends.

"Did he?" Gonzales was barely able to contain his rising anger. "Tell him I'm busy."

"Sir, I told him. He refuses to listen."

"Then"—Gonzales said it slowly, but frustration edged his voice— "tell him to keep his fat nose out of my business. Or I'll have him arrested for hampering the police in their duty."

He saw the young cop's eyes open wide at the angry disrespect.

Gonzales stubbed out his cigarette on the lawn. "Don't worry, I'll tell him myself."

He turned and left the young man standing there, walked slowly back up toward the villa, each step an agony.

PART FOUR

39

Volkmann awoke at eight in the morning and after breakfast checked out of the hotel and drove by Wilhelm Busch's house again.

The white Audi wasn't there, and when he rang the doorbell, there was no reply.

Snow was forecast in the next twenty-four hours, and he decided that if Busch hadn't appeared by the middle of the afternoon, he would drive down to the old monastery off the Salzburg road before the weather turned bad.

There was nothing to do but wait, but his mind was restless. He drove to the old Dachau camp, and the parking lot reserved for the tourist buses was empty. He parked the Ford and walked up to the gate. The railway tracks were no longer there but the camp was still ringed by the original concrete walls, barbed wire, and wooden watchtowers.

The metal entrance gates still bore the words ARBEIT MACHT FREI. The gates were open, but a sign on the wire fence said the camp was closed to visitors. He saw a truck with building materials parked inside, and decided to step through.

The camp remained much as it had looked during the war, but the *Blockhaus*, the U-shaped barrack house that had once served as the administration building, was now a museum and cinema. To the right were the cells that had housed the maximum-security prisoners, kept in isolation by the SS.

The only testament to the rows of prison huts that had once stood were two solitary wooden replicas, to show visitors how the prisoners had existed in the squalid camp. He saw the redbrick chimney where the crematorium still stood. A sign on the wall outside the modernized Blockhaus annex said in German: "Museum."

He opened the door.

Blown-up photographs hung from the walls, and there were several exhibits in glass cases. A tangled mound of eyeglasses in one, looking like some grotesque work of art; a tattered, striped prison uniform in another, a ragged yellow Star of David sewn on its sleeve. In the middle of the long room stood a grim reminder of the brutality inflicted in the camp: a wooden whipping block used by SS guards.

On the wall to the left was a series of photographs: victims of the camp experiments, a cattle train loaded with corpses, lines of emaciated flesh that had once been men, women, children, laid out in the sun. In one, a grinning SS officer, hands on his hips, stood looking down at a young mother, wide-eyed in death and clutching a dead little girl with matchstick legs.

He did not know why he had come here, but for a long time he stared at the pictures, until he was overcome by the images of brutality and torture.

A noise sounded behind Volkmann. A startled woman stood in the doorway, carrying a sheaf of papers. He guessed she was one of the administration staff.

"Are you with the building repair people?"

"No, I'm not."

"The camp is closed to visitors right now. Didn't you see the sign outside on the gate?"

He walked past the woman but said nothing and went outside.

As he drove out of the parking lot, he was thinking of his father, and he never noticed the dark green Volkswagen pulling out a hundred yards behind him.

When he drove by Busch's house again, there was still no car in the driveway, but he decided to stop and try the bell just the same.

When he rang for the second time, the door was opened by a man. Despite his obvious old age and his frail appearance, he was big and burly. He wore tinted, thick-lensed glasses and a woolen cardigan, his sparse snow-white hair combed back off his deeply wrinkled face.

He peered at Volkmann sternly. "Yes?"

The voice was sharp and aggressive. The man's skin was yellow from ill health.

"Herr Busch, I wonder if I might speak with you."

"About what? Who are you?"

Volkmann produced his identity card. The old man held out a wrinkled hand and stared at the ID for several moments before looking up at Volkmann.

"You're the fellow who called yesterday. My granddaughter told me. What do you want?" Impatience bristled in the old man's voice as he handed back the ID.

"I was hoping you could help me. I'd like to ask you a few questions, Herr Busch."

"Questions about what?" he demanded.

"Could we talk inside?"

Busch broke into a sudden wheezing fit of coughing. He removed a handkerchief from his pocket and covered his mouth. When he had recovered, Busch wiped his mouth with the handkerchief and said gruffly, "You better come in."

He led the way past a hallway into a living room. "This way."

The room was long and wide, and steps led down to a warm conservatory. Sunlight poured in through the glass. Framed photographs of Busch's family hung on the living room walls, and Volkmann saw an old one in black-and-white of Busch in officer's uniform.

Volkmann went to sit in a cane chair. Busch was still good on his feet considering his age, but when he sat opposite, he coughed harshly again and placed a hand on his chest.

"The consequences of old age and a former cigarette habit, Herr Volkmann. The medicine helps, if only for a while. Now, what's this about?"

There was a gruffness in the man's voice that irritated Volkmann;

it suggested he was used to giving orders. The images on the walls of the camp museum were fresh in Volkmann's mind, and when he glanced at the photograph of Busch in uniform, he felt a flush of anger.

"You're familiar with DSE, Herr Busch?"

"I've heard about it, yes."

"You were with the Gehlen Organization after the war. You were an intelligence officer."

"That is correct, yes. But what's this got to do with—"

"During the war, you were also an officer in the Abwehr."

Busch's watery blue eyes became suddenly wary. "That was a very long time ago. Maybe if you tell me what this is about?"

"A case I'm working on. I hoped you might be able to help me."

Busch seemed to mellow slightly. He half smiled. "Herr Volkmann, I retired from intelligence work many years ago. I don't understand why you'd want my help."

Volkmann explained about Hernandez's murder. When he told Busch about the house in the Chaco, he saw the confusion on the old man's face and said, "Herr Busch, the man who owned the house joined the Nazi Party in Munich in 1929. His party number was six-eight-nine-six. Twelve numbers away from yours."

The look on Busch's face went from puzzlement to understanding. "I see. How did you find me?"

"I had the Nazi Party membership files cross-referenced with the WASt. There are only two men still alive in Germany who had party numbers relatively close to the number of the man I spoke of. You're one of them."

The heat in the conservatory was stifling, and Busch shifted uncomfortably in his chair. "You said this man in Paraguay was dead. I don't understand. What relevance has he got to the journalist's murder you spoke of?"

"None, obviously, Herr Busch, but his past is very unclear, and someone related to him may be implicated in the murder." Volkmann paused. "For some reason the man who once owned the

Chaco property received large sums of money from Germany, both before and during the war. Your party number was close to his. I was hoping you might remember him and help me to shed some light on the matter." Volkmann looked at Busch. "I realize it's unlikely, but right now you're the only connection I have."

Busch half smiled and shook his head. "Herr Volkmann, we're talking about a long, long time ago."

"I realize that. All I ask is that you just look at the photograph and tell me if you recognize the man."

Volkmann removed the photograph of Erhard Schmeltz from his wallet.

The old man took the photograph. He looked down at it, then back up, shook his head.

"The face . . . I'm sorry, I can't remember. Besides, my eyes are not what they used to be. I'm sorry you've wasted your time." He went to hand back the photograph. "What was the man's name?"

"Erhard Schmeltz. He came from Hamburg."

Something flickered in the old man's watery eyes, and he stared down at the photograph again. When he finally looked up, Volkmann saw the look of disbelief on the wrinkled face.

"You remember him?"

Busch said slowly, "Yes, I remember him."

"You're certain?"

Busch's yellow skin had turned pale. "I met him many times." He paused for a moment. "And the name, yes . . . I remember. Erhard Schmeltz. From Hamburg."

Volkmann said, "Can you tell me anything about him?"

Busch suddenly looked very uncomfortable. He turned back and his tone softened.

"Would you mind if we stepped out into the garden, Herr Volkmann? The heat . . . I . . . I need some air."

When Volkmann nodded, the old man stood up shakily, and when they put on their overcoats he led the way to the door.

* * *

They sat facing each other on the wooden chairs at the picnic table. Busch looked down at the photograph in his hand. His voice sounded shaky.

"Erhard Schmeltz, from Hamburg. Yes, I knew him."

"What sort of man was he? How did you meet? Anything at all may help."

Busch looked back as if he were still lost in reverie. "He knew my father. Schmeltz served in the First War, so he was much older than I. He and my father worked together for a time. The kind of man Schmeltz was? Physically, he was a big man. Tough and dependable. But a peasant, not an intellectual. The type who takes orders, not gives them."

"How did you two meet?"

"It was the summer of 1929, just before I joined the party as a youth. In those days, the Nazi movement was gaining ground. Germany had come out of a war with nothing." Busch stared at Volkmann. "People say things are bad now, but in the old days it was worse, believe me. Do you know what it's like to see a man wheeling a barrow full of banknotes to the bakery shop to buy a loaf of bread? Crazy. But that's how it was in Germany in the Depression.

"Every day there were riots and protests and armed anarchists roaming the streets. No one could find work. And when people saw university professors reduced to selling trinkets and matches on street corners, they knew they were lost." Busch removed his glasses, rubbed his eyes. "My father was a soldier in the First War, like Schmeltz. After the war there was nothing for him but a long list of badly paid jobs. We went from lodging house to lodging house, barely eking out an existence, never enough bread in the house to feed a hungry family.

"And then came the Nazis. They promised prosperity, work, hope. To make Germany great again. Drowning men will grasp at straws, and we Germans then were drowning, believe me. There was a price to be paid, of course, but that came much later."

Busch stopped rubbing his eyes. "You might ask what all this has got to do with Erhard Schmeltz? Nothing, except that I want you to understand the background and how we came to meet."

"Tell me about him."

"Schmeltz worked in the same factory as my father. One day in the autumn of 1929, the factory closed down. That evening my father and his colleagues went out to get drunk to forget their sorrows, and later my father brought some of the men home to meet my family."

Busch paused. "My father's friends were very drunk. One of them was Erhard Schmeltz. They all sat around the table in our kitchen having soup and bread. They talked of Germany's hopelessness. I sat with them. Schmeltz had been a factory foreman. The loss of his position had upset him completely. At the table, he brought up the subject of the Nazis. Most of the other men present were communist or socialist party supporters. My father wasn't political. But Schmeltz declared that he was going to become a Nazi Party member. He said they were the only hope for Germany and suggested that my father and the others do likewise. Schmeltz even tried to interest me. I was a youth, easily impressed when Schmeltz said he served with Hitler in the First War and knew the top Nazis. A week later, I applied for membership and was accepted."

"How often did you meet Schmeltz?"

Busch shook his head. "After that night, I didn't see him again for at least another year. We were not close friends, but I got to know him."

"You say he knew some of the top Nazis personally. Who did he know?"

Busch looked out at the bare winter trees. "Himmler, Bormann. And he and Hitler were old army comrades. But I didn't hear Schmeltz mention his connections again after that night. He was really a very private man."

"What was Schmeltz's function in the party?"

Busch shrugged. "He helped at elections and played bodyguard. Many times I saw him at party rallies or in the Munich beer halls with some of the Nazi bigwigs. He was more brawn than brain, but a loyal and trusted party man."

"Did you know that Schmeltz emigrated to South America?"

"No, I didn't. And by telling me, you solved an old mystery."

"How?"

"Sometime in 1931, Erhard Schmeltz disappeared. No one knew where he had gone. But if what you say is true, now I know."

Volkmann paused, looked at the garden, then back again. "Do you know of any reason why a loyal Nazi like Schmeltz left Germany for Paraguay?"

The old man turned back, and said solemnly, "Why is this so important? All this happened so many years ago. What relevance has it to now, to the present?"

"I don't know how exactly, but I believe it has. Do you know why he ended up in Paraguay?"

"No, I don't. But I do remember there were rumors after he disappeared."

"What rumors?"

Busch shrugged. "But there were so many rumors. That he had been sent away on a mission. That he had got into someone's bad books and been forced to leave the country. But which story is true, I cannot say." Busch hesitated. "You said there was a photograph . . . of a woman? May I see it?"

Volkmann removed the photograph from his pocket. Busch squinted down at the image.

"Do you recall ever having seen that woman before?" Volkmann asked.

The old man looked up. "At my age, faces are difficult to remember. The young woman could be anyone. And my eyes . . . they're not the best. You know her name?"

"No. There was just a date on the back of the original photograph. July 11, 1931."

Busch peered at the image again, then shook his head. "I'm afraid she's not familiar to me."

"Could she have been a relative of Erhard Schmeltz's?"

Busch studied the photograph more closely, then shrugged, handed it back. "It's possible. I thought perhaps his sister. I met her several times, but it's not her."

"What about his wife, or a girlfriend?"

Busch smiled. "No, most definitely not. Schmeltz wasn't a womanizer. He was a big, awkward countryman always ill at ease around women." He paused, began to say something more, then appeared to change his mind.

As Volkmann replaced the photograph in his pocket, Busch said, "You're not telling me everything, are you, Herr Volkmann?"

The light was fading to gray now, the sun gone behind clouds.

Volkmann said, "Erhard Schmeltz emigrated to Paraguay in November of 1931. According to records in Asunción, he had with him his wife, Inge, and their child, a boy named Karl. Schmeltz also had five thousand American dollars in his possession. At six-month intervals afterward, he received bank drafts of five thousand American dollars from Germany. At first the drafts were sent privately. But after the Nazis came to power, they were sent secretly by the Reichsbank, right up until Schmeltz died in Asunción in 1943. After that, his wife received the money, until February of 1945, when the drafts ceased." Volkmann paused. "I'd like to know why Schmeltz received that money, Herr Busch. It may or may not have relevance to the case I'm working on, but I'd like to know. It's part of the puzzle."

Even in the fading light, he saw that the old man had turned pale again, and he stared into Volkmann's face. He opened his mouth to speak, then closed it.

Volkmann said, "Is something the matter? Did something I said surprise you?"

"Everything you have said so far about Erhard Schmeltz has surprised me." Busch looked away, stared out into the fading light. His face was as white as chalk. "Do you know who sent him the money from Germany?" he asked.

"I don't. But I'd guess it had to be someone with authority if the Reichsbank was involved."

"Why do you think the money was sent?"

"I've no idea." Volkmann looked at Busch. "But it surprises you that Schmeltz was sent such large sums?"

"Of course. He wasn't a wealthy man. At least not while I knew him. And I can't think of a reason why he would have received such amounts."

"You think it's possible Schmeltz was helping someone to put away money secretly? Someone high up in the party?"

Busch shrugged. "It's possible. After the war, Germans abroad helped Nazis set up secret bank accounts. But that happened toward the end of the war, when defeat was inevitable. Not before. And most of those accounts were kept in Switzerland."

Something seemed to be troubling Busch, but he remained silent, his brow furrowed.

Volkmann said, "Did you ever hear of something called the Brandenburg Testament?"

Busch's wrinkled face came up sharply. "Has this got something to do with what we're discussing?"

"Let's just say it came up in conversation. Why? You've heard of it?"

"Yes, I've heard of it. It's just old Nazi propaganda, Herr Volkmann."

"What do you mean?"

"In February 1945, two months before the war ended, a meeting was held in Hitler's bunker, near the Brandenburg Gate. It was supposed to be top secret, but we heard rumors about it afterward in the Abwehr. Hitler's most loyal SS were present. Mostly Leibstandarte SS, his bodyguard. Even they knew defeat was imminent, but none would dare admit it publicly. Instead, they talked about regrouping to carry on the war. The Testament was said to have been a legacy sanctioned by Hitler."

"What kind of legacy?"

"Herr Volkmann, it was really only propaganda nonsense, I assure you."

"Tell me anyhow."

"In the event of the Reich being defeated, gold and bullion held by the Reichsbank and SS were to be secretly shipped to South America and also hidden in parts of Germany. The belief was that when the time was right again, the party would be resurrected. You could say it was a blueprint to secretly reestablish the Nazi Party." Busch paused. "When we heard about the plan in the Abwehr, we laughed. It was the foolish hope of desperate men. The Testament came to nothing. Certainly gold and other bullion made its way to South America after the war. It was often used simply to keep a chosen few in comfort and security for the rest of their lives. But the amounts of money Schmeltz received and when he received it, that would eliminate him from any connection, surely?"

Volkmann nodded.

For a long time, Busch was silent. It was growing cold in the garden; he finally looked at his watch and stood. "I'm afraid I must take my leave of you. I have things to attend to."

Volkmann rose. "Thanks for your help."

Busch led him to the front door. "The smuggling operation you spoke of, you think it's gold?"

"I really don't know."

Busch hesitated. "There is one more thing you should know. I don't know if it's relevant, and I meant to say it earlier, but our discussion was somehow deflected." The old man paused. "According to your information, Erhard Schmeltz went to South America with his wife and child, is that correct?"

"That's what the records in Asunción say."

"The boy's name again?"

"Karl."

"And when was the boy born?"

"The records say four months before Schmeltz arrived in Paraguay."

Busch shook his head vigorously. "Herr Volkmann, it couldn't have been Erhard Schmeltz's wife, and it couldn't have been his son."

Volkmann stared back at the old man in confusion.

"Why?"

"Because Erhard Schmeltz never married. At least not in Germany. Nor did he have any children that I knew of. And the woman who emigrated to South America with him would have been his sister. I thought perhaps it was she in the photograph you showed me, but it wasn't. Her name was Inge, I remember. She was a rather unattractive, awkward countrywoman who never married or had children. She lived with her brother as his housekeeper, and she disappeared at the same time as Erhard Schmeltz." Busch paused, shook his gray head. "So whoever the boy was that you say they took with them to Paraguay, he wasn't their child."

40

MEXICO CITY. WEDNESDAY, DECEMBER 21, 12:00 A.M.

It was warm in the basement interview room, the atmosphere charged with tension.

Tension and frustration.

The gray walls were awash with bright light, and Gonzales gritted his teeth as he stared down at the Brazilian, Ernesto Brandt, seated behind the table. The man's left shoulder was bandaged, and he looked to be in pain.

Gonzales himself had been attended to by a paramedic at the villa; the man gave him a couple of yellow pills and told him to see a doctor immediately. The throbbing in Gonzales's arm wouldn't go away, but the doctor would have to wait.

He stared down at the Brazilian.

The man wore metal-framed glasses with thick lenses. His high forehead made him look like a professor. He sat impassively—except when his face showed pain—but silent throughout the one-sided conversation, which had gone on for almost three hours.

Gonzales put his two best interrogators on the job, and they questioned Brandt before Gonzales arrived. Now he glanced at his watch. After midnight.

The interpreter, a shy, young, bespectacled man, sat opposite, his presence a waste of time because Brandt was saying nothing. He had been read his rights, in Portuguese, by the translator. Gonzales spoke a little Portuguese himself, enough to get by.

There would be no lawyer until Brandt spoke. No food, no water, no painkillers. Nothing. But Gonzales might as well have been talking to a mute.

Brandt had already been interviewed by the two senior detectives using the translator.

"I'm talking to myself," one of the frustrated detectives said afterward.

"Tell me," Gonzales almost spat.

"His name's Ernesto Brandt."

"He told you?"

"He told us nothing. Not a single word. Just sits there. When we searched him, we found a key card for the Conrad Hotel. I had a man go over and check out the room."

"And?" Gonzales asked.

"Our dumb friend checked in two days ago off a flight from Rio. We found a Brazilian passport in the name of Ernesto Brandt. Age fifty, born in Rio. The passport looks good."

"You confirmed it with the Brazilian embassy?"

The detective nodded. "They're checking with Brasilia. They'll get back to us as soon as they have anything. Any luck with the roadblocks?"

Gonzales sighed, shook his head. But of course, they didn't know what they were looking for. A disadvantage in a city of more than 20 million. Brandt would know how many persons were in the villa at the time of the shooting and who they were. He would know what type of car the people who murdered Sanchez had escaped in.

The only ones at the villa who possessed identification were Lieber—the false passport in the name of Monck—and the two butlers.

The second butler, who survived, could tell them nothing. A business card in his wallet suggested he worked for a catering company used by Haider. But the butler was in a state of shock. Immediately after the villa shooting he swallowed a bunch of pills—a strong cocktail of tranquilizers. Now he was sedated to the eyeballs in the Valparaiso Hospital. A zombie. He wouldn't be able to talk for many hours.

And time was one thing Gonzales did not have.

The old man named Haider had suffered a heart attack. He was already dead as they stretchered him to the ambulance, just like Juales.

The detective nodded toward the interview room. "You want to try with Brandt? The guy's got glue on his lips. Personally, I think it's a waste."

Gonzales scowled. "We'll see."

The man watched him enter the room. Watched and said nothing. Gonzales wanted to beat the silence out of Brandt with angry fists. Juales dead. Cavales dead. Sanchez dead. And ten others. A bloodbath.

And yet this man said nothing. Calm. Controlled, despite his pain, despite hours of threats, and pounding the table in front of him.

Gonzales tried again. "Your name?"

Silence.

"Why were you at the villa?"

Brandt continued to look straight ahead at the far wall. Gonzales gritted his teeth. "Tell me the names of the men at the villa."

Brandt licked his upper lip, but his eyes didn't move.

Gonzales said, "The charges against you are serious. Complicity in the murder of six police officers. Resisting arrest. Attempting to flee the scene of a crime. I could go on but I'm losing my patience." Gonzales pounded his fist on the table. "So talk! Why were you at the villa? Who were the men meeting Lieber?"

Gonzales reached over, wrenched Brandt from his seat by the lapel nearest his wounded shoulder. Then he made a fist, clenched into a tight, angry ball.

For once, Brandt reacted. He screamed in agony.

Gonzales let fly.

The fist halted a hairsbreadth from the man's face. Gonzales let out a long sigh of frustration. Grudgingly, he let go of the Brazilian's lapel.

Brandt's face was contorted in pain. Slowly he sat down. Still no sign of fear, but a little anxious now.

Controlled again, Gonzales said, "Listen to me, Brandt, or whoever you are. Listen well. Thirteen men are dead. Some were policemen, close friends of mine. Good friends. Good men."

Gonzales took a deep breath, let it out, then went on: "The charges you face are serious. But if you help me I'll make certain it's considered by the court. Understand?"

Gonzales left the words hanging, waited for a response. In the silence that followed, he could hear his own breathing.

Finally, after what seemed like an age, there was a brief flicker in Brandt's eyes. He stared up at Gonzales.

He's going to talk, thought Gonzales.

Then Brandt opened his mouth, and the words came out in Spanish, contempt in every syllable. "I have nothing to say. Except that I want to speak with a lawyer."

Gonzales exhaled with a terrible frustration.

* * *

The man was tall and wore an expensive, well-tailored suit. His face was tanned and handsome.

They sat in Gonzales's office, the city's winking lights sprawling beyond the window.

In his left hand Gonzales held the gold-embossed personal card the man had handed him in the basement hallway minutes before. Gonzales ran a finger across its shiny rough-smoothness.

FIRST SECRETARY TO HIS EXCELLENCY, THE AMBASSADOR OF BRAZIL. The man's name below his title. When Gonzales met him in the hallway, he asked to see the prisoner, Brandt, but not to talk with him. The diplomat stared at Brandt silently for a long time. His face turned pale, then he nodded to Gonzales before being led back upstairs to the office.

The man said in perfect, cultured Spanish, "Perhaps you better explain the situation to me."

Gonzales ignored the niceties and told it straight. Thirteen people dead at the villa.

The diplomat reacted to the body count.

Gonzales finished, and the diplomat said, "After your detective phoned the embassy, we contacted police headquarters in Brasilia. The passport this man Brandt carried is legitimate. I believe our chief of police in Brasilia will be contacting his opposite number here in Mexico City to discuss the matter."

The diplomat hesitated, and Gonzales saw the perspiration on his upper lip. He was worried.

"Go on," prompted Gonzales.

The diplomat paused, uncertain. "This is a rather . . . sensitive matter. I believe I ought to speak with your commissioner first."

Gonzales took a deep, angry breath, then looked the man in the eye.

"I'm in charge of this case. You talk only to me. Thirteen people are dead, and your countryman downstairs is implicated. I want answers, fast. Who's Brandt? Why are you people so interested that the first secretary himself comes here? Tell me, and tell me quickly."

The diplomat's face flushed red. He wasn't used to being talked to in this way. But still worried. Perspiration glistening on his upper lip.

Gonzales said impatiently, "I haven't got all day, señor."

"Very well, Chief Inspector. Your superior will no doubt confirm this once he's spoken with our chief of police. However, I will tell you myself. What you are about to hear is highly classified and sensitive information." He paused, then added, "You may be aware that during the time the military was in power, Brazil developed a program for the production of nuclear weapons. After the return of democracy, the program was canceled, but not before several kilos of weapons-grade plutonium were produced. This material was not disposed of."

Gonzales watched the man without replying.

"Señor Brandt was involved in that program," the diplomat continued. "And it has come to light that he managed to steal some of that material . . . in small quantities. But over time, the small quantities add up."

"You're saying someone out there has enough Brazilian plutonium to build a bomb?"

"In short, yes."

Gonzales made a sign of the cross. "In the name of heaven . . ."

The story continued for several more minutes, the enormity of what the diplomat was saying making Gonzales understand Brandt's reluctance to talk.

When the diplomat finished, and Gonzales was satisfied that the man had told him everything, he thanked him and led him to the door, then moved back to his desk.

The call from the commissioner came immediately.

The conversation lasted for almost two minutes; then Gonzales tapped the receiver and made the necessary phone calls at once. All border posts, all air and sea ports—on alert.

As for the plutonium, the diplomat had no idea of where it was. Perhaps still in South America. Perhaps radical Muslims had it. Perhaps it was in Europe or North America. The proper, international authorities would have to be notified. Meanwhile, Sanchez's people in Asunción might have more immediate leads.

Gonzales swore.

In a moment he tried the number of the Central Police Office in Asunción himself, but the lines were busy. He called the operator on the ground floor, gave him the number, and told him to keep trying until he got through. He checked his watch. In a little while he would have to drive out to Tacubaya and tell Juales's widow of her husband's death. An unpleasant thought and deed. The man had been a good and competent policeman, and a close friend.

Sanchez's and Cavales's widows must be told, too.

His head ached. He lit a cigarette, inhaled as he crossed to the window. His arm throbbed, but he tried to ignore the discomfort.

Beyond the glass, stardust lights stretched to the Chapultepec Hills and the Sierra de las Cruces. So many places to hide in a city of more than 20 million souls, so many routes of escape. He didn't hold out much hope. People like Haider had connections, and there were other Haiders. What did they call it in the old days? *Die Spinne.* The Spider. He remembered hearing the stories told to him by the old detectives when he was a rookie. The Germans who came to Mexico with gold and money after the war and bought the big villas in the Chapultepec Hills and down along the coast. And their organization, the Spider, which was secretive and efficient in the extreme.

The chances of catching the men were slim. Without question, he would try—but something was telling him that the men from the villa were already gone. Still, he had to make the effort. For Juales and his men, for a dead Sanchez and his compatriot, all of them lying now in the police morgue.

The telephone buzzed. He turned, startled.

Asunción, he hoped. His call to Paraguay.

They would need to know about Sanchez and Cavales, how they died. And just as important, why.

And now that he himself knew, he shook his head in disbelief. No wonder the men were so desperate to escape the villa. No wonder they were prepared to flee at any cost. He crossed back to his desk, stubbed out his cigarette, and picked up the phone.

41

WEDNESDAY, DECEMBER 21

It was almost five-thirty when Volkmann's Ford drove up the gentle slopes toward Waldweg.

He consulted Ivan Molke's drawing. It placed the monastery eight miles going southeast.

Volkmann found it on a desolate road as the Ford's headlights swept across a narrow granite bridge. Beyond it were two massive wooden doors of the monastery entrance, set in high sandstone walls.

Some instinct told him to take the Beretta. He slipped the pistol in his pocket, and took the flashlight and the spare batteries.

The sandstone walls around the old monastery looked pretty solid. A metal crucifix hung above the ancient wooden gates. A judas gate was set in the middle, and Volkmann doused the headlights.

He shone the flashlight and when he pushed in the judas gate, it swung open on creaking hinges and he stepped inside.

He found himself in a cobbled courtyard. An ancient rusted handcart and mounds of debris littered the cobble. The flashlight picked out arched cloisters that ran along the sides. His footsteps echoed as he stepped under the dark archway.

The plaster was crumbled in places, and a door hung on broken hinges. Volkmann flashed the light inside an old office, cluttered with rotted furniture.

Nearby was a garden with a scattering of withered fruit trees. An old fountain stood in the center, its stone bowl filled with rainwater. Volkmann's flashlight swept over a belfry tower.

It was all part of the monastery church and graveyard, overgrown with withered ivy. He pushed open the church door, and the sound cracked inside like a roll of thunder. The place smelled of rot and decay. Broken stained-glass windows were set high in the walls, and a couple of ancient pews rested on their sides.

The wash from Volkmann's flashlight caught a stairway to his left. Stone steps led down into darkness. He followed the steps warily, until he found himself in the cellars beneath the church.

Bags of plaster and cement were stacked against the walls, along with cans of paint piled neatly. The storeroom was filled with building materials. Volkmann knelt and examined them. They appeared fresh and unused. As he stood up again, he heard a noise.

He froze.

Footsteps echoed from somewhere in the church above.

He flicked off the Beretta's safety and carefully climbed the stairwell. At the top, he heard a noise like the click of a shoe. He raised the Beretta. From somewhere outside he heard footsteps echoing hard on cobblestones. Volkmann raced back toward the courtyard.

He saw a figure dart between the cloisters. At that precise moment, the figure halted, turned, fired twice, all in one fluid movement. The bullets cracked into the wall above Volkmann's head.

He brought up the Beretta and fired off three quick shots into the dark, the bullets smacking into sandstone and ringing about the courtyard. The figure vanished.

Volkmann raced toward the monastery gates, and as he stepped through the judas gate, he saw the taillights of a car disappearing down the roadway. Some instinct told him to check the Ford, and when he reached it, he saw that the two front tires had been shot through.

He swore aloud as he saw a pair of red taillights fade through the trees before they disappeared into darkness.

It took him almost an hour to reach the service station on the autobahn, driving on one flat tire after fitting the spare. By the time he had two new tires fitted it was almost nine, and he drove back to the monastery to take another look around. This time he left the Ford three hundred yards from the road and walked back, taking the flashlight and spare batteries with him. Marks scarred the gravel where the fleeing car had burned rubber, but apart from that, he found nothing. At the stone bridge he shone the light and noticed a stream that ran in a moat around the perimeter.

He shone the flashlight where the fleeing figure had fired, but found no spent cartridge shells. He estimated that the monastery stood on several acres walled with sandstone and that despite its years, it was still in solid condition, and he wondered again what significance it must have to be drawn in Kesser's notebook.

He walked back up to the cemetery and flashed the light between the rows of headstones. Most of the monastery graves dated from before the war, and the most recent bore an inscription dated twenty years before. He saw no evidence of any freshly dug soil, and none of the graves appeared to have been disturbed.

It was almost three in the morning when he let himself into the apartment. The early morning traffic was thin and he spotted no one tailing him.

Erica was asleep, her blond hair strewn about the pillow. He realized that she was the only one who knew he was driving down to Dachau. He stood looking down at her face, doubt gnawing at him, wondering if he had been reckless in trusting her.

In the kitchen, he saw the note by the telephone: "André rang. He said to phone him."

He made the call to the duty office, and the Frenchman answered sleepily.

"The two names you gave me—Trautman, Klee—didn't turn up

on our computer, Joe. So I passed them on to the German desk like you said. They came back pretty quick."

"And?"

"They wanted to know what the story was. I told them I didn't know, but if we came up with anything, I'd get back to them."

"So what did the Germans say?"

"The two turned up as homicides."

"How did they die?"

"Trautman was a hit-and-run victim but they suspected homicide, three months ago. Klee was shot, two days later. In each case, the victims had no criminal background. Elderly middle-class men with no police records. No witnesses, no suspects. That's why the Germans were so interested to know if we had anything." The Frenchman paused. "What are you on to, Joe?"

"I don't know, André." He jotted details on the pad beside the phone. "Anything else?"

"Klee was a retired army major from Rostock, sixty-seven years of age. Trautman was a businessman, a year older, from Essen."

"What about a connection, André?"

"Apart from the homicide link, the German desk knows of no connection between both men, but they'd be very interested if you've found one. Does any of that help?"

"I don't know, André. What about Hanah Richter?"

"She retired some years ago, to Berlin. But I got a phone number and address."

Volkmann jotted them down on the pad. "Thanks for your help, André."

"Any time. Send my love to the woman. She sounds okay."

He sat on the couch sipping a scotch, thinking over André's information.

There was no doubt about Kesser now. He was definitely connected with the people in the Chaco, no question. The deaths of the two men on Kesser's list implicated him.

But why were the men killed? he asked himself. The only way to find out was to pull Kesser in.

He searched for any kind of pattern to the puzzle. The murdered men—Trautman, Klee—were middle class, with professional or business backgrounds. Like Rauscher and the woman, Hedda Pohl. The only connection Volkmann could see was that they would all have been born while the Nazis were still in power.

As he lay back on the couch, he thought again of the shadowy figure in the monastery courtyard. The car could have followed him on the main autobahn and then tracked him at a distance with its lights off, and he guessed that was what had happened.

He found the tape in his briefcase. He listened to it play through a half-dozen times, knowing the words before they came, knowing each inflection.

"The shipment . . . ?"

"The cargo will be picked up from Genoa as arranged."

"And the Italian?"

"He will be eliminated, but I want to be certain we don't arouse suspicion concerning the cargo. It would be prudent to wait until Brandenburg becomes operational. Then he will be dealt with along with the others."

Pause.

"Those who have pledged their loyalty . . . we must be certain of them."

"I have had their assurances confirmed. And their pedigree is without question."

"And the Turk?"

"I foresee no problems."

"The woman in Berlin . . . you're absolutely certain we can rely on her?"

"She won't fail us, I assure you." Pause. "There are no changes to the names on the list?"

"They'll all be killed."

Tiredness overcame him, and he removed the headphones.

He decided to sleep on the couch, too tired to move into the spare bedroom. He didn't want to wake Erica or talk with her just then, his mind too troubled and confused.

As he lay back, he massaged his temples and tried to empty his mind, but the recorded voices came in on him again. What was the shipment? Who was the Italian? The Turk? And who were the people to be killed? The people in Kesser's notebook list?

And who was the woman in Berlin?

As he lay there on the edge of sleep, he thought of the images on the Blockhaus walls at Dachau: the big, dark, lifeless eyes of the woman clutching her dead child to her breast, the grinning face of the SS man looking down at her.

He closed his eyes as if to erase the sight.

But the last thought on his mind as he lay on the edge of sleep was a line on the tape.

It came like a click in the back of his head, so obvious he wondered why it hadn't come to him before now.

Pedigree!

It was too late to do anything about it, and he would have to wait until morning to check with Berlin. But he wondered if it might be a glimmer of light in the darkness.

42

STRASBOURG. THURSDAY, DECEMBER 22

The business hours of government agencies in Germany are normally eight to four, and when Volkmann made the telephone call to the Berlin Document Center, it was exactly 8:00 a.m.

He asked to speak with Maxwell, and Volkmann explained the information he needed.

"What the devil's up with DSE that you're checking all these names?"

"I'm afraid it's classified right now, Mr. Maxwell, but Ted Birken told me to contact you if I needed any information. You think you could check?"

Maxwell sighed. "Well, I guess . . . but it may take a little time."

"How long?"

"It's Christmas. We're winding down. Can it wait until after the holidays?"

"I realize I'm asking a lot, but I need the information today. You think it can be had?"

Maxwell sighed again. "What you're looking for is a connection between these names, right? Klee, Trautman, Pohl, Rauscher, and the others. Where these people were stationed in the period you specified. And if they had any children, their names and dates of birth."

"That's it."

"It means going back through a whole bunch of files. You realize that? All you've given me is names. No dates of birth, no rank."

"I realize that, Mr. Maxwell. But as I say, it's important."

"I'll see what I can do. But I can't promise I'll get through them all."

Volkmann thanked the man and then punched in the number for Hanah Richter. She lived in Berlin's Nikolassee. A woman's voice answered, deep and commanding. She introduced herself as Hanah Richter.

"What's this about, Herr Volkmann?"

He explained he was with DSE and learned that she once worked for the German government during the Nazi trials of the 1970s, and that she was an expert on the period. "I have a favor to ask, Frau Richter. Would you take a look at a photograph of a young woman taken during the 1930s?" He explained about the Nazi armband in the picture. "Perhaps you might be able to identify her, or might know someone who could help."

"Is this something official?"

"Yes."

"Are you trying to track some Nazi?"

"No, Frau Richter. I can't explain any more than I have but I'd appreciate your help."

"You're going back a long time, Herr Volkmann. A very long time indeed."

"I realize this might be an inconvenience, but what if I flew to Berlin this evening?"

"Is this really that important?"

"Yes, it is."

"This young woman . . . you've no idea who she might be?"

"Perhaps the wife or girlfriend of a senior SS officer or Nazi official. But I'm only guessing. The photograph was taken in 1931."

He heard a deep sigh at the other end.

"I may be an expert, but my depth of knowledge does not extend to every friend of every Nazi. And you're talking about two years before the Nazis came to power, you realize that?"

"I appreciate that," Volkmann persisted. "But if you'd just take a look . . ."

There was a long silence at the other end of the line, and then finally the woman gave in.

"Very well. I better give you directions to my home."

He organized a return ticket to Berlin on the six o'clock shuttle out of Stuttgart. It was almost two when he got the return call from Maxwell.

The Document Center director gave him the information, and when he finished, said to Volkmann, "You still there?"

"Yes, I'm still here." Volkmann jotted down everything Maxwell told him.

"Does the information help any?"

"I think you could say that."

"Now, would you care to tell me what this is about, or is it still classified?"

"I still need to do some checking but as soon as I know for certain myself, I'll let you know. Happy Christmas, Mr. Maxwell . . ."

Volkmann cradled the receiver, looked down at his notebook, and started to make the phone calls.

It took him less than a half hour to get the information he needed, and when he finished making the calls, he could feel the sweat running down the back of his shirt.

He was aware of his heart pounding in his chest as he drove to the apartment. Erica had left a note to say she had gone for a walk in the park. He found her walking by the lake, and they went to sit on one of the benches.

He saw the look of surprise when he told her about Busch and the monastery shooting.

"There's something else that's strange," he told her.

"What?"

"I had a feeling about the place. As if I'd been there before. Not there exactly, but somewhere like it."

"What do you mean, Joe?"

"Like a feeling of déjà vu."

Her hand touched his face. "Tell me you'll be careful. It frightens me. What happened to Ivan Molke's men, you think the two incidents are connected? That it's the same people?"

"Maybe." He explained about Hanah Richter. "I'm flying to Berlin this evening. She may be able to help identify the woman in the photograph, or know someone who can."

"Was Busch certain about Erhard Schmeltz . . . and that Schmeltz's sister wasn't the boy's mother?"

"Adamant. The question is, who did the boy belong to if he wasn't theirs?"

"And the Brandenburg Testament. How can you be so certain that's still significant?"

"Because I checked with the Berlin Document Center. Let's take Manfred Kesser first. The records say he was a Leibstandarte SS colonel. He was stationed in Berlin at the time this Testament was pledged. I asked for seven names to be checked."

"What names?"

"The ones in Kesser's notebook. Trautman, Klee. And the others Lubsch was asked to kill. Massow, Hedda Pohl, and Rauscher. There was a word on the tape. Lubsch used the same word when he spoke of Kesser. *Pedigree*. That was what made it click into place. That and the Nazi armband in the Chaco photograph." Volkmann paused. "It was the only connection I could think of, apart from the victims' age group. But the Document Center connects all of the names."

"What connection? None of those murdered were Nazis, Joe. They were too young."

"But each of their fathers was a Leibstandarte SS officer, stationed in Berlin at the time the Testament was signed."

"But can you know that for certain?"

"The three people Kesser wanted killed: Massow, Rauscher, and Pohl. There were three officers on file with those names, Erica. The same applies to Trautman and Klee. There were two officers with those names, each with the rank of major or above. And they were all stationed in or near Berlin. My guess is that they could have been signatories to the Testament. And the people who were killed were the children of those officers."

"But how can you know that these people are the same children?"

"Because every SS officer's file recorded the names and dates of birth of their children, if they were married. All the names and ages match with their fathers' files. I telephoned our politician friend Walter Massow in Berlin, to be certain. His father was prosecuted and imprisoned for war crimes. Maybe that's why he's doing the work he's doing, trying to do penance for his father's sins."

"And Herbert Rauscher?"

"His father was a Leibstandarte major captured by the Russians in the battle for Berlin in April of 1945. He was sent to a German prisoner-of-war camp in Siberia and died there."

Volkmann let the information sink in, saw her hesitate before she looked at him.

"But Kesser's a neo-Nazi. Why would he want to kill the children of former SS?"

Volkmann shook his head. "I'm only certain of one thing. We're not just talking about the deaths of Rudi and the others. This is something that goes much deeper and goes back a long time. To the last months of the war in Berlin, when these people swore their allegiance to Hitler. There's got to be a reason why these people were killed. Maybe there's a secret someone still wants to hide. And there were other names in Kesser's notebook. Maybe that's what the voice on the tape was talking about when it said the names on the list would all be killed. The question is, why? What do the children of these officers know that makes Kesser want them dead?"

"Massow wasn't killed. Did you ask him what he knew?"

Volkmann nodded. "He was baffled by the whole thing. His father died in prison many years ago."

"Are you going to talk with Ferguson about all this?"

"Not until I find out why these people were killed. To do that I'm going to have to pull Kesser in and have a talk with him."

Erica looked at him. "You said there were seven names you checked besides Lothar Kesser's. You mentioned only six. What was the other name?"

He had been waiting for the question and he searched her eyes. "Your father's. He was stationed in Berlin at the same time as all the others, was posted there in January of 1945."

Erica looked away, toward the park, then back again.

He saw the expression on her face and heard the defensiveness in her voice. "Why did you check on my father?"

"Because if he was one of those who swore his allegiance, you might know something more than you're telling. And that something may even put you in danger."

"That's not the truth completely, is it, Joe? It was because you didn't trust me, and you wanted to see my reaction when you told me. And you still don't trust me, do you? Even though you're telling me all this. You look into my eyes, and I know you're searching for answers. You're searching to see if I'm telling the truth or lying."

"I want to believe you, Erica."

She said nothing for a long time, then she looked at him. "I've hidden no secrets from you, Joe. And I know none of my father's. If I was one of Kesser's people, why would I have come to you in the first place? Why would I have wanted you to investigate Rudi's death? Why, Joe? Why would I have done these things?"

He had no answer and he knew it.

"Joe, I hardly knew my father. I never believed in his ideals. You must believe this. The fact that my father was in Berlin at that time— I never knew of this until you told me."

He looked at the blue eyes watching his and remembered the warm body and the hands touching him in the darkness and how close he had felt to her. Looking at her now, he wondered how he could doubt her.

Her hand came up to his face, touched his cheek, and her voice was soft, almost pleading. "Prove that you trust me, Joe. Please."

"How?"

"Just believe me. And take me with you to Berlin. After what happened to you and Ivan Molke's men, I'd feel safer. Will you take me, Joe?"

He hesitated, aware of the blue eyes looking into his face.

He didn't notice the two men sitting in the parked car in the distance, observing them through the bare winter trees.

43

Meyer saw the lights of the small Tyrolean villages in the valley below as the Mercedes growled up the steep mountain road.

A sprinkling of snow dusted the thickly forested slopes, and as he came around the bend the headlights swept over the closed metal barrier gate. A sign was attached, the words EINTRITT VERBOTEN! in bold red lettering.

Meyer halted the car and switched off the motor. He flashed the headlights three times before dousing them completely, then pressed the button to roll down the electric window.

The scent of pine gum wafted into the car on the crisp, cold air, and he saw one of the guards come out from the wooden guard hut that was hidden behind the trees.

The man had a Heckler & Koch machine pistol draped across his chest. He shone a flashlight inside the Mercedes, before he nodded for Meyer to proceed.

Another guard appeared and unlocked the barrier gate. Meyer started the Mercedes, and the car slowly moved forward.

Kesser and Meyer crossed the gravel driveway together to the flat concrete building. Kesser opened the double dead bolts on the gray-painted steel door with a key from the bunch in his pocket. Once inside, he flicked the switch, and the room was flooded with light.

The interior of the building was ice-cold, but the contrast with the bland, functional exterior was stunning.

A wedge-shaped steel gantry stood in the center of the room. A metal launchpad cradled in the gantry held the gray-painted warhead at a 45-degree angle. Below the gantry was a concrete pit measuring three yards by three yards, the bottom and sides of the concrete lined with matted asbestos sheeting, and Meyer knew it was to damp the launch burn-off.

Two metal sliding doors were set in the flat roof, and the building walls were painted military gray. To the right of the gantry stood the IBM mainframe, its chassis a yard wide and a yard deep. A console screen and a standard keyboard stood on top, two swivel chairs set in front. A galvanized-alloy conduit ran to the bottom of the gantry, carrying the cables that would control the missile launch.

A gray telephone sat on top of a wooden desk beside the mainframe, and Kesser's briefcase was open, next to it a computer printout.

Kesser led the way past the gantry to the computer and sat in one of the chairs. He tapped the keyboard and the screen flickered and turned blue, lights flashing on the panels.

Kesser said, "I ran the program. It's fine. No bugs."

"Is it safe?"

"Of course."

Meyer looked alarmed, but Kesser shook his head.

"The warhead hasn't been activated." He pointed to the computer. "The program's simply loading up. It takes about a minute."

Meyer saw the computer screen go blank, then become blue again as a series of unintelligible figures began scrolling rapidly across it. Finally the scrolling stopped, and a white cursor blinked on the top left corner.

"Now the program's loaded," said Kesser. He pointed to the screen. "Watch."

He tapped in a series of commands, and the screen blanked again, then showed a graphic, white against blue. Meyer saw the grid map of Germany, gray lines crisscrossing the blue screen.

Kesser hit another key, and Meyer heard a sound like thunder overhead. The metal doors set in the concrete roof began to roll open on their steel runners. An icy blast of air gusted into the building; Meyer shivered as the cold night sky came into view, stars glittering.

When Kesser tapped the keyboard once more, the electric whirr of the stepping motor filled the room. Meyer saw the gray-painted missile twitch in the gantry until it assumed its programmed angle, and then the whirr of the stepping motor died and there was silence again.

Kesser said, "Now look at the center of the screen."

Meyer saw a white image in the shape of a tiny circle appear.

Kesser said, "Locked on target. The middle of the circle is the epicenter. I can expand the scale if you want to see the exact point in Berlin, but you know how it works. Right now the target center is between the Brandenburg Gate and the southern side of the Reichstag building."

Meyer took a deep breath. The air in the dark concrete building had become incredibly chilled; the metal doors above were still wide open. He pulled up his coat collar, felt a shiver run through him again. Cold or fear? He couldn't tell which.

Kesser said, "Of course it will never come to a confrontation. They will all back off—the Americans, the British, the others—once we tell them of our intentions, won't they?"

Meyer didn't reply. Suddenly the telephone by the console buzzed, the shrill noise echoing throughout the building. Kesser leaned across and lifted the receiver, listened, spoke briefly, then turned to Meyer.

"There's a call for you. Priority."

They took a taxi from Berlin's Tegel airport. Volkmann told the driver to wait while they checked into the small hotel off the Kurfürstendamm, then half an hour later they pulled up outside the lakeshore house.

It was one of the old, prewar properties that ring the Nikolassee shore, painted brown and white, the clapboarded windows shut to keep out the freezing blasts of Baltic wind that race across the lake in winter.

It was bitterly cold as they stepped from the taxi, dark clouds drifting across the moonlit water. Volkmann again asked the driver to wait.

A porch light came on, and an elderly woman appeared behind the glass door. She rubbed her hands to combat the cold, and waited until they came up the path before sliding open the door.

"It's kind of you to see us so late, Frau Richter."

The woman smiled at them both. "Please, come in."

The house was warm and she led them into a study that faced the lake. The walls were lined with shelves of books, and Volkmann noticed that most of them were on the subject of the Third Reich.

He introduced Erica, and the woman shook their hands and told them to sit down.

Hanah Richter was tall, with a face that was more handsome than pretty, her graying hair tied back, emphasizing her high forehead. But her eyes were bright Nordic blue and they sparkled with enthusiasm.

She excused herself, disappearing into the kitchen for a few moments, before she reappeared carrying a tray with three steaming cups.

"Hot chocolate," Hanah Richter explained. "It's my nightly ritual. I thought it might warm you both before your journey back."

She sipped her chocolate and looked at both of them, her keen eyes searching their faces. "So what's so special about this photograph, Herr Volkmann?"

"It's of a young woman, taken on July 11, 1931—"

Hanah Richter interrupted gently, "Perhaps you can show it to me?"

He removed his wallet and handed the picture across: the photograph of the blond young woman smiling out at the camera, the mountains behind her, the sun in her eyes, the unseen hand linking hers. Hanah Richter put down her cup and took the picture in both hands. She stared down at the image, and after a brief moment, she looked up.

"You said it was taken on July 11, 1931?"

"That's what was written on the back of the original. But I'm afraid we've no way of knowing for certain if the date is correct." Volkmann paused. "Why?"

Hanah Richter shook her head as if dismissively, then squinted down at the image once more as she reached into her pocket and removed a pair of reading glasses, then placed them carefully on her nose.

Her face showed a blank expression as she stared at the photograph for a long time. The wind gusted and whistled outside, lightly shook the clapboarded windows, but the historian didn't look up.

Volkmann said finally, "Do you recognize the woman in the photograph?"

When she looked up, Hanah Richter said, "Yes."

PART FIVE

44

"Her name was Angela Raubal."

Hanah Richter looked down at the photograph again as a gust of wind rattled the clapboarded windows.

"She was Adolf Hitler's niece. The daughter of Hitler's half sister, also named Angela Raubal. But the young woman was called Geli, to distinguish her from her mother."

Volkmann stared at the historian. "There's no doubt in your mind that it's the same person?"

Hanah Richter shook her head. "Absolutely none whatsoever. During my academic career, I wrote several papers on the period from 1929 to 1931, describing how it influenced Hitler's personal life. Geli Raubal figured largely in that period. I researched her background as thoroughly as possible. It was a very difficult time for Hitler. He was plagued by all sorts of problems, personal and otherwise. And this young woman was one of them." She looked at Volkmann. "May I ask where you got this photograph? I've never seen it before."

"From South America."

She raised her eyebrows for a moment. He thought she was going to question him further, but then she seemed to change her mind.

"You don't look very convinced, Herr Volkmann. About the identity of the young woman, I mean."

Volkmann glanced at Erica. She looked at him silently, then over at the photograph. He turned back to Hanah Richter. "It's a question of certainty. We need to be absolutely sure."

"If you won't take my word for it, I can show you several other photographs of the same young woman. Would that help?"

"That would help greatly, Frau Richter."

She crossed to a bookcase, where she searched along a shelf and finally selected two books, then came back. She laid the books side by side, then moved one under the reading lamp. Slips of yellow paper, reference markers, stuck out between the covers.

"These are fairly standard books dealing with the period. This first is Toland's biography of Adolf Hitler. The man's an absolute expert on the subject. This second book I wrote myself." She smiled. "My one brief moment of literary glory."

She opened the first volume, leafed through the plates of black-and-white photographs inside, and finally found what she was looking for. Her finger pointed to a snapshot of a young, dark-haired woman standing against a black Daimler. From the look of the car, Volkmann guessed it was a mid-1920s model. The woman stood with one foot on the running board, one hand on her hip. She wore a pale, sleeveless summer blouse and a darker skirt to knee length.

"This particular photograph was taken sometime in the summer of 1930."

Volkmann and Erica examined the image closely. The woman was dark-haired and pretty, her face square-jawed but attractive. A lighthearted young woman but trying to look serious for the camera. There was only a faint likeness to her in Volkmann's photograph.

He said to Hanah Richter, "She's not blond?"

The historian smiled and glanced briefly at Erica before looking back at him.

"It was common practice then as much as now for girls to dye their hair. Peroxide may change appearances, but the facial structure remains the same. She often changed her hair color. But if you look closely, you'll see it's definitely the same person."

Hanah Richter opened a drawer in the desk and took out a magnifying glass, handed it to Volkmann. "Please, be my guest."

Volkmann held the glass over the image. The basic facial structure of the young woman in Hanah Richter's photograph was without doubt the same: square-faced, high cheekbones, pensive eyes, thin, wide mouth.

"You see a resemblance?"

When he nodded, Hanah Richter said, "But you're still not convinced, are you? Perhaps it's the color of the woman's hair?"

"That, and her figure."

The historian smiled. "True. In this photograph, she looks much thinner. In yours, she appears quite plump. Let me show you another, taken in the spring of 1931."

Hanah Richter opened the second book. Midway through was a collection of photographs, and she found the one she was looking for and pointed to it.

The scene was a Bavarian restaurant. Four people sat at a table: two men, two women. Both women were blond, one young, one middle-aged. The younger of the two women definitely resembled the image in the Chaco photograph. Her features were fuller and remarkably similar, her hair blond and done in plaits in the style of young German girls. She wore a traditional Bavarian costume with lace collar. She smiled at the camera, as if someone had just made a joke.

Two of the people seated with her around the table Volkmann recognized at once. To her left, Adolf Hitler, his arms folded, a trace of a smile on his thin lips. Opposite sat the diminutive, grinning Joseph Goebbels, the Nazi propaganda minister. The older blond woman seated next to him had her arm linked through his.

Hanah Richter said, "The young woman with Hitler is Geli Raubal. This time with blond hair. The woman with Goebbels is his wife, Magda. And in this photograph there's something very interesting. A clue that relates to your photograph. Pass me the magnifier, if you would be so kind."

Volkmann did so, and Hanah Richter placed the Chaco photograph beside the one in the book.

"Now look closely, please." She positioned the glass over the new photograph, and Volkmann held it. The focus swam and settled.

Erica leaned in closer and Hanah Richter said, "If you look at her right wrist, I think you'll see something interesting."

A faintly glinting bracelet. Hanah Richter shifted the glass to Volkmann's photograph. Again, clearly visible, was a metal bracelet on the young woman's right wrist.

Hanah Richter said, "The bracelet was a gift from Hitler to his niece, in October of 1929, when he took her to a Nazi Party rally in Nuremberg. It was made of solid white gold with rubies and sapphires. Hitler mentioned it in a letter he wrote to a close friend. A white-gold bracelet that Geli Raubal later always wore on her right wrist." Hanah Richter looked up at them over her glasses. "Even besides all that, the facial features in your photograph are unmistakable, I assure you. It's definitely the same person—Geli."

Volkmann took the magnifying glass again, held it over the photograph as Erica stood beside him, comparing the two snapshots. The same cheekbones. The same eyes. The same-shaped face. He looked at Erica. She stared at him blankly before she addressed Hanah Richter.

"I realize the hour, Frau Richter, but can you tell us about her background? You said she was one of Hitler's problems. How was she a problem?"

"Because she committed suicide."

"When?"

"Almost two months after your photograph was taken. After a blazing row with Hitler in his Munich apartment, Geli shot herself through the heart. You see, the two had been lovers for a long time."

When Volkmann and Erica stared at her in disbelief, Hanah Richter said, "I'm afraid you've aroused my curiosity. Is this very important?"

Volkmann said, "It may be."

"Would you care to tell me why?"

"It has to do with a criminal investigation. I'm afraid I can't tell you more than that."

Puzzlement sparked in the historian's face. "When you say 'a criminal investigation,' what do you mean? To do with the young woman?"

Volkmann said, "Not her. Someone else."

"But what has Hitler's niece got to do with it? She died such a long time ago."

"I'm sorry. I can't tell you any more than that."

Hanah Richter frowned, her disappointment evident. Then she sat back and said, "Very well, what is it you wish to know?"

Volkmann said, "Everything you can tell us about Geli Raubal."

Hanah Richter pushed the books aside.

Volkmann sat forward. "You said she and Hitler were lovers. Can you tell us about that?"

The historian nodded. "Certainly there was a relationship between them. One that went far deeper than a normal uncle-niece relationship. You see, she lived in the same house as Hitler for a time, and they became very close. In 1927, when Hitler moved to his berghaus in the mountains at Berchtesgaden, his stepsister moved in with him to act as his housekeeper. Hitler distrusted many of those around him, so his half sister was an obvious choice. She tended to his housekeeping needs, organized his meals, his clothes. And with her came her daughters, Friedl and Geli."

Volkmann said, "What about their father?"

"He died when Geli was quite young. Perhaps that was part of her attraction to Hitler. Very early on, he became a kind of father figure. She was a high-spirited woman. Flighty, if one is to believe the history books." Hanah Richter smiled. "She was born in Vienna, so perhaps it was her Viennese charm. Of course, Eva Braun took center stage as far as Hitler's private life is concerned. She was the mistress all the history books record. But before her came Geli Raubal. She was Adolf Hitler's first real romantic attachment—I won't say love, because the man was incapable of human love. But let us say it was a romantic attachment. She adored her uncle, and he her.

"For a time they went everywhere together, and when Hitler moved to his apartment in Munich, Geli joined him. She was studying medicine at Munich University at the time, so the move was convenient, but close friends knew that the arrangement was more than simple convenience, that it was an excuse for them to remain together."

"What do you mean?"

The historian shrugged. "Think about it. It was rather a strange relationship. Just the two of them, uncle and niece, living in the same apartment together. And Geli was only twenty-three when she died. Naturally, tongues wagged in the Nazi Party about the arrangement. Hitler had always had a preference for young, fresh-faced girls—the younger, the better—because he couldn't relate to women of his own age. And besides, young women were more easily manipulated and fell easily under his spell. Of the seven women with whom we know he had intimate relationships, most of them were young. And of the seven, six committed suicide or made a serious attempt to do so. So Geli Raubal wasn't alone in that regard.

"Hitler seemed to have had a mesmeric effect on women. The ones he was intimate with as well as the mass of German women he was to appeal to when he became führer.

"And like a lot of German women at the time, Geli Raubal found his personality magnetic. She would have done anything for him. She most certainly wanted to marry him despite their being related. And for a time, Hitler plainly acted like a suitor. He hinted to some of his close party friends that he might actually marry her."

Hanah Richter looked at them. "Repugnant as that might seem, one must remember that this was before Hitler's true brutality began to show. His career was on the rise. He seemed destined to lead Germany. Geli Raubal would have gladly married her uncle, despite their age difference of nineteen years and despite the near-incestuous connotations it would imply. So she flirted wildly with him, seduced him, if you like."

The wind rattled at the clapboards again, and the fire embers flickered. Volkmann stared at the flaring coals for a moment, then looked back as Hanah Richter started to speak again.

"It was an absurd situation, of course, and it couldn't last. The people close to Hitler in the Nazi Party who knew what was going on were horrified: middle-aged uncle who intended on marrying his very young niece. In their public lives, most Nazis were outwardly moral, but we know that privately they were vipers. And they were against it all the more because Hitler was preparing to take part in the presidential campaign. A Nazi victory was absolutely vital. It was everything the party had struggled for. Geli Raubal was Hitler's niece and half his age. So marriage or the hint of scandal would have been disastrous for the party. It certainly wouldn't have helped Hitler's image in his public life. But I think that in the end he just led the poor girl in a merry dance until he got tired of her and moved on to Eva Braun."

Volkmann glanced over at the photograph lying on the table. "So why did Geli Raubal kill herself?"

Hanah Richter considered. "If we're to believe the history books, she was going through some kind of emotional disturbance. Probably because she realized Hitler was slowly but surely withdrawing from their relationship. On the seventeenth of September, 1931, the two had a blazing argument in Hitler's Munich apartment. When Hitler was leaving, Geli Raubal calmly said good-bye to him, then went up to her room. The next morning she was found dead, shot through the heart at close range. There was a small-caliber pistol on the bedroom floor next to her. The Bavarian police determined that she had died sometime in the early hours of the eighteenth.

"Hitler was in Nuremberg when he heard the news of her death. Outwardly, he appeared devastated, but those close to him in the party thought he was actually relieved that Geli was out of his life. And of course there were the rumors. The press at the time went wild and printed all kinds of stories. They ranged from the slightly believable to the utterly ridiculous."

"What kind of rumors?"

"That Hitler had her killed in a fit of jealousy because she was seeing someone else. Certainly Hitler was prone to violent fits of jealousy. On one occasion he broke her nose during a row. So it's possible he had her killed, of course. He would have been quite capable of that, and just as possible that his associates in the Nazi Party killed her because they saw the relationship with his young niece as a threat of scandal that might ruin their hopes of power. But it's more likely she killed herself out of some sort of desperation. If you want my opinion, I'd have to say a combination of accident and desperation—the fact that she realized Hitler was never going to marry her and wanted to end their relationship, all of which probably sent her into a fit of depression. But then, we shall never really know the true story."

"What else did the newspapers say?"

Hanah Richter smiled. "There were so many rumors, not all of them credible. The most scandalous suggested that Hitler had his niece killed because the affair had gotten out of hand and threatened his public image. The police were called in to investigate but nothing came of it and no charges were brought. There were allegations that the justice minister at the time, Herr Gürtner, had the file of evidence destroyed. Certainly it disappeared, and whatever evidence there was against Hitler was never found.

"After Hitler came to power, Gürtner rose very quickly within the ranks of the Nazi Party, so perhaps that speaks for itself and deepens the mystery. Perhaps he did help Hitler in some way to hide the real truth, whatever it may be." Hanah Richter shrugged. "Certainly there was some mystery about the death, but most people close to Geli thought the suicide was simply a dramatic accident that happened when she was at a low ebb. That she was playing theater with the gun when it went off. And I'm inclined to agree."

Volkmann stared down at the Chaco photograph, the mountains in the background, the unseen hand linking the woman's, the Nazi swastika emblazoned on the armband. "Who do you think the other person in the photograph might be?"

"Possibly Hitler. They were still seeing each other at that time, though for a period before that, Hitler tried to remove himself from the relationship because of pressure from the party. Geli decided to make him jealous and started seeing Hitler's chauffeur, Emil Maurice. She even became secretly engaged to Maurice. When Hitler found out, he flew into a rage and dismissed his chauffeur. Then Hitler started seeing her again secretly, until her death."

"The eleventh of July, 1931. Can you recall anything special happening on that date?"

"You mean special for Geli Raubal?"

"Yes," Volkmann answered.

Hanah Richter thought for a moment. "She died on September eighteenth, so your photograph would have been taken more than seven weeks before her death. Geli was in hospital for a minor problem a week before your date, during her medical school semester. And about two weeks later, I believe, she stayed with some friends in Freiburg. In between, she saw Hitler a number of times, but he was busy with the presidential campaign and didn't have much time for her." Hanah Richter's brow furrowed in concentration. "No, I'm sorry. The date you mention is not one that sticks in my mind. Believe me, if it were, I'd remember."

"One more question. Did Geli ever visit South America?"

"Definitely not. She traveled only in Germany and Austria." The historian looked from Erica to Volkmann. "Has your question got something to do with how you came to have the photograph?"

Volkmann nodded. "Yes, it has. Does the name Erhard Schmeltz mean anything to you?"

"In what connection?"

"In connection with Geli Raubal."

The historian frowned. "Who was Erhard Schmeltz?"

"A Nazi Party member. Someone Hitler knew well."

The historian shook her head. "Well, whoever he was, he mustn't have been very important. I don't ever recall hearing that name in connection with either Hitler or Geli."

"Have you any idea how a photograph such as this could have ended up in South America?"

"You're absolutely certain it was an original and not a copy?"

"Yes."

"So many Germans fled to South America at the end of the war. The photograph could have been taken there by someone close to Hitler or Geli. As to who, I haven't the faintest idea." Hanah Richter glanced pointedly at her watch. "Does that answer all your questions?"

Volkmann replaced the photograph in his wallet. "Thanks for your time, Frau Richter. Our apologies for keeping you up so late."

"That's quite all right." She shook their hands and led them to the door. The taxi was still outside, and as they stood in the open porch, Volkmann turned to the historian.

"Do you know where Geli Raubal was buried?"

"In Vienna. The old Central Cemetery."

"Is the grave still there?"

Hanah Richter shook her head. "I'm afraid the Nazi authorities in Vienna had that part of the cemetery destroyed in 1941. The grave and all the others around it were completely razed."

"Why?"

"Heaven knows. It seems most strange. No one I ever spoke to about the matter knew who issued the order. I suppose it only added to the whole mystery of Geli's death."

"Do you think the Nazis wanted to cover something up?"

"You mean about her death? It's possible, but then, we've no way of ever knowing."

Volkmann hesitated. "There is one last thing."

"Yes?"

"You said that Geli Raubal was a hospital patient. When?"

"In late June of 1931. She spent a few days in a private nursing home in Garmisch."

"What was she being treated for?"

"Some said depression, because Hitler had spurned her and was seeing his new mistress, Eva Braun. Others said she went in for minor surgery. But I have no way of knowing. Why do you ask?"

Volkmann felt the biting wind coming in across the lake, glimpsed the waiting taxi driver in his cab, drumming his fingers impatiently against the steering wheel as he stared at them through the glass. Volkmann turned back, saw Erica pull up her coat collar against the icy wind. Hanah Richter waited, shivering, for the question to be answered.

"This proposition may seem absurd, Frau Richter. But could Geli Raubal have been pregnant?"

Hanah Richter raised her eyebrows. "Actually, that was suggested as one of the reasons why she might have been murdered by Hitler or his cronies. But it was never proven. A journalist at the time, a man named Fritz Gerlich, claimed Geli was pregnant by Hitler and that Hitler had her killed for that reason. But the story was never published."

"What happened to the journalist?"

"He was arrested and later murdered in Dachau. But really his information was never proven. Why do you ask?"

Volkmann hesitated. "What if Geli Raubal already had a child?"

"You mean by Hitler?"

"Yes."

Volkmann saw the woman's expression change. She stood in the doorway, open-mouthed, the question totally unexpected, utter amazement on her face. Erica looked at him, too, a white, stricken look that for a moment made her appear ill.

Then Hanah Richter said incredulously, "Really, Herr Volkmann, something like that would never have escaped the history books."

He saw the woman's expression of amazement become disbelief. Then suddenly the disbelief turned to irritation as she hunched her shoulders against the biting cold and shivered. "You can't possibly be serious."

Volkmann said quietly, "No, of course not. You've been very kind. Thanks for your help."

45

They hadn't spoken during the entire journey in the taxi back to the hotel. Volkmann stared out at the lights of Berlin from the cab window, but said nothing.

As soon as they had stepped into their room, Volkmann poured each of them a drink. Erica stared palely at him as he handed her a half tumbler of scotch, the aftershock of the question he posed to the historian still evident on her face.

"What you said to Hanah Richter . . . you really meant it, didn't you, Joe? That Geli Raubal could have been pregnant? That she could have had a child by Adolf Hitler?"

"Yes."

"But Joe, that's absurd."

Tension braided Volkmann's voice. "Erica, it fits the puzzle. It fits everything we know and don't know about the identity of Karl Schmeltz. And you heard what Hanah Richter said. Geli Raubal could have been pregnant. It's also a likely reason why she might have been killed or committed suicide. Everything we heard tonight explains the mystery of Karl Schmeltz. Don't you see that?"

Erica stared back at him. "I can accept that Geli Raubal could have been pregnant. But that she actually had a child? Joe, how could it be possible? If Hitler fathered a child, it could never have been kept a secret all these years."

Volkmann heard the strain of incredulity in her voice. He swallowed his scotch and put down the glass. "It sounds crazy, Erica, I know, but it also makes some kind of sense. Think about it. Erhard Schmeltz and his sister immigrate to South America from Germany under mysterious circumstances in late 1931, two months after

Geli Raubal's death. They take with them a boy who's obviously not their son. Remember what Wilhelm Busch said about Schmeltz? He didn't have any children and had never married. As for Schmeltz's sister, she was older than her brother, most likely too old to have a child that young. So that discounts either of them."

She looked at him. "But the child could have belonged to one of them, Joe. Either of them could still have been the child's natural parent."

"Then why did they disappear from Germany so mysteriously? And what about the rumors Busch said went around when Schmeltz and his sister vanished? One of them was that Schmeltz had been sent away secretly. The circumstances suggest that the boy most likely wasn't theirs. So who did he belong to?"

Tension mounted in Volkmann's voice as he looked at her. "Erhard Schmeltz was a loyal and close friend of Hitler. Now consider what Hanah Richter said: Hitler had been having an affair with Geli Raubal, an affair that was well known among his friends and close acquaintances."

Volkmann crossed to the window and turned back. "According to Hanah Richter, two months before Geli Raubal was found dead in her uncle's apartment, she was a patient in a private nursing home. When she comes out, she's under stress, something troubling her. It must have been something significant, because two months later, she supposedly kills herself. Whether Hitler had her killed or she committed suicide isn't relevant.

"But what's relevant is what could have been troubling her. She's in love with Hitler. She wants to marry him. So why did she kill herself? Hanah Richter said Hitler had spurned her. That he was preparing for the presidential elections, and it was vital for the Nazis to win. The last thing he needed was the kind of scandal his relationship with his niece might have caused."

"But Joe, that she could have had a child? It's just not possible."

"Why not? You admitted she could have been pregnant. What if she was expecting a child by Hitler? What if the reason she went into the hospital in Garmisch was because she was expecting a child by her uncle? Hitler knows about it, realizes if news gets out that he's made his niece pregnant, the whole affair could ruin his career. Just like Hanah Richter said, he might have dragged the Nazi Party down with him because of the scandal. So he, or those closest to him, come up with a plan. Send the child away, somewhere far from Germany. And with someone Hitler could trust. A couple like the Schmeltzes would have been ideal. And a jungle region in Paraguay couldn't have been more remote, so the secret's safe."

He saw her look at him unbelievingly. "That kind of scenario would explain three very important things, Erica. One, the amount of money Schmeltz had when he arrived in Paraguay. Two, his sudden immigration. Three, the drafts from the Nazi Reichsbank sent to Paraguay until 1945. Someone high up had to sanction such large sums of money and keep it secret.

"If we're to believe Busch, Erhard Schmeltz wasn't a rich man. And a man who's fallen out of favor with the Nazi Party doesn't receive money from the Reichsbank. Nor does he keep his party membership." Volkmann looked intently at Erica. "And I don't believe Schmeltz was hoarding the money for some other Nazi, either. Or they'd have used some anonymous Swiss bank. Only Hitler or a very high-ranking Nazi would have had the authority to use the Reichsbank. So that leaves one strong possibility. The money was sent to support the boy. Geli Raubal's and Hitler's son.

"The very fact that we found the woman's photograph at the house in the Chaco confirms the link between Schmeltz and Geli Raubal. And you heard what Hanah Richter said: if she had an affair with Hitler, why couldn't it be possible that she had a child by him?"

Erica shook her head. "If that's true, why didn't Hitler have her abort the pregnancy?"

"Maybe she didn't tell him until it was too late. Maybe she wanted the child. And even if she did commit suicide, she must have been desperate over something. She also could have been depressed after the birth. If Hitler had refused to marry her and wanted the whole affair covered up by sending the boy away, it might have been enough to send her over the edge."

"But there must have been people who knew. It couldn't have been kept secret after all these years. It just couldn't."

"Geli Raubal was a medical student, Erica. She would have known people in the profession. People who helped with the birth and kept it secret. And you heard what Hanah said about the journalist sent to Dachau. What if he had heard the truth? What if that was the reason he was killed?"

Erica shook her head. "Joe, there are too many ifs. Believe me, part of me wants to accept what you're saying, because it makes some kind of sense. But another part of me is saying it's crazy."

Volkmann heard his own labored breathing, the thought of what he had said dizzying. "Then consider this. Why did the Nazis destroy the part of the cemetery in Vienna where Geli was buried? Why did they want to destroy all traces of her grave? There could only be one reason. A secret someone wanted to hide. Geli Raubal's secret. A postmortem could have determined if she had given birth. Destroying the grave meant destroying the evidence."

Erica was pale. "To keep the secret, why didn't they simply get rid of Geli Raubal's body? Why didn't they destroy the evidence that way?"

"Maybe they did."

"I don't understand."

"By removing the body and destroying the graves nearby, it would make it impossible to know whether her corpse was removed from the grave or not. All that remained would have been a tangle of unidentifiable bones. No forensic examination could ever have determined identities."

Perspiration beaded his brow as he looked at Erica. "Consider all I've said and how it connects to everything that's been happening. To Rudi's death, to the other deaths. Why sanitize a house in a remote jungle? Why destroy all traces of occupation in the Chaco property? Why be so obsessive about secrecy? What had those people in the Chaco really got to hide, Erica? Not a simple smuggling operation. Not simply a connection to Rudi's death and the others. But something that goes far deeper. Not only about the present, but the past. You sensed something at the Chaco house, remember? We all did."

"Joe . . ." Erica opened her mouth to speak, but she broke off.

He saw the tension in her, her mouth set grimly, before the blue eyes looked away. There was a hopeless look on her face that said it all, as if she had tried hard to convince him he was wrong and failed.

He knew that what he was suggesting was unreal, but it had a strange ring of truth and his voice was thick with emotion. "There's only one possible answer that can explain Karl Schmeltz's identity, Erica. Karl Schmeltz is Adolf Hitler's son."

For a long time neither of them spoke, as if the awesome possibility that had joined them in the stillness of the room lingered like a living thing.

"What are you going to do, Joe?" There was no emotion in her voice, and he looked back at her.

"Tell Ferguson and Peters, and just hope they believe me."

"You think they will?"

"When they hear the evidence, yes, I think they will."

Erica said flatly, "And then?"

"Find Karl Schmeltz. Because he's part of what's happening, Erica. He's part of everything that's happened and is about to happen."

He held her stare, spoke quietly, and for the first time he heard real fear in his own voice. "The voices on Rudi's tape and what Busch said was promised in Hitler's bunker. They're talking about the same thing, Erica. They're talking about the same Brandenburg. What happened all those years ago in Germany when the Nazis came to power." Volkmann paused, looked into her face. "Somehow I think it's going to happen all over again."

STOCKHOLM. DECEMBER 23, 6:15 A.M.

The young woman behind the SAS check-in desk at Stockholm's Arlanda airport watched as the man approached.

He wore an expensive camel-haired overcoat and a pale gray Armani suit that complemented his dark complexion. Good-looking, maybe thirty, good figure, but sad eyes.

The woman smiled. "Good morning, sir."

The Turk nodded silently and handed across his first-class ticket.

The woman typed in the details on the computer, Stockholm to Amsterdam, noticed the man had an onward connection to Berlin. As she checked in the man's leather suitcase, she smiled up at him. It was a pity he couldn't see her long legs tucked behind the desk; maybe she could have coaxed a date.

She completed the details on the computer and handed the man back his boarding card. As the man took it she noticed his hands. Strong hands, but crisscrossed with a web of thick pink scars that made her shudder inside. A definite turnoff.

"You may board straightaway, Mr. Kemal."

"Thank you."

She forced a smile. "Are you traveling on business or pleasure, Mr. Kemal?"

"Business."

"I hope you have a nice trip."

"I'm certain I will," the Turk replied, and turned toward the boarding area.

46

GENOA. THURSDAY, DECEMBER 22, 11:57 P.M.

"Franco . . . ?"

The voice came to him out of the darkness.

Franco Scali turned over sleepily in the warm bed and muttered, "What . . . ?"

A finger prodded him. "Franco, there's someone at the door."

Franco opened his eyes. The bedroom was pitch black.

"What time is it?" he called out to his wife.

"Midnight."

Franco moaned as he heard the buzzing doorbell in the distance. The bedroom curtains were closed, but through a chink he could see the moonlit sky. He and Rosa had gone to bed early after spending the day Christmas shopping. Now he felt his wife's hand on his shoulder, shaking him.

"Franco . . . ?"

"I heard you, woman."

Franco threw back the sheets and dragged himself from the warm bed, felt the chill. He flicked on the bedside lamp, blinked as the harsh light flooded the bedroom. Rosa moaned as she pulled back the bedcover, and the bell rang again downstairs, a couple of short, urgent bursts.

"Who the devil is it at this hour?" Franco grumbled.

"I think it's Aldo Celli. When I heard the bell I got up and thought I saw his car outside."

"Then why didn't you answer the door?"

"I said I think it's him. I'm not sure," his wife grunted, then turned over again, dragging the covers with her.

Franco sighed and scratched himself.

Aldo. Aldo the Eagle. The craneman at the docks. What did he want at this hour? Franco dragged on his dressing gown and went downstairs. When he unlocked the front door he saw big Aldo standing under the porch light, his collar pulled up against the cold.

"What is this, Aldo? You know what time it is?" Franco shivered.

"Can I come in, Franco?"

Franco sighed and led the big man into the sitting room. He turned on the light first, then dragged up a chair for Aldo.

Franco said, "So what's up?"

Aldo's big, fleshy face showed concern. "One of the juggernauts brought in a container this evening. Il Peste was on the late shift.

After I dropped the container, Il Peste came and looked at the number. Then he had us open the container, and he started using the duster and sniffing around."

"So?"

Aldo blinked. "I asked him what was up. He said it was the same container that came in from South America twelve days ago. One he wanted to recheck."

Franco's stomach jolted.

"He found something, Franco," Aldo went on.

Franco raised his eyes in mock surprise. "What do you mean?"

"The side of the container, there was a hidden compartment held in by some screws. Pretty neat job, you never would have thought it was there. But Il Peste kept tapping away until he found it."

Franco tried to hide his fear. He felt his palms sweat. "Why you telling me?"

"The cops came. They took all our fingerprints. Said they want us to stay back after our shift if necessary, in case they needed to talk with us. Something about the container . . ."

Franco swallowed. "Go on . . ."

"Then Il Peste wanted to know when you were rostered on again. I told him you had a couple of days off. I heard him mention your name to one of the cops. A detective named Orsati. Then I heard one of them say they'd call on you sometime this morning."

Franco felt his stomach churn, tried not to throw up all over Aldo's shoes.

The big craneman stood. "I just thought I'd slip out and tell you, seeing you're the boss. I told no one I was coming. But I got a feeling there's going to be trouble, Franco. The cops and customs, they're swarming all over the place like flies on dung."

Franco nodded, managed a faint smile. "You did right, coming here, I mean. If there's going to be trouble, I'll need to be prepared."

"That's what I thought. I'd better be getting back. The cops might get suspicious if I'm away for long."

Franco pushed himself up from the chair. He put a hand lightly on the craneman's big shoulder. "You'll tell no one you came here, right?"

"Hey, what are friends for?"

"Thanks, Aldo. I owe you."

Franco went back to the bedroom, threw off his dressing gown, and dragged on his clothes, feeling ill, like he wanted to die.

Rosa came awake. "What's wrong? Who was at the door?"

"No one. You must have been dreaming, woman."

"I heard the bell, voices downstairs."

"You heard nothing. I gotta get some air. I'm up now, I can't sleep."

Rosa protested, but Franco wasn't listening. It took him less than three minutes to dress, get down the stairs, lock the front door, and reach the Fiat. He had told Rosa not to answer the door if anyone called. The woman knew better than to argue.

He drove to the deserted Piazza della Vittoria, found a kiosk, and used one of the phone cards he kept in the glove compartment. He punched in the number from the slip of paper in his wallet.

The number rang. A couple of seconds of fearful, crushing silence before the receiver was lifted and Franco heard the voice at the other end.

"Ja?"

Franco didn't speak German. He felt his legs shaking as he panicked. Again, the voice said, "Ja?"

Franco said, "You speak Italian?"

A pause. The voice said, "Sí."

"Then listen, amico. We've got us a big problem . . ."

FRIDAY, DECEMBER 23

They managed to get seats on the 7:00 a.m. shuttle from Berlin.

He parked the Ford in the DSE underground garage, and when they went up, he left Erica waiting in his office while he went in search of Peters.

He found him in his office.

"Joe, I'm glad you made it back, something's come up—"

"We need to talk, Tom."

Peters saw the look on Volkmann's face. "Is everything okay?" he asked.

"Where's Ferguson?"

"Gone to a meeting with the section heads."

Peters saw the look of frustration on Volkmann's face. "What's this about, Joe?"

"I'd prefer if Ferguson was here. I'd like to discuss it with you both."

Peters recognized the stress in Volkmann's voice but said, "I'm afraid it'll have to wait. Something's come up, something important maybe. And Ferguson won't be back until later."

"What's come up?"

"You're going to love this. I got a call from the Italian desk. The police in Genoa may have found something that fits in with our request. They want us to take a look at a container that came in on a ship called the *Maria Escobar* on the ninth of this month."

"Where from?"

Peters smiled. "Montevideo. I told them you'd be on the next available plane."

"How long have I got?"

"There's an Al Italia flight from Frankfurt in under three hours. A return flight tonight at nine. You ought to just make it back unless something develops. I've arranged a private charter from Strasbourg to Frankfurt. It's waiting at the airport now."

"What about our meeting?"

"I'll set it up for this evening. Phone me the minute you get back."

Volkmann said, "Do me a favor. While I'm gone, stay with Erica."

Peters frowned. "Any particular reason?"

"This thing I'm working on—it's beginning to make sense, Tom, but it's looking more bizarre and dangerous by the second. She could be at risk. I want someone I can trust to watch over her. I'll explain when I get back."

He spoke with Erica, told her not to talk with anyone about the case until he returned.

Peters came into the office and he introduced them.

Peters said charmingly, "How about I take the young lady to lunch, Joe? Then I can drive her back to your place." He smiled. "Pretty much everyone's finishing early for the holidays. I'll leave a note for Ferguson about our meeting, tell him it's imperative we talk."

Five minutes later, as Volkmann drove to the airport, there was a knot of tension in his stomach like a ball of steel.

47

BONN. FRIDAY, DECEMBER 23, 9:30 A.M.

Chancellor Franz Dollman grimaced as he sat in the back of the black Mercedes. Beyond the bulletproof windows of the stretch limousine, a police escort guided the car through the streets of Bonn.

As the car passed the Münsterplatz, Dollman looked up from his paperwork. The lights of a Christmas tree winked on the platz. The thought of Christmas approaching normally depressed him, but this time he looked forward to a few relaxing days away from his grueling state duties. Already his cabinet was a week behind the scheduled holiday recess; so many problems remained to be dealt with.

Dollman massaged his temples as he sat back. He had been up since six assembling his paperwork, then breakfast, followed by a quick glass of schnapps to help brace himself for the emergency cabinet meeting.

The Wednesday morning meetings in Bonn's Schaumburg Palace were always the same of late, had been for the last year—an utter shambles. Dollman expected the same of this one, wondered how the country had managed to survive, put it down to the resolute, hardworking nature of the German people. They had seen adversity before and were certainly seeing it now.

As the car sped past the Marktplatz, Dollman glimpsed the broken shop windows, the littered glass, the paint daubed on walls. All the hallmarks of another riot. He turned to Ritter, his personal bodyguard, sitting beside him. The man was disrespectfully chewing gum.

Dollman nodded gravely toward the scene beyond the glass. "What happened?"

Ritter's jaws moved slowly as he chewed. "It started off as a protest march about unemployment. Then the right-wing groups joined in. Before long, it was a riot."

Dollman sighed. "Anyone killed?"

Ritter shook his head. "Not this time. The riot squad cracked a few skulls, that's all. If you ask me, these demonstrators ought to be locked up."

It was getting out of control, Dollman reflected as the Mercedes headed south toward the Schaumburg Palace. More shattered windows along the route. Pavement slabs had been torn up, shopfronts vandalized.

Dollman didn't bother replying to Ritter's remark. The man was an excellent bodyguard, tough and discreet, but he had a limited intelligence, and so Dollman always kept their conversations to a minimum. If Ritter had his way, half the world would be behind bars.

And it was the same everywhere these days: Riots. Marches. Protests. The immigrant problem.

"Lock the lot up and throw away the keys. That's the answer," Ritter added.

If only it were possible, Dollman reflected. He'd start with half of his bickering cabinet.

The Mercedes turned slowly into the courtyard of the Schaumburg Palace and slid to a halt outside the imposing entrance. His wife would be in their residence on the grounds. There would just be time to see her after the cabinet meeting before he left for Berlin. Another boring function to attend, before Weber's special security meeting the next morning. Still, Weber's meeting suited him perfectly. He would spend the night in Wannsee with his mistress, and that at least Dollman looked forward to. The thought briefly lifted his spirits as the chauffeur stepped out smartly and opened the rear door. Dollman gathered up his papers, closed his briefcase, and handed it to Ritter.

As he climbed out, he saw a sober-looking Eckart, the finance minister, waiting in the doorway to greet him. No doubt there was more bad news even before the meeting began.

Dollman sighed and strode grimly toward the palace entrance.

The meeting was no different this morning as Dollman observed the drawn faces of the men seated at the large oval table.

Riots the previous night in Berlin, Munich, Bonn, and Frankfurt. And the latest financial news was depressing. Eckart wrung his hands in despair as he imparted the details.

Dollman removed a fresh white handkerchief from his pocket and dabbed his brow; the cabinet room was hot, the heating turned up to counter the chill outside. Beyond the bulletproof windows, he glimpsed a harsh wind whipping the trees.

A tall, distinguished-looking man in his early sixties, Dollman had been chancellor for eighteen months. He would gladly have resigned but knew that he was the only one in the room capable of leadership in these difficult times.

He looked up now from the reports lying in front of him on the polished oval table and replaced the handkerchief in his breast pocket. All of the ministers were present—except for Weber, the vice chancellor, who was expected later. A fresh outbreak of rioting in Leipzig had demanded his presence. He didn't envy Weber his task of overseeing federal security. He suited it because he took no nonsense, but a security job was just asking for trouble. Still, that was Weber's problem.

Eighteen men at the big table, including himself.

Dollman heard a cough and turned his head to see Eckart trying to catch his attention.

"The economics reports, Chancellor. Do you wish me to start?"

Dollman glanced at his watch. "What else is remaining?"

"The report on federal security. But we're still waiting for Vice Chancellor Weber. If he's further delayed, we'll have to reconvene after lunch."

Dollman sighed. "Very well, Eckart, you may begin." Dollman knew what was coming as Eckart's dry, monotonous voice called the ministers to attention.

Dollman's mind was elsewhere. On the house in Wannsee. There would be time to call on the way to Charlottenburg, then come back after the civic function. Lisl was a politician's dream. Discreet, beautiful, lustful in bed. He always found her company invigorating.

Dollman suppressed the smile of contentment that threatened to cross his lips as Eckart's depressing monologue droned on. He saw the assembled ministers stare ahead or look toward the windows.

He was past trying to make sense of the chaos. At that moment, all he hoped was that he could make it to Berlin by evening. He looked up as Eckart's speech finally came to an end.

"And that concludes the economics reports. Thank you, ministers, for your attention."

What attention? thought Dollman. Half of them were sleeping, or trying to, or bored to death. There was a sudden eruption of coughing, and then a hushed silence.

Dollman deflected any questions by looking pointedly at his watch. "Gentlemen, I suggest we reconvene after lunch to hear the vice chancellor's report. As interior minister, I believe, he has some important points to discuss."

As Dollman finished speaking, the door to the cabinet room opened and Konrad Weber stepped into the room. He carried a thick folder in one hand, his briefcase in the other. A tall, grim-looking man; his face looked serious, as always. But a good vice chancellor. One who took his responsibilities seriously. Dollman was glad to have him on his side, but from the strained look on Weber's face, it looked as if he were about to impart doom.

"Chancellor, gentlemen, my apologies for being late . . ."

"Take a seat, Weber. You're ready to read your special security report?"

Dollman felt glad of the interruption, but dreaded Weber's report. At least it saved him from any questions. Now Weber could take some of the flak.

The vice chancellor nodded to Dollman as he moved to his place at the table but remained standing. He placed his briefcase on the floor beside him. As he opened the folder in front of him, Dollman saw that several of the papers inside bore official red security stamps. Highly confidential.

Dollman sighed quietly. Weber had already informed him privately on the phone that the news would be grave. From the look on the cabinet's faces, Weber's security reports would send them all rushing toward the windows.

Dollman tried hard to relax, wondered where it would all end. He thought of voluptuous Lisl, lying on the bed in the house at Wannsee, waiting for him.

If it weren't for that woman, he felt certain he would have rushed toward the windows himself long ago.

48

STRASBOURG. DECEMBER 23, 3:02 P.M.

It started to snow as Peters drove up outside the apartment on the Quai Ernest.

He parked in the courtyard, and he and Erica went up. She was subdued during their lunch in Petite France, and Peters guessed that something was troubling her, but he hadn't pressed her to talk.

When they stepped into Volkmann's apartment, he could see that she had made herself at home and had tidied the rooms; here and there small items rearranged since he had last visited. *Very interesting,* he thought. *So she and Volkmann have something going here.*

A little later he excused himself as she made coffee, and he went to the bathroom. On the way back, he paused in the hallway and stepped into Volkmann's bedroom. He could smell the lingering scent of her perfume. Her clothes and her makeup bag lay by Volkmann's bed.

As he stepped back into the living room, she came out of the kitchen. "I never asked if you take sugar and cream?"

Peters smiled. "Both. Two spoonfuls."

She moved back into the kitchen, and Peters lit a cigarette and went to stand at the window. Flakes of snow drifted against the glass, and he stood there reflecting on the relationship between Volkmann and Erica. On the one hand, it wasn't surprising. She was quite beautiful and intelligent. On the other hand, she was a German, and her father had been in the SS . . . which ordinarily would have been disqualifying marks where Volkmann was concerned. But he figured she must be something special to have broken through Volkmann's walls.

As he moved away from the window and went to flick on the remote control for the television, Erica came back in holding two mugs of steaming coffee. As Peters leaned forward to take one he saw her stare at his waist. He looked down. The holstered Beretta was visible, clipped to his belt. He smiled up at her. "Do guns bother you?"

"I guess."

"No problem." Without another word, he stood and unclipped the weapon, tucked it under his overcoat he'd left folded on the chair, then sat back down again.

* * *

The Mercedes drove up and down the quay four times and then halted outside the apartment building. Snow brushed against the car's windows, and the wipers were on.

The passenger checked the address again and then nodded to the driver before he pulled up the collar of his raincoat and stepped out into the snow.

As the man disappeared into the courtyard, the driver sat tapping his fingers on the steering wheel, the motor still running.

Three minutes later, the passenger returned and climbed back into the car, his hair and raincoat flecked with snow. He wiped his face with a big hand and said in German, "It's the right apartment. Volkmann's name's on the doorbell. There's a window at the back. Two people inside. A man and a woman."

The driver checked his watch. "Okay. Once more around the block, then we come back."

As the Mercedes pulled away, the passenger reached under his seat and took out the two silenced pistols.

GENOA. 3:15 P.M.

A tall Italian detective with a bushy mustache introduced himself to Volkmann at a warehouse by the docks. His name was Orsati, and he seemed confident that he had broken the case: the container on the *Maria Escobar* had a hidden compartment.

"There's a customs official—his name's Paulo Bonefacio—who found it." He pointed out the man, who was standing off to the side. "We can show you the container; it's nearby."

Volkmann nodded.

"So Bonefacio did some checking, and it turned out that the container has been back and forth to Montevideo several times over the past year. He figured that an inside man must have taken the contents of the hidden compartment. He did some further checking and found that the container has been handled exclusively by Franco Scali. He's a senior clearance clerk here."

"He's the inside man?" Volkmann asked.

"It seems so. Though we haven't finished interviewing him yet, I'm sure he'll have a great deal more to tell us."

"Let's hope so," Volkmann said.

"So anyhow, let me introduce you to Scali." Orsati made an over-here motion with his hand to another detective. A moment later, the detective led a very frightened-looking clearance clerk to Orsati and Volkmann.

"Signore Volkmann, meet Franco Scali."

Scali nodded a greeting. "Ciao," he said.

"Scali," Volkmann said quietly.

Orsati said, "Let's start with the container."

Scali forced a smile. "Sure."

The detective led the way.

The Fiat carrying Beck and Kleins drove into the dockyard and came to a halt a hundred yards from the warehouse. There had been so many police cars on the apron that no one had bothered to stop them.

As Beck switched off the engine, Kleins studied the cars parked outside the warehouse. A hundred yards away, a knot of men stood gathered around the big blue container.

Kleins reached behind him for the powerful Zeiss binoculars and focused on the men.

Volkmann stood on the docking apron, a soft breeze blowing in from the harbor. Powerful security lights flooded a part of the apron sealed off with rolls of yellow crime-scene tape.

Then the customs official, Paulo Bonefacio, led them across the apron to a blue container with three gray-striped markings.

Volkmann saw that a plate had been removed from the side, and it lay on the ground, perfectly matching the gaping, quarter-yard-wide hole it had covered. The customs official beamed over at them.

Volkmann asked the detective, "How did he find it?"

"He has a metal knuckle-duster. He uses it to tap containers. Hollow spaces sound hollow. On this one, there was a slight difference in the metal sound toward the right-end wall. Last time this container was on the docks, he suspected it, but didn't have time to do a thorough check."

Orsati knelt beside the container, stared in at the small chamber within the gaping hole. Then he looked up at Volkmann and said, "You want to take a look?"

Orsati handed across a slim pencil light. Volkmann knelt down and flicked it on, probed inside the empty chamber. He saw the twin brackets welded onto the inner metal frame, left and right sides, maybe one quarter of a yard apart. The chamber smelled of paint and rust. He stood and turned to glance at Scali. The clerk looked at him uncertainly.

Volkmann asked Orsati, "Does Scali speak English?"

The detective questioned the clerk. Scali shrugged, said something in reply.

Orsati said, "He says he doesn't."

"Then I won't be very useful when you interview him." Volkmann looked at Scali for a time. "How do you plan to get him to talk?" he asked Orsati.

"The evidence against him is circumstantial, but solid. Like I said, no one else had access to the container. That's leverage enough, I think."

Volkmann saw that Franco Scali looked anxious, no question about it.

"There's an office in the warehouse," the detective said. "I'll talk to him there. When I'm finished, believe me, I'll know everything Franco Scali knows." He smiled. "Why don't you wait outside? Get some fresh air. After Scali's made his speech, I'll call you in."

Kleins saw the knot of people around the container move away toward the warehouse. He picked out Scali with the Zeiss. He nodded to Beck, who reached behind on the seat for the two briefcases.

It didn't take long to ready the two Heckler & Koch MP 5K machine pistols and slam home the magazines. When they looked up, they saw the group reach the warehouse.

Kleins slapped the cocking handle of his weapon and flicked his safety catch to off; Beck did likewise.

STRASBOURG. 3:55 P.M.

Ferguson sat in the office, snow falling outside. He arrived back late from lunch and saw the note from Peters about the meeting with Volkmann, stressing it was urgent. A postscript said that Peters was at Volkmann's apartment with Erica Kranz. He guessed it had something to do with Volkmann's investigation, and was about to telephone Volkmann's apartment when the telephone rang and he picked up the receiver.

Jan de Vries came on the line. "A classified communication arrived from Asunción for your attention, sir, and it's marked 'Urgent.' I thought I'd bring it up personally."

"Do that, Jan."

Three minutes later, De Vries arrived. He appeared subdued, and Ferguson waited until the man left the office before breaking the waxed seal and opening the envelope.

Inside he found the signal and he read it slowly, ashen-faced. He stood there for a full minute in silence, in disbelief, oblivious to the snow brushing against the window; then he read the signal again.

When he finished this time, he picked up the telephone and rapidly punched in the numbers. When he got no reply, he thought for a moment, then he hit the receiver cradle smartly again and began to punch in numbers once more.

Had he stayed at the window, he would have seen the black Mercedes draw up in front of the building and the two raincoated men climb out, one of them carrying a briefcase.

They entered the building ten seconds later, showed their identity cards at the security desk, then crossed the lobby to take the elevator to Ferguson's office.

A mile away on the Quai Ernest, another two men stepped out of their parked Mercedes into falling snow.

They walked across the white courtyard and climbed the steps. When they halted outside Volkmann's apartment, the driver of the car nodded to his partner. Each man opened his raincoat and withdrew a silenced pistol.

While the driver scanned the courtyard below, the second man took a heavy bunch of keys from his pocket.

He selected one and tried it in the lock.

49

GENOA. 3:55 P.M.

A cold breeze swept in from the sea, and it washed Volkmann's face. As he stepped out onto the apron from the warehouse, he realized he had left his overcoat in the unmarked police car.

He reached the parked car ten yards away, and saw the figure of a man move toward the warehouse from the harbor side, caught for a moment in the sweep of silver light from the lighthouse out in the bay. The man was fifty yards away, maybe less, a dark Fiat obscured behind him.

Volkmann saw the machine pistol in his hands, and for a brief moment he thought the man was one of the Italian cops, but the man moved at a trot and he wore no uniform.

Volkmann froze. Something was wrong. The man's stride was too purposeful, too determined, the weapon in his hands held across his chest at the ready.

Volkmann turned and glanced back at the warehouse. Lights blazed in the tiny office where the Italian detectives and the customs man had taken Scali—looking like characters in some drama beyond the lit glass, Scali's lips moving, the others listening. Easy targets.

Volkmann looked back again toward the man. Forty yards from the warehouse now, moving fast.

Volkmann started to reach for his Beretta, realized he hadn't taken the weapon with him.

He swore, moved rapidly back toward the police car, yanked open the driver's door, and searched frantically in the glove compartment for a weapon. He realized that the man with the machine pistol had a clear line of fire toward the warehouse, realized that Scali was the target, the voices on the tape echoing like an alarm bell in his head as he tried to find a weapon.

"And the Italian?"

"He will be eliminated."

Apart from papers, the glove compartment was empty. He tried to think. Detectives always carried weapons in an unmarked car; Italian cops were no different. But where? Sometimes in the trunk; sometimes overhead in a zipped compartment. Volkmann felt along the coarse vinyl. No zip. No weapons compartment. He felt under the seats.

Nothing.

He checked for the keys in the ignition.

None.

Volkmann swore again as his right hand shot down to the side of the driver's seat, felt for a trunk release, found one, pulled it hard. Then he looked back out through the rear window, seeing the man twenty yards away now as the trunk yawned open.

As Kleins moved at a trot across the apron, he saw the knot of men standing in the lighted office window, saw the faces plainly beyond glass, two men standing, two sitting, one of them looking like he was talking while the others listened.

Scali.

Fifteen yards to go now, and still the men in the office hadn't seen him.

He had left Beck sitting in the parked Fiat, watching his back, ready for the getaway; the second car parked in a side street four blocks from the harbor entrance, ready for their escape.

But a difficult hit. Not impossible, but too many people, too many things to go wrong, but the kill imperative, according to Meyer.

Twelve yards from the warehouse window and still the men beyond the glass hadn't noticed him. His finger slid around the trigger as he ducked under the line of yellow tape.

Kleins hesitated, animal instinct telling him something was wrong. He saw a movement out of the corner of his eye. As he looked to the right, the trunk of the unmarked police car opened. Kleins glimpsed the figure of a man, crouching as he moved toward the trunk, his hand reaching inside, searching frantically. Kleins couldn't see the man's face, but in those split seconds, he knew the man was marked for death.

He swung the Heckler & Koch around and fired in one swift motion. The apron erupted with a thunderous volley as the man darted back for cover, lead ripping into the police car, shattering glass, puncturing metal.

Kleins swung the weapon back toward the warehouse window, saw the people behind the glass react to the sound of gunfire, mouths open as they froze in disbelief and stared out at him.

He squeezed the trigger.

The office window shattered, glass fragmenting, lead hitting concrete and wood and flesh as the Heckler & Koch's deadly chatter sprayed the tiny room, the figures beyond the window dancing like crazed puppets as Kleins fired one long, sustained burst.

Click.

The magazine emptied. Kleins tore it out, slammed home a fresh one from his pocket, cocked the Heckler again.

Suddenly he glimpsed the figure move out again from behind the car, his hand coming around to pull something from the trunk.

Kleins swung round the machine pistol and squeezed the trigger again.

Volkmann crouched helplessly behind the car, eyes flicking from the man to the open car trunk, to the shattering office window and the figures dancing in the deadly burst of gunfire.

As the man concentrated on the targets beyond the window, Volkmann saw the opportunity, crouching low again as he moved toward the trunk, hand reaching inside, fingers probing for metal, for the hard form of a shotgun, a machine pistol.

Nothing.

Then the cold metal of a wheel jack.

Then . . .

Something hard in his fingers, an L clamp, then another, then the outline of a weapon, fingers touching the hilt of an Uzi, grasping the comfort of cold, hard metal.

Volkmann heard the chatter of the Heckler & Koch suddenly stop, saw the man tear out the magazine, slam in a new one.

Volkmann swung around and up, saw the Uzi held in the L clamps with two rubber stays, tore them off, wrenched out the weapon, praying it was loaded.

The volley of gunfire that came just as he grasped the Uzi sent him reeling back behind the car, and he hit the ground, hearing the jackhammer crack of bullets as they ripped into metal. As he fell back and rolled along the side of the car, the fingers of one hand fumbled wildly for the safety catch, found it, then the cocking handle.

He flicked the Uzi onto automatic fire with his thumb, bullets cracking into the ground around him.

The man with the Heckler & Koch moved forward, firing wildly; Volkmann rolled to the right on the asphalt, and on the third roll he aimed and squeezed the trigger.

The Uzi exploded in his hands.

Bullets ripped into the man's chest, his body lurching, hammered back onto the ground as Volkmann kept the pressure on the trigger.

Click.

The magazine emptied.

Silence.

Volkmann dropped the Uzi, stood, and looked back toward the warehouse window. No movement beyond the shattered glass, but he heard the moans of pain and the cries for help.

At that moment, he heard the roar of a motor and saw the head-lights of a car flash onto his left.

Beck saw everything happen from where he sat in the parked car.

He swore. He saw Kleins fall under the hail of fire, saw the man drop his weapon, stand, and move out from behind the shattered police car.

Beck gunned the Fiat's engine and flicked on the headlights.

As he reached for the Heckler & Koch on the seat beside him, he hit the accelerator hard and the Fiat lurched forward.

Volkmann heard the screech of tires and saw the blinding beams of light race toward him.

Eighty yards.

Seventy.

He crouched as a burst of fire suddenly raked the ground to his left, chips of stone flying as lead cracked into asphalt.

Fifty yards.

Forty.

The Fiat growled toward him, headlights like the glaring eyes of some crazed wild animal, blinding him.

The empty Uzi lay five yards away.

He raised his hand to shield his eyes from the piercing lights, glimpsed the Heckler & Koch beside the man's pulped body, flung himself down, and rolled the last five yards, his hands scrabbling wildly for the weapon as another burst of fire raked the ground to his left.

Thirty yards.

Twenty.

Volkmann grasped the Heckler & Koch, rolled to the right, aimed, squeezed the trigger just as the Fiat appeared under the wash of the apron's lights.

The burst from the Heckler & Koch shattered the left side of the windshield, turned it white, but the car kept coming, weaving crazily. Volkmann glimpsed the face of the driver beyond the half-shattered glass, the barrel of his weapon spitting flame.

At the last moment, Volkmann released the pressure on the trigger, rolled to the right again, squeezed the trigger hard, felt the weapon chatter madly in his hands as the bullets ripped across the shattered windshield.

The second burst almost decapitated the driver, sent his head flying back hard against the headrest as the Fiat veered wildly out of control, screaming past Volkmann with a rush of air. There was a grinding screech of metal hitting metal as it smashed into the unmarked police car, and then came a sharp crack as the gas tank exploded and a geyser of orange flame erupted.

A wave of intense heat rolled toward Volkmann as he pushed himself up and raced back toward the warehouse. The light was still on in the tiny shattered office, but no sign of life.

And then he saw a figure stand up shakily. Orsati—blood streaming down his face, his hand covering a head wound as he tried to steady himself against a wall.

Suddenly the harbor came alive. A siren screamed, and seconds later a ghostly blue light swirled as a police car raced out of nowhere and screeched to a halt.

Two uniformed police stepped warily from the car, pistols at the ready as they cast disbelieving looks at the shattered warehouse office, then at the tangle of blazing metal.

As the men rushed forward, unsure of their enemy, Volkmann slowly raised his hands over his head.

And then another police car wailed into view, and then another. More cops jumping from cars, until finally all the sirens died and were replaced by screaming voices, the twilight streaked by the corona of revolving blue lights and the shadows of cops everywhere.

STRASBOURG. 4:03 P.M.

The two men stepped out of the elevator into the empty corridor.

The one carrying the briefcase led the way. It took them less than twenty seconds to find the office, the name on the plaque on the door.

Ferguson was on the telephone and clutching a sheet of paper when the door burst in. He saw the men and the silenced pistols in their hands and started to open his mouth to speak.

Four times he was hit in the chest, twice in the head, the force of the bullets sending him flying backward, dragging the telephone and papers with him, his body hurled against the wall.

The receiver was still clutched in his hands when the man with the briefcase stepped forward and coldly fired another two shots into his head.

The two men remained in the office no more than twenty seconds, one of them searching through the unlocked cabinets and desk drawers, the other opening the briefcase he carried, setting the bomb's timer, then closing the briefcase again and placing it under Ferguson's desk.

Neither man noticed the classified report from Asunción lying on the floor, the page streaked with blood.

They checked the hallway, saw that it was clear, and stepped outside, closing the door after them.

*   *   *

Erica sat alone in the bedroom.

When Peters had started probing her with a few gentle questions, she had excused herself, saying she was tired.

A gust of wind rattled the glass, and a flurry of snow brushed against it. As she went to draw the curtains, she heard the noise from the hallway: a sudden rush of heavy footsteps.

She moved quickly across the room. As she opened the bedroom door, she heard the television, saw Peters rising quickly from his chair, staring at some point toward the hallway, saw the color drain from his face.

Peters said, "Who the devil are you—"

And as he reached for the pistol lying on his coat, Erica saw the two men with guns in their hands rush toward him, saw the backs of their pale raincoats.

As Peters grabbed his pistol, there was a strange whistling sound, and then another and another as both men fired rapidly into Peters's body, blossoms of red erupting on his chest and face as he was flung back against the chair.

Erica screamed.

The Mercedes halted on the Quai Arpège, and the man in the passenger seat checked his watch.

Fifteen seconds later, both men heard the huge blast in the distance as the air ruptured with the sound of the explosion. The man nodded, and the driver pulled out from the curb.

Minutes later came the wail of sirens behind them in the distance, but neither man looked back.

And neither saw the dark-colored sedan that pulled out quietly fifty yards behind them.

50

Volkmann waited his turn to speak as he sat in the police commissioner's office on the Plaza di Fortunesca.

The tension in the room was as thick as the cigarette smoke that rose like a gray cloud to the ceiling. Orsati sat in the center of the brightly lit office; broad strips of flesh-colored plaster ran from just below his left eye to the middle of his cheek where a bullet had rutted flesh.

"It could be worse," he had said to Volkmann after the doctor and nurse tended to him on the dock apron, white teeth flashing behind his mustache, but the detective looked badly shaken.

Apart from Volkmann and Orsati, there were two other men in the room. One was the Genoese police commissioner. A bespectacled, handsome man wearing a smart gray business suit with a pale blue tie and white handkerchief. A touch of flamboyance, but the man totally in control.

The fourth man present was the chief of detectives, tall, with metal-rimmed glasses.

Orsati explained that Scali had talked before he was shot. One small box, the last consignment. A heavy box, concealed in the false side of the container. Several other consignments over the past year—weapons, Scali had guessed, or maybe even gold. But Scali claimed he wasn't sure, the contents a mystery.

Orsati told them that the forensic people were still conducting tests. The commissioner sat behind the desk, chewing an unlit cigar. The chief of detectives was talking now to his commissioner. Volkmann waited for the man to finish, waited for him to translate.

Volkmann had told his story in English, corroborated by Orsati.

As far as the commissioner was concerned, it came down to four bodies and two wounded detectives. One of the dead was an official of the Italian customs service, Paulo Bonefacio; the others were Scali and the two armed men on the apron.

The assassin's clothing was of German manufacture. But he carried no identification papers of any sort.

"Like a suicide squad," Orsati remarked of the men's action. "Crazy."

Now the chief of detectives stopped talking, turned to Volkmann, and said, "I have explained everything to the commissioner as you and Detective Orsati told it to me. But something's unclear. Do you have any idea why the two men wanted to kill Franco Scali? What their motive was?"

Volkmann glanced toward the window, darkness outside. "I can only tell you what you know already. We learned about a cargo from South America, with Genoa as the possible destination. We requested that a thorough check be made on all cargoes from Montevideo and São Paulo." Volkmann stared at the man. "I gave you the name and telephone number in Strasbourg. Have the commissioner contact Ferguson at once and tell him what's happened."

The man sighed. "Signore Volkmann, we are trying to make contact. But in the meantime, your help would be greatly appreciated. Isn't there anything else you can tell us?"

"Nothing."

The man said impatiently, "We have been more than cooperative. But four men are dead, and I want to know why."

Volkmann recognized the frustration in the man's tone. But he needed Ferguson to decide how much he could tell the Italians.

Volkmann said, "I need clearance."

The man's face showed his frustration. "Then what has happened goes much deeper?"

Volkmann nodded.

The chief of detectives looked at him. "We've tried to contact your headquarters, but with no luck. The operator thought there was a faulty line, but the exchange knew nothing."

A knock came on the door, and a detective entered. He asked to speak with the chief of detectives. Both men stepped out into the hallway, their heads bowed in whispered conversation. Moments later, the chief came back into the room, his face pale. He looked at Volkmann.

"We contacted one of our DSE liaison officers in Strasbourg at his home number." The man paused. "He said there has been an explosion at your headquarters. Our officer knows nothing concerning casualties, only that all his own people are accounted for."

The man hesitated again, flicked a glance at the others before he saw Volkmann's face drain to white.

"There is something else, Signore Volkmann. Something important, I believe. Our forensic people at the harbor, one of the tests they carried out on the container . . . they used a Geiger counter. It registered a high reading." The man paused. "It suggests that the cargo Scali removed contained radioactive material."

WANNSEE, BERLIN. DECEMBER 23

The stretch black Mercedes turned into the large private grounds of the house in Wannsee just after six.

Set back off the lakeshore road, the property was not overlooked by any of the big old prewar houses that ringed the lake.

Ritter stepped from the car and led Dollman to the front door, the two other bodyguards in front of the Mercedes remaining in their seats.

The beautiful young woman who opened the door greeted Dollman with a smile but ignored Ritter. Once the two men were inside, Ritter was consigned as usual to the comfortable front study on the ground floor, while Dollman and the young woman waited a respectful five minutes in the sitting room at the back of the house before they went upstairs.

Ten minutes later, Chancellor Franz Dollman lay on white satin sheets in the master bedroom, a glass of champagne in one hand. Lisl slid the disc into the music system, the sounds of Mozart filling the room. His favorite music to relax by.

An expression of pure pleasure lit his face as he admired Lisl's sensual figure, and she came to lie beside him, her blond hair flailing his chest, her pink nails stroking his arms. She was a rare specimen indeed, his Lisl, and helped him dissipate all those tensions of high office.

Until he had met her almost a year before, there had been a physical void in his life: he and his wife hardly ever made love. There were public expressions of endearment, for the television cameras, for the newspapers, but his Karin was not a sexual woman, a trifle dowdy, yet an ideal chancellor's wife: loyal, moral, conservative.

But Lisl.

Twenty-three and a body made in heaven.

Her pink-nailed fingers raked his chest, intensifying his pleasure. She was playing with him, something she liked to do now and then, the feline in her.

"Good?"

"Exquisite."

"What if you're late for the palace?"

"Do I look as if I'm worried?"

The thought of spending Christmas in a boring house, with a boring family, when he could have this woman.

Another mistress would have complained about the important times when a family came first. Lisl, as ever, hadn't complained. "I understand, liebchen. That's where you should be at Christmas."

Dollman managed to keep her out of the limelight with no great effort. Besides, it was an understanding among cabinet members: one's private life was just that, private. Unless the press got hold of it. In which case, you swam with denials or sank like a stone. Much depended on the woman in question. In Lisl's case, her desire for secrecy was on a par with his own. It was the answer to a prayer.

"Tell me about your meeting."

"As usual, Weber sees extremists under every bed. He's scheduled an emergency security meeting for tomorrow morning."

"In Bonn?"

Dollman smiled and shook his head. "The Reichstag."

Lisl frowned. "Is it serious?"

"Weber seems to think so."

Dollman didn't elaborate. Federal security was not a subject to be discussed with a mistress. He didn't tell her that Weber was putting the finishing touches to an emergency decree that very night; his plans to intern all extremists would put the final nail in their coffin.

The meeting in the Reichstag was to be held in room 4-North, the secret room. The place always intrigued Dollman; so few Germans knew about it. Specially designed to counter any possibility of bugging or electronic eavesdropping, suspended in midair on eight steel wires from each corner so that no part of it touched walls or floors.

Lisl purred, "That means you've no excuse not to stay tonight."

Dollman smiled. The function at the palace would be finished by midnight, no later. Then he could spend the night with Lisl before the Christmas holiday and family beckoned.

She turned her magnificent figure toward him.

"I'll cook supper. Just the two of us, alone."

Dollman glanced toward the curtained window. Even as they spoke, he knew there were three armed men stationed in the two cars outside in the driveway, another three positioned along the cold street in an unmarked car. Ritter, as always, in the study below. In the brains department, the man might be lacking, but his loyalty and discretion were beyond question.

The tiny transmitter Dollman carried everywhere with him was on the bedside table. The 9 mm pistol he was supposed to carry he had left in the Mercedes. The thing troubled him, made him think of violent death. A necessary precaution, but one he often disregarded.

She smiled. "What time will you be back?"

"A little after midnight. No later."

"You promise?"

Dollman let his eyes wander over Lisl's voluptuous curves. At that moment, he would have promised her the vice chancellorship.

"I promise." He leaned across, turned up the volume higher, and took Lisl's hand. "Meanwhile, we still have a little time together, so let's enjoy it."

In the darkened study below, Ritter relaxed on the couch with his feet up. The phone was in his pocket, and he had turned down the volume on the walkie-talkie that lay on the coffee table in front of him; his holstered SIG Sauer pistol draped over the end of the couch.

He heard the rising sounds of Mozart upstairs, and he smiled to himself.

51

STRASBOURG

It was after seven when the Learjet touched down.

Volkmann called his apartment and let the number ring out. No answer. When he tried the office numbers, the same happened. He guessed that the lines had been damaged, and he wondered if Peters had heard the news and taken Erica with him to the building.

He picked up the Ford from the airport lot, and thirty minutes later he was standing at the corner of the headquarters. A half-dozen police cars were parked outside, their blue lights flashing. Lights blazed in the lobby, where temporary lighting had been rigged up, and he heard the whine of a mobile electric generator, but most of the building was in darkness.

The snow had stopped and the streets were covered in gray slush. Two fire trucks parked nearby, the firemen reeling in hoses. A couple of forensic cops in white overalls were still sifting through the debris that littered the platz.

More forensic people moved in and out of the rigged lights on the third floor. It had taken most of the damage. Ferguson's office windows were shattered, and blast flames had stained the external walls.

As Volkmann stood in the shadows, he saw several faces he recognized in the crowd, but he saw no sign of Erica or Peters. His heart raced and his mind was in turmoil. One of the German officers, tieless and wearing casual clothes, stood chatting with one of the policemen, smoking a cigarette. Volkmann thought of approaching him, but instinct made him hesitate.

He decided to try calling the duty officer once more. He walked to a public phone at the end of the street and this time he got through on a crackling line.

He heard the voice of the young French officer, Delon, answer, and gave his name.

Delon asked urgently, "Where are you, Joe?"

Volkmann ignored the question and said quickly, "Tell me what happened."

Delon gave a deep sigh. "Ferguson's dead. A bomb went off in his office two hours ago. I was on duty in the basement. What's left of him is in the police morgue, and Jan de Vries is in the Civil Hospital with a severe concussion. He was on the second floor when the bomb went off. I've taken over as duty officer."

"How did it happen?"

"The guy on the front desk admitted two men fifteen minutes before the blast. They had Belgian Section IDs that looked bona fide. They took the elevator up to the third floor but never came down. We found a fire-escape door on the first floor open. They must have left that way." Panic sounded in Delon's voice. "It's crazy here, Joe. No one knows what's going on."

"Are you the only one on duty?"

"No, one of the guys from the Belgian Section's in the next room talking to Brussels about the IDs. But no names so far."

"Who was on the front desk when it happened?"

"A young guy from the French desk. He's been with us only three months. The idiot never even got them to sign in."

"Did he give descriptions of the men?"

"It was snowing outside, and the men wore overcoats with their collars up. Both tall, fair-haired, mid-thirties, that's about it. They didn't speak, just showed their IDs."

Delon paused. "I've been trying to contact Peters, but there's no reply from his number. There was a security signal for Ferguson. It came in just before the blast."

"From where?"

"South America. Ferguson saw it just before the place went up." Delon paused again. "I think that either Peters or you should see it, Joe. It's important. Not something I want to discuss over the phone. I've got a copy in the basement safe."

"You don't show the signal to anyone, André. Not until I've seen it. Do you understand?"

"Of course."

"My place is on the Quai Ernest. Meet me there. Come alone, and tell no one where you're going. And bring the signal copy."

"What the heck's up, Joe?"

"Just do as I ask." He gave Delon the address. "When did you last see Peters?"

"This afternoon. He left early with some woman. Why?" Volkmann heard the pause and then the young Frenchman said, "Is everything okay?"

"For now, just do as I say. I'll talk to you later."

It took Volkmann two minutes to drive to the Quai Ernest. Peters's Volvo was parked in the courtyard, caked in snow, and as he went up the steps, he saw the smudged footprints in the slush leading down to the courtyard.

The front door to the apartment was closed, and faint noises came from inside. The light in the small bedroom was on beyond the curtained window, and he rang the bell. When no one came to the door, he retraced his steps down to the Ford.

He found the Beretta under the driver's seat, and cocked the weapon. He walked around to the small garden at the rear of the building and looked up at the windows. He saw no movement, just the blue flicker beyond the curtained glass that told him the TV was on. His heart was pounding as he walked back around and climbed the courtyard steps once more.

He unlocked the front door warily and stepped inside, the Beretta ready, aware of the stench of lingering cordite as he went through the rooms, his heart pounding wildly in his chest.

He saw Peters's body lying across the settee and the room in disarray. He felt a jolt of fear, then caution, as his eyes flicked from the bloodied corpse to take in the room. Blood drenched the carpet, and it was clotted and caked on Peters's face and clothes. There was a bullet wound above Peters's right eye and two more in his chest cavity. He touched Peters's left wrist. The flesh was ice-cold.

It took him ten seconds more to check the apartment. He saw the splintered wood of the bedroom door, the telephone off its cradle, and one of Erica's shoes by the door. When he didn't find her body, he felt relief, and then a terrible anger took hold.

He thought of what might have happened to her and felt his hands tremble with rage, and he was aware of an overwhelming need to act, knowing Kesser's people had taken her.

And then for a moment, he felt his insides wrench and fall, as a surge of doubt swamped him. *What if Erica is one of them? She fits the pedigree. What if she brought Peters's killer here?*

For a time, that thought burned within him. *But betraying me doesn't make sense. Unless there's something to this I don't see?*

It took several minutes before his self-control returned.

He flicked on the safety catch of the Beretta, found a towel in the bathroom, placed it over Peters's face, and went to sit in the chair by the door.

He waited for Delon to arrive.

Volkmann removed the bloodied towel and then replaced it. "He's been dead for maybe a couple of hours."

The Frenchman was pale, his fists clenched tight by his sides as he stared at Peters's body. "Who did this, Joe?"

"The same people who killed Ferguson."

Delon looked badly shaken. Suddenly the sharp blue eyes regarded him with detachment, and his professionalism took over. "Joe, I think you had better tell me what's happening here."

Volkmann ignored the question. "You brought the signal copy with you?"

Delon took an envelope from inside his overcoat pocket, opened it, and handed it across.

"You think this information has something to do with tonight?" he asked. "Because if you do, you better tell me. I'm the acting duty officer. This happened on my watch."

Volkmann took the signal copy and read it slowly.

TO: Head, British DSE.

FROM: Chief, Seguridad Paraguayan, Asunción.

The following information is classified and urgent:

(1) Regret to inform the deaths of Captain Vellares Sanchez and officer Eduardo Cavales in Mexico City, approx 20:00 hours local time, Dec. 20. Deaths occurred in the course of police raid on residential property in suburb of Chapultepec, during attempted arrest of one Franz Lieber, traveling on alias passport of Julius Monck, from Asunción. Lieber also confirmed dead. Lieber known acquaintance of Nicolas Tsarkin. In course of raid, two occupants thought to have escaped. Both male

Caucasian. One believed named Karl Schmeltz. Second escapee believed named Hans Kruger. Chief Inspector Gonzales in charge of case in Mexico City. Gonzales mounted immediate search but suggests that the two may have already fled Mexico. The Chapultepec property owned by one Josef Haider, naturalized Mexican citizen, but formerly wanted for war crimes. Haider also died in course of raid. Investigation proceeding. Will contact if further information from Gonzales, Mexico City.

(2) Priority and highly classified: Confirmed to us by Gonzales, Mexico City, that one of the men arrested at above residence identified as Ernesto Brandt, Brazilian passport holder. Subject refuses to cooperate, but Brazilian Embassy confirms that Brandt is employed by Brazilian government civil nuclear research establishment and suspected of involvement in disappearance of 12 kilos—REPEAT: 12 KILOS—weapons-grade PLUTONIUM. Investigation proceeding. ENDS.

Volkmann looked up, and as Delon saw the look on his face, he said, "This has something to do with what happened?"

"Yes," Volkmann answered. For a moment, sickeningly, he felt very alone, and very exposed. "I want you to listen to me. The people who did this to Peters—the people who killed Ferguson—they've taken someone else."

"Who?"

"The woman you saw Peters leave the building with. Her name's Erica Kranz. She was staying here, and Peters was playing guardian."

Delon frowned. "Who is she?"

"A journalist. She put us onto this." Volkmann held up the signal. "I'm guessing that's why she was taken. Whoever's behind it, they want to find out what she knows, who she told her story to. And it's probably why Ferguson and Peters were killed. The two men who were killed in Mexico City, Sanchez and Cavales, they were working the case."

The Frenchman saw the look of anger on Volkmann's face, then shook his head. "Joe, you're telling me very little." He glanced uncomfortably at Peters's body. "Who did this?"

"They're neo-Nazis." Volkmann saw the look of confusion on Delon's face. "The German names I had you check. The same people who took the woman were responsible for their deaths. Why they were killed, I don't know, but it's tied in with what's happening."

Delon said hoarsely, "What are you saying? The people who killed Peters have this plutonium?"

"They've been taking it into Germany in small consignments from South America over the past year." Volkmann told Delon what had happened in Genoa, saw the man turn paler still.

When Volkmann explained about the tape, Delon said angrily, "Why weren't we informed?"

"Because until today, I didn't know there was radioactive material involved. And until you showed me that signal, I didn't know the material was plutonium. Until now, the pieces of the puzzle didn't fit together."

The Frenchman shook his head. "Joe, this doesn't just concern the British desk. It's too serious a matter. I'll have to inform my superiors."

"André, I need time before the alarm bells start ringing. If these people learn that we know about the material, then who knows what they might do?"

"What do you mean? How could they know?"

"Because they're planning a coup. A putsch."

The Frenchman's head shook slowly, as if not daring to believe what he had heard. He stared into Volkmann's face, his voice a hoarse whisper.

"How do you know this?"

"Trust me, André. It's going to happen. The signal confirms it.

The people behind this have sympathizers in the German police and army. They must, if they intend to succeed."

Delon looked at him doubtfully. "I don't understand. Why the plutonium?"

"To stop others from interfering. It's the only reason that makes sense."

Delon's hand massaged his brow in an act of indecision.

Telling him about Schmeltz would totally bewilder him, and Volkmann decided not to. For a long time Delon just sat there. When he seemed to finally realize he was being told the truth, he sat forward.

"What you ask, I can't do it, Joe. I can't take the chance. It's too much to ask." The Frenchman regarded Volkmann keenly. "You're close to the woman?"

"Yes."

"Then emotion is clouding your judgment. You must realize that?"

"You're wrong, André. Believe me."

"Then I have a question. How much support do these people have?"

"I don't know, but they don't need it. With plutonium they can hold everyone to ransom."

Delon thought for a moment. "You say you need time, but what do you propose to do?"

"One of their people in Munich, a guy named Kesser—he may know where they have the material. Give me eight hours. If I can find out, I'll call you. In the meantime, you contact every section head personally. Tell them what I told you. But stay clear of the German desk, just in case. There are people in Berlin I'd trust, but I'd want to talk with them personally. The first thing we need to do is to locate the material. You have the signal from Asunción. Explain what I intend."

"And when is this coup going to happen?"

"My guess is soon. It's Christmas; every army in Europe will have most of its personnel on leave. No one would be expecting something like this."

Delon said anxiously, "And what if I don't hear from you within eight hours?"

"Then it's up to our governments. If it means crossing German borders to stop these people, I hope they're capable of making that decision."

Delon sighed and wiped his brow, and Volkmann knew the Frenchman had given in.

Volkmann said, "Can I keep the signal copy?"

"Yes. The original's still in the basement safe."

"Give me a number where I can contact you, André."

The Frenchman wrote a number on a piece of paper. "I'll stay at headquarters. That's my own private line, in case you can't get through. The lines were damaged by the blast, but we patched up the emergency ones. I'll call the section heads on a secure line as soon as I get back. Here's hoping they believe me. You're sure you don't want any backup?"

"There isn't time, André." He saw the beads of sweat on the Frenchman's face.

"You think this is the right thing, doing it this way, Joe?"

"It's the only way, believe me."

"Then good luck, my friend."

Volkmann took the autobahn to Munich.

It started to snow, and two hours later it was coming down heavily, the fields ghostly white.

The traffic was thin, and as he passed Augsburg, a column of twelve German army personnel carriers and six supply trucks lumbered in single file in the slow lane, heading toward Munich.

Volkmann's heart pounded as he overtook the army trucks slowly, trying to glimpse the stenciled divisional markings, but the vehicles were caked with snow and mud. Fifteen minutes later, he pulled into a filling station and made the call. It lasted less than a minute.

As he climbed back into the car, he checked his watch before he turned back onto the Munich road. It read ten-fifteen.

52

BERLIN. 8:15 P.M.

The Turk stepped out of the crowded train station at Wannsee.

Kefir Ozalid carried the briefcase and wore his overcoat, scarf, and woolen gloves. He crossed the street toward the lake, the tourist boats tied up for the winter. The wind coming in off the choppy water was biting cold, but he scarcely noticed, adrenaline coursing through his veins.

At the station exit he hesitated, to make sure he wasn't being followed, pausing to light a cigarette as he looked back over his shoulder.

He saw only workers and Christmas shoppers coming out of the station, returning late from the city, but no one remotely interested in him. He reached the house ten minutes later.

The lights were on downstairs, and a Christmas tree flickered in the window. As he walked past, he saw that the porch light was off, as it should be. A footpath led around the back and he found the rear gate.

Flipping up the wooden latch, he let himself in, eyes alert and watchful. The houses nearby were bordered with high evergreens, and their privacy ensured that no one could see him.

He had spent an hour that morning walking through the Wannsee streets and footpaths that bordered the lake, getting his bearings, and studying the house.

No lights were on at the rear, but he could see the open basement window and he walked smartly across the lawn and knelt down. There was enough room for him to squeeze through, and moments later, he was standing in the basement.

He closed the window and made sure the latch was firmly locked before he removed the slim flashlight from his pocket and shone the beam around the room.

Lime-green walls, a couple of wooden boxes stacked against the wall farthest from the window. He saw the bare wooden stairs that led up. He placed the briefcase on the floor and climbed the stairs carefully, keeping to the side so the boards didn't creak.

When he reached the top, he gripped the door handle. As he opened the door a crack, faint music came from somewhere in the house. He felt a pleasant wave of heat against his face, and he saw the stairs leading up to the bedrooms. He couldn't hear the woman, but he knew she was somewhere in the house, a faint scent of perfume lingering in the hallway.

He closed the door, descended the basement stairs, then flicked open the briefcase locks. He removed the Beretta pistol, the silencer, and the two loaded magazines, then closed the briefcase again and placed it beside him.

It took him less than ten seconds to screw on the silencer and slide a magazine into the pistol butt. When he felt it gently click home, he slipped the second magazine into his pocket. He had not taken the prayer mat with him, but there was a small red foot carpet at the end of the basement stairs and he carefully turned it to face the wall before he knelt down. He said one final prayer for Layla before he touched the rug gently with his lips and stood up.

Now, as he waited in the cold basement, adrenaline raced through his veins. He checked his watch: eight-forty-five.

He flicked off the flashlight and waited patiently in the darkness.

Four more hours.

Four more hours and Dollman would be dead and Layla would be avenged.

MUNICH

It was 10:45 p.m. exactly when Volkmann pulled up outside the house in the Starnberg district.

Ivan Molke came out to stand under the porch light in the lightly falling snow. He quickly led Volkmann into a paneled study, where a fire blazed in the grate.

When they were seated, Molke said seriously, "Your phone call was very brief, Joe. Has this got something to do with what happened in Strasbourg? I heard it on the news."

When Volkmann spoke, his voice was thick with emotion. It took him almost five minutes to explain everything, and he saw the reaction on Molke's face, disbelief mixed with fear, and when he had finished, Molke stared at him with incredulous eyes.

"No, it can't be . . . ," he said. "You're certain about the woman in the photograph?"

"Hanah Richter identified her, there's no question. The other part's guesswork, Ivan, but it makes some kind of sense. It's like a puzzle fitting together."

"Karl Schmeltz is Adolf Hitler's son?" Molke shook his head as he stood up. "It sounds crazy, Joe." His face was pale. "A neo-Nazi putsch I can imagine as possible, yes. But not another Hitler, Joe. Never that. No way."

As Molke continued to shake his head, Volkmann took out the signal copy from Asunción and placed it on the desk. Molke read the paper. After a time, he looked up as if in a daze.

"Do you think the people who trailed my men belonged to the same group?"

"I don't know, Ivan. Have you been tailed since we last spoke?"

"Not that I'm aware of. And I've been careful after what happened with my guys." Molke slipped his right hand into his pocket and removed a Glock, weighed it in his palm. "I haven't been taking any chances. I keep this with me." He swallowed hard as he placed the pistol on the desk. "Do you have any idea where Erica is now?"

"Assuming she's still alive, Kesser's people probably have her."

"Where's Schmeltz, do you know?"

"After what happened in Mexico City, my guess is that he's already in Germany. Or soon will be."

Molke looked at Volkmann blankly; then he said, "What do you want me to do?"

"Do you know someone with authority in the State Ministry? Someone you'd trust your life with?"

Molke said, "I don't know if I'd go that far with those guys. They're career types. But there's a politician named Grinzing I'm on first-name terms with. He's the only one I can think of right now who might listen to me."

"Then I want you to deliver a letter to him by hand, tonight. See that he reads it. In the letter will be everything I've told you, every-thing I suspect, except what I told you about Karl Schmeltz. Because no doubt Grinzing will want to ask you a few questions about me." Volkmann paused. "Like if I'm crazy. If the letter is some kind of joke. The contents he'll have to judge for himself. Regarding me, make him know that he can trust me." He looked directly at Molke. "We worked together in Berlin for four years, Ivan. You know my character. That I can be trusted. Simply tell him that when he asks. But above all, tell him it's vital that he act on the letter. The signal from Asunción can be verified by Strasbourg. His own state security people can make contact there directly."

"Why don't you want me to tell him about Schmeltz?"

Volkmann shook his head. "He'd never believe it, Ivan. You must know that. And explanations will only waste time. I don't know how long we've got before these people start to move, but I can guess from what's happened that it's going to be soon."

"And if Grinzing doesn't believe me, what then?"

"You still know people in Berlin. Contact them. The same with state security. Tell them everything you're going to tell Grinzing."

"You honestly think they'll believe me, Joe?"

"I don't know. But you're the only hope I have, Ivan."

"What are you going to do?"

"Drive over to Kesser's place. If he's not at the apartment, his girl-friend may be. One of them's got to know something. If neither one is there, I'll drive up to the place at Kaalberg."

"And do what?"

"Find Kesser. He'll know what's going to happen."

Molke shook his head vigorously. "Joe, you saw the armed guards up there. It's too dangerous. Let me call a couple of my people in as backup."

"There's no time to lose, Ivan. It would complicate things further. Just deliver the letter."

Molke sighed and looked at Volkmann solemnly. "You know, I never thought this would happen again in Germany. Not in my lifetime. Sure, there've always been the crazy, extremist groups like the ones who burn down immigrant hostels. The shaved heads with swastikas who march and give the Nazi salute at the Brandenburg Gate every anniversary of Hitler's birth." Molke shook his head fiercely. "But not this. Never this."

He tried not to think of Erica, but she was still in his thoughts when he reached Kesser's apartment twenty minutes later. The snow had stopped falling and he tried to check his anger as he stepped out of the car, forcing himself to figure out how to handle the situation.

Christmas candles burned in the windows of the apartments and nearby houses, and here and there the lights of a Christmas tree winked on and off. The lights were off in Kesser's apartment, and he saw no sign of the gray Volkswagen in the parking lot. His heart skipped a beat when he thought Kesser or his girlfriend might not be at home.

He had the Beretta in his pocket. This time he used the copy keys Ivan Molke had given him, and he let himself in the front entrance and went up to the second floor.

He hesitated before knocking on the apartment door, but when he knocked three times and got no reply, he let himself in, the key offering a little resistance before it turned in the lock.

The apartment was in darkness and when he tried to flick on the light switch, suddenly he was caught in the glare of a powerful light beam. As he wrenched the Beretta frantically from his pocket, he felt the stinging blow across the back of his neck. He heard muffled voices and felt strong hands immobilize him, and then something sharp jabbed his left arm.

He was barely conscious as he was carried back down the stairs and out into the cold air; then he heard the far-off sounds of car doors opening as he was bundled into a narrow space.

After that, the blinding whiteness took over and it smothered him.

53

MUNICH

It was almost 11:40 p.m. when Ivan Molke pulled up outside the driveway of the imposing house in the exclusive suburb near the Isar River.

A uniformed policeman was on duty in the hut that stood inside the gates. Molke showed his ID, and the man phoned through. Moments later a police bodyguard walked down from the house. He recognized Molke, walked over to the car.

"What's this all about, Ivan?"

"I need to see Grinzing. Private business. Tell him it's urgent."

"You've no appointment?"

"No."

"He'll have to give me clearance first, Ivan. I'll see what he says."

The bodyguard telephoned through, and one minute later, Molke found himself in Grinzing's study, the walls lined with expensive, leather-bound tomes.

Johann Grinzing was forty-two, tall, with blond, thinning hair. An ambitious man who exuded an air of confidence, he wore his expensively tailored suits well. His face was rugged, and his slim hands perfectly manicured.

Grinzing lit a cigarette and sat down behind his desk, gesturing for Molke to be seated opposite.

He glanced at his watch and regarded Molke with questioning eyes. "So, what brings you here this late, Ivan? Is there a problem?"

Molke nodded. "I need your help, Johann."

Grinzing said simply, "Tell me."

Molke reached inside his overcoat pocket and took out the buff-colored envelope. He saw Grinzing stare at it, and before Molke handed it across, he said, "I want you to do two things for me, Johann. First, listen to what I have to say. Then I want you to read the envelope's contents."

"What's this, Ivan?"

"A friend asked me to give it to someone I trusted in the State Ministry. Someone with influence. Once he had told me what it was about, I chose you."

"I'm flattered, but go on."

"The man's name is Joe Volkmann. He works for the DSE in Strasbourg."

Grinzing raised his eyebrows. "This has something to do with national security?"

"Yes. I'd like to contact Weber, the interior minister, but I don't know him personally."

Grinzing lifted the cigarette to his mouth, drew on it slowly as if considering something, before he blew out smoke. "So, how can I help you?"

"Before you read what's in the envelope, I want you to know two

things. One, there was a bomb planted at the DSE offices this afternoon."

Grinzing said solemnly, "I heard it on the news earlier. Has this
got something to do with it?"

Molke nodded. "Then you may also have heard that the head of
the British DSE was killed. Plus another man. Also British."

"I thought it was two missing. That's what the last report said."

"That's Volkmann. He hasn't contacted his people in London."

Grinzing raised his eyes again. "Go on, please."

"Number two, Volkmann is totally trustworthy. I worked with
him in Berlin. He's one of the few people I'd trust with my life."

"Why are you telling me all this?"

"Because after you read the signal here, probably the first question you're going to ask me is, do I trust him? I want that clear from
the start. I do. Absolutely."

Grinzing averted his eyes for a time, thinking. Then he said, "May
I see it?"

Ivan Molke handed the envelope across. Grinzing opened and
plucked out the contents, unfolded the pages promptly and read.

Molke watched Grinzing's tanned face become waxen, and then
the politician looked up.

"And you really trust him?" There was a tone of incredulity in the
question.

"I told you already, Johann. Please believe what you read."

Grinzing shook his head slowly, his voice a whisper. "It's
almost beyond comprehension." He looked down at the pages
again and then up at Molke. "You really expect me to go to the
state prime minister with this? Tell him that a group of neo-Nazis
is planning to take over the country? That it may have a nuclear
weapon?"

"If you don't, then I will. There isn't much time. A matter of hours
perhaps."

"And where's Volkmann now?"

"In Munich."

Grinzing put down the pages. "I'd be laughed at. You must realize that."

Molke said grimly, "And you must realize that if these people carry out what they intend, this entire country is in danger of repeating the past."

"I find that difficult to believe. And even if what you said were true, a democracy like Germany cannot be dismantled overnight. It's absurd."

Molke looked pointedly at his watch, then back at Grinzing. "They'll have supporters. In Parliament. In the armed forces. In the police. They have to have, because it's the only way they stand a chance of succeeding. And it only takes a small number to lend their support to this act of madness for the whole country to be plunged into a nightmare again."

Grinzing shook his head, but his face was pale and his voice hoarse. "I really can't believe that, Ivan. It's not possible."

Molke let out a deep sigh. "Very well. May I have the letter back? I'll take it to the minister myself, even if I have to kick down his bedroom door."

Grinzing hesitated. For a long time he looked at the papers in his hand, and then he looked up at Molke slowly, as if reconsidering. Grinzing said, "What if the minister believes you? What do you expect him to do?"

"Alert Berlin and Bonn. The federal office will have a list of loyal army and police officers the country can rely on. Every sensible democracy takes that precaution to counter such a situation as this—a coup that threatens its existence."

"And if the minister doesn't believe you?"

"I think he will. But if he doesn't, I still have friends in Berlin who might listen." Molke's voice became strained. "For heaven's sake, Grinzing, we have to do something."

There was an uncharacteristic anger in Molke's voice, and Grinzing hesitated, looking as if a great weight were pressing down on him. "I want you to do something for me, Ivan."

"What?"

"Give me five minutes alone to think this through. You must understand my position. Such a decision cannot be taken lightly."

Molke looked at his watch, saw the anxiety on Grinzing's face. He nodded. "Okay."

Grinzing stood, clutching the pages. "I'll leave you here alone. You'll have my answer within five minutes."

As the door closed softly after Grinzing, Ivan Molke let out another deep sigh. At least the man was beginning to take him seriously.

Johann Grinzing stepped out into the hallway, past the bodyguard sitting in the chair reading a newspaper under the portrait of Grinzing's father.

The guard went to rise out of respect, but Grinzing gestured for him to remain seated. He stepped toward the back door, opened it softly, and moved outside.

The gardens were white and the air crisp and cold, the branches of the bare apple and pear trees at the end of the garden covered in fingers of snow and the house behind him eerily quiet. His wife had gone to her mother's with their two daughters for the holidays. He nervously lit another cigarette.

For eighteen years, he had been a public servant. For all those years, he had never been faced with a decision as grave as this one. He stared down at the pages in his hand, legible in the wash of light from the security floodlight on the back wall of the house. What Molke had said was true. There was a list of people loyal to the government. They could be activated quickly, if necessary. Cover all the major cities and ports, air and sea.

He thought of making a call first to seek advice but reconsidered. He was on his own. It was his decision to expedite the matter if he chose. Any delay would be on his shoulders.

He would have to inform his superiors, and urgently. But he would extract the most from it, of course. If he came out of it well, there was opportunity here.

But how to approach it? How to resolve it?

Three minutes later, he had figured out what to do. He stepped back inside, and into the hallway again. This time the bodyguard didn't rise but simply gave a respectful nod and went back to reading his paper. Late-night visitors were common in Grinzing's household.

For a few brief seconds, Grinzing glanced up at the painting of his father. The blue-suited man stood erect, the state flag flying behind him in the portrait. A loyal Bavarian to the core. It was strangely appropriate, Grinzing reflected. The man had been dead some twenty-five years. The portrait's blue eyes stared down and seemed to warn him. What he was about to do could ruin him if it went wrong. His future could hang on this.

His father's eyes looked on just as he remembered them. Blue. Honest. True. A loyal servant to his Fatherland and state. Only the blue business suit looked out of place.

All that was missing, Grinzing reflected—recalling the old photographs he had kept since childhood—was the black uniform of the Leibstandarte SS.

Molke turned as Grinzing stepped back into the study. "You've reached a decision?"

"Yes." Grinzing sat down behind the desk again.

"Which is it?"

"There are a few matters I wish to discuss first."

Molke saw Grinzing's hand reach over slowly behind the desk. In an instant the drawer was opened, the Walther pointing at Molke's chest.

Molke stared and went to speak, but no words came.

Grinzing said, "I want you to listen to me very carefully, Ivan. What I have to say and how you react may determine whether you live or die in the next few minutes."

Molke still said nothing, simply stared at the man and then at the Walther again, his mouth open in disbelief.

Grinzing said calmly, "You're surprised, I can see that. I have a confession to make, but one that by now you've guessed. The people you fear, I belong to that group. I and many, many others."

Molke said simply, "Why?"

A grim smile flickered on Grinzing's lips. "Because for the first time in years, this country has a chance to be truly strong again. To reinstill the old virtues we once prided ourselves on. To stop apologizing for our past. To cleanse our country of all the filthy, stupid imported breeds our politicians had the audacity to invite here. To reawaken a sense of pride in being German. And I wish to be part of that change that is about to take place. It offers a great future for someone like me, I think you'll agree."

"You're a fool, Grinzing. It can't succeed."

"On the contrary, it can. Too much planning has gone into this. It can't fail."

"Dollman would never sit back and allow this country to be dragged into the gutter again."

"Dollman won't be alive to obstruct us. As for his cabinet . . ." Grinzing shrugged. "I think I've said enough already. Suffice it to say that they won't stand in our way."

"And you think the German people would support any of this?"

"But they will, Ivan. Our strategy's been worked out. The people will rally behind us. Once they see we're capable of elevating this country to its former greatness, building a new and prosperous and powerful Reich that will stand tall and proud and strong again, they'll thank us. It can and will be done, I assure you, and that's all you need to know. Doesn't the prospect excite you just a little?"

Molke ignored the question. "A nice speech, Grinzing. Did it take you long to rehearse it?"

Grinzing's thin smile widened. "If you're trying to anger me, Ivan, trying to deflect me in an attempt to make a run for it, forget it. You'd have a bullet in you before you'd gone one pace. And believe me, I'm a capable marksman. But you can take your chances if you wish. It would be my word against the word of a dead man. A dead man who arrived anxiously outside my home asking to see me. Pretty suspicious, don't you think? One of the guards even asked me if I wanted him to be present. He said you looked troubled. And troubled men are capable of strange behavior. Like attempting to murder a state politician." Grinzing smiled again nervously. "I'm certain I could come up with a plausible reason as to why you tried to kill me and how I was forced to defend myself."

Molke said bleakly, "I want to hear your reasons."

Grinzing raised his eyebrows before he spoke. "You just heard them."

"And the nuclear material? Tell me why."

"I would have thought that was obvious. There is a warhead. It will give us the leverage to seize NATO nuclear missiles on German soil and foil any attempt by outside powers to interfere. If they attempt to stop our progress, they face the possibility of a holocaust. And Germany still has the largest army in Western Europe, don't forget that." Grinzing paused. "There's nothing more to say, except that after the coup, there will be a reckoning. Those with us, those against us. Those against will be dealt with harshly, I assure you."

"No doubt, Grinzing, you're going to start building concentration camps once more."

Grinzing smiled again. "I'm sure that will be on the agenda if these imported breeds refuse to leave our country. A necessary evil, I'm afraid, to rid us of unacceptable elements." He paused. "You're a sensible fellow, Ivan. I've always thought you so. You have an option now. There's a door off to my right. It leads eventually to the garage. I can phone through to the guard and tell him we're leaving. You come with me quietly and sensibly. If you make no fuss, I promise that by noon tomorrow, I shall make those who will be in power aware of your . . . shall we say, silent compliance. You'll be a free man."

Molke glanced toward the door, then back. "I'm a free man now."

Grinzing smiled. "Of course you are. Except that I have a gun pointed at your chest and won't hesitate to use it if you try to call the guards or attempt to escape."

For a long time Molke looked blankly toward the far wall; then he turned back to stare at Grinzing. "I want to tell you something, Grinzing. And to ask your advice." Molke looked hard at the man seated opposite. "It concerns my father." He saw the frown on Grinzing's forehead and then went on: "I'm sure you understand father-son relationships, don't you? The portrait on the wall outside. Is it of your father?"

"Yes."

Molke nodded. "I thought as much. So you were close. He influenced you."

"Of course."

"If you told me he was a Nazi Party member, I doubt if it would surprise me."

"Both Nazi and Leibstandarte SS." Molke saw the look of pride on Grinzing's face. "Do you know anything about that SS organization, Molke?"

"They were murderers."

"On the contrary. They were the most loyal soldiers this country ever had. The cream of Germany. The chosen few. And their officers were the elite. The most dedicated, unswerving men the Reich had. Let me tell you something, Molke. My father and many others like him took an oath to Adolf Hitler and the Reich. To perpetuate the ideals they fought for and made sacrifices for. To serve their Fatherland with every atom of their being. And the only people who have the given right to lead this country to greatness again are their children and their children's children. I am one of them. We've waited a long time for the right moment, and now it's come.

"Look at what's happening in this country, Molke. Not only on the streets. Even ordinary Germans are saying the Reich had its merits. Why? Because they know it's time to clean this country up. Time to wake up and be Germans again. Time to shake off that stupid mantle of pious remorse for the past. To purify this country and clean up its mess. And yes, you were right, there are people, many in positions of power, people like me, men and women who have waited a long time for this moment. They are bound in blood to fulfill their fathers' pledges. And when the time comes, and it will come within the next hours, they will do their duty."

Molke looked at Grinzing palely. "I can't believe you think that every German thinks like that, Grinzing. If you do, you ought to be certified. Or that every son and daughter of every SS officer will support this madness."

Grinzing half smiled. "Those who don't will be dealt with. Some already have been. They disgraced their fathers' testimony by refusing to help us plan for the days ahead. But those with us will help mold the future and create an even greater Germany. I'm talking about a formidable force, Ivan, not some half-baked group of anarchists."

Molke said nothing. There was an almost maniacal look on Grinzing's face. Finally Molke said, "Then I think you're going to appreciate what I have to say."

"Go on."

Ivan Molke hesitated. When he spoke, his voice was calm, almost without emotion. "Before the war my father was a young man with a wife and a baby. Once the Nazis came to power, they began to purge anyone who was anti-Nazi, but doubtless you know that . . ." Molke paused for a second, saw Grinzing stare at him quizzically. "My father was called on one night by the Gestapo. They took him to Spandau and beat him to within a breath of his life. Why? Because he had dared not to join the Nazi Party, and in fact spoke out against it. Because, in the words of the Nazi propaganda writers, he was 'an antisocial element.' For that privilege, he spent twelve years in concentration camps. At Flossenbürg he broke and carried rocks and was treated worse than a pack mule. He was beaten, humiliated, starved. He was treated as less than human. He was whipped on the whipping block until he couldn't walk, and that for simply losing a button on his camp uniform. All these things, the endless beatings, the humiliations, the erosion of his privilege as a human being, they affected him deeply. He saw men being killed on the whim of a guard. Men being killed for no reason other than the sadistic pleasure of a camp commandant. He saw boys of no more than fourteen being hung from gibbets because the SS guards wanted some fun to liven up their dull afternoons— place a bet on who would squirm the longest before death."

"You're trying my patience, Molke."

"I'm nearly finished. My father survived the camps. But he wasn't my father anymore. He was dead." Molke raised a finger, put it to his head. "Up here he was dead. A ghost walking in our house. A father we could never get close to because his pain was like a wall around him." He looked intently at Grinzing. "There are no Jews worth talking of in Germany, Grinzing. Not anymore. But there are Turks and Serbs and Poles and others whom your neo-Nazi comrades would no doubt class as racially inferior. Scapegoats to blame. Impurities to cleanse. Will they be the new Jews? Will they go to the ovens, too?"

There were tears in Molke's eyes, and very slowly he leaned a little forward toward Grinzing. He saw Grinzing move back slightly in his chair and raise the Walther.

"So I have a question for you, Grinzing. What would you do in my situation? Would you keep your mouth shut and believe in someone like you? Or even in this man Schmeltz? This man you believe to be Hitler's son. Would you, Grinzing? Or would you take your chances?"

There was a brief, quizzical smile on Grinzing's lips, and then Molke shifted his hand quickly to his right pocket and moved left just as the Walther in Grinzing's hand exploded.

The first shot clipped Molke's right shoulder blade, shattered bone, the force of the bullet jacking his body backward, the second bullet nicking the aorta above his heart.

But the third shot was from Molke's own Glock, which he carried in his right pocket. One shot before the weapon jammed on the reciprocating load.

The bullet hit Johann Grinzing square in the face, striking him just above his right eye. As the impact drove the other man backward, Molke slumped on the floor.

His head thudded against the carpet, there were screams and shouts from outside, and then the door burst in and he heard cries and the sound of rushing feet. Hands gripped Molke, shook him, wrenched his hand from his pocket.

As consciousness went from him, he heard voices swearing, saw hands moving about Grinzing. The politician's body had been flung back before collapsing on the floor behind the desk, his shattered face lying directly across from Molke's.

The last thing Ivan Molke saw before his sight faded was the look of utter surprise on Grinzing's dead face.

54

It was snowing as the car jerked to a halt, and Volkmann became conscious again.

The headlights were extinguished, and the car doors opened. He saw the secluded house beyond the driveway, the front door already open.

City lights sparkled beyond a flank of trees. He guessed they were somewhere in the mountains near Munich. When he looked back, he saw the figure of the terrorist Wolfgang Lubsch step out of a lighted doorway and into the falling snow. He wore a heavy parka, and his glasses glinted under the light.

Volkmann was dragged from the car and into a comfortable living room. Glass doors led to a balcony, and the lights were on. On a table were a half-drunk bottle of schnapps and some glasses.

Lubsch kicked forward a chair. "Sit down, Volkmann."

When Volkmann ignored the command, the terrorist said, "Under normal circumstances, I'd have no hesitation in putting a bullet in your head. You're not a journalist, are you, Volkmann?"

The icy blasts of air that hit Volkmann as he was dragged from the car had brought him quickly awake, but he was still fighting to regain his senses.

Lubsch lit a cigarette. "It wasn't difficult to discover who you are. People like you and me scent each other like cat and dog. After our talk at the lake, you worried me. Why were you so interested in Winter's death? So interested that you'd risk coming after me."

Volkmann looked into the terrorist's face. "Those were your people at Zurich airport?"

Lubsch blew smoke out into the air. "And at the monastery. We've been watching every move you and Erica Kranz made since that day at the lake."

"How?"

Lubsch sat down. "How did we follow you? Erica was easy. But you . . ." He reached into his pocket, removed a small electronic device with an aerial, held it between two fingers. "A simple transmitter attached to your car so we couldn't lose you. The same with your friend Molke and his men. You see, you confounded us, Volkmann. Everything about this business confounded us. Until now."

"You're not with Kesser and his people?"

"Give me some credit, Volkmann."

"Where are we?"

"Someplace where we won't be disturbed."

Two men stood in front of the door that led out. One held a Glock in his hand. Volkmann recognized them both. One was Hartig; the other was the scar-faced man with the truncheon. Both looked over at him, their faces expressionless. Volkmann turned back to face Lubsch. "Why have you brought me here? To settle old scores?"

"Hardly. We have matters to discuss."

"Such as?"

"Something important to both of us." Lubsch paused. "You must forgive the behavior of my men, Volkmann. But you see, we thought Kesser's people would turn up looking for him. Instead, you showed. It was quite a surprise."

"Where's Kesser? Do you have him?"

Lubsch ignored the question and stood. He crossed to the window, snow flurrying against the other side of the glass, and turned back to face Volkmann. "We Germans sometimes have a dramatic nature. We can be loud, aggressive, unfeeling. But we're not all beasts, Volkmann. And we don't all want another Reich."

"You know what Kesser's people intend?"

"Yes, Volkmann, I know."

"Did Kesser tell you?"

"Hardly. He's dead."

Volkmann began to speak, but Lubsch interrupted. "Two of my men were waiting for him outside his apartment. My instructions were to take Kesser alive. I was hoping he'd tell us what we needed to know. Kesser came out and drove to the mountain. Halfway there, my men overtook his car and blocked the road. When Kesser realized what was happening, he pulled a gun and shot one of my men. They fired back and hit Kesser in the head. He was still alive when they took him to one of our safe houses. But by the time I got there, he was dead."

Volkmann shook his head in anger. "Do you know what you've done, Lubsch?"

"The world's a better place without him, believe me."

"Did you kill Winter, too?"

"Hardly. I told you at the lake, Volkmann. Winter was a braggart. Especially when he was drunk. He liked to talk about the new world order he and his friends were going to create. Except he talked too much. So Kesser had him hit."

"Why try to take Kesser?"

"The same reason as you, Volkmann. To find out what his people intend. Two of my men were watching your apartment in Strasbourg. They saw Erica Kranz being taken by two men in a black Mercedes. They heard an explosion and decided to keep tailing the Mercedes, but they lost it in bad weather near Augsburg. We figured Kesser's people were behind it."

Volkmann stared at Lubsch. "Do you know where Erica is?"

"At the Kaalberg."

"She's alive?"

"I've no idea, Volkmann."

"How do you know she's at the mountain?"

"Kesser's girlfriend told us. Once we showed her Kesser's body, the rest was easy. She's involved, but her loyalty didn't extend to losing her own life. Taking Erica was part of their plan. To find out how much she and your people knew."

"What else did the girlfriend tell you?"

Lubsch looked steadily at Volkmann. "Everything she knew. Who's behind it. What they intend."

"Tell me."

Lubsch reached for the bottle of schnapps. He splashed liquid into one of the glasses and handed it to Volkmann.

Volkmann pushed it away. "I don't want a drink, Lubsch. I want the truth."

"Take it, Volkmann. You're going to need it when I tell you. And then, my friend, I'll tell you what we're going to do."

Volkmann emptied the glass and replaced it on the table. Lubsch poured himself a drink and went to stand by the fire.

"They've got a missile sited at the Kaalberg. The nuke variety, not a conventional warhead. They've got neo-Nazi cells in the army and police, and politicians who are supporting them. The man you asked me about at the lake, Schmeltz. He's there, at the mountain; he's the one who's pulling the strings. They're trying to repeat history with a putsch, just like the Nazis. Only this time there's a missile as a lever. If any outside power tries to march over German borders and interfere, it risks a calamity."

Lubsch swallowed the liquid in one gulp. "Kesser's girlfriend wasn't privileged enough to know everything. But she knew enough. To start with, they're going to kill Dollman and his cabinet." Lubsch saw the look on Volkmann's face.

"How?"

"There's a house in Berlin's Wannsee where Dollman keeps his mistress. Her name's Lisl Henning. She's one of their people. Dollman's due there sometime after midnight. There's a Turk named Kefir Ozalid waiting to put a bullet in his head."

"And the cabinet . . . ?"

"She didn't know. Only that it happens after Dollman gets hit. They'll all be killed."

Sweat beaded Volkmann's face, the voices on the tape suddenly clear. "Why Ozalid? Why not one of their own people?"

"Because they've been very clever. As soon as Ozalid pulls the trigger and the cabinet gets hit, the streets are going to be full of righteous Germans baying for immigrant blood. Kesser's friends have set it up perfectly. They'll blame the deaths on immigrant extremists. They pit German against immigrant and in the chaos, make their coup a walkover." Lubsch put down his glass. "They've everything worked out down to the last detail. The monastery you saw. You know what it's for? It's to be a detention center . . . for undesirables. Immigrants and others. Another Dachau, no doubt. Kesser had a long list of such places to fill once they take over."

Volkmann stared back at Lubsch. "Tell me what you intend doing."

"The only thing we can do. The Kaalberg is half an hour from here. My men and I are going to try to take out the missile. Neutralize it. And find this Schmeltz."

"You're making a mistake, Lubsch. You'll never succeed on your own. Let me call Berlin . . ."

Lubsch shook his head. "How long's it going to take you to convince them, Volkmann? And by then, it may be too late."

"What makes you think your men can do the job?"

"Volkmann, in this weather, we'll be lucky even to make it up the mountain. But if we do, we stand some chance. By simply informing Berlin, we have none. If Dollman's killed, this country can still stop what's happening. But without a government, there isn't a chance. Kesser's girlfriend didn't know how the cabinet will be hit, but someone up there will know. According to her, there's never more than a half-dozen armed guards on the property. There are four of us, including me. You make five. All we need is the element of surprise."

"You'll need more than that. What about weapons?"

"We have them. Machine pistols, grenades. Well, what do you say, Volkmann?"

Volkmann looked past the window, at the city lights beyond the mist of slanting white. He turned back, searched the terrorist's face. "You know, I had you down as a nutcase, Lubsch. Which only goes to prove that I'd have made a lousy psychiatrist."

Lubsch laughed. "I've been called worse. That's probably a compliment."

"Why are you doing this? Why are you helping me?"

"For the reason I told you. I don't want another Nazi Reich or anything like it. I don't want the mistakes of the past repeated. Because if that happens, there would never be another Germany. Not ever." Lubsch smiled grimly. "Absurd, I know, you and I joining forces, but there you have it. So, are you with us?"

Volkmann hesitated. "There are two things I want to make clear."

"What?"

"I make my call to Berlin."

Lubsch considered. "And the second?"

"If we make it up the mountain, Schmeltz is mine."

Lubsch said, "It's not only because of Erica Kranz, is it, Volkmann?"

"There's something Kesser's girlfriend didn't tell you about Schmeltz."

The terrorist grimaced, his voice suddenly strained. "She told us, Volkmann. I didn't mention it, because I thought you'd think I'd lost my reason." Lubsch shook his head as if in disbelief. "Part of me wants to believe what she said, and yet another part of me is questioning my sanity. Still, I know she didn't lie. They say that history repeats itself. Only, in this case, who would have believed it?" He paused. "What do you want, Volkmann? A chance to speak for the dead?"

55

BERLIN. SATURDAY, DECEMBER 24, 12:16 A.M.

The Mercedes braked to a halt on the gravel driveway.

The porch light was on outside the house, and as Ritter opened the car door for Dollman, the chancellor slid out of the warm limo.

Lisl was waiting in the hallway, and while Ritter disappeared as usual into the study she led Dollman inside.

On the dining room table supper was laid. A bottle of Dom Perignon stood in a silver bucket of crushed ice. Next to it were fresh flowers and two lit candles. Lisl had drawn the curtains to stop the prying eyes of the bodyguards, and as Dollman crumpled into a leather armchair by the fire, she said, "You had a difficult day?"

"Exhausting."

She went to stand behind him, massaging his shoulders.

Dollman groaned with pleasure. Moments later she felt his hand grasp her arm, and he pulled her around. She saw the look of impatience on his face and said, "Let's eat first."

Dollman's hand started to slide along her thigh, but she smiled, and led him to the table.

Dollman wolfed down his food and drank three glasses of champagne. When it came to dessert, Lisl served him chocolate mousse. He looked longingly at her and let his hand slide down the curve of her hip.

She smiled down at him. "What about dessert?"

"I'd much rather have you, my sweet."

The chancellor managed a weak grin, but tiredness and alcohol crumpled his face. She smiled back, took Dollman by the hand, and led him upstairs to the bedroom.

Five minutes later, Dollman watched as Lisl slid a disc into the sound system. Then the strains of Mozart filled the room.

She came to lie beside him on the silk sheets. Dollman's energy was spent, it was obvious, and when he made a weak attempt to touch her she gently pushed his hand away. "It's better you sleep for now, liebchen. Time to recharge your batteries. I'll be waiting for you when you wake."

Dollman murmured gratefully and turned over, exhausted.

She waited for several minutes before she slid off the bed, crossed to the window, and peered out through a parting in the curtain. Three cars were parked below: one in the street, the others in the driveway, though there was no movement. But Ritter's men were out there. And Ritter himself was downstairs in the study, as usual.

As the curtain fell back into place, she heard Dollman begin to snore, his big body rumbling under the covers. She checked her watch before she crossed to the sound system again. She lowered the volume to near silence, waiting for the second hand to sweep past for one minute exactly, aware of her heart beating furiously; then she raised the volume again gradually until the music resumed its former pitch. She went to sit at the dressing table, her hands trembling as she stared down at her watch again.

1:10 a.m.

In another ten minutes, it would all be over.

In the basement, Ozalid tensed as he heard the sounds of Mozart die and flicked on the pencil light. He watched the second hand sweep around: one minute, then the music volume rose again.

He had heard the cars pulling into the driveway, heard the sounds of footsteps in the hall, then moving up the stairs to the bedroom. But nothing this last half hour. Until now.

He tensed again. His watch read 1:10. He flicked off the light and stood in the darkness, a knot of expectancy in his stomach, but every sense alert.

He would wait five minutes, just to be certain.

Then he would move.

12:46 A.M.

Christian Bauer was director of the Berlin Landesamt, a tall, lean man in his mid-fifties with gray sleeked hair and a handsome face. He wore a dressing gown over blue crumpled cotton pajamas, but even so, he had the well-groomed look of the diplomat about him.

He had made coffee, but Werner Bargel ignored the steaming black liquid. Bargel had telephoned him to say he was coming over. That it was urgent.

It was strictly business and Bauer saw that his assistant's face was ashen, but Bauer spoke calmly, as if he were used to emergency calls to his home in the early hours. "Tell me what's so urgent, Werner."

"I got two telephone calls just before I called you, sir. Both from Munich. The first was from a man I know named Volkmann. He's with DSE."

"Go on."

"According to Volkmann, a man named Kefir Ozalid is going to assassinate Chancellor Dollman." Bargel paused briefly, saw the look of alarm on the director's face. "He also said the entire cabinet is going to be killed."

Bauer's mouth was open. "When?"

"Tonight. Now. He didn't know how, only that it's going to happen after the attempt on Dollman's life." Bargel swallowed. "All the cabinet are staying in Berlin, sir, for Weber's security meeting in the Reichstag this morning."

Bauer put down his cup, his face draining of color.

His assistant director flicked a glance at his watch, as if for emphasis. "Before I came here, I had Ozalid's name put through our computers. We're also trying to locate the chancellor."

"What did the computers say?"

"There's a Kefir Ozalid listed under security-risk category two. He's Turkish. Immigrated to Germany in his teens. Thirty years old."

Bauer stood up anxiously. "Okay, so we've got a file on him, but why would he want to assassinate Dollman?"

"Two years ago Ozalid spent three months in prison for seriously assaulting an Interior Ministry official in Bonn. The sentence would have been longer, only the court took into account extenuating circumstances."

Bauer's eyebrows rose. "What extenuating circumstances?"

"According to his file, he and his wife were the victims of a group of right-wing thugs who firebombed an immigrant hostel. His wife died from her injuries. She was also pregnant. The thugs involved were never apprehended." Bargel paused. "Dollman was interior minister at the time, responsible for federal security. Apparently, Ozalid wrote to him, blaming Dollman for not having the thugs brought to justice. The official Ozalid attacked was one of Dollman's staff."

"Good grief . . . ," Bauer said. "Did the computer say anything about Ozalid's whereabouts?"

"He left Germany a year ago, last known address in Stockholm. But he could have slipped back into Germany on a false passport . . ."

Bauer thought for a moment. "Do you trust Volkmann?"

"Yes."

"Can we speak with him?"

Bargel shook his head. "He just made the call to my home number, pressed on me the absolute urgency of the situation, and then he hung up." Bargel paused. "But there's something else, sir, tied in with Volkmann's information. Something very disturbing."

"What?"

Bargel took a deep breath. "According to Volkmann, the threats to Dollman and the cabinet are only part of it. There's going to be an attempted coup."

Christian Bauer looked at Bargel disbelievingly. "By whom?"

When Bargel told him, Bauer shook his head slowly and said, "You . . . you can't be serious?"

Bargel didn't stop; he explained all he knew about the missile and its location. Then he caught his breath nervously, drew in a deep lungful of air, saw Bauer's shocked reaction.

The director asked quickly, "Where's Dollman now?"

"With Lisl Henning." Bargel swallowed. "Volkmann said she was involved."

"He mentioned her by name?"

"Yes, sir. I ordered security to contact Dollman's bodyguard Ritter and tell him what's happening. However, because of the complexity of the situation and the protocol involved, the other orders I gave await your confirmation."

"What orders are those?"

"I gave the duty officer a list of senior military officers and security personnel to contact. On your command, they're to come here immediately. There's a team already on its way to Lisl Henning's house in Wannsee—I took the liberty of issuing the order as soon as I heard from Volkmann." Bargel quickly checked his watch. "They should be arriving within the next few minutes. Another team is making ready in Munich to move to the Kaalberg." Bargel paused. "You may, of course, countermand my orders."

"What about the cabinet?"

"I've already ordered that their personal security be increased and put on alert."

Bargel looked at his superior expectantly. Bauer's face was tense. He nodded quickly.

"Okay. Confirm your orders, with my approval."

"What about the interior minister, sir? He'll have to be informed."

Bauer was under pressure, and he spewed out his words. "I'll contact Weber myself. But for heaven's sake, get onto Ritter."

At that moment the portable buzzed in Bargel's hand. He listened, and then spoke sharply into the receiver. "Keep trying! Do you hear me? Keep trying!" Bargel covered the mouthpiece and looked up.

Bauer said urgently, "What is it?"

"It's about Ritter, sir. We're getting no reply from his phone."

Karl Schmeltz stepped out onto the snow-swept balcony and buttoned up the green loden coat to the collar. He crossed to the end of the low wall and stared out at the snowy darkness.

Ghosts.

Ghosts everywhere.

An icy wind gusted, eddying the snow falling thinly in the valley below.

He had been in these mountains before, listening to the Föhn wind, knew it with certainty. Osmosis. Absorbed in his bone jelly. The memory ached there now like a soft pain.

Flakes of icy snow brushed against his cold cheeks. Chilled, invigorating.

Bone-cracking coldness.

He sucked in a deep breath, felt the chilled air probe his lungs like icy fingers.

Good.

Twice, in youth, he had been brought here, to the south, remembering faces and names before his journey began: Bormann, Mengele, Eichmann. Secret trips and safe houses and furtive meetings. *Yes, here's the boy. Take a good look at him. Someday, not in your lifetime perhaps, but someday . . . when the time is right, when the opportunity presents itself . . .*

The Prussian snapping of heels, the firm shaking of hands, the pledges of allegiance. Old faces and new faces that kept the flame burning.

Who would have thought it would take so long?

An icy blast blew across the balcony. He sucked in another deep breath of the chilled air.

So close, so very close.

A noise sounded and he turned toward the French windows. Meyer stepped out onto the balcony, his footsteps crunching on snow.

"The woman's here."

Schmeltz nodded, and both men strode back into the house.

Ozalid flicked on the pencil light.

1:14 a.m.

Four minutes had passed. He flicked off the light.

In the darkness, he took a quiet, deep breath. Impatience was setting in.

Do it.

He began to climb the basement steps very slowly. When he reached the top, he flicked off the Beretta's safety, switched off the light, and slid it into his left pocket, then gripped the door handle lightly.

He opened the door a crack. The table lamp was on in the hallway, the study door closed, and he could see no light under the door where the guard would be resting.

He stepped out into the hallway.

Above him, the landing was in darkness, but he could hear the music coming softly from the bedroom. He moved up the stairs, reached the landing. The music was louder now, the bedroom door open a crack, revealing a thin splinter of light.

Ozalid took a deep breath as he raised the silenced Beretta.

He stepped toward the light.

In the study darkness, Ritter was asleep on the couch when his phone buzzed. He came awake with a start, exhausted after a hectic schedule with Dollman, resting his eyes but falling asleep in the process.

Now he fumbled for his phone, found it in the darkness, said sleepily, "Ritter."

"Ritter, this is Werner Bargel. Where the devil have you been? Are you with the chancellor?"

Ritter found the lamp and switched it on, almost knocking it over as the voice crackled with urgency.

"Why? What's up?"

"There's no time to explain, just listen, Ritter. There's going to be an attempt on the chancellor's life. Stay close by him. Do you hear? Stay close! Don't let him out of your sight. Support will be with you in minutes. But stay with Dollman!"

Ritter dropped the phone, grasped the walkie-talkie on the table, and spoke into it rapidly, not waiting for a reply from the bodyguards in the cars outside.

"Watch units . . . Alert Red! . . . Repeat, Alert Red! Watch units!" Ritter shouted into the mouthpiece, his voice strained. "Cover entrances and exits, now!"

He reached the door in one big stride, stepped out into the hallway, the SIG Sauer pistol already raised in his free hand, eyes scanning the ground floor. Music, but other sounds, too, doors opening outside in the driveway, the other bodyguards responding to his call.

As Ritter moved toward the stairs, he glimpsed the open door leading down to the basement, his every sense signaling danger. He hesitated, but only for a split second. The door hadn't been open earlier, he was certain, and if it was open now, then someone must have . . .

No!

He could hear the men moving frantically about outside, but he ignored the sounds as he raced up the stairs. Pistol at the ready and taking three steps at a time, Ritter bounded toward the landing.

As Ozalid stepped into the bedroom, he saw the man sleeping in the white silk sheets, the beautiful young woman wearing the pink nightgown sitting by the dressing table.

She stared over at him silently, not making a sound, but with fear in her eyes.

There was something surreal about the scene, the music playing on, and for an instant Ozalid hesitated as he stared back at the young woman.

Their eyes met, and her gaze shifted nervously to the figure lying on the bed, as if pointing out the target.

Ozalid saw Dollman's body half covered by the bedclothes, his white shoulders, his back and part of his torso visible, the gray chest hair and his belly rising and falling as he breathed.

Ozalid stepped forward, aimed the Beretta, and heard racing footsteps on the stairs.

Then other sounds from below the landing, wood splintering, a door crashing in . . .

Ozalid turned instantly as the bedroom door burst in and the bodyguard appeared, clutching a pistol.

The bodyguard saw the gun in Ozalid's hand swing around, his face registering his shock and his disadvantage.

As Ritter rolled suddenly to the right, Ozalid fired two quick shots, one of them clipping Ritter's left shoulder. The bodyguard screamed as the bullet cracked into bone. Then the Turk turned back to face his target.

He aimed as Dollman came awake with a startled look on his face, the big body rising from the covers.

Ozalid fired twice before the chancellor could speak.

The bullet struck Dollman's left cheek just below the eye socket; then he was flung back in the bed as the second shot blasted his chest.

As Ozalid started to fire a third time, out of the corner of his eye he saw the bodyguard raise his pistol.

Before Ozalid could aim again, he heard the explosion and felt the piercing hot lead enter his right side. And then he was punched sideways by a quick series of shots, lead tearing into his flesh as the bodyguard emptied his pistol.

Ozalid reeled back, glimpsing the woman in the nightgown, hearing her screams. As he was spun around by the force of another bullet, the gun went off in his hand. The shot tore into the woman's throat, and she was flung back against the wall.

As the last burst of lead hammered into Ozalid's body, he pitched forward onto the silk sheets on top of Dollman, not aware of the sounds of the men bursting into the room, or of the harsh voices screaming frantically, but dimly conscious of the hands tearing at his body, pulling him off the chancellor.

Forty seconds later Vice Chancellor Konrad Weber got the emergency call in his sixth-floor suite in Berlin's Kempinski Hotel.

Despite the hour, Weber was still dressed and reading through his papers, and he sat up expectantly and placed his leather briefcase on the bed beside him.

Weber listened on the phone as Christian Bauer described the chancellor's assassination in Wannsee and explained what he knew about the intended coup.

A stunned silence followed, until Weber said hoarsely, "Oh no . . ."

Konrad Weber, a pragmatic and precise man, was clear about his duties as vice chancellor despite the shocking news of Dollman's assassination, and he left Christian Bauer in no doubt as to what had to be done to protect the German state. By law, Weber would assume the position of chancellor immediately and convene an emergency cabinet meeting within the next hour at the parliament building.

The threat to the cabinet's lives was a grave and real one, and Weber agreed with Bauer's strategy. Reichstag security officers were already contacting ministers staying at hotels throughout the city. Security at the Reichstag itself was to be stepped up in case of an attack on the building during the coming hours.

A state of emergency would be declared by Weber and those in the army and police whose loyalty was without question would be contacted at once, and the borders sealed.

Weber ordered Christian Bauer to confirm the location of the site in Bavaria but to hold off on any attempt to seize the missile until Weber and the cabinet decided on a course of action. He was quite adamant about that, despite Bauer's protests: Konrad Weber said he wasn't going to risk the decimation of Germany and its people until he had all the facts concerning the coup and who the plotters were.

The next minutes and hours were of grave importance, and Bauer was to answer only to him and to no one else. Weber would assume control of the armed forces and police.

When he finally terminated the phone conversation six minutes later in his suite at the Kempinski, Konrad Weber looked over at his brown leather briefcase on the bed, certain he had everything he needed to convene the emergency cabinet meeting at the Reichstag.

56

The driver pulled in under a clump of trees on the mountain road. Switching off the engine, he doused the headlights, and five men climbed out of the cramped Opel. There was a sudden burst of activity, the car's trunk opening, and weapons were dispensed in the snowy darkness.

One of the terrorists thrust a Kalashnikov into Volkmann's hands. He took the weapon and checked that the safety was on, made sure the magazine was loaded. Lubsch returned his Beretta, and he slipped the automatic into his pocket.

He looked up toward the Kaalberg mountain. The weather was turning worse, the snow coming down heavily. A thick clump of pine trees faded into a mist of snowy whiteness, the visibility down to no more than ten yards. The snow was an ally, Volkmann knew. It was worth a dozen men. The driver had kept the engine revs low for the last two hundred yards to mute the noise of their approach.

Volkmann tried not to think about Erica, but focus on the climb ahead. Flakes of snow stung his face. Lubsch was giving orders to Hartig, who then disappeared into the swirl of snow, a Kalashnikov draped across his chest.

Lubsch came to join Volkmann. "The two of us will go up through the trees. Once we get close enough, I use this." Lubsch held up a Sony transceiver. "When my men below get the order, they'll start firing on the plateau, to try and pin down whoever's up there. Hartig's gone ahead to cut power to the cell phone transmitter nearby, and to try and sever the telephone and power-line junction boxes. If he can do that, Kesser's friends will be cut off from the outside world. If we need to use the phone line, Hartig can reconnect us."

"Why the power lines? They may have an emergency generator."

"No doubt they will. But Hartig's the expert, and he says to cut them. If an emergency generator kicks in, Hartig says the supply will only be connected to the lighting circuits and power sockets. But nothing heavy-duty, like electric motors, because the emergency circuit wouldn't take a heavy load. That way, the missile will be out of operation." Lubsch smiled. "But let's not count on it, Volkmann."

Lubsch took a deep breath and exhaled, the air around him fogging in the icy coldness. "We'll have to play the cards as they fall. But we have the advantage of surprise, so let's just pray the guards on the plateau barrier don't hear my men coming." He glanced up toward the trees and the blanket of white, then checked his watch and called the rest of the men together. He had them synchronize their watches. "Okay, let's go over everything one more time. Any mistakes could be lethal."

The Reichstag parliament building on the Platz der Republik was lit up like a Christmas tree.

Werner Bargel had never seen so much activity. Not since the Wall had come down and the crowds had swarmed over toward the Reichstag building from the Brandenburg Gate, two hundred yards away. That was a night to remember.

So was this.

Bargel stood on the steps outside the double glass doors at the Reichstag's south entrance, his breath fogging in the December air as he paced the concrete nervously, the shock of Dollman's death still on his mind.

On everybody's mind.

The massive, imposing granite building had witnessed much history. The Reichstag fire. The storming of Berlin by the Russians. The Berlin Wall going up and coming down. And it was witnessing history in the making again right now.

It seemed as if half the cops in Berlin were swarming around the parliament building.

At least sixty green-and-white Volks and riot-squad Mercedes vans, hundreds of police dressed in full riot gear, some with leashed German shepherds, at least four helicopters hovering overhead, their noisy rotors throbbing in the darkness.

Green-uniformed cops milled around in nervous clusters, talking, worried looks on their faces; other groups raced off into the trees in the small park opposite, flashlights sweeping in the dark, dogs barking, voices calling out, walkie-talkies crackling. Everywhere, frantic activity.

Unbelievable!

The threat to the cabinet's lives was daunting enough without having the missile threat to worry about, too.

Bargel checked his watch: 2:10 a.m.

Three of the ministers had already arrived without incident. Gaunt-faced, all of them, as they climbed the Reichstag's stone steps, flanked by a deep wall of antiterrorist police. Dollman's death had shattered them. The threat to their own lives wasn't helping their nerves.

Bargel looked out toward the waves of green uniforms and plain-clothes. All of them wore yellow discs on their lapels, marking them as part of the security teams. But a yellow disc meant nothing. Anyone in the street could be waiting for the right moment, including someone in uniform. Bargel scanned the faces of the cops, chatting nervously in groups, some of them watching the entrance.

Any one of them, or more.

Whom to trust?

But Bargel doubted that anyone in his right mind would risk an assault on the cabinet now. It would be suicide. Security at the Reichstag was as tight as a rusty nut.

No one was allowed in or out without the personal permission of the Berlin chief of police, or Bargel himself. The chief of police stood outside on the cold street, ten yards away—his bleached face looking as if someone had cut his arteries. No one looked sure of anything, despite the precautions. The security teams scoured the Reichstag building three times with specially trained dogs in tow, checking all the rooms and every cranny, the basement, every floor, every wing of the building.

Nothing.

No one there who shouldn't be, no bombs or explosives.

Bargel had decided with the chief of police what would happen next. As the cabinet arrived, they would be led to an elevator that would take them to the third floor and the north wing of the building, to the room designated 4-North. The route was two minutes' walking distance from the entrance. When Weber arrived, accompanied by his bodyguards, Bargel would lead him there personally.

The room called 4-North had another name in the Reichstag. The Wire Room, they called it. Used only in emergencies and for high-security meetings.

Not so much a room as a big soundproofed box with one double-door entrance, the room was suspended on eight thick steel wires above the floors of the Reichstag. There was no way to bug it because the walls, ceiling, and floor touched nothing. No telephones. No communication. Only one way in and out, sealed by oak doors with bullet- and bomb-proof sheathing. And that entrance would be heavily guarded.

Bargel glanced over at faces in the swarms of cops, thinking again about Volkmann's warning. Any one of them could be an assassin, waiting for the moment to strike.

But that was too risky, too unlikely.

It had to be a bomb, Bargel thought. But the building had been thoroughly checked, even room 4-North, even the security staff's own personal lockers. Three bomb-squad teams went over the same ground, one after the other. Nothing. Clean. Not a trace of explosive.

So if not a bomb, how?

A scream of sirens made Bargel's heart jump. A cavalcade of Mercedes and motorcycle cops arrived. More cabinet ministers, worried men stepping out of black limos, cops surrounding the cars, helicopters hovering lower overhead, radios crackling.

Bargel greeted them at the door, eighteen of his armed men waiting inside, ready to guide each minister to room 4-North, along with one of his bodyguards.

More wailing sirens, blue lights.

The next car was Konrad Weber's.

A buzz of activity erupted as faces strained to see Weber arrive, a rush of men from the antiterrorist squads surrounding the car to protect him.

Bargel prayed that none of the A-T squad were there to kill Weber.

Bargel deftly unbuttoned the jacket under his raincoat where the SIG pistol was clipped to his belt, ready just in case, though he somehow knew that nothing would happen here. He waited at the double glass doors until Weber had climbed the steps, the man's long, dark winter overcoat flapping about his legs, a bleak look on his white face, the two bodyguards flanking him trusting nobody, not even the Berlin chief of police leading the way.

Once inside the glass doors, Bargel gestured at the elevator that led to room 4-North. What did he call Weber now? Vice chancellor, or chancellor? Stick with the safe one.

"This way, sir," he said gravely.

Bargel led the way, and Weber and his bodyguards followed.

* * *

Meyer left the house and walked across the lit snowy driveway to the concrete building.

As he stepped in, he hit a switch, and light flooded the cold room. He crossed to the console and telephone, his eyes flicking to the gray missile gantry standing in the center of the building as he picked up the receiver, aware of his heightened anxiety.

The phone line in the house had gone dead.

Twenty minutes earlier, when his head of security had relayed the news, Meyer's face drained. Not only Dollman was dead. Grinzing was dead, too.

And Kesser and his girlfriend gone, their apartment in disarray.

The head of security said he would call back within ten minutes; his men were searching Kesser's apartment, hoping to find some clue, trying to get further news on Grinzing.

But still no call.

The lines dead; even the cell phones had no coverage.

Meyer swore as he tried the only other line, aware of the beads of sweat on his face, of the others waiting in the house for him to return before Kruger went down to the barrier to find out if anything was wrong.

Dead.

He tapped the cradle a half-dozen times just to be certain, but still nothing. Slamming down the receiver, he heard the far-off crackle of gunfire . . .

His heart jolted as he paused to listen, hardly breathing, like an animal scenting the wind. More gunfire raging in the distance.

Meyer pulled himself together and hurried toward the door.

Snow fell heavily as Volkmann and Lubsch came out of the bank of trees to the right of the driveway.

Floodlights blazed overhead, washing across the snowed-under driveway, tire marks on the white carpet, empty except for two Mercedes caked in snow. Off to the right, the roof of the flat concrete building was covered in white. They crouched low behind the first Mercedes.

Beyond the veil of snow, Volkmann saw lights on in the house, but no movement in the windows. Lubsch flicked on the CEL, spoke quickly, then turned to Volkmann.

"Hartig cut the phone communications. Let's hope he can find the power lines. Ready?"

Volkmann nodded.

Lubsch said, "Then let's do it," and he barked a command into the CEL.

Seconds later the valley below erupted into a riot of gunfire and small explosions.

Volkmann moved forward across the snow-covered gravel toward the berghaus, Lubsch after him, just as they heard the door open behind them.

As he stepped out into the falling snow, Meyer saw the two men standing there, a surprised look on their faces. Each pointed a Kalashnikov at him.

Meyer froze in shock.

The dark-haired man put a finger to his lips, said quietly, "Not a word. Hands by your side." He took a step toward Meyer. "Where's Erica Kranz? And where's Schmeltz?"

Meyer hesitated. The man pointed the barrel of the weapon directly at his head.

Meyer's legs began to buckle. The man grazed the Kalashnikov's cold tip against his cheek.

"Answer!"

"Inside the house."

"Your name?"

"Meyer."

The man with the Kalashnikov flicked a glance back toward the gray concrete building, light spilling out from the open steel door. "Move back inside."

Meyer sweated, his mind in turmoil. He glanced at the second man, the light from the floodlamps reflecting off his glasses. The gunfire grew louder, and Meyer wondered why the others hadn't heard it and come out of the house.

This time the cold Kalashnikov barrel pushed painfully hard into his head, and Meyer faltered.

"Move or I blow your head off."

Anger in the man's eyes, a kind of madness, but controlled; he would squeeze the trigger, no question.

Meyer was pushed, and stumbled toward the building.

A noise sounded just as Kruger came running out of the house, reacting to the distant gunfire, the Walther in his hand, alarm on his face.

There was the briefest second of indecision as Kruger took in the scene and then he raised his gun.

Before Volkmann could swing the Kalashnikov around, Kruger fired wildly.

Meyer's body was punched back, and the Kalashnikov was wrenched from Volkmann's grasp as a bullet pierced his hand.

Bullets ripped through the frozen air, a scream from behind as Lubsch took the brunt of Kruger's fire, bullets cracking into concrete and flesh.

As Volkmann crouched and rolled to the right in the snow, he felt another round hammer into his right arm, glimpsed Kruger moving back frantically toward the house, still firing wildly.

Volkmann gripped the Kalashnikov in his left hand, brought it up, and fired in one fluid movement just as Kruger reached the door.

The Kalashnikov bucked wildly, the hail of bullets tore into Kruger's left side, and he spun violently.

Volkmann squeezed the trigger again.

The second burst caught Kruger in the neck, almost decapitating him, and his body arched and fell.

The gunfire echoed and died.

Volkmann stood, aware of a numbing sensation in his arm. Blood oozed from his right hand, where a bullet pierced his palm; a second bone-shattering wound just below the elbow. All he felt was a dull sensation, no pain yet, but it would come soon enough.

The bodies of Lubsch and Meyer lay on the snow. Meyer's eyes were open in death, and a gaping hole drilled Lubsch's face, his glasses lying in the white snow powder.

Far below, Volkmann heard sustained gunfire—Lubsch's men, meeting stiff resistance by the sound of it, but it seemed far away, as if happening in another time, another place.

There was a timelessness to everything, but he was aware of the ticking seconds, aware of the pain now flooding into his arm and hand.

Suddenly he was plunged into darkness, every light extinguished. Volkmann stood in the dark, feeling cold snow on his face, his heart pounding.

Seconds later, the area flooded with intense white light, blazing through the falling snow as the floodlamps came on again.

Hartig had cut the power lines; the emergency generator was kicking in now.

The house porch light and the floodlights overhead flickered a couple of times, then came bright again as the generator settled.

Volkmann looked back at the concrete building. The door was still open, but the inside was in darkness.

If Hartig was wrong . . .

The sound of gunfire rose, raging, eddying, dying, rising again.

An awesome silence suddenly filled the snowy darkness like a force as the firing died abruptly.

He turned back toward the house, light spilling out from the hallway, dropped the heavy Kalashnikov, fumbled as he wrenched the Beretta from his pocket with bloodied fingers, felt a sudden weakness engulf him, his mind fogging. He closed his eyes as unspeakable pain began to surge into his wounds.

He opened his eyes again, inhaled deep lungfuls of chilled air, tried desperately to remain conscious.

Volkmann stepped past Kruger's body, and into the house.

57

A log fire blazing, French windows leading to a balcony. White flakes dashing against glass.

The man stood by the fire, a surprised look on his face, but no fear. Erica stood beside him. As Volkmann moved into the room, she saw the Beretta, went to speak.

Volkmann said, "Nobody move."

He held the weapon at arm's length, took a deep breath, tried to take in the scene. Erica and the man, standing close together. She looked at him palely, shock on her face, and Volkmann felt the confusion. Blood draining from his shattered arm, senses blurring.

He stared over at the man. Fit-looking. Tanned skin, wrinkled face, intense stare. Handsome. Silver hair. Schmeltz, no question.

Volkmann watched as the man's eyes flicked to the Beretta, then back at him.

Erica started to move toward him, and the man made no move to stop her.

"Joe . . ."

Volkmann swung the Beretta to point at her, said hoarsely, "I said nobody . . . not unless I tell you. Just do as I say."

Erica froze, her face white.

Volkmann aimed at the man's head, gestured toward the table. "Step away from her. Slowly."

Schmeltz did as he was told. He glanced up as the lights flickered overhead, then settled.

Volkmann said, "Sit. At the table. Hands on top."

Schmeltz moved to the table, placed slim hands on the polished wood as he calmly looked over.

"Who are you?"

"My name's Volkmann."

For several seconds Schmeltz stared at him. "Yes, Joseph. I know of you." The blue eyes became hard; then he looked toward the floor between Volkmann's feet.

Volkmann glanced down. Blood trickled onto the carpet. Red spots. His face burned.

He looked back up as Erica said, "Joe, listen to me, please."

Concern in her voice. Or was it his imagination? Volkmann felt his senses slipping away, his vision going. An unreality about the scene.

He blinked, tried to focus. Erica moved toward him again, slowly this time. He swung the Beretta around sharply. She stared at him in astonishment.

"I told you. Don't move. Don't speak."

Schmeltz said quietly, "If you came here to stop us, you can't." He shook his head, the knowing eyes watching Volkmann. "You really can't stop us."

"Why not?"

"It's gone too far. If you kill me this moment, it would make no difference. Do you intend to kill me, Joseph?"

Volkmann ignored the question, tried to keep his eyes focused, to fight the darkness threatening to engulf him. "I've told Berlin. They're already moving to stop you."

Schmeltz looked toward the French windows. Snow dashing against glass. A look on his face as if nothing mattered. When he turned back, he shook his head. "It hardly matters. Dollman is already dead, believe me, Joseph."

"And his cabinet? How do you intend on killing them?"

Schmeltz's eyes opened wide as he reacted to the words. He glanced over at Erica, then back at Volkmann. When he spoke, his voice was almost a whisper.

"How did you know?"

"Just answer the question. What's going to happen?"

"That doesn't matter now. It's too late to stop it, believe me."

Volkmann's finger tightened on the trigger. "It matters if you want to stay alive."

Schmeltz paused, as if considering. "You didn't come alone, did you?" He looked over at the telephone. "Your people cut the lines?"

Volkmann nodded.

Schmeltz looked back. "That was stupid, on your part. The telephone would have been your only chance of warning Berlin of what's about to happen."

Volkmann's barrel touched Schmeltz's forehead. The man's head jerked back in alarm but Volkmann kept up the pressure, pushing the Beretta hard into his flesh.

"Tell me, and tell me quickly. Or so help me, I'll squeeze the trigger."

Konrad Weber looked at the stunned faces seated around the table in room 4-North. In the harsh neon lights, every one looked like death.

The doors were locked and Weber was on his feet, addressing the seventeen men.

"Gentlemen, I have several proposals to deal with this extraordinary emergency. Very firm action must be taken." His voice was resolute. "I hope to have your full cooperation in each and every one of these proposals. The president has been informed of the situation and those senior officers in the army and police force whose loyalty we can depend on are already at their posts. All the forces at our disposal are ready to act. Those responsible for these outrages must be swiftly dealt with. I need hardly remind you that all our lives may be in danger."

Weber cleared his throat, saw heads nod in solemn agreement.

"First, a state of emergency will be declared. Second, a decree for the protection of the people and the federal state will be enacted. All civic and constitutional rights will be suspended until those elements that threaten our democracy have been purged. Third, I want every known neo-Nazi and every extremist, regardless of political leanings, rounded up and interned at once."

Weber paused, wiped the sweat from his brow with a pocket handkerchief. "The problem of the missile is an alarming one. As soon as we have identified the organizers behind this outrage, we shall act immediately."

Weber saw the frightened nods. He knew that the pressure was telling on his face. In the silence that followed, he heard a faint ticking noise and looked down, alarmed. The sound grew louder. Weber looked up, realized the noise came from the electric clock on the wall, the second hand ticking away. He let out a sigh, recognized his paranoia, looked at the faces at the table.

"Gentlemen," he said firmly, "I must inform the president before we enact these emergency measures. So are we all agreed?"

Weber looked at the sober faces around the room and quickly asked each minister by name in turn, as protocol demanded.

Every one of them agreed.

Snow dashed in flurries against the French windows, and the log fire crackled.

Volkmann kept the Beretta pointed at Schmeltz's head. He felt the faintness begin to sweep in again, the butt of the weapon sticky with blood, dripping onto the floor. Eyes losing focus, images fading. He blinked, sucked air deep into his lungs, tried to clear his head. He heard panic in Erica's voice, but she seemed to speak from far away.

"Joe . . . let me help you."

If she came closer, she could distract him, allow Schmeltz to make a move. He forced himself to ignore the voice.

Suddenly a surge of pain flooded his entire body, and he faltered, slumped back in the chair. He snapped open his eyes, kept the pistol pointed at Schmeltz as she spoke again.

"Joe, please."

Volkmann said, without looking at Erica, "Stay where you are."

He saw Schmeltz lean forward in his chair, heard him speak softly. "You'll bleed to death, Joseph. Listen to what she says."

"Just tell me what's going to happen."

"You're a remarkable man, do you know that?"

"Tell me."

"To have unraveled what is happening. To have found me. I admire your ability, your tenacity. Your courage." Schmeltz paused. "Your name is German, but you are not German, are you, Joseph?"

"Tell me, Schmeltz. Whoever you are."

"You know who I am, Joseph. Just as I know who you are. Just as I know about your father."

Anger flashed in Volkmann's face. Erica said, "Joe, he made me tell him everything."

He saw what looked like pain in her face.

Schmeltz leaned closer. "Forgive me. But I wanted to explain. The mistakes of the past won't be repeated. What happened to your father won't happen again, Joseph. Not ever."

"I don't believe that, Schmeltz. And neither do you. It may not happen to Jews, but it will happen to others. Time's up. No more talk. Tell me what's going to happen in Berlin, or I kill you right now."

Schmeltz looked toward the telephone, sat back in the chair, the soft blue eyes more confident. "It's pointless. You have no way of stopping what is about to happen."

"Tell me, quickly." Volkmann's finger tightened, went to squeeze. *"Tell me!"* Volkmann's scream rang around the room. Schmeltz's eyes dilated as he swallowed. "The cabinet is meeting in the Reichstag. Weber has assumed Dollman's position. He is proposing emergency measures to stop what is happening. But the meeting is a charade."

"Why?"

"Because once Weber has made his proposals, he will excuse himself. Leave the room. Go to his office on the pretense of making a phone call to the president."

Schmeltz hesitated. Volkmann tightened his finger on the trigger again.

"Keep talking."

"Weber will leave his briefcase behind. When he reaches his office, he will detonate a device in the briefcase. A bomb will explode, killing only those inside the cabinet room. The structure of the room makes it impossible for anyone to survive. They will all be killed. Weber will have assumed complete control."

Schmeltz paused. There was a long silence, and Volkmann looked away, toward Erica.

A pleading look on her face, tears at the corners of her eyes.

His mind began to fog again, pain rolling in. He looked back at Schmeltz.

"And where do you figure in this?"

"Weber's position will be temporary." Schmeltz looked directly at the Beretta. "But my part is not important. Not now." His eyes shifted back to Volkmann. "Even if you kill me, it would make no difference. The seeds have been sown. There is no going back once the bomb goes off. Only Weber can hold Germany together. Weber and others like him. Men and women who will uphold their fathers' testimony." Schmeltz leaned forward. "And they will do it, Joseph. Believe me, they will."

There was a hint of excitement in Schmeltz's voice. Volkmann stood up, Schmeltz's face clouding in front of him. He looked away, tried to focus, couldn't. When he looked back, Schmeltz's features were a blur.

Volkmann flicked a look at Erica, her features hazy, too, like seeing her through frosted glass. He filled his lungs with air, short, deep bursts, blinked hard, cleared the fog. He tried to concentrate on Schmeltz's face.

"Not all Germans are Nazi supporters. Not all of them will support you."

"Enough will. You think we haven't planned this to the last detail?"

"How?"

"Weber will denounce the murders as a treasonable act by immigrant extremists to destabilize the nation. There will be a surge of nationalist fervor that hasn't been seen in this country in decades." Schmeltz paused, looked at him. "Listen to me, Joseph. Do as I say, and you won't be harmed. You can walk away from here—"

"Stand up."

Schmeltz stood up, his tall frame towering above Volkmann, his eyes cautious. "What are you going to do?"

"It's what you're going to do. You're both going to walk to the car outside. If any of your people are left and try to stop us, I'll put one in your head."

Schmeltz licked his lips nervously. "If you're trying to reach a telephone, you're wasting your time. Others will come here, because they cannot reach me. You won't get far."

"Move."

As Volkmann flicked the Beretta, blood dripped onto the carpet from his wounds. He started to feel himself go under, gripped the back of the chair.

"Joe, please . . . you'll bleed to death."

Volkmann didn't see Schmeltz's hand move until the last moment. It came up smartly and gripped the Beretta, twisted, pointed the weapon toward Volkmann.

Erica screamed.

As Schmeltz grasped the Beretta, Volkmann gripped the man's arm blindly with his good hand, clung to it, oblivious to pain. Schmeltz tried to wrench himself free. Volkmann pulled down hard, heard the sharp crack as the bone broke, heard Schmeltz scream in agony as he squeezed the trigger.

The weapon exploded.

The bullet tore into Erica's side, and Volkmann watched with horror as she was slammed back against the wall.

As Schmeltz struggled to release himself, Volkmann pushed with all his weight into the man's body, both men tumbling back, shattering glass and wood as they crashed out through the French windows, the weapon flung from Schmeltz's grasp as they rolled across the breadth of the balcony, snow and shattered glass crunching under their entangled bodies.

Volkmann struck the concrete rail, the force knocking him breathless, Schmeltz's weight crushing into him a fraction of a second later.

Icy blasts of wind, flurrying snow.

Pain. Piercing cold.

As he struggled to move, Volkmann felt Schmeltz's weight come off him. He closed his eyes, opened them again; the image of Schmeltz swam before him, crawling back across the balcony, scrabbling wildly in the snow, breath rising in hot, panting bursts like an animal's.

Volkmann forced himself to stand, saw Schmeltz's hand reach out for something.

Volkmann lunged. He landed on Schmeltz's back, and the man exhaled air like a bellows.

Volkmann clambered over him, fingers groping in the snow, eyes searching frantically for the weapon.

And then Schmeltz's arm came out of nowhere, and his weight landed on Volkmann's back, knocking him breathless, arms locking around Volkmann's throat, strangling him, knuckles digging into his windpipe, crushing throat muscles.

Volkmann felt himself go under as he fought for breath, tried to grasp Schmeltz's arm, the effort painful, impossible.

Someone else was there. Volkmann turned his head and saw Erica, her side drenched with blood, her hands on Schmeltz, dragging him. Volkmann twisted his body, and with Erica's help, wrenched the other man up and off.

Schmeltz's body tumbled into snow.

Volkmann glimpsed the dark metal against white, a yard away, turned toward where the pistol lay, fingers scrabbling in the snow, cold, so cold, difficult to discern metal, difficult to move.

Please, Lord.

Something hard, still warm.

He found the butt of the weapon, gripped it in his left hand.

He turned, saw Schmeltz crawling back toward the balcony.

Volkmann held the pistol at arm's length, aimed at the back of Schmeltz's head, trying to judge distance, two yards, less.

"Stop." The words painful.

Schmeltz ignored the command, stood up, chest heaving as he fought for breath, blood streaming down his face from the shattered bridge of his nose, eyes wide and staring.

"I said stop."

Snow swirling. Silence except for the labored breathing of the three people on the balcony and the gusting flurries of snow.

"Listen to me, Joseph—"

Volkmann stood panting, looking into Schmeltz's face, fought the nausea sweeping over him.

Erica was huddled against the rail, her face clenched with pain. The left side of her sweater and skirt were covered with blood. A wave of anger gripped him.

And then there was a sudden throbbing of helicopter blades from somewhere in the swirl of snow above. Volkmann heard it and glanced up. The sound coming closer, coming in fast. More than one craft. Swishing of blades as they cut the icy air.

Bargel's people.

Or Schmeltz's.

Volkmann aimed the pistol at the center of Schmeltz's forehead.

Schmeltz's eyes opened wide.

Volkmann thought of the pictures hanging on white walls. A woman clutching the lifeless body of her child. The grinning SS man standing over her.

His father's pain.

Schmeltz's voice, coming to him faintly now.

"Joseph, listen."

Schmeltz moving closer.

Volkmann felt himself start to go under again, his eyes beginning to cloud. His body winding down, a terrible, excruciating wave of pain almost suffocating him. He gritted his teeth, fought the pain. A chill went through him, making him shiver. He took a deep breath.

Let it out.

Slowly.

Schmeltz moved closer.

"Don't move."

Schmeltz stopped.

Volkmann aimed between Schmeltz's eyes.

The dull, chopping noise of blades coming closer. Schmeltz's eyes flicked up to the swirling heavens, then came back to Volkmann.

Volkmann wanting to scream the words aloud, but instead, said them softly. "They say every sin has its own avenging angel. Do you believe that?"

Volkmann looked at Schmeltz's face.

He didn't wait for the reply.

The Beretta exploded.

When he came to, he was lying on a stretcher.

He was aware of the ghostly swirl of flashing red and blue lights in the thinly falling snow; he heard the wailing sirens, and a harsh, metallic clatter of blades somewhere overhead. A babble of loud and desperate voices faded in and out, orders being shouted and carried on the icy wind.

When he tried to look around, he saw ghostly figures in white arctic fatigues appear out of nowhere, weapons at the ready, but then they began to blur and he lay back again.

A rugged-faced man in white fatigues and with a Heckler & Koch machine pistol draped around his neck loomed over him suddenly, looked down into his face. He smiled briefly, and his hand touched Volkmann's shoulder as if to reassure him. Volkmann tried to speak, tried to tell him about Weber, tried to tell him about Erica, but the words would not come.

The man looked away. There was a voice, telling him something, then a burst of gunfire from somewhere out in the whiteness and the man grimly barked an order, and he was gone.

And then all life seemed to go from Volkmann again. A feeling of lightness in his head, as moments later he felt the stretcher lifted, or so it seemed, and he was suspended in midair.

And then a wave of intense pain washed in and smothered him.

* * *

It took Konrad Weber three minutes to walk to his private office on the third floor of the Reichstag.

Werner Bargel accompanied him and his two bodyguards.

When they reached the office, Weber unlocked the door and stepped inside, then locked it again, leaving the three men outside in the hallway. In the oak-paneled room, he crossed to his desk and sat down. His hands were shaking as he opened the drawer and removed the remote-control transmitter, placed it in the palm of his left hand.

As he clenched the fingers of his free hand, he took a deep breath.

The phone buzzed in Werner Bargel's hand.

Bauer's voice, frantic. "Where are you, Bargel?"

"Outside the vice chancellor's office."

"Bargel, listen to me, for heaven's sake . . ."

Konrad Weber heard the frantic voices in the hallway, heard the crash of splintering wood as the door burst in, saw the SIG pistol in Bargel's hand.

As Bargel raised the pistol to aim, Weber grinned and touched the button.

The distant explosion, when it came a split second later, cracked through the Reichstag like a clap of thunder.

58

Volkmann came awake in the private ward in Munich General Hospital a little after 10:00 a.m. two days later.

He heard a radio on somewhere, music beyond the closed door.

"Tannenbaum." The carol that had always made his father cry, and he wanted to cry, too, not because of the music, but because he was breathing, alive.

He was connected to tubes, probes wired to his arms and chest and linked to a machine, his heart beating in tandem with white blips on a green screen. He touched the cotton dressing on his numbed right hand, the hard bond of white plaster around his right arm.

Werner Bargel was seated at the end of the bed. A nurse appeared out of nowhere, a sudden rush of activity. He heard Bargel's voice.

"How do you feel?"

His lips stuck together; it was an effort to part them. "Lousy."

It was another twenty minutes before Bargel spoke again, after the doctors had been called and examined him, after the nurse had offered sips of cold water to wet his cracked, parched lips. A couple of yellow pills to swallow. A damp cotton cloth dabbed on his face and neck. Refreshing. Cool.

He saw Bargel talk with the doctors out of hearing range, and then the room emptied, and he and Bargel were alone.

Bargel sat in the chair beside the bed. "The doctors assure me you'll make a speedy recovery. But for a while there, it was touch-and-go. You'd lost a lot of blood. You put more stress on your body than it was designed to take."

Volkmann raised himself, then slumped back in pain. The throbbing in his right temple became a blinding ache.

"Take it easy, Joe. They've given you something to ease the pain, so it should take effect soon."

Volkmann said, "Erica . . . ?"

Bargel sat forward. "She's in a private room a floor below us. The medical team got to her in time. Don't worry, Joe, she's going to be all right."

He saw Bargel smile faintly, and he went to turn his head, tried to take in the room, but there was a fuzzy quality to everything.

Bargel said, "I don't know what she must have thought when you staggered into the room up on the mountain, but I suspect she was glad to see you." He smiled. "And she was worried sick . . . you were a bloody mess. It was a miracle you stayed conscious. And then when you waved her off when she tried to help, she thought you must have lost your mind."

"I wasn't thinking clearly," Volkmann admitted.

"As for her," Bargel continued, "she went through an ordeal of her own. They'd pumped her full of that truth drug, scopolamine, to make her talk . . ."

"Did she tell you that she saved my life?"

"No, she didn't."

Volkmann explained.

Bargel leaned closer. "She's a terrific woman, Joe. But I suppose you know that. And when two people with such conflicting pasts like yours can find reconcilement, it tells me that there's always hope."

"She told you about Schmeltz?" Volkmann asked then, changing the subject.

Bargel nodded, his face pale and serious. "She told us everything she knew. The rest we were able to piece together."

"How long have I been unconscious?"

"Two days."

"Tell me what I missed."

It took ten minutes to explain. Dollman and the cabinet were dead, except for Weber, who was in a high-security cell in Moabit Prison. The president had taken over the duties of chancellor, and formed a caretaker government. A list of conspirators was found in the safe in Grinzing's study. All known extremist neo-Nazis and their supporters were under arrest. The terrorist Lubsch and one of his men were killed in the assault; the others escaped into the mountains before the all-weather choppers landed.

When he mentioned Ivan Molke, Bargel saw the look of pain on Volkmann's face.

"Ivan was a good man, Joe. And a good German." Volkmann looked away, toward the white wall. Bargel's voice brought him back.

"And so was Lubsch," he went on, "in his way. What he and his friends did for you—for all of us—was heroic." Bargel leaned forward. "When the woman told me about Schmeltz, at first I didn't believe her. It sounded so crazy. I thought she had cracked after her ordeal."

"What made you believe her?"

"One of the people on Grinzing's list talked. Everything you deduced, everything Erica told us, it's true. Geli Raubal had a son. The Schmeltz couple took him to South America."

"What about the body?"

"It's been disposed of, secretly."

"Where?"

Bargel shook his head. "Even I can't tell you that, Joe." Bargel paused. "The army's on the streets, restoring order. Most people don't know what's happened. We've imposed a newspaper blackout until things are under control. The measures are extreme, but we want to make certain there's no chance of this country repeating history."

"I don't get it. Erica's father was Leibstandarte SS. Why wasn't she contacted like the others?"

Bargel nodded. "She was on their list but was only one of many. It seems it was Winter's job to make an approach to her but he didn't make it a priority. Maybe because he knew her personally, and that she wouldn't be the kind to help." Bargel shrugged. "Whatever the reason, it probably saved her life."

Bargel saw the strain on Volkmann's face and stood. "We'll talk again, Joe. For now, get some rest. I owe you a great debt of gratitude. Not only me, but the country. I just want you to know that."

Bargel crossed to the door and smiled. "I'll tell her you're awake. She's anxious to talk with you."

The snow started to fall as they traveled in the taxi from Heathrow, but by the time they had reached the neat square of Victorian houses, it had stopped.

Everywhere white, deserted. New Year's Eve.

The flight from Frankfurt had been delayed, and when he telephoned and told her he was coming, he heard the surprise in her voice, saying how good it was to hear from him.

When he told her they'd have an extra guest staying for a few days, he recognized her excitement, like the young woman on the beach in Cornwall he always remembered, with her hair tied back, always a smile on her lips, an aura of happiness about her that made him know why his father had married her.

It was four o'clock in the afternoon when the taxi pulled up at the top of the square. Darkness was falling, the gates of the tiny park were open, branches heavy with snow, here and there footprints where a child had strayed and an adult followed. But no one there now. Empty.

He led Erica in through the park gates, placed the two overnight bags beside the bench, brushed away snow. As she sat beside him, through the trees he could see the house, lights on already, a plume of gray smoke rising faintly from the chimney.

There were lights on in other houses, too. Candles burning, Christmas trees winking in the twilight through fogged windows, the vestige of Christmas. Another eight hours and a new year.

A pigeon cooed in the branches above. A fir tree rustled. The sound of beating wings.

Erica asked, "Which house is yours? You never told me which one."

Volkmann pointed to the redbrick house, and she studied it for a long time.

"It suits you."

"How?"

She smiled. "Solid. A little old-fashioned. But dependable."

He smiled back and Erica looked about the park.

"This is where you played when you were a boy?"

"Yes."

She closed her eyes and said, "I can picture you, you know. From the photograph I saw in your apartment."

"Tell me what you picture."

"A boy who is quiet and very serious. A loner, but curious. And a boy who loved his father and mother very much."

"You see all that?"

She smiled again. "It's what I picture." She opened her eyes, brushed a strand of blond hair from her face, looked across at him. At the handsome face she wanted to touch as he looked silently about the snowy landscape. She said, as if reading his thoughts, "This place is special for you, isn't it, Joe?"

"I used to come here with my father."

He felt the touch of her hand, the silky warmth of her fingers twining through his. Comforting. He wondered how he had ever doubted her.

She said, "His pain has been repaid now. And the pain of all the others who suffered."

"You believe that?"

"Yes, I believe it. Because you stopped it from happening all over again. And now you can bury your father's pain."

Volkmann looked at her face. He took her hand in his, brought it to his lips, kissed the cold fingertips. "I'd like to believe that."

Through the trees, he could see the house. His mother would be waiting. He looked down at the blue eyes watching him.

"Come. She's expecting us. And I'd like you to meet her." Volkmann picked up their bags, and they started to walk back across the park toward the row of redbrick houses.

The suite on the top floor of the Hilton hotel had a clear view to the mountains beyond the city. It was a cold, clear New Year's Day in Madrid, and both men sat by the window.

The younger of the two was in his early thirties, lean and fit-looking. His briefcase was open, and a sheaf of papers lay on the coffee table in front of him.

The second man was in his early fifties. His tired face looked haggard after almost two days without sleep. The hotel recorded his name as Federico Ramirez, but as a precaution the man changed passports twice in the last twenty-four hours during his connections from Asunción.

He wasted no time on small talk, nor did he offer his young visitor a drink. "The number of arrests and detentions, you have the latest figures?"

The younger man glanced briefly at his notes. "We estimate twenty-three thousand, as of midnight last night."

The older man betrayed no emotion at the figures, and his visitor carried on talking.

"But the situation is still fluid, and the figures may increase. Apart from those on the list, the authorities are simply pulling in those with a strong past record of support, so it's likely they'll be released if charges can't be pressed."

The older man said impatiently, "And the cells, how are they holding up?"

"In the eastern region, they remain pretty much intact. The other three points of the compass are the ones really affected. But the damage isn't that great. We've been relatively lucky."

The older man stood up and said sharply, "Lucky? What happened, Raul? How the devil did it go wrong? We were that close." The older man held up two fingers, the tips close together.

The younger man sighed at his superior. "You got the preliminary report in Asunción. I'm afraid it's the best we can do for now. Over the next few days we ought to have a clearer picture. Certainly the man and the woman, Volkmann and Kranz, were largely responsible."

The young man paused, then leaned forward. "But something positive has actually come out of this. Something that wasn't in the report you got. I wanted to tell you personally."

"What, for heaven's sake?"

"Many of the rank supporters didn't really believe we would attempt what we did. Now that they've seen it can happen, they're more determined than ever to carry on." The young man leaned forward more eagerly. "We were unsuccessful this time, but when it happens next time we'll be even more prepared. We'll have learned from our mistakes. You know the Western democracies can't sustain their problems. Immigration. Unemployment. Recession. They're already crumbling. It's only a question of time before we try again."

"What's the estimate?"

The young man shook his head. "I can't give you a definite answer on that. Not just now. But in the meantime we continue to try and strengthen our position."

"I can confirm that to Asunción?"

"Absolutely. You know we have the resources. It's really only a question of time."

The older man sat, lit a cigarette. "Do we know what's happened to Schmeltz's body?"

"Five days ago it was cremated. And buried in a forest near the Polish border."

The gray-haired man sighed and shook his head. "The couple, Volkmann and Kranz, how did they find out?"

"A photograph they found at the Chaco house of Geli Raubal. That was the clue they worked from. That and the journalist's death." The young man met his superior's stare. "You want us to take care of them?"

"Not right now, Raul. But later, I promise you, they'll pay the price."

The older man studied his watch and then his visitor. "You're flying back to Germany this afternoon?"

The young man shook his head. "I have a meeting with our neo-Nazi comrades in America. They're interested to hear our damage reports and our future intentions for cooperation. The same with our other contacts in Europe. They believe their immigrant problem is getting worse, and want our advice. And you?"

"London tonight. Then Asunción, via Rio."

The young man looked at him. "They've got the preliminary report, but impress on them we still go ahead with our plans. Assure them of our determination, sir."

The older man placed a hand on his visitor's shoulder. "I'll let them know; don't worry, Raul. And thanks for coming."

The young man picked up his briefcase, replaced his papers, clicked shut the security lock. He picked up his overcoat, and the gray-haired man led him to the corridor.

They shook hands firmly. The young man pressed the button for the elevator, and the doors had already opened when he heard the older man call after him.

"And Raul . . ."

"Yes?"

"I almost forgot. Happy New Year."

"The same to you, sir."

AFTERWORD

In the winter of 1941, ten years after Geli Raubal was found dead in her uncle's Munich apartment, the Nazi authorities in Vienna issued a secret instruction that her grave and those around it in the Vienna Central Cemetery were to be completely destroyed. No reasons were given, and the order was carried out.

To this day, plot 23e is an unused expanse of green in the midst of a cluttered maze of family vaults and graves in the old cemetery. Whether the remains of Geli Raubal are still buried there is a mystery. There have been numerous attempts to have the remains found and exhumed, but the Viennese authorities have consistently denied permission, thus prolonging the mystery.

In the months and years after the "suicide" of Hitler's niece, several people claimed to know the truth behind her death, a "secret" that had ultimately led to her murder.

All died violent deaths, including the journalist, Fritz Gerlich, mentioned in this book.

But what was the "secret"?

There are clues.

In late 1931, one month after Geli Raubal's death, Erhard Johann Sebastian Schmeltz, a fervent Nazi and a close friend of Adolf Hitler, disappeared mysteriously from his home in Munich, along with his sister. The couple was never seen again in Germany.

Seventeen years later, and more than two years after the war had ended, a former SS officer, wanted by the U.S. Army's then Counterintelligence Corps for his involvement in the disappearance of a quantity of Nazi gold bullion and for secretly transporting it to South America, wrote to a friend in Munich from his new home in Asunción, Paraguay. In his letter he said that he had been shocked to come across the sister of an old friend from before the war; the woman was now living in a remote town in a region north of the Paraguayan capital.

The friend's name was given as Erhard Schmeltz.

Accompanying Schmeltz's elderly unmarried sister, the writer noted with some surprise, was a pensive, dark-haired youth no more than seventeen.

ACKNOWLEDGMENTS

To all those in Europe and South America who gave their assistance in the researching of this book, my sincere thanks. In particular, I would like to acknowledge the following:

In Berlin: the staff of the Berlin Document Center; Axel Wiglinsky, Acting Director, Reichstag Security; Dr. Bose and Hans-Christopa Bonfert; the Berlin Landsamt für Verfassungsschutz (Office for the Protection of the Constitution).

In Vienna: the administration staff of the Vienna Central Cemetery.

In Strasbourg: Jean-Paul Chauvet.

In Paraguay: Carlos da Rosa.

Also, Janet Donohue, and Professor Jim Jackson, of Trinity College, Dublin. Thank you all for your help.

BRANDENBURG

GLENN MEADE

READING GROUP GUIDE

INTRODUCTION

In this riveting international spy thriller, master storyteller Glenn Meade (*Snow Wolf*) weaves a complex, fast-paced story. British intelligence agent Joe Volkmann crisscrosses the globe to solve what he thinks is a drug-smuggling operation but soon realizes that he is up against something much more sinister—a plot to establish the Fourth Reich of the Nazi Party, with tentacles reaching from Paraguay to Berlin. Suddenly dark secrets from the past begin spilling out into the present, bringing Europe to the very brink of disaster. Meade shows with chilling clarity how conditions in Nazi Germany bear an eerie resemblance to events unfolding in our world today.

TOPICS & QUESTIONS FOR DISCUSSION

1. Discuss the significance of the title, *Brandenburg*. To what does it refer?

2. What drives Joe Volkmann in his relentless pursuit of justice?

3. What accounts for Volkmann's initial distrust of Erica Kranz? Is that distrust justified? Why or why not?

4. Briefly discuss what you know about the Nazi period in Germany. Volkmann says to Erica, "[N]o people became as brutal as they did during the Nazi period. I simply can't understand it—how your countrymen could let it all happen." Do you see how this might have been possible? Why or why not?

5. As university students, both Lubsch and Winter claimed to be concerned about "the future of Germany" (p. 211), yet they stood on opposite sides politically. Discuss how political opposites can have a common goal, yet propose radically different solutions to reach that goal. Do you see a similar situation happening in the world today?

6. The elderly former Nazi, Wilhelm Busch, describes a depressed Germany by saying, "Every day there were riots and protests and armed anarchists roaming the streets. No one could find work. . . . And then came the Nazis. They promised prosperity, work, hope. To make Germany great again. Drowning men will grasp at straws, and we Germans then were drowning" (p. 334). In what ways do today's headlines echo some of the problems plaguing Germany during the rise of Hitler? Can you think of any groups today who feel strongly that they have the perfect solution to the world's problems?

7. What is the significance of the "pedigree" that all the murder victims had in common? (p. 351) For what reason were they killed?

8. What is the ultimate goal of the neo-Nazi group? Do you think it's true that the German people will rally behind them, as Grinzing claims? (p. 431) Why or why not?

9. It has been said that one man's terrorist is another man's freedom fighter. Review the description of the Nazis offered by Grinzing (p. 433). Have you ever heard the Nazis described in this way? In their own estimation, did the Nazis intend to destroy Germany or improve it?

10. What sorts of unrest do you see happening around the world today? Do you think that a destabilized country leaves itself open to a takeover by anyone who claims to have the answers? Discuss.

11. What was the purpose of assigning Kefir Ozalid to assassinate Chancellor Dollman? What effect did the neo-Nazis hope this information would have on the German people when it became public?

12. Do you hear today of immigrants being blamed for society's ills? If so, what do you think the solution might be?

13. While planning their approach to Kaalberg, Volkmann tells Lubsch, "If we make it up the mountain, Schmeltz is mine" (p. 441). Why does he say this? Discuss the role of revenge and whether you think it will truly satisfy Volkmann.

14. Toward the end of the book, speaking of the neo-Nazis, the man called Raul says, "You know the Western democracies can't sustain their problems. Immigration. Unemployment. Recession. They're already crumbling. It's only a question of time before we try again" (p. 478). Do you think he is correct? Why or why not?

15. What did you think of the ending of *Brandenburg*? Did it surprise you?

ENHANCE YOUR BOOK CLUB

1. If you know an older person who remembers World War II and the Nazi era, invite him or her to join your discussion.

2. For an overview, watch an introductory documentary about Nazism, such as Episode 1 of *The Nazis: A Warning from History*, available online at http://topdocumentaryfilms.com/the-nazis-a-warning-from-history/.

3. Discuss some actions that ordinary people can take to ensure that something like the Holocaust never happens again.

A CONVERSATION WITH GLENN MEADE

1. How were you inspired to write *Brandenburg*?

Some years ago I was in Garmisch in southern Germany writing a newspaper article for the *Times*—about the mysterious disappearance of huge amounts of Nazi gold bullion at the end of World War II—when I met an elderly former SS man who told me an incredible wartime story.

As a young recruit he was stationed in Vienna in 1941. One night he and his comrades were given secret orders to proceed to Vienna's old Central Cemetery, where they were to completely destroy a section of the graveyard—raze it to the ground with bulldozers and earth-moving equipment, obliterating all trace of the graves in that part of the cemetery.

The "secret" behind the reason for the SS destruction inspired me to write the book.

The bulldozed area of the graveyard actually held the grave of a woman named Geli Raubal—Adolf Hitler's niece, with whom he had a close relationship—and who died in mysterious circumstances just before Hitler came to power. (Rumors circulated at the time that Geli Raubal was actually murdered, on Hitler's orders, because she was pregnant with his child, or had already given birth.)

This "secret"—that Hitler may have had his niece killed in order to hide the fact that she had fathered a child by him, a child who survived and might be still living today—formed the central "mystery" that must be uncovered in *Brandenburg*. It also has a chilling significance in today's world, in which Europe is once again being ravaged by neo-Nazi groups that are looking for a leader to rally around.

It's historical fact that Hitler personally gave the order in 1941 for the grave in Vienna to be destroyed—some believed it was to frustrate any subsequent autopsy that might reveal that his niece was pregnant or had given birth. To this day, the ravaged section of the cemetery still exists—it remains a barren patch of land, the gravestones long obliterated.

2. Many of the social conditions of pre–World War II Germany—high unemployment, a weak economy, the "immigrant question"—sound disturbingly familiar. What do you think is the likelihood that another Nazi-like entity could rise to power in the twenty-first century?

History often has a habit of repeating itself, so never say never. When I met with Germany's national intelligence organization during the research for the book, several officers I spoke with privately expressed their grave concerns about the neo-Nazi groups that are still on the rise in Germany. They continue to simmer dangerously in the background since their resurgence in Europe in the 1960s and '70s. And it's not just a European phenomenon—Russia, Eastern Europe, the U.S. all have the problem. I believe it will worsen worldwide with these groups attracting even more followers among the disaffected as economic conditions and unemployment deteriorate.

3. Did you have a favorite character or scene in *Brandenburg*? If so, which one, and why?

That's a difficult one. Like a good parent, I love all my "children" equally. But some characters or scenes will always stand out in the author's mind. I may have a slight fondness for Joe Volkmann and Rudi Hernandez, but for different reasons. Volkmann because he's complex, and Hernandez because he's not.

Scene? The one where Volkmann and Erica learn the true identity of the mystery woman in the photograph taken in the 1930s. It's a real shock, an enigma revealed, and all the more enjoyable to write because it's based on a real character and a true revelation.

4. How long did it take you to research and write *Brandenburg*?

About a year, which involved several trips to Germany, where I met a bunch of shaven-headed neo-Nazis in Berlin—one of the scariest experiences I've ever had because of the absolute ease with which they boasted about their acts of violence, their hatred of immigrants, and their denial of the Holocaust. It ranks up there with meeting hard-line Al Qaeda supporters in Istanbul, while researching another book of mine, *Resurrection Day*. They were both chilling, sobering experiences, and served to remind me of the potential danger we all face from such fanatics.

5. What is your research process? How do you know when to stop researching and start writing?

I read as much as I can on the subject and visit any important locations that will feature in the book. Research is hard work but fun—you're constantly discovering facts and details that may be of use to you in the writing. I usually take along a video camera and record images of the locations I will use in the book. They help jog my memory when I'm writing.

I've got most of the research done before I start the writing process—but in truth, you're often still discovering interesting morsels of research until right before you hand in the manuscript to your editor.

6. Were there any surprises for you in the writing of this novel? Did you uncover any startling facts or glimpses of history that were new to you?

Discovering the central "secret" behind *Brandenburg* was a big revelation to me. I hadn't known a lot about Hitler's private life, or about Geli Raubal.

It was a shock that was all the more disturbing when I visited Vienna's old Central Cemetery and saw the ruined plot where Hitler's niece was buried.

7. How have readers responded to *Brandenburg*?

Pretty well; it certainly generated a lot of mail. One of the surprising things about it is that my German publisher declined to publish the book at first, fearing German sensitivity about the subject matter. Only when they had successfully published several other of my books did they decide to take the risk. It became a bestseller in Germany.

8. If readers take away one primary message from *Brandenburg*, what do you hope it will be?

That old cliché, learn from the past. The Nazi period was truly horrific—probably *the* most evil and brutal episode in human history. The same conditions that caused fascism's rise could well happen again; neo-Nazism has been on a definite rise in the last decades. I hope it helps even in a small way to remind readers that we must never allow that part of our history to repeat itself.

9. *Brandenburg* remains suspenseful all the way to the end. Is there a sequel?

History also has a habit of repeating itself where authors are concerned. So you never know.

10. What advice would you offer to a novice fiction writer?

Read, read, read. Write, write, write. Don't just read a book or see a movie once—do it twice or more. The first time should be for pleasure; the second and subsequent times for craft. Study how writers achieve the effect they want to achieve on the page, and try to do the same kind of thing in your own writing, if not better.

11. Many of your books deal with historical themes. What attracts you to writing about historical events?

An interest in history since I was a kid—I was always a daydreamer, constantly taking myself off to other worlds, where I imagined myself existing. I guess it's still a trait, and I still daydream, except now I'm lucky enough to make a living from it.

12. What book are you working on now?

The question no writer likes to answer . . . in case a wicked spell is cast upon his work. Let's just say it borrows elements from my other works, and there's certainly a historical element, but it's more contemporary, and set in the U.S. and Europe.

AN EXCERPT FROM

THE SECOND MESSIAH,

ANOTHER THRILLING READ FROM

GLENN MEADE

1

Leon Gold didn't know that he had two minutes left to live and he was grinning. "Did anyone ever tell you that you've got terrific legs?" he asked the drop-dead-gorgeous woman seated next to him.

Gold was twenty-three, a tanned, good-looking, muscular young man from New Jersey whose folks had immigrated to Israel. As he drove his Dodge truck with military markings past a row of sun-drenched orange groves, he inhaled the sweet scent through the rolled-down window, then used the moment to glimpse the figure of the woman seated next to him.

Private Rachel Else was stunning.

Gold, a corporal, eyed Rachel's uniform skirt riding up her legs, the top button open on her shirt to reveal a flash of cleavage. She was driving him so crazy that he found it hard to concentrate on his job—delivering a consignment to an Israel Defense Forces outpost, thirty miles away. The road ahead was a coil of tortu-ous bends. "Well, did anyone ever tell you that you've got terrific legs?" Gold repeated.

A tiny smile curled Rachel's lips. "Yeah, you did. Five minutes ago, Leon. Tell me something new."

Gold flicked a look in the rearview mirror and saw sunlight igniting the windows and the glinting dome of a fast-disappearing Jerusalem. There was only one reason he stayed in this godforsaken country with its endless friction with the Palestinians, high taxes, grumbling Jews, and searing heat.

The Israeli women. They were simply gorgeous. And the Israel Defense Forces had its fair share of beauties. Gold was determined that Rachel was going to be his next date. He shifted down a gear as the road twisted up and the orange scent was replaced by gritty desert air. "Okay, then did anyone ever mention you've got seductive eyes and a terrific figure?"

"You mentioned those too, Leon. You're repeating yourself."

"Are you going to come on a date with me or not, Private Else?"

"No. Keep your eyes on the road, Corporal."

"I've got my eyes on the road."

"They're on my legs."

Gold grinned again. "Hey, can I help it if you make my eyes wander?"

"Keep them on the *road*, Leon. You crash and we're both in trouble."

Gold focused on the empty road as it rose up into sand-dusted limestone hills. Rachel was proving a tough nut to crack, but he reckoned he still had an ace up his sleeve. As the road snaked round a bend he nudged the truck nearer the edge. The wheels skidded, sending loose gravel skittering into the rock-strewn ravine below.

Alarm crept into Rachel's voice. "Leon! Don't do that."

Gold winked, nudging the Dodge even closer to the road's edge. "Maybe I can make you change your mind?"

"Stop it, Leon. Don't fool around, it's crazy. You'll get us killed."

Gold grinned as the wheels skidded again. "How about that date? Just put me out of my misery. Yes, or no?"

"Leon! Oh no!" Rachel stared out past the windshield.

Gold's eyes snapped straight ahead as he swung the wheel away from the brink. A white Ford pickup appeared from around the next bend. Gold jumped on the brakes but his blood turned to ice and he knew he was doomed. His Dodge started to skid as the two vehicles hurtled toward the ravine's edge, trying to avoid a crash. The pickup was like an express train that couldn't stop and then everything seemed to happen in slow motion.

Gold clearly saw the pickup's occupants. Three adults in the front cab, two teenagers in the open back—a boy and a girl seated on some crates. The smiles on their faces collapsed into horror as the two vehicles shrieked past each other.

There was a grating clang of metal striking metal as the rears of both vehicles briefly collided and then Gold screamed, felt a breeze rush past him as the Dodge flew through the air. His scream combined with Rachel's in a bloodcurdling duet that died abruptly when their truck smashed nose-first into the ravine and their gas tank ignited.

Fifteen miles from Jerusalem, the distant percussion of the massive blast could be heard as the army truck's cargo of antipersonnel mines detonated instantly, vaporizing Gold's and Rachel's handsome young bodies into bone and ash.

The Catholic priest was following two hundred yards behind the pickup, driving a battered old Renault, when he felt the blast through the rolled-down window. The percussion pained his ears and he slammed on his brakes. The Renault skidded to a halt.

The priest paled as he stared at the orange ball of flame rising into the air, followed by an oily cloud of smoke. Instinct made him stab his foot on the accelerator and the Renault sped forward.

When he reached the edge of the ravine, he floored the brakes and jumped out of his car. The priest saw the flames consume the blazing shell of the army truck and knew there was no hope for whoever was inside. His focus turned to the upturned white Ford pickup farther along the ravine, smoke pouring from its cabin. The priest blessed himself as he stared blankly at the accident scene. "May the Lord have mercy on their souls."

His plan had gone horribly wrong. This was not exactly what he had intended. If the pickup's occupants had to die, so be it—the priceless, two-thousand-year-old treasure inside the vehicle was worth the loss of human life—but he hadn't foreseen such awful carnage.

He moved toward the pickup. A string of deafening explosions erupted as more mines ignited. The priest was forced to crouch low.

Seconds later his eyes shifted back to the upturned Ford pickup. He could make out the occupants trapped inside the smoke-filled cabin. One of them frantically kicked at the windshield, trying to escape. Nearby the sprawled bodies of a teenage boy and girl lay among the wreckage.

When the explosions died, the priest stood. His gaze swung back to the burning pickup. The desperate passenger had stopped kicking and his body had fallen limp. As thick smoke smothered the cabin, the priest caught sight of the leather map case, lying wedged inside the windshield.

He knew it contained the ancient scroll that had been discovered that morning at Qumran, and that the pickup was on its way to the Antiquities Department in Jerusalem with its precious cargo. But the priest was desperate to ensure that the scroll never reached its destination.

His orders from Rome were clear.

This was one astonishing secret that had to be kept hidden from the world.

Flames started to lick around the map case. "Dear God, no."

He scrambled down the rocks toward the wreckage.

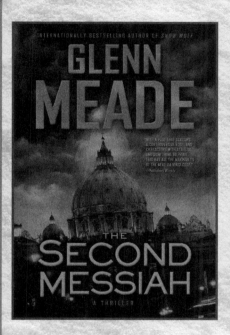